James B. Thomson

# Joseph Thomson, African Explorer

A biography

James B. Thomson

**Joseph Thomson, African Explorer**
*A biography*

ISBN/EAN: 9783337308438

Printed in Europe, USA, Canada, Australia, Japan

Cover: Foto ©Raphael Reischuk / pixelio.de

More available books at **www.hansebooks.com**

# JOSEPH THOMSON

## AFRICAN EXPLORER

A Biography

BY

HIS BROTHER

(Rev. J. B. Thomson, Greenock)

WITH CONTRIBUTIONS BY FRIENDS

MAPS AND ILLUSTRATIONS

SECOND EDITION

LONDON

SAMPSON LOW, MARSTON AND COMPANY

LIMITED

St. Dunstan's House

FETTER LANE, FLEET STREET, E.C.

1897

TO

# His Friends in Many Lands.

# PREFACE.

I HAVE written this biography of my brother for the
following among other reasons: (1) because I desired to
satisfy my own heart and to fulfil what I have felt to be
a personal duty; (2) because I believe that the reading
public will find it healthful and stimulating, even as his
friends found it pleasant and profitable, to know the man;
(3) because the work which he did, great as it is
admitted to be, cannot be fully understood apart from an
acquaintance with the character and aims of the worker.

My private relation to the explorer has enabled me
to write of him with a full personal knowledge, but I
recognise the fact that there are various aspects of his
life-work upon which the public will naturally desire the
opinion of experts. Fortunately, he numbered among his
friends men who can speak with the highest authority in
every department, and I have been happy in receiving
contributions from them which enable me to present to
the reader an estimate practically complete.

In this connection I make here my warm acknowledg-
ments to Sir Archibald Geikie, Mr. J. M. Barrie, Mr.

Ravenstein, Mr. J. Scott Keltie, Dr. J. W. Gregory, Mr. J. A. Grant, and Mr. G. F. Scott-Elliot.

A hearty word of thanks is also due to Mr. J. G. Bartholomew, for the specially prepared maps in which he offers his suggestive tribute to the geographical work of his friend; to Mr. Alexander Anderson, for the poem which he has written for the book; to Mr. Fergus, for the two photo-portraits; to Mr. T. L. Gilmour, who has kindly assisted in the reading of proofs and in other ways; to Mrs. Calder and Mr. Armstrong, who have favoured me with their valuable co-operation; and to all who have obliged me with the loan of letters.

GREENOCK,
    *9th October,* 1896.

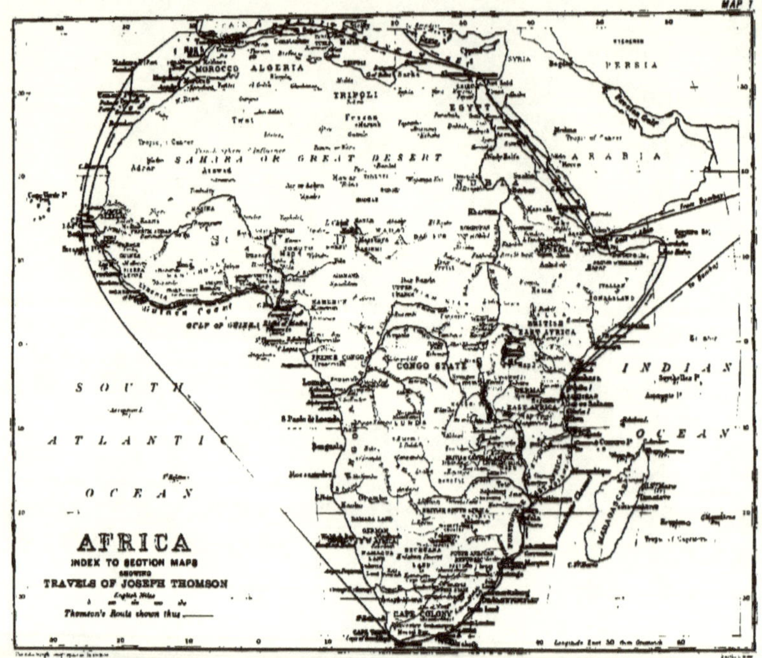

PERSIA
SYRIA
ARABIA
EGYPT
TRIPOLI
ALGERIA
MOROCCO
SAHARA OR GREAT DESERT
SOUTH ATLANTIC OCEAN
INDIAN OCEAN
CONGO STATE
FRENCH CONGO
BRITISH EAST AFRICA
CAPE COLONY
MADAGASCAR
Guinea Coast
GULF OF GUINEA
AFRICA
INDEX TO SECTION MAPS
SHOWING
TRAVELS OF JOSEPH THOMSON
English Miles
Thomson's Route shown thus

# CONTENTS.



## APPENDIX.

# LIST OF MAPS.

# LIST OF ILLUSTRATIONS.

He sleeps among the hills he knew,
  They look upon his early rest;
The winds that in his childhood blew—
  They stir the grass upon his breast.
His grave is green in that sweet vale
  Where the fair river gleams the same;
It rolls, and gathers to its tale
  The added memory of his name.

And youth is his: though time extends
  The growing years from spring to spring,
He still will be to all his friends
  Secure from what their touches bring.
Calm, then, will be his wish'd-for rest,
  After the weary toil of feet,
To sleep—the grass above his breast—
  And know that perfect peace is sweet.

O better thus than he should lie
  To mingle with no kindred earth,
In the lone desert where the sky
  Burns all things into fiery dearth,
And where not even one kindly eye
  Could note the grave wherein he slept;
The dusky savage passing by
  Would mark it not as on he swept.

But this was not to be: he lies
  Near to the murmur of his rills,
He sleeps beneath our Scottish skies,
  And in the silence of his hills.
His grave is green in that loved vale
  Where the fair river gleams the same;
It rolls, and gathers to its tale
  The dear possession of his fame.

Alexander Anderson.

# JOSEPH THOMSON, AFRICAN EXPLORER.

## CHAPTER I.

### CHILDHOOD.

JOSEPH THOMSON was born on the 14th of February, 1858, in the village of Penpont, Dumfriesshire. He was the youngest of a family of five sons. His father, William Thomson, was a native of the neighbouring parish of Keir where for some generations his forebears had lived in honoured simplicity and good repute. William Thomson was originally a working stonemason, but by dint of diligence and wise carefulness he had by this time attained to the position of a master-builder on his own account, and was patiently laying the foundation for still larger enterprises than the demands of mere local trade made possible. The mother of the future explorer, Agnes Brown, was a native of the parish of Penpont. She belonged to a family which had long been known and respected in the neighbourhood, and which carefully kept up the traditions of a godly ancestry. Both father and mother were plain, unassuming persons, content to do their own work faithfully and to be kind and friendly towards their neighbours. If they had an ambition beyond that of providing things honest in the sight of all men and being useful and respected in their station, it was that they might be able to do well for their children, and to give them advantages, educationally and otherwise, which they themselves had not enjoyed. This honourable aim, so characteristic of the better class of the Scottish common people, was not denied its fulfilment. From the day of founding their home they had quietly and steadily prospered. At first they occupied a little cottage in the country, but after a few years they built for themselves a pleasant house in the village, and there it was that the subject of this memoir first saw the light.

Heredity always counts for something in a man's career, and certainly it counted for not a little in the case of Joseph Thomson. Those who were familiar with the family could very easily trace in his individuality elements of character which were more or less prominent in his parents. Training, environment, choice, opportunity, and the leading of circumstances had all, of course, their own influence in making him the man he came to be ; but, undoubtedly, no inconsiderable measure of the success he attained in his special sphere must be credited to qualities of mind and body which he inherited.

His father was a man of no ordinary force of character. Outwardly, he was, in his prime, a figure to take note of. Very tall, powerful in physique, and with a constitution of iron, he was one with whom very few could compete in either strength or endurance. But animating this massive frame there was a heart of the tenderest and a mind keenly alive to high thoughts and all things beautiful. He had a distinctly poetical temperament, and loved to read poetry. Burns he had "at his finger en. 's." He had, however, a special leaning to the solemn and grand in this department. It was believed among his children that he could repeat 'Paradise Lost,' or Young's 'Night Thoughts,' from memory. His favourite subjects of study were such as appealed to the imagination—for instance, astronomy and geology—and there was nothing more familiar than the sight of him poring for hours in the evening, with a perfect oblivion of all else, over such a book as Dr. Dick's 'Sidereal Heavens,' or Hugh Miller's 'Testimony of the Rocks.' Two qualities were notably characteristic of him—power of concentration and simplicity of purpose. Whether in reading or in working he was "a whole man to one thing"; and when he had made up his mind that this or that was the right thing to do, he went with an undivided heart straight on his course, quite unconcerned as to what people would say or think.

In the mother, too, could be discerned traits which re-appeared in the son. She was less ardent in temperament than her husband, but she had that quiet, steady, staying power, which breaks down difficulties with the sheer force of patient gentleness. It was much more to her mind to win her way by kindliness than by will-power, and many a notable victory she won among her children by a charm which they did not understand at the time, but which they remembered in maturer life as a pattern to imitate —the charm of sweet, tactful, unhasting reasonableness.

Looking back upon the circumstances of that home-life into which Joseph Thomson was born, one cannot but feel that they were well fitted to develop in him the promise of a vigorous and healthful manhood. Simplicity ruled in all the arrangements of the household. Hardship was not known there, but luxury just as little. Duties had to be done without question, though, if possible, they were made to wear an aspect of graciousness, as of things worthy to be done because they were right. The inevitable friction among a family of five energetic boys tended naturally towards self-reliance and independence of character. This was wisely encouraged. Precept and authority were never obtrusively prominent, but there was ever pervading the household an atmosphere of wholesome example, which, if subtle and silent, operated towards moral results with a mightier effect. And there never could be any mistake as to what the meaning of that example was. Reverence, truthfulness, honour, were virtues which lived continuously before the eyes of the family, and their beauty could be seen and felt. Certainly Joseph Thomson would have sadly belied his upbringing if he had not become the courageous lover of truth and the man of chivalrous straightforwardness which he proved himself to be.

From his childhood, Joseph Thomson was of a singularly gentle and lovable disposition. He was full of energy and vivacity, but never self-assertive. In more than one respect the child was distinctly father of the man. Even in opening boyhood he exercised a noticeable ascendency over his playfellows, thus unconsciously foreshadowing the subtle power of personal influence which afterwards stood him in such good stead, when, amid circumstances of difficulty and danger, he had to manage men. It is well remembered by those who watched the early years of the lad that he had continually a troop of his compeers about him, and that, although some of these were bigger and older than himself, he was always the unquestioned leader in their boyish pranks and "ploys." It was in no sense by forwardness or rough ways that he occupied that place, for there was nothing of the overbearing character about him. No doubt the fact had its explanation partly in his force of initiative—he always knew exactly and decidedly what he wanted to do; partly in his fearlessness and enthusiasm; and partly in his overflowing love of fun— that genuine brightness of spirit which disarms ill-will and makes jealousy impossible.

The village of Penpont, where he spent his first nine years, preserved a quiet, self-contained existence of its own. The events of the great busy world only touched its life as a distant echo. No rush or rumble of traffic broke its slumberous monotony, except when an occasional couple of farm carts would pass in a leisurely clattering way to or from the distant railway station, or the farmers themselves— for the most part an easy-minded, free-living lot of men under the mild, uncommercial estate *régime* of the dukedom of Buccleuch in those days—would dash through the place with their stylish gigs and horses on their way to the weekly county market, or after the compulsory emptying of the village inn. There the children could grow up in simple homely ways, and on the plain unsophisticated diet of the country accompanied with unrestricted exercise in the fresh air, lay the foundation of manly vigour in brain and muscle.

In due time Joseph Thomson made his acquaintance with the village school, under its excellent teacher Mr. Robson, who for a generation has presided over the educational destinies of the neighbourhood. He took kindly enough to the simple tasks given him, and disposed of them in an easy, off-hand fashion. But when the school day was over, there was no doubt about the energy which he threw into his play. With his inevitable troop of companions he was here, there and everywhere —now up to one childish exploit, now bent upon another. Soon the resources of enjoyment in the village were used up, and he must needs go further afield for outlets to his buoyant spirits. In the neighbourhood there is no lack of matter for interest and amusement to an intelligent boy, and in a very short time every nook and curious place in the surrounding woods and ravines was familiar to him.

The scenery around Penpont is very beautiful. The village stands picturesquely, just where the river Scar, after alternately brawling among the rocky defiles and sulking in the deep dark pools of Glenmarlin, passes the richly-wooded grounds of Capenoch, and glides into an open valley which gradually widens out till it merges in the broad fertile dale of the Nith. To the west of the village the ground slopes up into a range of hills, notable among which is Tynron Doon, overlooking the valley like a huge Cyclopean mound, seen as a striking feature from afar, with its curious conical shape and its flat top, upon which once stood an almost inaccessible Roman camp, and, later, a stronghold of some sort associated with traditions of King Robert Bruce. Eastward, the outlook over the fair expanse of field and forest to the distant hills of Closeburn, backed up by the grey height of Queensberry, is attractive in the extreme.

Born with an eye keenly sensitive to the beautiful, Joseph Thomson manifestly became in very early years conscious of the exquisiteness of his surroundings, and felt within him the stirrings of a response to their charm. He was never so intent upon his boyish quests as to be insensible to the spell which Nature had woven for his spirit, as from some point of vantage new aspects of loveliness in the landscape would claim his attention. He loved to ramble about in the open air, and in his pryings into the secrets of woods, and hills, and picturesque river-banks, he was receiving without knowing it an education. Silently impressions of an indelible sort were being made upon his mind and heart.

So the time fared on, and the lad, bright, frolicsome, venturous, restless, grew in strength and in the liking of his fellows. His daily school tasks and evening exploits, varied by a whole Saturday's outing now and then, and punctuated by the inevitable attendance in all weathers at service and Sabbath-school, in the United Presbyterian Church at Burnhead, a mile away from the village, constituted the weekly round of his life up to his tenth year. Once in a while, on the occasion of a fair, or show, or other public event, there would be a much-prized visit to the adjoining larger village of Thornhill, where he had, according to his boyish conception, an opportunity of "seeing the world." But, except for such mild excitements as this, the stream of his child-life flowed on in unruffled quietude.

# CHAPTER II.



THE year 1868 saw the opening of a fresh chapter in the boy's experience. It came through the removal of the family to Gatelawbridge, a place about four miles from Penpont, at the base of the hill range which skirts the eastern side of the Nith valley. An opening had occurred in the lease of the farm and freestone quarry there. The quarry was at that time a place of no great importance. It had a traditional interest from its having been once worked by " Old Mortality "—a name familiar to all readers of Sir Walter Scott, as having provided the title and substratum of legend for one of his most fascinating novels—but no attempt had been made to take out of the quarry more than sufficed for the supply of purely local wants. William Thomson, knowing the quality of the stone, and foreseeing the possibility of largely developing the business, resolved to offer for the tenancy. He was accepted, and entered upon the occupancy to the advantage of all concerned, for under the management of himself and two of his sons, the works have, in the process of time, become the most important centre of employment in that part of the county.

The coming to Gatelawbridge was a kind of epoch in the mental development of the inquiring boy, who was just at an age when the traces and tokens of the historic past were beginning to exercise a kindly quickening influence upon his imagination. Within a radius of

three miles or so from his new home as the centre,
lies a patch of country teeming with points of manifold
interest.  You cannot walk half a mile in any direction
in this area without finding that which recalls some
quaint and curious reminiscence of a remote or recent
past.  There are half-obliterated, grass-grown roads, and
the remains of camps large and small, to send you back
to the times of Picts and Romans.  There are hoary
ruins and sites of ancient castles and forts, redolent of
memories of the most stirring and glamorous periods
of Scottish history.  There are ravines and hillsides and
glens and passes consecrated by stories of the brave
Covenanters who, amid persecution, were ready to dare
and suffer all for conscience' sake.  There are spots whose
names have been enshrined in literature by the magic
words of poets, from Blind Harry to Burns.  There are
nooks by wood and stream where linger legendary traditions, fanciful, humorous, or pathetic.  And at no point
are you permitted to forget the spirit of beauty which
haunts you everywhere, and which on a summer or
autumn day seems to pervade the very atmosphere of
the whole dale.

The entire district is a veritable land of delights to
one gifted with the seeing eye and the responsive fancy;
and, from what has already been said, it was but to be
expected that the embryo explorer's interest and curiosity
should be speedily aroused.  The romance of his environment gradually took possession of him, and more and
more ruled the thoughts of his boyhood and youth.  In
a passage with a very recognisable element of the auto-
biographical about it, which occurs in " Ulu," he depicts
the impressions and experiences of the next few years in
a characteristic way.  Describing the scenes amid which
Gilmour (the hero of the story) grew up—"a peaceful
valley amid the southland Scottish hills "—he says :—

" Probably throughout the length and breadth of

Britain there is no other spot so perfect in itself, so complete in every natural charm, as that broad lowland valley. Far surpassed in any one feature by a score of places, the scenery of Carrondale, in its varied assemblage of pleasing characteristics, stands alone. Stretching away from the little village in their midst the fertile fields spread their rich mosaic of green and gold around cosy farmhouses breathing of peace and plenty. There the broad home park with its stately array of oak and beech and broad-leaved chestnut, gives added dignity to lordly mansions, stern with the pride of high degree. Beyond, the well-clad ridges lose themselves in purple heath or desolate moorland, or rise into swelling hills, over whose towering shoulders the fleecy clouds linger in loving dalliance, to cast a mantle of magic shadow athwart their hoary sides. Below, in broken reaches, gleams the river, loitering seawards between wooded banks or smiling cornfields. Its tributary streams in haste to join it, rush headlong over riven rock and linn, making glad music in many a dim retreat, the sacred haunt of poetry and love.

"Every glen, almost every field, has its story of the romantic, half-forgotten past."

Then, after setting forth the historic associations of "Carrondale," he proceeds:

"What more could Nature afford or history supply to fire the fancy and rouse the romantic instincts of a lad naturally prone to poetic imaginings? Eagerly Gilmour drank in every tale of knightly chivalry in love and war, every legend that appealed to the imagination by its terror or its pathos, supplying the gaps in the record by much erratic reading of poetry and prose, better fitted for the education of a Don Quixote than for the training of the more practical knight of the nineteenth century.

"As the years passed by, however, he began to think

less and less of the romantic aspect of his surroundings, and more and more of the wonderful lesson they had to teach of Nature and Nature's ways of working. In his attempts to decipher the rock-told story, he was led into every secluded corner of the valley, every wild nook of the hills and moorlands. Nature became his religion. In a sense he was a Pantheist, worshipping everything, from the storms to the sun and the hidden soul which unites them.

"Happiest when alone, he would climb to some distant height, to revel in the glorious freedom of the fresh mountain air, or gaze in ecstasy on all the varied loveliness of the valley at his feet. Or he would spend the long slow hours of summer noon lying among the heather, his senses lulled to dreaminess by the far-off bleat of sheep, the whirr of grouse, the mournful call of the curlew, as they blended harmoniously with the restful sound of unseen burn, or the distant sough of brawling torrent.

"What longings and aspirations filled his soul the while! Vague and crude enough, no doubt, but all upward, all towards the light. His heart was all in the future, all in the coming battle of life, all in the strife against falsehood and wrongdoing, and on the side of truth and right."

This passage, in so far as it refers to Joseph Thomson himself, somewhat anticipates the course of our narrative; but it summarises in a useful and expressive way the inner history of his life for the next six or seven years.

For the first few months after the settlement of the family at Gatelawbridge, Joseph Thomson attended the little school which had been erected in the hamlet mainly for the benefit of the workers' families. Circumstances, however, led to his being transferred to the public school at Thornhill, where he received almost the whole of his education.

This school was superintended by Mr. Hewison, a fine specimen of the now almost extinct type of parish "dominie." He was a man of distinct vigour and independence of character, with a shrewd eye for "a lad of parts"—and not a few of such has he in the course of his half century of professional service passed educationally through his hands. A former pupil thus describes his personality :

"A sturdy old Scotsman of hardy Norse origin. Born and reared in the Orkney Islands, with muscular frame and upright bearing, steel-grey hair and kindly face, he looked the ideal Viking of the northern seas. . . . His pet aversion was smoking, which he held was a most disgusting practice, and woe betide the delinquent caught indulging in the fragrant weed."

Modern educational methods in national schools have no doubt brought many advantages for the general mass. But there were some things about the old parochial school system which wise educationists would not willingly have let die, if they could have been made compatible with the underlying idea of the new system. We suspect that Mr. Hewison at least was one who would gladly have retained the old elastic *régime* whereby some regard could be had to the individuality of a promising pupil; and we are not sure but that, in the hands of so capable and conscientious a teacher, this would have been preferable to the "steam roller," levelling action of the code.

"My earliest recollection (says Mr. Hewison) of the world-renowned African explorer is that of a rubicund, open-countenanced boy appearing in the playground on a fine May morning of 1869 as 'the new scholar.' From the day he entered till the day he left some years afterwards, he was indubitably the favourite of the school. His good nature, kindly disposition, cheerful give and take spirit, soon secured for him the respect of all. He rode to school on a pony, and it was a common occurrence to see him draw ' Donald' close up to a gate to enable one little fellow to get on before him and another behind him, for a cantering lift homewards."

We cannot, in the case of Joseph Thomson, repeat the record of aversion to lessons and of truant ways which has signalised the schooldays of not a few men of mark. Undoubtedly, indeed, when in after days he came to measure himself with others in the university, he became conscious of many educational deficiencies which needed to be remedied, and he severely blamed himself as having, all through, dealt with his school tasks in too easy-minded a fashion and never having brought his real strength to bear upon them. His teacher, however, saw no cause to find fault with him ; for the impression he retains of him is that of a boy "obedient and diligent, and in home preparation thoroughly trustworthy." It has to be confessed, nevertheless, that the latter duty was one which sat very lightly upon him indeed, and was more frequently neglected than honoured in the observance. The truth, we believe, is that under the mechanical influence of a prescribed system which regulated the progress of a whole class by the pace of the dullest pupil, the lessons were to the sharp-witted boy so easy that they failed to make the impression upon him they would have made if it had been possible really to put him on his mettle.

As for his general bearing among his fellows, it is remembered by those who were intimate with him in his schooldays that there were two things which he stead-fastly set himself to combat.

The first was the bullying of the girls. In a mixed public school like that at Thornhill this was only too common. But Joseph Thomson's whole nature rose against it. All through life, one of his distinctive traits was a chivalrous reverence for womanhood, and this spirit was just as noticeable on the playground. If ever he felt inclined to fight with other boys, it was, more often than not, as the champion of the weaker sex. This, it may easily be conceived, was a thing calculated to expose him to the sneers of coarser natures; but, as he was felt to be quite capable of holding his own, he never seems to have been troubled in that way.

The other thing to which he vigorously objected was profanity and indecent talk. He was no prude, and made no affectation of the "good boy" character, but swearing and foul language he simply hated, and very soon those who wanted to be friends with him got to know that they must eschew these things in his presence. "Many a punching of a good-natured kind he gave his classmates for using bad language, and the punishment was never resented, as it was admitted by all that he had a right to constitute himself *censor morum*." So testifies his chosen companion and, afterward, fellow-student, Robert Armstrong.

For the rest, he was one of the most companionable of boys. To his friends he was simply "Joe." It seemed unnatural to call one so simple and hearty and un-affected by any more formal name. To this day, indeed, his intimates, one and all, speak of him in no other way. The familiar title has, to not a few, a depth of tender meaning which no other designation, however honourable, could have; and the fact has, in its own fashion, a kindly significance which cannot be mistaken.

At Thornhill, just as at Penpont, "Joe" could always at will gather around him a band of followers, and as occasion offered, he was ever ready to lead off in any piece of genuine fun, or to indulge in a daring frolic. As illustrating this, an incident of his early schooldays may be here related.

It was the day of the parliamentary election in Dumfriesshire—the last of the old open elections, whose rude humours have been banished into oblivion by the sedative

influences of the Ballot Act. The whole of Mid Nithsdale had emptied itself into Thornhill for the day, and the
voting had to be conducted amid scenes of excitement,
rough play, and riotous hilarity that would have required
the describer of the Eatanswill election to depict them
adequately. The district being in sympathies essentially
radical, the Liberal candidate (Sir Sydney Waterlow) was
of course the popular favourite, and whoever dared to
oppose him had to run the gauntlet of a demonstration of
disapproval which was not a little trying to the temper.
The boys entered *con amore* into the amusement. To
them the sum of duty for the day was to impress every
fresh arrival on the Tory side with a proper sense of
their contempt. Some took the hooting good-naturedly
and escaped easily. Others, not so tactful, got angry, and
suffered accordingly. Among these was Captain John
Jones, Chief Constable of the county—a name usually
spoken only with awe by the boys. Irritated, and feeling
his dignity insulted by the laughing satirical company of
youngsters that followed at his heels, he suddenly turned,
seized the foremost of the boys, and administered a good
shaking to him. The victim was none other than Joseph
Thomson, who, as the scion of a Liberal household, felt
that it became him to show himself on the right side, and
whose characteristic enthusiasm had carried him to the
front. In a moment, however, the Captain's good sense
prevailed, and realizing the humour of the situation, he
marched off his youthful prisoner to the village book-
shop, from which the said prisoner presently emerged,
amid cheers, carrying a volume with an inscription com-
memorative of the adventure.

Incidents like this, however, were but spice to season
the serious business of his schooldays. That business was
not lessons, but the reading of books.

The fever of reading early infected him, and ran its
course with a consuming ardour. At home, and at school
for a time, it was always the one thing—every spare

moment was occupied with poring over some kind of literature. In the long winter evenings he would, at home, lie stretched out full length upon the hearthrug, with elbows upon the floor and head supported by his hands, and would read for hours until bedtime. As summer drew round, he would, in fine weather, exchange the hearthrug for a sunny knoll in one of the fields, or a quiet place in the Sandrum Wood, and there spend his time until the dim twilight fell and compelled him to desist. For a time, indeed, his health seemed likely to be injured by the intensity of his devotion to books; but when his mother in her anxiety took to hiding them, he, not to be baulked of his joy, would read all the way home from school, deposit his treasure in some secure place of concealment, start an hour or two earlier in the morning, get into the school-house by a window or otherwise, and there in silence indulge his passion until the classes would assemble. Then during the hour of recreation it was the same thing continued.

"To many of the boys," writes one of his schoolfellows, " his preference for books even during play-hours was a matter of surprise. It was the regular thing, whenever his presence was essential to some boyish game or argument, for him to be aroused from the greensward underneath the shady chestnut-trees in the playground, where he had retired and stretched himself at full length to pore over a book by some favourite author. He was constantly reading, not the trashy penny dreadfuls so dear to the heart of the schoolboy, but solid and instructive books."

The novels of Scott and the stories of R. M. Ballantyne were read and re-read, ' Ungava ' being a special favourite. In Shakspere he delighted, and the ' Ingoldsby Legends ' he could nearly say off by heart. " A common scene on the playground (says his teacher) was a closely wedged group, male and female, with ‘Joe’ in the centre volubly rattling off the last story he had read.”

In his reading he was as omnivorous as he was insatiable. Nothing came amiss to him. He had an instinctive liking for good literature, but he found something to interest him in any kind of book. The writer has found the little fellow wrestling eagerly with the unattractive pages of ‘Dwight’s Theology’ when other and brighter matter failed him. On the other hand, he was just as ready, upon occasion, to go to the opposite extreme, and to absorb himself with even the crudest stories of backwoods adventures. Indeed at one time this kind of book had an influence upon him which proved more useful than he or any one else could have anticipated.

His imagination became fired with the marvellous feats of horsemanship which form part of the stock material of such stories. Being himself full of the spirit of adventure, he would try to reproduce some of those feats. Many an extraordinary performance he and Donald (the pony) had on the quiet. He would, for instance, place objects here and there on the ground, and then, in the rush of full gallop round the field, he would practise bending over from the saddle and picking them up with his hand. One day a friend, who had himself been in a regiment of dragoons and was an expert in equestrianism, was struck dumb to see him on Donald’s back tearing along the very edge of a high precipitous bank, where one slip or false step would have instantly precipitated horse and rider, probably with fatal results, into the stream many feet below. In fearless escapades of this kind, however, he was unconsciously giving himself a training which would some day stand him in good stead, besides exercising his nerve and giving him confidence and coolness in presence of peril.

It was when he was about eleven years of age that the bent of mind which was practically to determine the drift of his life became discernible to himself. His eldest

brother, the writer of this narrative, returning home at the
close of one of his college sessions, happened to bring to
him, as a present, a volume descriptive of travel in strange
lands. He was fascinated and wanted more. The lives
of the explorers were eagerly sought out by him. With
the narratives of Mungo Park, Bruce, Moffat, and others,
he was soon perfectly familiar. Then the works of
Livingstone fell into his hands. He greedily devoured
them, and they seem to have awakened new thoughts
within him. In those simple, unconventional records of
the patient, large-hearted missionary-pioneer, he realized
something more than the glamour belonging to adventures
and hair-breadth escapes. The mystery and pathos of
Africa's darkness here came near to him and laid hold
of his imagination. He was touched with a feeling of
Livingstone's compassion for the benighted tribes, and his
mind wandered, in a tender questioning way, over those
large spaces on the map of that long-neglected continent
marked " unknown."

Very soon after this the newspapers began to voice the
anxiety of the country about the prolonged silence of that
great explorer, and the fears that were being entertained
lest some evil thing might have befallen one whose name
all revered. Nowhere did those notes of concern find a
more sympathetic response than in the heart of the ardent
schoolboy at Gatelawbridge. When, at last, it was announced that an expedition was to be sent out to search
for the lost traveller, his enthusiasm became uncontroll-
able. Coming to his mother with the news, he eagerly
asked her to intercede with his father to give him money
that he might go and join it. It was in vain that
she gently explained that one so young could be of no
use, and that they would never take him on board the
ship. With tears he pleaded his case. He would get on
board somehow! and when he appeared at sea they would
be bound to take him, and he was sure he would be able
to make himself useful! When the expedition set out he

eagerly scanned the daily papers for every scrap of news regarding it; and when at last the veteran explorer was reported to have been found by Stanley, his delight knew no bounds.   Those who saw the lad rushing into the quarry, his face beaming with excitement and heard him enthusiastically shout out the glad tidings to his father long before he got near to him, recall the scene now with a pathetic interest.  At that time it seemed to them amazing that one so young should manifest such vivid concern.

Now these incidents may, to the reader, seem to be mere freaks born of a boyish imagination. But they really represented no passing whim.  He had taken his resolution and he never departed from it.  He would be an African explorer!  He would some day, if possible, see for himself what those blank spaces on the map represented!  There never was a more notable case of a boy instinctively discovering his vocation and resolving to prepare himself for it.

From this point the operation of his purpose can be traced without a break.  It ran as a continuous power of motive and guidance and control in his life through all the years that followed, up till the moment when he actually entered upon the career which in his heart he had craved for himself.

And he had practical, although they might be sometimes amusingly boyish, ideas about his self-training.  He would abjure the delights of soft mattresses and lie sometimes even upon the floor of his bedroom "to harden himself," as he explained.  And, though he devotedly loved his mother, not a few anxious vigils did he unintentionally prepare for her, when, as the summer night overtook him in his rambles among the hills, he would determine to make his bed in the heather or among the brackens, that he might anticipate the experience of resting under the open sky and of going to sleep in the watching of the stars.

So the years wore on, and his schooldays began to

draw to a close. The course he had followed in his classes contained no novelties. It was simply intended to put him in possession of a plain ordinary education. Besides the various branches of elementary English, he learnt a little of mathematics, mensuration, and drawing. The rudiments of Latin he had to get up, but for the subject he had no liking. In French, however, he took more interest, and in this language he made a good beginning, which in after days he followed up to some purpose, as we shall see.

About the year 1872 a new influence began to tell upon him and to mark a further stage in his mental development. This was the Young Men's Literary Society in Thornhill. It was formed by a number of lads like-minded with himself, such as his class-fellow Armstrong and his intimate associate Wallace Williamson (now minister of St. Cuthbert's, Edinburgh), together with two of his own brothers and some of the more studiously inclined youths of the village of Thornhill. The society started with great vigour, and, from the accounts obtainable of its meetings, it must have contributed in no small degree to the intellectual quickening of its members.

Its nights of debate were notable and memorable occasions. With the freedom and fearlessness of youth, the stripling disputants tackled all manner of subjects. No topic was too recondite or august or sacred to deter them from discussing it. As this got to be whispered abroad some of the more orthodox and "unco guid" in Thornhill began to shake their heads and even to suggest that the religion of some of the more venturous speakers was not in a good way. On one occasion this found a rather ludicrous expression.

A circus had just come into the village, and the day happened to be that of the regular meeting of the society. The temptation was too great for the youths, and they resolved to adjourn to the place of entertainment. They came up in a body laughing and ready for a little sport.

Finding the entrance crowded, they began in a playful fashion to push forward, when suddenly the mirth of the whole company was violently aroused by the shout of a half tipsy mason "Stand back, ye gomerals, and let *thae young infidels in!*"

But, if the members of this society claimed for themselves considerable liberties, they undoubtedly turned their meetings to good purpose. At these Joseph Thomson found himself thoroughly in his element. He threw himself with characteristic enthusiasm into every department of its work. In numerous essays which he contributed to its manuscript magazine—"Ours"—he began to try his "prentice hand" at literary composition, and it is interesting, in reading these still existing numbers, to note, amid youthful crudeness of style, and solecisms of grammar and syntax, distinct foreshadowings of that fluency and that aptness of literary allusion, which were so characteristic of his writing in after days. The debates, however, were his chief joy. Into these he threw himself with the intrepidity of a Rupert. Opposition showed him at his best, and brought out reserves of strength with which his ordinarily quiet demeanour would not have led one to credit him. In common intercourse he did not much indulge the gift of speech; but when the spirit of discussion took possession of him, he could be articulate enough; and, as he was by no means phlegmatic in temperament, his words often did not err on the side of tameness.

But, while the literary society thus afforded scope, exercise and stimulus for such gift of writing as he possessed, and, by frank fellowships and strenuous argumentative conflicts, helped to give him command of his own intellectual resources, there was another society which tended in a quieter but no less effective way to minister to that ideal of a life-work which he had begun secretly to cherish for himself. This was the Society of Inquiry, an association which was formed at the same time as the one to which we have already referred, for the encouragement of scientific study and observation, and which, for the following twelve or fifteen years, maintained a healthy and serviceable life.

The membership of the Society of Inquiry consisted originally of a score or so of the more intelligent gardeners at Drumlanrig Castle, together with a number of young men in the district who indulged a taste for science in one or other of its branches. The society comprised not a few earnest and successful local workers. But the high priest of its mysteries, and the life and soul of it generally, was its president, Dr. Thomas Boyle Grierson, in whose museum it held its meetings.

Dr. Grierson's name calls for more than a passing mention in this narrative. He was a man of a very marked individuality—one of those men who give flavour and character to the life of a place. Certainly the Thornhill of those days had no figure so outstanding, no character so interesting.

The picture of that familiar personality must still linger in the memories of many. The roughly and carelessly clothed figure enveloped in the inevitable dark-coloured Scottish plaid, and walking with a rapid gait, as of one absorbed—the mass of straight brown hair hanging heavily as a curtain to the one side of his brow, and made more noticeable by the forward stoop of the head—the face, spare and serious, that spoke of simple living and much thinking —the pensive mouth with its drooping extremities, and the blue-grey eyes with a far-away, mystical, dreaming look about them—such were the characteristic lineaments of the man, as he moved before the eyes of his fellow-villagers for thirty years or more. A man compelling observation!

In his relation to the intellectual and educational life of Thornhill, Dr. Grierson was no less a man *sui generis*. He was full of plans for the mental and social elevation of the people, and his ideals were often of the highest. In his advocacy of these, however, his zealous temperament

carried him up into such a cloud of rhetorical, and sometimes even rhapsodical, discourse, that it was difficult for
his unimaginative hearers to take him quite seriously.
Hence, not infrequently, when he was most in earnest, he
provoked a wondering smile in place of responsive action,
and gave an air of the unpractical to many schemes that
were well worthy of experiment. Thornhill loved him,
but he had the misfortune to be often " speaking over its
head," and consequently to be voted by the slower-moving
local mind a bit of a visionary.

But it was in his love of science and his efforts to
popularise it that the doctor found his vocation, and was
enabled to become a real power in the district. He had
not the kind of mind that makes a specialist; but he
looked at science precisely from that point of view which
fitted him for interpreting it and giving it an aspect of
interest to ordinary people. He was cosmopolitan in his
reading. Every "ism" and "ology" had some point of
fascination for him. His brain was seething with the
most miscellaneous conflux of ideas, and his memory was
an encyclopædia of quaint and curious knowledge, which
it was an ineffable delight to him to pour out, whenever he could find the receptive and sufficiently patient
listener.

The focal point of his scientific interests lay in his
museum. That museum was indeed a wonderful collection
for a single individual to have amassed, working alone in
a secluded country district, and with no resources to rely
upon except the modest profits of a limited and gradually
dwindling practice. But what Dr. Grierson lacked in
external advantages he made up for by enthusiasm, and
by faith in the value of his scheme. The scientific and
educational usefulness of local collections was a subject on
which he was never tired of dilating. This idea, which he
held in common with not a few distinguished scientists,
such as Sir John Lubbock and others, was more than once
advocated by him before the British Association ; indeed,

we believe, he was the first to press the matter upon the attention of the Association.

His faith had at least this practical effect, that it delivered him from all excess of modesty in applying for contributions to his curious store. Being fully satisfied that he represented the interests of science, he foraged boldly. He had the keenest scent for what would serve his purpose, and if any one in the district for ten miles round became possessed of any article of antiquarian or scientific interest, it was just as well for him to make up his mind at once that its only proper resting place was the museum at Thornhill, for the doctor's visit was inevitable, and the doctor's logic was generally irresistible. Indeed, at one time afterwards, Joseph Thomson had almost to quarrel outright with him for the retention of some of his valuable African curiosities. In this and other ways there gradually grew up, under his fostering care, an institution of which Thornhill felt that it had reason to be proud.

But, to the doctor, collecting was not an end in itself. Here at least he had a very practical object in view. What was the good of antiquarian treasures and scientific specimens, if there were not students to use them? Hence the formation of the Society of Inquiry. It was the natural complement of the museum; and only when it had once been fairly established did the quaint *savant* feel that he had attained to his educational ideal.

Dr. Grierson being, *par excellence*, the father confessor of the neighbourhood on matters scientific, it was but natural that Joseph Thomson should take him into his confidence. The lad, in his eagerness to peer into the secrets of nature, as hidden in rocks and plants, wanted encouragement and sympathy. The doctor's ear was open and interested; and so there speedily sprang up between the two a fellowship of a very close kind. The young inquirer was felt to have the right stuff in him, and his zeal and success in doing original work surprised and delighted his older friend.  The doctor was, in fact, not a little proud of his confidant, and in later years it was one of his amiable weaknesses to pose as his patron and to claim him as a *protégé*—an experience to which the explorer submitted with good-natured amusement.

When Joseph Thomson joined the Society of Inquiry either at, or immediately after, its formation, he was the youngest on its roll; but from the first he was not only one of the most devoted but also one of the most efficient of its members.  In its meetings he found a much-prized opportunity of giving articulate utterance to his ideas and of putting to the test of discussion his theories and the result of his observations.  The fact that he could find an appreciative audience gave him an immediate object to work for; while, at the same time, the fact that his statements would be keenly scrutinised, not only put him on his mettle but trained him to accuracy and caution.

The value of these things he fully recognised, and during the four or five years of his association with the society, there was no worker more in evidence.  His name during those years is continually recurring in the records of the society, now as the donor to the museum of some valuable antiquarian " find," now as the describer of some interesting specimen, now as the narrator of some scientific excursion, now as the reader of a paper or as the leader in a discussion.

The records of the society show, as might have been expected, that the subject of geology was one which very specially occupied his attention, and that his father's quarry formed a very useful exercise-ground for his meditations and observations.  His father's delight in Hugh Miller's works had possibly infected him.  Be this as it may, he was, as a boy, thoroughly conversant with ' My Schools and Schoolmasters ' and ' The Testimony of the Rocks.'  Passing from these to Page's ' Text-Book of

Geology,' he soon had that stiff treatise pretty well assimilated.

But he was not content to store up knowledge without applying it to use. This was made evident by his contributions to the proceedings of the society. 'The distribution of Peroxide of Iron in the Sandstone of Gatelawbridge Quarry,' 'Some peculiar markings in the Sandstone of Gatelawbridge Quarry,' 'The Stratification of the Sandstone of Gatelawbridge Quarry, with special reference to the unconformable character of certain Strata';—these are among the titles of the communications which he presented; and they indicate that, while he was a greedy reader of the literature of his favourite science, he was, from the first, resolved to be a practical reader of the book of Nature.

Thus it happened that, at an early period, he became quite an expert observer. He was so constantly in the habit of bringing the knowledge he had acquired from books to bear upon whatever lay under his eyes, that he was soon able to take in at a glance the geological character of any piece of country, and to determine with substantial accuracy the significance of its various features. This faculty, as it ripened, brought increasingly a true delight to him, and added a fresh and powerful motive to extend his rovings.

So heartily did he revel in this new sense of vision, that there was hardly a hill or glen for twenty miles round which he had not visited and studied. From Enterkin Pass to the Solway, from Cairnsmore to Queensberry, from the cliffs of Glenwhargen to the peak of Criffel, he had wandered in exploration before he was more than seventeen years of age. He was indefatigable as a pedestrian, and when to the joy of walking he could add the joy of increasing his earth-knowledge, his exploratory excursions were an endless attraction to him. The shepherd in lonely unfrequented spots, or the zealous gamekeeper suspicious of poachers, would curiously watch the solitary lad, as, hammer in hand, he clambered over rocks or peered into forbidden places.

Though he worked much alone, he enjoyed not infrequently the fellowship of his classmate, Robert Armstrong, who was also a member of the Society of Inquiry. Concerning these occasional outings with his friend, Mr. Armstrong thus writes :—

" Though geology ever held the chief place in his heart, he had a love for all kinds of science. His first enthusiasm was given to the collection of our local ferns. 'The Linn' and 'The Cleugh,' and other glens among the hills, yielded many treasures, and only those with similar tastes can fully understand the boyish glee with which caps were thrown in the air when a new or rare fern was found. The district is not very rich in fossils, but every possible locality was visited and carefully examined. The Silurian shales away beyond Mitchelslack yielded various species of Graptolites; the White Quarry stigmaries and sigillarias ; the limestone of Closeburn and Barjarg gave various shells ; and in the Carboniferous clays at the foot of Crichope Linn he discovered two or three fossil ferns, which, if not new to science, were new to the Lower Carboniferous limestone of Scotland. Several excursions were made to Wanlockhead and Leadhills in search of minerals, the best of which he arranged in a glass case. These excursions were usually made on Saturdays. But often in the summer evenings we went right from school, and, merely halting at Gatelawbridge, went on to the Linn to search for ferns and fossils, and explore the burn up to its source in Townfoot Loch."

It was probably the happiness of these untrammelled wanderings that suggested to his mind the idea of fitting himself for an appointment on the Geological Survey. The employment seemed to him an entirely desirable one, and, as he gradually realized how precarious was the possibility of his ever being able to satisfy his childhood's ideal of being sent to search unknown lands, he was fain to fix his mind upon the more attainable ideal of exploring his own country.

This aspiration was further accentuated by a casual meeting which he had with the director of the Geological Survey himself—Professor Archibald Geikie, at Crichope Linn. Crichope Linn, we may say in passing, is one of the most interesting and remarkable linns in Scotland. It is a deep, narrow, richly-wooded gorge about a mile in length, where the rocks of Permian sandstone have been rent asunder by some natural cataclysm. A stream flowing through has worn the soft stone, now into curious circular cavities, and anon into quaint channels, through which it rushes as a swift current, or hurls itself as a noisy cascade into some deep pool, whose dark surface and fern-bedecked sides the visitor can only dimly discern from his standpoint thirty or forty feet above. This picturesque ravine—the prototype, by the way, of the hiding-place of Balfour of Burley in 'Old Mortality'—was a favourite haunt of Joseph Thomson. It appealed both to the romantic and scientific sides of his nature; for, while it had its Elf's Kirk and Covenanters' place of refuge, it had also in secret recesses its cryptogamic and geological treasures. Often had he clambered through its dangerous places in search for rare specimens. And not without reward dear to the scientific spirit, as we have already seen. It happened that Professor Geikie, busy with his survey of Nithsdale, visited the Linn one day, and came upon the lad at his solitary self-appointed task. It goes without saying that the master, as full of unconventional *bonhomie* as of scientific enthusiasm, was interested in the youthful worker, who on his part was only too delighted to guide the unexpected visitor to all the points of importance. The interview ended in an adjournment to Gatelawbridge, half a mile off, where the three new fossil ferns, already referred to, were duly examined, pronounced to be a genuine "find," and carefully noted for insertion in the printed results of the Survey.

An incident like this, with its memory of words of approval and encouragement, spoken by so high an authority, could not fail to have a great effect upon Thomson's mind. Apparently it is from this point that we must date the definite resolution to have a University training in science, so as to fit himself for some more congenial career than seemed likely to open for him at home.

All this time, however, Joseph Thomson was not living otherwise an idle life. He had, in the end of 1873, left school; but the energy of his nature was too great to permit of his being content without a definite employment. So, in default of a more suitable occupation presenting itself, he resolved to try his hand at work in his father's quarry.

In this sphere, however, he was pretty much a "chartered libertine." As for his hours of work, he came and went as he pleased. Many an afternoon, as some interesting quest would occur to him, he would silently vanish from his place and be off to the hills, not to be seen again till late at night, or even, sometimes, till next morning. Then as for the manner of his working, it is to be feared that it did not conduce to the profit of the firm. In his handling of the stones he certainly did not lack vigour; but he indulged in a "breadth of treatment" which did not square with conventional ideas of the art of stone-cutting. The effect was described with unconscious humour by one of the masons in the quarry, when he said contemptuously of a stone which the young "impressionist" had finished, that "it looked as if it had been sputten up by an earthquake." The truth is that his heart was not in this sort of task, though it served very well to save him from the sense of being idle. He had never that serious view of it, as a possible life employment, which alone could have given him a desire to excel in it. While his hands were busy with mallet and chisel, his thoughts were often upon other objects. He was dreaming of far different uses for his powers, and wondering on what hand Providence was to open a door into the future of his dreams.

None of his friends was surprised, therefore, when he intimated that he had made up his mind to go to college and have a course of the science classes. Probably his father had anticipated this decision, and when it was mentioned he met it with prompt approval. He was shrewd enough to see that his son had not yet entered into his vocation, and as he himself, plain man as he was, sympathised to the full with every aspiration after mental culture, he was heartily willing to supply the wherewithal for the gratification of his aim. The beginning of the winter session 1875–76, therefore, found Joseph Thomson enrolled as a student in Edinburgh University.

# CHAPTER III.

## COLLEGE DAYS.

JOSEPH THOMSON began his college career with the two classes of geology and mineralogy, and of chemistry, Professor Geikie being the teacher of the one, and Professor Crum Brown of the other. He had probably intended to keep himself strictly to these two subjects. But very soon, as the nature of the class demands became clear to him, he began to realise vividly his deficiencies in relation to elementary education. The mistake he had made in taking his tasks at school in such a light-hearted fashion stood out very plainly. However, the mistake was, as he thought, not beyond remedy, and remedied it must be. Hence we find him promptly enrolling himself in such extra-mural classes as seemed needful; and these did much for him, although he never quite overcame the disadvantages under which he had thoughtlessly placed himself.

As for his chosen science classes, he threw himself into the work of them *con amore*. He had come to the University for a very practical purpose—not to glide through it for the name of the thing, but to fit himself for an already formed life-purpose. He must therefore allow himself no idle hours. Now that he had waked up to the reality of life and to serious thoughts of his future, it behoved him to be earnest, just in proportion as he had dallied with his school work in days gone by.

In view of his extra-mural work it was fortunate for

him that the class of geology made no great strain upon him. His previous reading and practice had made him familiar with the elements, and thus enabled him easily to keep abreast of the daily lessons, while giving time for other things. But, taking one thing with another, his hands were abundantly full, and he was glad when the Sabbath came round with its release from toil, and its call to quiet thought about other things.

How he felt about this will be best described in his own words. Writing to his intimate friend and schoolmate Miss Bennett—with whom he corresponded confidentially all through his college days, and to whom were addressed nearly all the letters quoted in this chapter—he says :—

"What a glorious thing is a Sabbath in town! No sound breaking in upon the holy calm, except the musical chime of the church bells and the occasional tramp of people going to church. Now and then the rattle of a cab helps to make the stillness more impressive, as it reminds one of the dreadful din of the rest of the week. What a grand institution it is! Released from the cares of the past week one recruits his energies for the next. Then one has more time to think of religious questions—to read that glorious old book the Bible."

At such times, when the sounds of city traffic were hushed, he loved to let his heart and imagination wander away to the open country, and to live for a little in imaginary communion with the rural scenes he loved so well. It needed little to wake the responsive chord of memory. He speaks of posting himself often on Sabbath mornings at the window of his lodging "to listen to the glorious sound of the organ" from a church which just faced his window, "and of a woman's voice singing in the choir." "I would rather," he says, "hear that any day than the best concert. It always makes me think of home, of the solemn loneliness of the hills, of the mingled gloomy and cheerful beauties of Crichope Linn, of the singing of the birds, the sighing of the trees and the rippling of water over its rocky bed."

In the solitude of his lodging during this first session, he found his hours of relief from study taken up with other and deeper thoughts. For now, in a special sense, he became conscious of the awaking of his spiritual nature, and of the persistent surging up of questions about the unseen, and about the mystery of life and duty. He had been brought up breathing daily an atmosphere of unostentatious religion in his father's house, and he had never known anything but reverence for things sacred. But hitherto habit had been the dominant factor in his attitude towards these matters; he had been conscious of no stirring of profound personal interest. Now, however, when his life was lifted out of its old setting, when he was thrown in upon himself and compelled to a sense of his individuality, he began to realise the throbs of his spiritual being, to feel the existence of a world behind the visible, with its great facts and problems pressing for attention. He had, in fact, reached that momentous stage in a man's evolution when the voices of the soul become articulate, and when "deep" begins to "call unto deep."

"I hope (he writes to his friend) that my learning of science is not entirely ape-work—a mere exercise to the memory—which, alas, in seventy out of every hundred turns out to be the case—but an education in the true sense of the term; and that, while it is more immediately connected with the intellect, it may react upon the emotional, moral and religious nature. The latter, I fear, you will hardly consider, from various expressions used in this letter, to have been much attended to. But that is a mistake. Since I came here, I have thought more of religion than ever I did before."

His letters reveal him as greatly exercised in quiet moments with the ever-recurring question of faith *versus*

reason, and groping after the point of reconciliation
between the two. They represent him as looking back
with tender memory to what he had been taught, but
realising that the simple views of the Bible in which he
had grown up were hard to hold against the arguments
of science and philosophy—praying for guidance, yet
feeling that the forces arrayed against the unquestioning
faith of his childhood were looming up more and more
formidably.

One thing that early impressed itself upon him was the
sacredness of a man's personal convictions, from whatever
point of view he may arrive at those convictions, or after
whatever form he may find it needful to express them. It
was his own God-given right as a free, spiritual, responsible being to question and reason and judge about the
deepest problems of truth and duty for himself; but it
was no less the inalienable privilege of every other man
to do the same. It seemed to him, therefore, to belong
to the essence of true charity that no man should attempt,
even by the strong assertion of dogma, to restrict his
neighbour's liberty.

This was a position from which he never swerved.
Indeed, the feeling only deepened as the years went on,
and as circumstances threw him into contact with men of
widely varying views on religion; and it largely accounts
for the reticence which he persistently maintained upon
all mere points of doctrine, as distinguished from the ever-
pressing necessity of pure and noble living. "I would
not for the world," he writes, "attempt to overturn any
man's religious views, whether I thought them to be right
or not." For himself, he wanted some profounder and
nobler motive in life than the hope of heaven or the fear
of hell. Yet there seemed to him to be many who could
only have their conduct shaped to better things by
such motives—and who was he that he should judge
them ?

There were times when, in his wrestlings with the

problems of the unseen world, he felt overwhelmed and humiliated at the helplessness of human reason, and to be possessed with the feeling that one could not be sure of anything. But, anon, that which is deeper and more insistent than reason would return quietly to assert its sway, and to re-awaken the consciousness that God and truth and eternity are realities, which loom up calm and changeless, like the broad-based heaven-piercing mountains, when the morning breeze has swept aside the enveiling mists that hid them.

More and more he became convinced that doctrinal formulas, however helpful to many minds, are not the things to put to the forefront, and, increasingly, his own religion resolved itself simply into a devotion to goodness in all its forms. He had in him a deep vein of devoutness; but for him the one supreme thing was to be true and live beautifully, and no man ever strove more honestly to honour his ideal. It was not in vain that he registered thus early his purpose of "hoping always for the best, striving to attain to as high a standard of life as possible, making truth my guide, and following it wherever it may lead or to whatever issue it may tend."

Ere we pass from this subject, it may be well to quote, as illustrating the trend of his thoughts in those early formative days, a letter to a distinguished fellow-student. This correspondent, who was of a somewhat metaphysical turn of mind, had in a letter been discussing the question, Why do I exist at all? "This," replies the embryo scientist, to whom living was greater than theories of life, "is an eminently unprofitable subject."

"Allow me," he continues, "to lay down a few rules for your guidance. In the first place, overhaul your conscience, and find out what your convictions are regarding your duty. Having done so, prepare to act up to them as far as is in your power. And then ask yourself the question, What is your true origin? Are you merely the result of blind natural forces and laws, or are you the result of intelligent design—in fact, were you *made* (whether by evolution or by an instant act of creation) by a Supreme Being?  If the former is the case, then truly it is a black lookout.  If mind and soul are the result of an evolution from matter, then with it they must return to their constituent particles, and a theory of existence is vain. . . . The thought is repugnant to all that is good and great and true in man's nature, and we turn with a sigh of relief to the more hopeful side of the question. This, too, no doubt, has its difficulties, but how few and how small compared with the materialistic theory !  Think of the bright hope gleaming through the darkness in the idea that we have, as the Author and Finisher of our being, One who is our Father, our Shepherd, our Protector, who is Love, Truth, Goodness.  And then, what a future for us there is on this theory !

"Think of these things.  Casting away all thought of the *why*, consider that you *are*.  Consider that you *have* a future, and that everything in that future depends upon the way in which you act up to your honest convictions of right and wrong.

"It is the sad fate of all people who search out the unknowable, instead of grappling with the realities of life, that they lose themselves among words.  Turn to Nature, and like Longfellow you will soon exclaim :—

   ' These in flowers and men are more than seeming;
      Workings are they of the self-same powers
   Which the poet in no idle dreaming,
      Seeth in himself and in the flowers.

    *        *        *        *

   And with childlike, credulous affection
      We behold their tender buds expand ;
   Emblems of our own great resurrection,
      Emblems of the bright and better land.'

Begin and read the ' Psalm of Life ' immediately ; also ' The

Prelude,' 'The Light of Stars,' 'Footsteps of Angels,' and 'Flowers.'   Think also of 'The Law of Life':—

> 'Live I, so live I,
> To my Lord heartily,
> To my Prince faithfully,
> To my Neighbour honestly,
> Die I, so die I.' "

We may reasonably infer from the above letter that the simple healthful philosophy of Longfellow's poetry had had its own share in the moulding of the writer's views of life.   It may also be noted that there was one other book which had a great influence upon him.   That was Dr. Walter C. Smith's 'Hilda among the broken gods.' He felt it to be "a most delightful work."   "I am not a great reader of poetry," he says, "but over this work I became positively enthusiastic."

Considering the leeway which he had to make up, and the need he recognised of improving his education all round, he seems in this first session to have had no idea of aiming at class honours, pitted as he was against many whose previous literary and technical preparation had been so much more favourable than his own.   It was not according to his nature to be a mere "crammer" for honours.   "I have no ambition for medals and that sort of thing," he writes.   "My aim is knowledge, and exams. merely serve as knowledge-gauges, by which I may get a more definite idea of what I have learned."

Nevertheless, the close of the session found him occupying a good place.   In geology he obtained a certificate of "high distinction" in the ordinary class works, honourable mention for mineralogical analysis, and also for his essay on the class excursions.   In chemistry he likewise acquitted himself with credit, and obtained second class honours.

After a short holiday he returned to Edinburgh for the summer session (1876).   This time his subjects of study were botany, under Professor Balfour, and practical natural history under Professor Huxley, who for the session took the place of Professor Wyville Thomson in his absence with the *Challenger* expedition.

The experience of studying personally under Huxley was a privilege to which he had been looking forward with eager anticipation; for he had already been fascinated with the charm of Huxley's writings, and had received from them no small amount of mental stimulus. Nor were his expectations disappointed. But he found the work to be unexpectedly hard, and very soon he had the sense of panting to keep pace with the demands of the lecturer. It was not merely that the texture of scientific reasoning in the lectures was so closely knit—although that was a very palpable fact—but the character of Huxley's terminology was entirely strange to him. It met him on his weakest side, for it presupposed a knowledge of Greek (being little else than Greek compounds with English terminations), and of Greek he had none.

"Huxley's usual lectures," he writes, "are something awful to listen to. One half of the class, which numbers about four hundred, have given up in despair from sheer inability to follow him. The strain on the attention at each lecture is so great as to be equal to any ordinary day's work. I feel quite exhausted after them. And then, to master his language is something dreadful. It is equal to learning a new tongue. But, with all these drawbacks, I would not miss them, even if they were ten times more difficult. They are something glorious, sublime."

Again he writes: "Huxley is still very difficult to follow, and I have been four times, in his lectures, completely stuck and utterly helpless. But he has given us eight or nine beautiful lectures on the frog. . . . If you only heard a few of the lectures you would be surprised to find that there were so few missing links in the chain of life, from the *amœba* to the *genus homo*."

He felt the strain of this session to be very great, and complains of being kept dreadfully close at work. "My hours at college," he writes, "are from 7.30 A.M. to 5.30 P.M. I never get half an hour to myself except at the end of the week."

But when the Saturday came he did enjoy it to the full. When released from the restraints of class and city his pent-up animal spirits fairly overflowed. With the superabundant energy characteristic of him, he explored, in long walks, all the country round about Edinburgh, often starting in a frolicsome mood at absurdly early hours. In one of his letters he says: "I have done quite a feat *à la* Weston. Yesterday morning I walked fifteen miles before 6.30 A.M. to Carlops, and had the pleasure of waking up some friends there at what they doubtless thought a dreadfully unseasonable hour. After a short rest I had another walk of seven miles over some hills, which in ordinary walking would be equal to ten or twelve." And of course he had the return journey to make!

Then there were the periodical excursions of the botanical class. Every one knows how unconventional students are when thus out in the open; and in all the frolic he was in the forefront. He would come home as hoarse as a crow from a variety of vocal performances, and find infinite amusement at the concern of his sympathetic landlady over "the bad cold he had got."

He finished this session also "with distinction," at least in the natural history class, and at the close returned to Gatelawbridge.

He did not resume his University work in the winter of 1876, as he felt that his father needed him at home. Probably, even from the educational point of view, he was just as well employed in securing and consolidating what he had learned, and in putting his acquired knowledge to the test of practical experiment. Book knowledge could at the best be but a scaffolding by means of which he might build up his actual capacity as a scientist; the real building could only be done by the practical use of his eyes, and by the application of his mind to the problems around him.

He resumed his attendance at the Literary Society and the Society of Inquiry in Thornhill, and exercised himself in the preparation of a number of essays. But the task which specially occupied his time and thoughts was the practical working out of a theory of the geology of Mid-Nithsdale, which he early recognised to be in some respects peculiar, and whose special features had never been explained. Here was lying to his hand an opportunity of doing congenial and truly original work. To this, therefore, he devoted himself with his wonted concentration and carefulness during the autumn and early winter months. The result of his observations and reflections he embodied in an elaborate paper entitled 'The Origin of the Permian Basin of Thornhill,' which he read before the Dumfries Scientific Society on February 2nd, 1877.

Subsequent to the reading of this paper, another subject of no less attractiveness presented itself. In the development of the business of the quarry at Gatelawbridge, his father was having a branch line of railway constructed to Thornhill station, a mile off. In cutting through a ridge of drift, the workmen exposed a geological formation of a decidedly unusual character. The quick eye of the young student at once noted the deposit as being different from any known accumulation of the same age in Dumfriesshire, and probably even in Scotland. The elucidation of the enigma thus suggested was therefore his next work. The facts and his conclusions formed the subject of another paper, which he read first to the Society of Inquiry at Thornhill in October 1877, and afterwards to the society in Dumfries in the January following.

These two papers were at once recognised as of more than common interest, not only as being in themselves fine specimens of scientific induction, but as revealing in so young an observer a quite exceptional capacity for independent work. They were printed together in the transactions of the Dumfries society, and constitute his first appearance in type.

In the winter of 1877 he was once more at college in Edinburgh. He joined Professor Geikie's advanced class of geology and mineralogy, and also that of natural history under Professor Wyville Thomson, who had now returned to his post. The long interval which he had had for private study and practice had given him increased strength and confidence. In both classes he felt the ground, as it were, more firm beneath his feet, and he threw himself into the labours of the session in both with the encouraging consciousness that, even though he had an unusual number of clever competitors, he ought to be able to give a good account of himself.

On this occasion his former schoolfellow, Armstrong, shared his rooms, and from reminiscences by him we quote the following :—

"He was a most conscientious student. He wrote out his notes in full immediately on coming from the class, and engaged me to look them over and make any corrections in spelling or grammar that might be necessary —for he was most anxious to improve himself in English. He was also most methodical in his work; every hour had its appointed task. Even the stroll along Princes Street—his 'constitutional' he called it—was always taken at the same hour, 4–5 P.M.; and woe betide the landlady if coffee was not on the table at 9.30 P.M. prompt. In the evenings, when no exam. was near to make us burn the midnight oil, we made calls on mutual friends, or received visits from them. At other times a good novel would form the evening's relaxation. I remember he got through 'David Copperfield'—it was the first time he had read it—at one sitting. In this, as in more weighty matters, 'Joe' broke the record. When any star, such as Irving or Toole, visited Edinburgh, an occasional evening would be devoted to the theatre. Miss Wallis, in her *rôle* of Shaksperian heroines, was a great favourite, and the Italian Opera, on its annual visit was always patronised. It is needless to say that he was most regular in his habits; he did not smoke, and of course he never touched drink. He had such a well-balanced nature that he felt no need for an artificial stimulant of any kind. He was no faddist; the desire simply did not exist."

At intervals during the session there were the usual class excursions for "field practice" in geology, which were no doubt full of instructiveness, notwithstanding that they were by no means solemn performances. If they were valuable as means of giving practical knowledge of the earth's crust, they were also interesting as revealing how much of genial humanity lurks responsive beneath the academic crust of professorial nature. One of these excursions he describes with great gusto:—

"A glorious one . . . when we went to North Berwick, explored the coast there, and finished off with a grand dinner at the principal hotel. There were twenty-two of us, including Professor Geikie, Mr. Murray of the *Challenger*, and a Dr. Purvis. After dinner nearly every one sang comic songs. Geikie gave 'The Three Jews,' and Murray gave, among others, 'The Costermonger's Donkey.' The singing in the train was perfectly terrific. All the students' songs that could be raked up were done in chorus, in which the mild and melodious voice of yours truly was not the least conspicuous. We finished up at the Waverley Station with every one standing up, hats off, and singing as loudly as our already exhausted voices would allow 'God save the Queen.' It caused an immense sensation, which would hardly have been lessened if it had been known who were among the singers."

When the end of the session drew near, the tussle for first place was very keen. He was conscious of knowing his subjects, but he knew the brilliance of some of the men he had to reckon with, and he was aware of his own points of weakness; hence he suffered himself to indulge in no over-confidence. But in the end the issue was clear. He emerged as Medallist in Natural History and Medallist in Geology, besides having won the first prize for blowpipe analysis and the fourth prize for an essay on the class excursions. And no man grudged him his honour.

The following notes by Sir Archibald Geikie give an interesting glimpse of Joseph Thomson the student, and indicate suggestively enough why none of his fellows could be jealous of him. After referring to the course of his class-work, the *quondam* professor says :—

"It was in the excursions into the field, for practical geological work, that I saw most of Thomson, and formed my high opinion of his capacity. He was always the first to climb a crag or scale a quarry, showing in these early days the daring and physical endurance which stood him in such good stead in after life among the wilds of Africa. He had likewise a quick eye for geological structure, and rapidly seized the salient points of each section as we came to it. He displayed, too, an exuberant enthusiasm for geology, and seemed never so happy as when he was striding ahead of his fellows to get at the next section, where he felt sure some fresh light would be thrown upon the structure of the district.

"There was such a frank open-heartedness about him, such a love of fun, and so much kindly humour, that he became a great favourite with his class-fellows, who liked him for his companionableness, while at the same time they respected him for his ability. I shall never forget one scene in particular, where these pleasant relations between them showed themselves in a very striking way.

We had gone, at the end of the work of the winter, to take an April holiday in the Western Highlands for some ten days. One day, as we were sauntering up Glen Spean, a member of the party found a penny tin-whistle on the road. In the course of the evening it was discovered that Thomson could play a little on this musical instrument, and from time to time discordant notes and shouts of laughter were heard from a back room, where he was made by his companions to play Scottish airs to them until far on into the morning. When we started to resume our tramp next day down Glen Spean, he was placed at the head of the procession, and with his whistle in his mouth, but hardly able to play for laughter, he marched ahead, to the wonderment of the peasants in the fields, who seemed to look on the company as a detachment from the county lunatic asylum.

"Thomson preserved this tuneless instrument as a memento of the first geological expedition in which he had ever taken part. Two years afterwards, when we were tramping through the east of Fife, and studying the cliff section of the East Neuk, he one day, when we had sat down for luncheon, perched himself on the edge of the low cliff, and, to the amusement of the party, produced his whistle, and began again the discordant ditties which had so roused his class-fellows in the Highland glens. I can, in imagination, see him now as he sat then, with his legs dangling over the crag, his cloth cap pulled over his ears to shield them from the biting east wind, his cheeks distended with the effort to extract audible notes from his instrument, and his face showing the utmost gravity, as he swayed his head from side to side to keep time with the air he was trying to coax out of the refractory whistle.

"I used to have parties of the students at my house and I remember the last of these gatherings at which Thomson was present. He volunteered a series of short recitations, personating different characters and ranks of life.    It was an exceedingly clever performance, which showed him in an entirely new light, and indicated a versatility of adaptation and a knowledge of men and manners which greatly surprised and interested me.

"After he left college I saw him only rarely.  When Keith Johnston asked me about a geologist to accompany him on his African expedition, I had great pleasure in strongly recommending Thomson.  We all know how admirably he justified the choice that was made of him."

# CHAPTER IV.



THE college session being finished, Joseph Thomson once more turned his footsteps homewards. For a few weeks he was content to rest, and, in the renewal of old associations and the revisiting of familiar scenes, to recover tone after the labours of the winter. The pleasure of these occupations kept him from the immediate sense of self-dissatisfaction. But, as the weeks passed by, and the superfluous energy of his nature craved for outlet, he became increasingly aware of an anxious and unsettled feeling. What next? was a question in relation to his life which pressed itself upon his thoughts with fretting insistency. It haunted him, and was, as he said, "eating the life out of him."

It was open to him, of course, to join in his father's business and to throw his energies into the work of its development. But, whatever prospect of profit there might be in that course, his heart turned from it. His likings lay in a wholly different direction. He could be satisfied with no career in which full scope was not to be found for the exercise of his scientific tastes. His college experiences had only deepened his devotion to research, and in the success which he had attained he had caught glimpses of a possible future for himself far removed from commerce. But where was the way of entrance into that future to be found?

The only hope that seemed to have any likelihood of

translating itself into reality was that of his being appointed to the staff of the Geological Survey. But an opening in this line might be long enough in presenting itself; and how was he to exercise himself in the meantime?

It was while he was thus despondently "mooning about in his native valley," that his opportunity came. One morning he noticed in the newspaper a paragraph which made his heart bound with excitement and interest. It was to the effect that an expedition under Keith Johnston was in course of preparation to proceed to East Central Africa. The news came upon him with all the force of a summons to service. Here, if Providence was kind, was the very opening for him. The thwarted ambition of his childhood leapt up into life again, and, under an impulse which he felt to be resistless, he forthwith wrote off, volunteering to go in any capacity whatever and without salary.

At this time he was just twenty years of age, and with his fair, fresh complexion he looked no more. When, therefore, in the course of a few days he received a request to meet with the president and African committee of the Royal Geographical Society, he went with much trepidation, anticipating that his boyish appearance would at once put him out of the running. Undoubtedly his youth did present a serious difficulty. The committee naturally felt some doubt and hesitation as to whether they were justified in appointing him. However, his testimonials were undeniably good, his physique splendid, and his enthusiasm manifest, and these all made their due impression. In the speech which Sir Rutherford Alcock, the chairman of the committee, made at the presentation of the gold medal of the Royal Geographical Society seven years later, he said, "I well remember scanning Mr. Thomson and thinking I could see a good deal of character and determination in his face." Meantime influential friends, hearing of his application, strongly interested themselves in his favour, among these being Professor Geikie, who could speak with fullest knowledge, and also Professor Seeley, who had somehow met him at the British Association and, struck by his youthful devotion to science, had become one of his correspondents. His two geological papers, as printed in the transactions of the Dumfries Scientific Society, were heard of and sent for. The result was that, after an interval of racking uncertainty on his part, he received intimation that his application had been entertained.

But the appointment which he had received was one which brought with it some elements to temper his pleasure. To his surprise and annoyance he found himself designated, "Geologist and Naturalist to the Expedition." This was more than he bargained for, and, with his modest views of his own attainments, he could only feel humiliated by the responsibility so unexpectedly laid upon his shoulders.

"I am in great tribulation of spirit," he writes to a correspondent, "and I come to unburthen my woes to your sympathetic ear. My disease arises from a too rapid development of my fame. The first shock to my sensibilities was received when I figured as ' Geologist' in *The Academy*. Then I was struck all of a heap by finding that *Nature* and *The Times* were both so unfortunate as to ' believe that I had received an excellent training as a geologist,' and that they ' expected I would make important contributions to our knowledge of the geology of the region to be visited.' And then, to make confusion worse confounded, Bates, the secretary of the Royal Geographical Society, describes me as ' Geologist and Naturalist' to the four principal scientific societies here.

"Now, what is a poor unfortunate to think who is next to launched on the ocean without a compass at the age of twenty, new from a short term on the irons and with no experience? Don't you think it really too hard to raise expectations of such a brilliant character? I am continually asking myself if I am not like a mushroom which appears suddenly in the night and disappears nearly as rapidly under the light of day. It is not often that people have to complain of a too rapid development of their fame, but I find myself in that predicament. May heaven grant that all expectations be realised! but I would have thanked heaven very heartily if there had been no expectations."

He was, however, not the person to become faint-hearted under responsibility, or to shrink from a task because of its mere difficulty. So, as was to be expected, he calmly accepted the situation and proceeded to make the most of the time at his disposal. He took a lodging at Kew on September 15th, and from that day until his departure, two months later, he spent every available moment in museums, libraries, or the Botanic Gardens, ascertaining what was already known of the natural history and geology of East Africa. With respect to geology, he found the information available to be of the most meagre description. To Armstrong he writes: "I have been hunting about for geological scraps over the entire libraries of the Geographical and Geological Societies, and you would be surprised at the little that is known." These scientific grubbings he varied by the taking of lessons in swimming and boxing.

During those two months he was introduced to a number of distinguished men of science, including Sir Joseph Hooker, who drew out a list of instructions for his use, Professor Oliver, Mr. Smith and Dr. Woodward of the British Museum, Sir Rawson Rawson and others. His chief mentor and helper, however, during that time of preparation was Mr. Bates, of Amazon fame, the acting secretary of the Royal Geographical Society, whom he describes as "an exceedingly pleasant old gentleman, ever ready to be of service, and continually priming me with valuable confidential hints."

To Keith Johnston, as his chief, he came prepared to stand on the most loyal and kindly footing.  He saw him for a little every day, and was anxious to develop some sense of comradeship—apparently, however, not with conspicuous success.  He thought Johnston "a very nice fellow, hating all fuss," but felt that "his conversational powers were not very remarkable, which made it somewhat difficult to get along sometimes."  This reserve he hoped would wear away, as they entered more fully into the fellowship of their appointed work, and got to know each other better.

The work appointed for the expedition was the exploration of the unvisited region between Dar-es-Salaam and Lake Nyassa, with the view of finding a practical route to the interior by which the great chain of central lakes might be connected in some better way than hitherto with the east coast.  If the stores held out, they were to continue their investigations as far as Lake Tanganyika, the nature of the country between the two lakes being as yet quite unknown.  It did not seem probable that more than this could be accomplished with the funds at the disposal of the expedition.  Even this scheme, however, gave promise of no small experience of perils and hardships.

But, to the ardent and light-hearted young enthusiast rejoicing in the exuberance of health and energy, of how little account were all possible privations when compared with the joys of peering into hidden regions and of reaping a rich harvest of knowledge in the interests of civilisation and science?  Moreover, as he was only second in command, the sense of burden did not weigh so heavily upon his mind.  He had, indeed, in the agreement which he signed, bound himself to take command and carry out the objects of the expedition, in the event of anything happening to deprive it of Johnston's leadership.  But a look at his chief's athletic form, so thoroughly inured by hardy exercise and by experience of travel elsewhere, was

sufficient to banish every anxious thought and make the
bond seem more a name than a reality.  It was therefore
only with the spirit of cheerful anticipation that he viewed
the advent of the day when he was to set sail for the scene
of his chosen life-work.

At 3 P.M. on the 14th of November, 1878, the ss.
*Assyria*, with Johnston and himself on board, cleared out
of the Victoria Docks, London, amid drenching rain.  The
last adieus were waved to his father and friends on shore,
and he was fairly started on his long and hazardous
enterprise.

The voyage began in a tempestuous fashion, and for the
first three days the experiences of the passengers were
anything but enviable.  On the 18th, however, the
weather greatly improved, and from that time on to the
12th of December, when Aden was reached, pleasure and
merriment reigned on board.

To the young man, who had hitherto known nothing but
insular quietness in his life, but who was saturated with
the spirit of romance, and open-eyed and responsive to all
the wonder of the new world into which he was being
borne, every new scene was an object of delight and
interest.  His first glimpse of Africa was one fitted to
fascinate his mind, when, on the morning of the 21st,
"the notched and grooved peaks of the Atlas appeared
in the south, lighted up with the roseate hues of the
rising sun," and calling up "picturesque imaginations of
the wandering Moors who peopled its rocky recesses."
He thought not that some day in the yet hidden future
he was to see it without the poetic gilding.

He enjoyed a few hours ashore at Algiers, where, hastily
passing by the boulevards and everything that reminded
him of Europe, he plunged into the native quarter, and,
amid the sights and sounds of a purely Mohammedan
scene, he revelled in the varied sensations of mingling
with North African life.  A day and a half were spent at
Port Said, which he found to be, morally and physically,

a sickening place, "evidently used," he said, "as a harbour for the earthly agents of the devil and an easy entrance to and from the lower regions." Similar rambles were permitted to him in the tropical Arabian towns of Jidda and Hodeida, which he eagerly took advantage of to familiarise himself with other aspects of the East.

There was a fortnight of delay at Aden before the steamer for Zanzibar would start. This he utilised in paying a visit to Berbera, 150 miles off on the African coast, where a great native fair was being held, and where, in the characteristic commingling of the wild Somali and other interior tribes, he could feel himself for the first time face to face with the native barbarism of the Dark Continent, and get some idea of the real people he would have to deal with. In this little trip he had also other foretastes of the realism of African travel, in the miseries of two days and a half spent each way in an open native boat packed with filthy Arabs, he being sick all the time and lying amid the never-ceasing fumes of hateful tobacco smoke, without a shelter from the blazing sun in the daytime or from the chilling dew at night. He had compensations, however, in the variety of interesting characters which he met at Berbera, and in the opportunity of making a geologising excursion to the hills under an escort of cavalry—a full account of which he sent home in the form of a paper for the Royal Geographical Society, entitled, "Four days in Berbera."

Zanzibar was reached on January 5th, 1879. There the travellers were received with characteristic kindness by Dr. Kirk, a man not only distinguished in many callings, as doctor, explorer, scientist, diplomatist, but one who, by his wise, energetic, untiring efforts as consul-general at Zanzibar, has made his mark more indelibly upon the history and destiny of East Africa than any other single individual. He, of all men, was in sympathy with their mission, and made every provision for rendering their sojourn agreeable.

The five months that must elapse before a suitable season for beginning their journey should arrive, they spent in various useful ways. While Johnston was busy studying the different possible routes, inquiring, planning, purchasing, Joseph Thomson was no less busy in his own special line. Besides throwing himself heartily into the study of Kiswahili under the able and kindly guidance of Bishop Steere, he went out in all directions about the island on natural history excursions. These useful occupations, together with a variety of sight-seeing and sport, the frequent enjoyment of Dr. Kirk's splendid hospitality, a grand reception by the Sultan, and the meeting with all kinds of interesting people, including several distinguished travellers, kept the time from hanging heavy on his hands.

By the end of February the necessary preparations were well advanced. It was then resolved to make a sort of trial trip to the famous forest region of Usambara on the mainland. This would give them a foretaste of coming experiences, and help them to realise more clearly the conditions of African travel.

The marvellous scenery, which unfolded itself as they toiled up and up among the mountains, filled the young explorer with enthusiasm. Now they passed through precipitous gorges rich with every feature of natural beauty. Anon, they moved with awed step amid the gloom and eerie stillness of the primeval forest, where every tree was a monster shooting up from a hundred to two hundred feet in height. The sights of the day and the sounds of the night awakened, as with a magic influence, all the poetry of his nature, until he was almost weary with pure enjoyment. And when, to the rich supply of natural delights, there was added the spice of varied adventures, it may well be imagined that this brief exploratory excursion was one fitted to inspire him with eager anticipation of what was yet to come. "Never shall I forget my first sight of this grand forest," he writes to Armstrong. "I do not exaggerate when I state that I

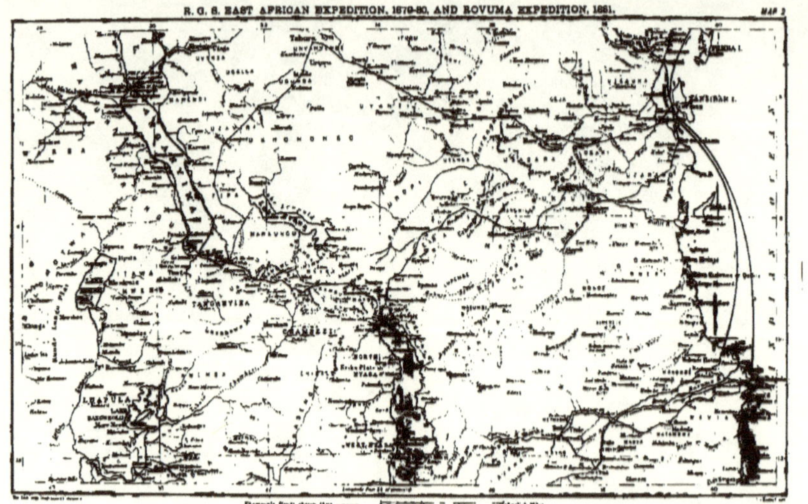

R. G. S. EAST AFRICAN EXPEDITION, 1879-80, AND ROVUMA EXPEDITION, 1881.
MAP 2

felt stunned, and that in my five days' sojourn in it I walked as one in a maze."

Immediately on his return from this interesting region he embodied his observations on its *fauna* in a paper for the Society.   He also wrote a paper on the geology of the district.

In Zanzibar, he was, of course, not without experience of the fevers and other disagreeable accompaniments of African life.   But in his exuberant health and buoyancy he made light of these drawbacks, and only took them as part of the necessary seasoning which was to fit him for his chosen task.

In the two months following the Usambara trip, however, Johnston seemed very much out of sorts.   He went on doggedly with the necessary preparations; but as he became increasingly taciturn and morosely reserved, his young companion began to regard him with anxious misgivings.   Evidently his leader felt that there was something seriously wrong with himself; but as Johnston was entirely uncommunicative he could only look on sympathetically and hope for the best.

By the time when the rainy season was approaching its close, he had had quite enough of the life of Zanzibar, however interesting in itself.   He had got all that could be obtained in the way of education for his task; he had learned to have confidence in himself, and he was eagerly longing for a final start.

At last the day came for which he had wearied.   On the 13th of May a farewell visit was paid to the Sultan, who treated the travellers with charming courtesy.   Next day the expedition, with all its *impedimenta*, was embarked on board the Sultan's steamer *Star*, for transport to the starting point at Dar-es-Salaam.   A day or two was usefully spent there in giving the final touches to the work of organisation, with the valuable help of Dr. Kirk. On the 19th the travellers bade adieu to their friend and began their hazardous march.

The caravan numbered one hundred and fifty men, at their head being the experienced and faithful Chuma (whose name has become familiar to all readers of Livingstone's life), and the cheery and energetic Makatubu. Some seventy-eight of the men carried guns. In every respect the equipment of the expedition was practically perfect. "A better organised caravan," said Dr. Kirk, "never left the sea-coast for the interior." All were full of hope and enthusiasm and high spirits—too soon, alas, to be shadowed by anxiety and sorrow!

For the first month, the marching, though dreary and trying enough, amid the rough and swampy coast lowlands, was without mishap. But the rains continued three weeks longer than had been expected, and in an atmosphere reeking with malarial poison, poor Johnston's illness (which had reasserted itself at Dar-es-Salaam), in place of passing off developed into an alarming attack of dysentery. As he was eager to get to Behobeho before resting, they pushed on, carrying their disabled leader, and trying to alleviate his sufferings as best they might.

He did reach Behobeho; but it was only to read with dimming eyes the letters from friends which had reached him from the coast, and then, after a day or two of increasing weakness and frequent unconsciousness, to pass into the last silence. He had but crossed the threshold of his great enterprise and he had fallen, leaving the ripening harvest of his hopes unreaped, and giving one more sad illustration of the pathos of death's inexorable call.

Now had come the supreme crisis of Joseph Thomson's life. It had come in an agonising form, and it had come not only with appalling suddenness, but with an imperative demand for instant decision, which left little space for thought. It is not often that the "tide in the affairs of men," which makes or mars their future, comes upon them with such an overwhelming flood of distractions. But the crisis had to be faced and grappled with! What was he to do?

The arguments against going on were plain enough.
The way before him was long and dark.  The difficulties
and dangers of the enterprise were enormous.  Then, he
was but twenty-one years of age, without experience or
the special knowledge required in a leader—a mere boy,
whose explorations had all been done in his dreams.  To

GLIMPSE OF CAMP LIFE.

proceed might simply mean disaster and death.  Yet,
what if it did?  Could he purchase escape from such a
possible end at the cost of admitted failure and humiliation in his own eyes and of the eclipse of his aspirations
in their very dawning?

The occasion was, indeed, one of those emergencies
which cannot be paltered with, but which go rudely right

down to the reality in an individual and reveal him to himself and to the world.  In an instant, Joseph Thomson discovered his own manhood.  With his foot at the portal of the unknown, he could not linger a moment on the thought of going back.  Was he not a Scotsman?  A countryman of Bruce, Park, Grant, Livingstone?  Was it not a prize worth suffering for to join that noble band of self-denying men, who in the Dark Continent had made the name of their country famous?  Moreover, could he doubtfully consider consequences in the doing of his duty?

The answer of his heart was clear and firm.  Though at the time he was physically prostrate with fever, there was no wavering of purpose.  Moreover, his men must see nothing to suggest such a thing.  Calmly he arranged to give his fallen chief reverent burial and to mark for future seekers the place of his rest; and calmly he gave the orders to march forward.

No doubt Chuma and some of the more shrewd and experienced of his followers wondered.  But there is, in the right dealing with a great crisis, not only that which gives a man the mastery of himself, but a subtle something which makes others feel the spell of his mastery too.  Manifestly, this was a case in point.  Not a word of doubt or questioning was uttered.  Joseph Thomson might be but a boy in years and looks, but his men felt that in tone and bearing he was every inch a master; and at his word they unquestioningly resumed their journey.

His own condition, as they left Behobeho on the morning of July 2nd, was not reassuring.  His brain was reeling, and his limbs felt so weak that he had "incontinently to sit down to prevent a fall."  A few minutes in the open air, however, soon steadied him, and with a resolute heart he set forward.

The nature of his marches before and after Behobeho is vividly described in one of his letters written at that place.  Over large tracts at first, he says, "it was one continuous tramp through marshes, with water from ankle to waist deep." Succeeding this was "a soul-wearying stretch of country, one uniform level sandy plain, covered with scraggy stunted trees, and quite devoid of flowers."

"If you want," he continues, " to get some idea of what an African road is like, I would advise you to go out to some moorland place after rain, and march up and down in one of the drains for two or three hours. If there is a loch near at hand, vary your walk with a ramble into it, and now and then perambulate over some piece of dry ground. The effect will be highly realistic.

"At five o'clock in the morning the drums beat as a sort of *reveille*, and in half an hour we are ready for breakfast—tents down, boxes tied up. Another half hour sees us under way. We generally make one march of it, stopping for the day, according to circumstances, between 11 A.M. and 1 P.M. Up go the tents and into mine I crawl, where, after an infinite amount of perspiration and wriggling, I contrive to get into dry clothes. I then emerge on carnivorous thoughts intent.

"We rejoice in a wonderful sameness in our food. Fowls and rice greet us morning, noon and night, with sometimes an egg or two as a variety. But, what won't go down with a good appetite? If you could look into my pocket on the march, you would probably there find a cob of boiled Indian corn, to allay the pangs of the inner man while pushing along.

"We have got a remarkable 'boy' who attends on us, and glories in such vagaries as cleaning the plates with the skirt of his *kanzu* (the shirt-like dress of the Zanzibari). When that *kanzu* was cleaned, or what other articles it has cleaned, we have resolved never to inquire, as the knowledge might be disastrous to our appetites. Of course, he has been supplied with innumerable cloths, but I suppose the bartering spirit is too much for him.

The knives and spoons he wipes clean (!), when not observed, with his fingers."

The quality of Joseph Thomson's leadership was soon put to a sharp test by the sudden appearance of a war party of the much-feared Mahenge. The word, Mahenge! spoken with bated breath, and hoarsely whispered along the line of porters, was enough to produce a panic. Down went the loads, and in a moment the caravan was on the verge of a calamitous rout. Fortunately the dreaded warriors had not yet caught sight of the company, and hastening to the front, the leader, partly by threats, but mainly by his own coolness, reassured his terror-stricken men. Prompt measures one way or another were needed, and it required but a moment or two of thought to enable him to take his decision. The natural impulse of a weaker man would have been to trust to his guns. But Joseph Thomson took a bolder course—a course which was not only nobler, but which proved in this and many a similar crisis to be safer by far, though it required infinite nerve to take it. Leaving all weapons behind him, he stepped out into the open among the naked, hideously-painted, feather-crowned savages, very much to their astonishment. Proclaiming that he and his party were friends, and acting as if he took it for granted that the Mahenge meant to be equally friendly, he carried his point instantly by a mere *tour de force;* and thus an emergency which might have ended the expedition was, to the infinite relief of all, turned into an occasion of fraternising. We mention this incident because it illustrates in a typical way the fearlessness of the young explorer, the spirit of self-control and tactful forbearance in which he entered upon his life-work, and the basis of moral influence upon which was gradually built up his men's boundless confidence in him in times of peril.

Leaving the dreary district of Uzaramo behind, and traversing, amid a variety of trials and adventures, the richer countries of Ukhutu and Mahenge, he at last reached, about the beginning of August, the base of the great central plateau.  His attainment of that point was to him an infinite relief, for it marked the completion of the first, and in some respects one of the most trying parts of his journey, "where the European is first brought face to face with the hardships of travel, and where he must ever be ready to do battle with disease and danger, and be ever on the alert against desertion and stealing."

His retrospect of the journey thus far was in every way encouraging.  He had in these months gained valuable experience.  He had, partly by firm treatment, and partly by a wise humouring of their prejudices and weaknesses, got his men disciplined to loyalty and trust.  He had established his own faith in gentle methods, in dealing with the ignorant and wayward tribes.  And it was with no small satisfaction that he could say he had "left behind him nothing but goodwill and friendship, teaching the natives that his mission was peace and that the word of the white man could be trusted."  This good beginning was representative of all that was to follow.

On the details of the journey for the next eight or nine months it would be impossible to dwell here.  These must be read in his own book; we can but give the barest outline of his stirring story.

Entering upon the inner plateau, he traversed with infinite difficulty the great desolate moorland region of Uhehe and Ubena, 4000 to 5000 feet in elevation.  It was a veritable life and death struggle.  He was ill all the time with rheumatic fever, and could often only keep himself erect with the support of two men; indeed several times he did fall through sheer exhaustion.  Yet march he must, for the spectre of hunger ever shadowed them, and the bleak winds by day and rains by night were chilling the life out of his men.

The first plateau led to a second and higher one, with

a general level of 7000 to 8000 feet, inhabited by negro tribes of the most miserable and degraded type, representing in fact both physically and mentally almost a caricature of humanity.  Descending from these hideous and inhospitable regions, they pressed on eagerly for the lake. Nyassa was at last sighted; its shore, nearly 4000 feet below, could, however, only be reached by the most precipitous and perilous descent.  They did contrive to get safely down; but every man of the company was completely worn out.

After resting a few days at Nyassa he pushed on over the rich, and hitherto quite unexplored, tract between that lake and Tanganyika, now rejoicing in the arcadian simplicity of one tribe, anon having hard work to protect himself against the perverseness and rapacity of others, but everywhere finding that persuasion was mightier than wilfulness, and that patience was a panacea for most of their troubles.  Patience he found to be indeed a virtue hard to maintain in many a situation, for his continued fevers made him weak and irritable.  But he had laid down a law for himself in this matter, and however provoking the people might be, he was always able by an effort of will to keep the mastery of his spirit.  It was not the people alone that tried his temper.  The follies and little tricks of his men kept him continually on the stretch, and made it hard for him not to lose his self-control.  When it came to a test of wits, however, he was generally "one too many" for them, and the laugh was pretty sure to end on his side.  So he traversed in order the countries of Makula, Nyika, Inyamwanga, Mambwe and Ulungu.

On the 3rd of November Tanganyika was reached at its southernmost point—an event which was celebrated with due demonstrations of delight.  On the lake he launched his collapsible boat, which he had named *The Agnes*, in honour of his much-loved mother far away, and rowed round to Pambete, the caravan following by land.

At this place his career nearly found an inglorious termination, for, while bathing in the lake, he had the narrowest escape from being eaten by a crocodile. Not many days later, at another place, he was in equal peril from the visit of a lion, which paced, and sniffed, and growled round his solitary tent for a good part of a night, he expecting every moment that his flimsy protection would be rent asunder, and himself torn to pieces.

The arrival at Tanganyika marked the completion of the duty set by the Society. But there was no thought of return until many more mysteries should have been solved. Two things, at least, there were which he could not return without attempting to deal with; these were the exploration of the unknown western side of the lake, and the final settlement of the moot question of the Lukuga outlet, concerning which Stanley and Cameron had propounded such conflicting theories. Then, after these, there was the survey of the Congo, which had been begun by Livingstone, and carried further by Stanley, but still waited to be finished. Might not he, if fortune was favourable, strike westward, and endeavour to crown that interesting work?

Camping the majority of the men therefore, under Chuma, at Iendwe, on the southern shore of the lake, he proceeded with a picked company of thirty men. The circumstances under which he began this self-appointed part of his work were certainly anything but pleasant. He was ill from the very start; so much so, indeed, that he says he "could often have walked with the most philosophical resignation into the lake." As a matter of fact, he could only keep going by the sheer determination of an indomitable will. Moreover, in the Warungu he had a most excitable and suspicious set of savages to deal with. Every hour thought and nerve were on the strain, and again and again it only wanted a momentary failure of presence of mind, or an ill-considered word, to bring about the most lamentable consequences.

The Warungu had, of course, never seen a white man, but they knew what an Arab slave-trader meant, and not unnaturally they took the traveller and his followers for a slave-hunting party—a fact which roused them to a demoniac excitement. More than once the axe was uplifted to dash out his brains, and the arrow drawn to the head to pierce his heart. It was only his perfect coolness that saved him. It inspired even the most furious with a kind of superstitious awe. They could have understood any resort to arms in self-defence, and would have finished their deadly work in a moment. But they knew not what to make of this calm white stranger, who bore no weapon in his hand, and who met their frenzied demonstrations only with a smile and a word of friendship. He seemed to them a being "uncanny," and they *dared not* hurt him.

The elements of Nature were as unpropitious as the people, and the travelling had to be done amid the *maximum* of physical discomfort. As they toiled on, over mountains running to 7000 feet high, they seemed to be passing through the very home of storms. To quote his own words :—

"The rainy season had fairly set in, with all the fury characteristic of the tropics, and the very floodgates of heaven seemed to have opened to deluge the land ; yet through the remorseless downpour we must march hour after hour, and day after day. The huge rolling thunder-clouds overspread the heights, and the thunder, with appalling roar, echoed and re-echoed on every side. Now it was above us—the lightning flashes ever and anon splitting the clouds open with their awful power. Then we were in the midst of it, with view circumscribed by the enveloping darkness, while the ground shook, and we instinctively cringed with dread, as the gloom was suddenly dispelled for an instant with blinding effect. Passing upwards, we would next stand triumphant upon some savage peak, and look down on the incessant war of elements.  And with what a wild exultant excitement did we watch the grand scene beneath!  The rugged mountains and valleys, with the murky clouds rolling in intense masses around them; the swollen, headlong torrents adding their monotonous roar to the ever-renewed thunderpeals; while the resistless wind whistled through the trees, bending them like straws."

After a five weeks' journey, involving labours and trials in which the life of months seemed to have been expended, he at last, on Christmas Day, stood beside the Lukuga outlet.

What he saw came to him with all the piquancy of a great surprise.  He had come expecting, from Cameron's account, to find a " swampy lazy stream, winding imperceptibly amid huge sedges, papyrus, and jungle tracts," but lo! there rushed past at his feet "a swift resistless current," bearing its broad mass of waters onward with swirling eddies.  Stanley's prophecy had been verified. The mud barrier which he saw damming up the waters of the lake had, as he said it would, been swept away, and through the opening had poured such a body of water, that already there were evidences of Tanganyika having lowered its level as much as eight or ten feet.

The satisfaction of having finally settled this much-debated problem was to him a sufficient Christmas feast, and he gladly gave himself up to a day or two of well-earned rest at Kasengè.  But it was only for a brief time that he could allow himself for a breathing space, and presently we find him afloat in a slave-trader's boat, bound for Ujiji on the eastern side of the lake.  The voyage was a miserable one, and it culminated in a frightful midnight storm, after which he was literally washed ashore into the arms of the London Missionary Society's agent there.

His troubles and illnesses, however, could not dry up the fountain of his geniality.  He had nothing but his wonted playfulness in writing to his friends.  In a letter from Ujiji to his sister-in-law at Greenock, on the birth of her eldest child, he says :—

"On New Year's Day, feeling somewhat gloomy as I thought of home and the annual gathering there, there was put into my hand a packet of letters, and among these there was one containing the interesting intelligence of the appearance of another Joe ready to replace me, etc. This cheered me immensely. I may now go forth, thought I, and fearlessly penetrate into the wildest parts. There is a Joe at home—like me, of course—and what use is there in keeping human duplicates in this world of distress, where elbows have to be used so constantly to get through the world at all? But there! I think I have gone far enough in a letter intended to be congratulatory. I can hardly tell you how pleased I was to read the news, or what soothing thoughts it had raised in my mind. I have sat and pictured Master Joe in jolly mood—of course he must be a jolly fellow—sitting on your knee, while you sing to him ' Oh, let us be joyful,' and rejoicing in your own happiness. Such thoughts, I assure you, do one a world of good after the rough scenes, the almost daily quarrels with one's own men, not to speak of the thousand and one troubles and annoyances which beset one's path. I shall often, in my weary or sick hours, transport myself to Greenock, and, unknown to you, see Master Joe in the various pleasing phases which childhood presents ; and if I find him crying and in pain, I may draw the comforting reflection that even this helpless babe has its troubles—why then need I grumble at my hardships? And so on.

"I have spent quite a jolly New Year's holiday at Ujiji. Delightful time. Mr. Hore, the missionary here, has just devoted himself to me.

"I will have a glorious route to go back—completely unknown, but believed to be of the most interesting character. The Society have added £500 to the original grant, and left me to go where I please.  If my calculation holds good, I shall be home within seven months."

At Ujiji he managed to secure some fresh stores, preparatory to his dash for the Congo.  Thereupon he recrossed the lake, and set his face westwards.

For the first sixty miles or so, among the Waguha, he contrived to get on fairly well.  But in the Warua tribe he found an obstacle against which neither courage nor diplomacy could prevail.  For once he had to confess himself baffled.

For weeks the party marched in ceaseless peril of their lives, the victims of endless maddening annoyances.  It was like forcing one's way through swarms of angry hornets.  The men were all armed with guns, but their ammunition was exhausted, and probably, if the Warua had had the slightest idea how harmless they were, not a life would have been worth an hour's purchase.  Coolness and "the game of bluff" were their only resources, and the young leader kept up the superstitious fear of the white man's weapons by judiciously using his few remaining cartridges in making as impressive a show of marksmanship as he could with his express rifle.  Thus day by day he warded off an impending catastrophe, though never for a moment unconscious of its shadow.  At last, his men, in terror, fairly mutinied just as he was within a day's journey of the river, and there was no course left him but to take a Pisgah view of what he believed to be the great Congo valley and retrace his steps to the lake, where he arrived despoiled and humbled, but thankful to find himself in the flesh at all.

A sail of two hundred miles in a canoe along the eastern shore of Tanganyika supplied a romantic as well as healthful variation of his exploratory adventures, and brought him back to the camp at Icndwe.  There he found all well, and met with a reception that brought tears into his eyes.  His men had given him up for lost, and they were simply wild with delight to see him again.

Homeward! was now the word of order. War made it impossible to carry out his plan of proceeding straight east to Kilwa, so he had no choice but to strike northward to the caravan route at Unyanyembè. The intervening three hundred and fifty miles of unexplored territory—through Fipa, Ukhonongo and Ugunda—he covered with great rapidity, making, in course, a flying visit to Lake Leopold (Lake Hikwa), which he was the first white man to see, and to which he gave the name it now bears.

At Unyanyembè he paused for a few days, in preparation for the final rush to the coast. In a letter dated 27th May, 1880, which he wrote from this place to his fellow-student Williamson, he says:—

"My march is nearly over. I have got back into well-beaten tracks, and am even occupying a house where nearly every Englishman who has entered this region of Africa has lain and groaned over his fevers, his delays, and the thousand and one troubles incidental to African travel. Livingstone waited here with patient resignation for months, ruminating no doubt now on the great lake, anon on the 'great open sore of the world.' Stanley barricaded and loopholed its walls in the war with Mirambo. Here Cameron groaned over his fevers and his delays; and before me rises the picture of Murphy, stout and burly, sinking with a groan to the ground, and Dillon, blind and helpless, lying wearily on his couch. In later times Captain Carter, of elephant fame, had to flee from the house as from a house infected, and but a few days ago his Scotch assistant and two Belgians were on the point of shooting each other with their revolvers; and last of all, to close this 'strange eventful history,' here lies yours truly resting from his long and lonely march, and feeling as if his work was o'er. Since I wrote to you

REVIEWING THE EXPEDITION.

I have had an eventful and romantic time of it with hard marches and hard fare—now flying as from a valley of the shadow of death, anon knocking about among the romantic creeks and bays of Tanganyika in an old 'dug-out,' paddled in time to the wild songs of the Wajiji, living on beans or Indian corn or cold sugarless tea, and sleeping as comfortably as bare planks and acute angles in a cramped position would allow, exposed without shelter to wind and rain.   But in whatever position one is placed in this world something of beauty appears—a daisy meets the eye, or a sweet sound the ear.   And who would have thought that in those far-off wilds the sounds of a fine 1200 franc hurdy-gurdy would meet the ear and charm it, as the tunes of one's own native land swell, and like some sweet afflatus waft you into dreamland ?

"I have had a great reception amongst the Arabs, all expressing their astonishment at the route I have covered, the short time I have taken to do it, and all on my own legs. . . . We really made a brilliant display in our entry to Unyanyembè, and took the place by storm.   I hold quite a levée all day long—Arabs flocking in, from the governor downwards.   I feel quite amused when I look around and see my guards at the door, a crowd of well-dressed servants, marshalled by the famous Chuma, all ready to attend my utmost wish, while every now and then a gorgeously-dressed Arab appears with his train of followers.   The governor and his brother are a pair of glorious old gentlemen, and have taken me under their wing entirely.   I say, when I see all this and look back into other years, 'Certainly the days of romance are not yet past.'"

The remaining five hundred miles from Unyanyembè to the coast were as nothing to the men, who were in splendid condition, and in the highest spirits.   After a journey of unprecedented speed, they reached Bagamoyo on the 10th of July, and entered it "with all the pomp of a bloodless victory."

Joseph Thomson had indeed accomplished a notable feat, and he had done it in a spirit which not only his Scottish countrymen, but all lovers of humanity, could heartily approve. He had led his men over some three thousand miles, more than the half of which lay through regions unknown to the geographer. He had tactfully, and with unstained hands, dealt with hostile and troublesome tribes so as to make it easier for other men to follow him, and he had returned with his caravan unbroken and loyal. He had, as yet, hardly passed the threshold of manhood, but he had already established for himself the right to be considered a worthy successor of Park and Livingstone.

The authorities at Bagamoyo treated the weary travellers with great distinction and lavish hospitality; and when, two days later, the caravan marched to the Consulate in Zanzibar to be formally disbanded, the Sultan not only sent by a messenger his salaams and congratulations, but took the unusual course of gladdening the men's hearts with a present of money.

All the thoughts of the young leader were now of home and friends, and the first departing steamer bore him as a passenger.

# CHAPTER V.

## UP THE ROVUMA.

THE closing days of August found Joseph Thomson once more in London, *en route* for his native valley, whose well-loved scenes he was eager to see again. To step ashore from the ship was to feel himself immediately in touch with home; for there on the landing-stage was his father, who, joyful to know of his son's survival of all perils, had come from Scotland to meet him. He only remained in London long enough to report himself at the headquarters of the Society, and then he was off northward to realise his cherished dream of "revisiting the clear flowing Nith and wandering upon its banks."

The father's eye was quick to note the change which toil and trial and the burden and responsibility of command had wrought upon him. He had set forth from home the ruddy and exuberant youth. In the course of a short year and a half he had been transformed into the thoughtful, decided, self-reliant man, but with the laugh as of old ever ready to light up his bronzed features.

As they passed Dumfries on the evening of August 30th, there were awaiting him quite a number of friends, including, among others, his old confidant, Dr. Grierson, and his fellow-student, Williamson. Here also was introduced to him one who soon became his intimate, Alexander Anderson, "The Surfaceman," of poetic fame.

At Thornhill a pleasant and affecting surprise had been prepared for him. As the train drew in to the station,

the passengers were startled by a series of loud explosions
from fog signals which had been placed on the line.
When they hastened to the windows they became aware,
from the banners flying and the playing of a band, that
some local demonstration was afoot, the centre of interest
being a quiet-looking youth who had just stepped from
the train, and with whom everybody was eager to shake
hands. A single inquiry made the situation clear to all,
for the papers had all been chronicling in eulogistic
terms the success of the expedition; and as the train
moved on, the passengers mingled their hearty cheers
with those of the assembled crowd.

The district had felt itself honoured and had risen to
the occasion. The Town's Committee of Thornhill led
the way by resolving to present the returning traveller
with an address of welcome; and it was this graceful act
which the great concourse had gathered to endorse with
their cheers. The recipient of these flattering attentions,
having no idea of the honour in store for him, was wholly
taken aback. When he attempted to reply to the warmly
expressed greetings of the address, he found his heart too
full for words, and could only utter a single sentence of
thanks. The procession then reformed, and, placing him
with his friends at the head of it, escorted him to Gatelawbridge. There his father's workmen had planned to show
their enthusiasm by the erection of a triumphal arch, and
through that, amid honourable demonstrations, he was
borne to the old home, which he had sometimes almost
despaired of ever seeing again.

This kindly exhibition of goodwill was not all. His
old comrades in the Literary Society felt that they had
quite a special interest in this home-coming, and that it
behoved them also to have their *feu de joie*. A few days
later, therefore, they entertained him with a supper, at
which they could express after their own fervid fashion
their sense of the fact that "Joe" had done worthily and
helped the society to make its mark. In the warm

atmosphere of renewed fellowship he "found his tongue," and in his reply spoke even eloquently. We only quote a sentence or two of his speech, but they contain the keynote of his whole career as a pioneer of civilisation.

"With regard to the results of the expedition I prefer to say nothing. These have yet to be brought before competent geographers, and till then the less said the better. But, gentlemen, this I will say; my fondest boast is, not that I have travelled over hundreds of miles hitherto untrodden by the foot of white man, but that I have been able to do so as a Christian and a Scotsman, carrying everywhere goodwill and friendship, finding that a gentle word was more potent than gunpowder, and that it was not necessary, even in Central Africa, to sacrifice the lives of men in order to throw light upon its dark corners."

In the month of November, the members of the Royal Geographical Society met to hear from the explorer an account of his stewardship. There was a large and distinguished gathering, attracted not only by the intrinsic interest of the story that was anticipated, but by the special circumstances which had marked the history of the expedition, and the fact that the leader who was to address the assemblage was the most youthful who had ever enjoyed that honour. The occasion was a trying one for him, and he anticipated it with not a little trepidation. When the moment came, however, something in the look of the company suggested sympathy, or confidence in him, and he felt he was safe. He became as cool as he beforehand had been nervous, faced the audience without a shake or quiver of the voice, and read his paper so that not a point was lost.

His narrative was received with enthusiasm; for he had to tell of a satisfactory settlement of all the geographical problems to which the expedition was to direct its attention. And not only had he filled in blanks in the map, he had brought back rich spoils in scientific results, for, though the character of his responsibilities had been entirely changed by the death of Johnston, his original aim had never been allowed to fall out of sight. He had examined the rocks and formations over the whole ground which he had traversed, and was able to give for the first time an intelligible and comprehensive theory of the geology of East Africa. Botany had also been enriched by his collection of plants, and conchology by the shells which he had gathered on Nyassa and Tanganyika. Thorough work all round had been done, and it received its reward of unreserved appreciation. At the close, Sir Rutherford Alcock said that the Society had been extremely fortunate in their selection of a leader, and he had worthily performed the task he undertook. He (Sir Rutherford) did not know that there had ever been a more successful exploration in Central Africa, or one more complete in all its parts.

In recognition of the manner in which the work of the expedition had been carried through, and in commemoration of what the president had declared to be "the most remarkable geographical event of the year," the Society resolved to strike a medal for distribution among the members of the caravan.

The character of his address to the Society aroused in not a few quarters a keen desire to have a detailed narrative of his journey and researches in book form. From this proposal he strongly shrank. The idea suggested a most irksome task. Moreover, while he wrote with great fluency and natural vivacity, he was keenly conscious of certain literary deficiencies which might have stood in the way of his success. Means of overcoming both difficulties, however, were promptly found, as explained by himself in his preface, and forthwith the preparation of the book was proceeded with. In his journals he had abundance of material, for it had been his habit—a habit which he kept up in all his expeditions, and which gives the impression of vividness and vivacious-ness to all his narratives of travel—to make his notes on the spot wherever possible, and to chronicle all incidents at the first available moment after they happened. The work, therefore, made rapid progress during the winter and spring months.

In the early summer of 1881, 'To the Central African Lakes and Back' was published. It obtained a very cheering reception, several editions being speedily disposed of. It was also translated into German, and issued in Jena, shortly after its appearance in England.

As a variation from his literary labour, he spent some time in Edinburgh during the winter, renewing old associations. There it was that he made the acquaintance of Mr. J. M. Barrie, who was then finishing his college career and making the beginnings of his brilliant success as a *littérateur*. It was the recollection of " forgatherings " with the young explorer, in the company of Anderson and other kindred spirits in Edinburgh and London, that furnished the material for the delicately humorous sketch of him in " An Edinburgh Eleven."

It was probably at one of those happy meetings that Alexander Anderson jokingly said that when he died in the heart of Africa he would write a sonnet to his memory. The event seemed in those light-hearted days so far off, that Joseph Thomson laughingly insisted upon the sonnet being written on the spot; which it was, and we give it as it flowed from the facile pen. It was a frequent subject of humorous allusion afterwards, but alas, it was more prophetic in substance than either writer or subject anticipated, for though Africa was not to be the traveller's final resting-place, he was indeed to lay down his young life in its interests.

J. T. Obit. 18—.

" Dead in the wastes of Africa, while yet
    Youth with its numbers lay upon his brow,
    And unreaped age before him. He is set
    Among the fresh young pioneers; and now

He will be with them evermore.  And we
Who lag behind, homesick, weary with longer life,
Watching that continent that yet shall be
Ploughed into smiling harvest fields, and ripe
With what is now around us, shall we not—
With all these rich ripe wonders in our eyes,—
Shall we not link his name and that dear spot
Where, far from home and kindred graves, he lies,
To all the good and nobler breadth of sway
Which crowns that dusky nation of to-day?"

A few lectures on his African adventures were delivered by him at Thornhill, Lochmaben, Greenock; and, when the book was fairly off his hands, he went up to London that he might perfect his equipment as an explorer by taking lessons in astronomical observation, photography, and the like.

In quiet life like this, however, he could not long remain content.  He could enjoy for a while the pleasures of the drawing-room, but a little of this went a long way with him.  He had an honest dislike to being lionised. It bored him to be made to speak about his own exploits. His strength was long ago thoroughly recruited, and he craved for some fresh outlet for his overflowing vigour of mind and body.  It was just when that feeling began to become acute that a new employment presented itself which seemed entirely to his mind.

In his East African expedition of 1862, Livingstone had visited the river Rovuma and found what he supposed to be clear evidence of the existence of coal.

"At Michi," he says in his journal,* "about a hundred miles from the coast, a few small pieces of coal were picked up on the sandbanks, showing that this useful mineral exists on the Rovuma and on some of its tributaries.  The natives know that it will burn.  At the lakelet Chidia we noticed the same sandstone rock with fossil wood on it, which we have on the Zambesi, and

* 'The Zambesi and its Tributaries,' pages 427, 430.

know it to be a sure evidence of coal beneath. We mentioned this at the time to Captain Gardiner, and our finding coal now seemed a verification of what we then said: the coal-field probably extends from the Zambesi to the Rovuma, if not beyond it."

The great traveller did not pretend, of course, to speak with the technical knowledge of an expert; but a report of this kind, if adequately confirmed, pointed to possible results of great importance to that part of the Sultan of Zanzibar's dominions. To find a genuine coal-mine in his section of the continent would, at least, be to that potentate a manifest source of wealth, for the replenishing of his never-too-full treasury. We need not wonder that the imagination of successive sultans conjured up in connection with it all manner of pleasant prospects.

First an Arab and then a Parsee engineer were despatched by Sultan Seyed Barghash after his accession, to make observations with respect to the reputed source of enrichment. These behoved to report in terms agreeable to His Highness; and, although neither knew anything practically about the subject, they spoke in glowing language as to the abundance of the valuable mineral, and as to the ease with which it could be obtained. His Highness had only to make a little preliminary outlay, and presently his coffers would be swelling with a great return. The Sultan was naturally elated at these brilliant prospects. Why should he not forthwith begin to realise his treasures?

But the impulse was meantime checked by a counsel of caution. Dr. Kirk, being apparently consulted by the Sultan, thought it well that some further advice of a more skilled character should be invoked. There, for instance, was Thomson, whom His Highness had so recently seen, a man trained to know all about rocks, and whom his countrymen were praising for his skill and insight in such matters. He would tell him the whole truth. Let him be sent for.

And so it came to pass that, just when time was beginning to hang heavy on his hands, Joseph Thomson received the offer of an appointment "to determine and report upon the nature, extent, and economic value" of those reputed coal formations in East Africa. The Sultan was quite sanguine in his own mind, as events proved. He apparently only expected the young scientist to confirm, and perhaps outrun, his own anticipations. Joseph Thomson knew nothing of all this, and gladly accepted the commission. It chimed in exactly with his own wishes; for it bore him back to the work of exploration in Africa under most favourable auspices, and very specially it gave him the opportunity of following out his geological researches in an interesting part of the continent. Almost exactly a year, therefore, after he had left Zanzibar, on the conclusion of his former expedition, he again appeared there, ready and eager for active service.

Hurry, or even prompt action, is, however, a thing not understood in the official surroundings of Eastern princes. He wanted to get the necessary men at once engaged, and everything in order for a business-like start. "But," he says, "the eccentric machinery of an Oriental Government was hard to be moved. During the first fortnight nothing could be done. First, 'I must rest after my voyage,' then 'I must wait till the mail had gone'; finally, 'Everything would be arranged when something else was settled.'" After about a hundred communications had been sent without visible effect, he was beginning to think of letting things drift, when all of a sudden the orders of the Sultan came, to the effect that he was to be off to the Rovuma in three days.

It was rather a large order to fit out a caravan in such a space of time. But there was a piquancy in the very bigness of the task, and he was not the man to be beaten. Within the appointed three days he was ready for the road. But his anxieties were not yet ended. He was ready, but his men were not. They had somehow got it into their heads that they had another day, and, in prospect of their departure, every one of them, Chuma among the number, had gone in for a carousal, and they were scattered over the city. Where to get them was a mystery. However, in his resolution to be up to time, he impressed some four hundred of the Sultan's soldiers into detective service for the occasion. And then ensued a search royal. Any porter seen was to be seized, and *identified afterwards.*

"There were of course some curious mistakes," he writes in a letter describing the affair, "but our numbers gradually rose. After nightfall the hunt became exciting. I gained an insight into Zanzibar life such as I could not have obtained in a year. Every drink shop, every bad place, every native house was visited. Two of the men we found had just been married that day, and the brides had to be left disconsolate. After twelve o'clock at night, we had the satisfaction of conveying all my men, except two, on board closely guarded. I was dead beat, but next morning at daybreak I had the satisfaction of sailing out triumphant, the men themselves enjoying the recital of the incidents connected with their own capture, and looking upon the whole as a good joke."

The expedition, started after this lively fashion, was, despite all its toils, thoroughly enjoyed by its leader from beginning to end ; for all through he revelled in good health, and his experience saved him from many troubles and enabled him to evade many difficulties, which otherwise might have taken a considerable discount off his happiness. The starting-point was Mikindany, some thirty miles north of the Rovuma. There also Livingstone had begun his journey, but a quite different route was now chosen. The caravan numbered in all seventy-four, fifty-four of these being of his old men, under Chuma and Makatubu as before ; and the march began on the 17th of July, 1881.

Striking up to the plateau of Makondè, " the country

of bushes and creepers," they traversed with much painful labour the tantalising tangle of thorny undergrowth which covers its whole surface for about eighty miles inland. After eight days of twisting and wriggling in this confused jungle, they emerged on the further side of the plateau to find the Rovuma valley spreading itself out in a vast expanse to the south and east. Descending into the plain, which seemed to be quite uninhabited—thanks to the desolating slave raids of which Livingstone tells such a sad tale—they pressed on to the river. This they found to be "three quarters of a mile broad, with great stretches of yellow sandbanks glittering under a vertical sun," the banks being "particularly charming, from the beauty and variety of the trees with which they are clothed"—yellow-wood trees and tamarinds, elegant palms and grotesque baobabs giving endless contrasts of shape and hue. Following the course of the river, the line which now forms the political frontier between the German and Portuguese spheres of influence, they reached the point where the Lujendè blends its waters with those of the Rovuma.

The Lujendè proved to be much the larger of the two confluents. At the point of union it was quite a mile across. Every here and there rapids occur, which make navigation a thing out of the question; but in point of picturesqueness the Lujendè is very interesting. One of its most striking features is the number of islands—some of them three or four miles long—which dot its course, and which give an appearance of great richness to the scenery. "These islands," as Last tells us in his description of the district, "are not submerged during the wet season, and therefore they form the permanent homes of the people. Some of them are very beautifully wooded, covered with large forest trees garlanded and festooned with creepers."

Keeping to the course of the Lujendè, and passing through a fertile tract, many parts of which have the appearance of "a long string of gardens," they found themselves after a few marches on the spot where the so-called coal was to be found, the Maviti village of Itulè.

Alas for the Sultan's dream of commercial enrichment! The suspicion of the young geologist that the coalfields would prove mythical received only too complete fulfilment. "To our disgust," says he, "we discovered that the coal was nothing more than a few irregular layers of bituminous shale, which when placed in a wood fire emitted a flame, but remained almost unchanged in bulk. It does not even burn alone. Accompanying the shale, we found small quantities of a curious anthracite-like substance, which could be set on fire only with great difficulty, but left more than fifty per cent. of ash."

Proceeding to a point two days further up the Lujendè, where the coal was said to be specially abundant, they made further anxious observations and experiments; but, sad to say, with no better result, and as the series of beds containing the shale finishes abruptly at this place, as it had commenced abruptly at Itulè, it became clear to Joseph Thomson that the coal-beds of the Rovuma had no existence.

Yet while, as regards its main object (the finding of coal), the expedition, from the Sultan's point of view, was a blank failure, it was, from the explorer's point of view, valuable in its results, both in the matter of profit and enjoyment.

Not that the journey was destitute of the ordinary hard and trying experiences of African travel; for at one time he marched for some days in agony with a painful ulcer on his leg, and at another time he and his men had to face the terrors of journeying for days without water, reducing them to a condition in which they were glad to pay a heavy price for liquid mud, in which, at another time they would hardly have condescended to wash their hands. Truly, as he says, "African travelling, even in the most favourable circumstances, is no rose-water work.

To see any ' fun' in it at all one must not only be largely endowed with the imperturbable optimism of Mark Tapley, but have a frame healthy and robust and fitted to bear fatigue and heat and hardship in no ordinary degree, besides rejoicing in an appetite neither delicate nor fastidious."

Both in the outward and homeward journey he was able to make most useful additions to his knowledge of the geology of East Africa as well as of other matters less recondite.

As for interesting sights, there were not a few " rare noteworthy objects" in his travel which stay-at-home people might well wish to see—such as the extraordinary hills which dot the great Rovuma valley, and which shoot up abruptly from the plain in every variety of shape as peaks, domes, cones, needles; and very especially the extraordinary mountain of Lipmmbula, which rises like a huge broken column 970 feet high, "a perfectly compact mass of granite, almost without a single flaw or joint except on one side," where the daring climber was able to make a difficult and perilous ascent to the summit.  Then there was that " wonderfully picturesque gorge, grand and weird in the extreme," through which the Rovuma flows at Undè (the furthest point in his journey'), where the immense rocks and boulders fill the bed of the roaring river, and the smooth, symmetrical, dome-like mountains of granite rise on either side with scarcely a crack or irregularity.

Sport too was here ideal.  The great plain, though destitute of human life for the most part, was a perfect hunter's paradise, for " it literally swarmed with game" of every variety that the most enterprising Nimrod could sigh for.  After enjoying his exciting encounters with sundry wild creatures through the day, he could read his Shakspere or Tennyson or make his astronomical observations in the evening camp to the romantic accompaniment of the roaring of the king of beasts.

MOUNT LIPUMBULA.

G 2

Then, as for ethnological and social studies, there was in the inhabited parts no small variety to interest the inquirer. There were the ugly, low-grade, massively tattooed Makondè, with their curious combination of sexual morality with periodical *pombè* (native beer) debaucheries. There were the Maviti, the raiders and bullies of the region, with their Zulu war customs and destructive genius. There were the intelligent and industrious Wayao (to which tribe Chuma belonged), with their cleanly habits and keen trading instincts. There

CHIEF WITH PELÈLÈ.

were the Makua with their advanced ideas on the rights of woman. There were the Mawia with their slender well-made figures, the most exclusive tribe in East Africa. And there were, finally, the Matambwe, wild and ghastly in appearance, from their practice of rubbing themselves with wood ashes in place of washing with water. All these were more or less contrasted, yet nearly all united in the observance of one strange habit, the wearing of the *pelèlè*—a round piece of wood about an inch and a half in diameter inserted in the upper lip, which make it stick out like the bill of an Australian ornithorhynchus. This extraordinary ornament, so characteristic of the Rovuma region, is highly prized.

"I found it quite impossible," he says, "to obtain more than a single specimen, and that had not even been worn. It was believed that if a *pelèlè* fell into my possession I would certainly work some black magic on the seller and produce dire mischief generally. Doubtless they are all the more valued by the wives because they are invariably the affectionate handiwork of their husbands. A Makondè lady would no more think of disposing of her *pelèlè* than a European lady of her marriage ring. When a woman dies, this much-prized adornment is always most religiously preserved by her husband or near relatives; and when they go to water the grave—with beer not tears—the *pelèlè* is likewise taken to show that her memory is still faithfully cherished."

Joseph Thomson no doubt carried away from his four months' tour in the Rovuma region many pleasant memories and much information which others would be glad to hear. But what about the reckoning with his august employer? Truth to tell, it was not pleasant. He was too simply straightforward and undiplomatic for such a master. The Sultan was mightily disappointed, and took childish ways of showing his feeling. He had asked for coal and he had got shale! Was he not ill-used? It afterwards transpired that the Sultan believed he had really found coal, but for reasons of his own was keeping back the truth. And so, under a sense of royal disfavour and of suspicious surveillance and irksome restriction, the offender was kept dangling aimlessly about Zanzibar, to the mortification of mind and body— all of which he relates with rueful pleasantry in one of his letters :—

"I am in despair. I feel that all the lightness of touch

and the playful fancy, which I sometimes flatter myself belong to me in some slight degree, have fled into the infinite azure of the past. . . . I am at the present moment a prey to that horrible scourge prickly heat, making me feel as if needles were oozing out of every pore of my *corpus*. Mosquitoes by the million buzz about my ears, but sing no pleasant love songs to my maddening brain. I am also a martyr to certain volcanic eruptions vulgarly known as boils, which prevent me from sitting, lying, walking, or standing with any degree of comfort. Then the temperature is so high that at midday I have not got out of my pyjamahs, while to get a breath of air I have continually to resort to the fan. I need not enlarge the list by referring to my acute troubles of spirit, and telling how my mental and moral equilibrium has been completely upset. . . . For the last two months I have been kept a prisoner on parole, and classed in the ranks of the unappreciated. My report on the coal of the Rovuma has thrown the Sultan into the sulks. He won't even believe in me, and has kept me all this time doing nothing, sending me a daily hash of lies. . . . I am determined to cut with him at the first opportunity."

In view of experiences like these it is not surprising that the New Year of 1882 saw him once more under the paternal roof in Scotland. The ways of Eastern potentates had not been to his mind; for with all his look of un-hurrying leisure, he was too much in earnest about his life-work to be content to waste his time in enforced idleness. As soon as he was satisfied, therefore, that there was no prospect of his being able to continue with satis-faction the work which he had undertaken, his resignation was promptly sent in.

For the next three months after his return, he devoted himself to study and general reading at home and in Edinburgh, and to the cultivation of congenial acquaintanceships.   By way of literary exercise, he also prepared two articles for *Good Words*.

As the days lengthened out, however, and the weather became brighter, he was glad to entertain the idea of a little continental trip.   An intimate friend, who was proceeding to Kreutznach, was anxious to enjoy his fellowship on the way, and as this opened up the prospect of visiting the fabled Rhine, he promptly made his arrangements to go.   That April holiday, with its memories of sympathy in sight-seeing, of amusing incident, and of discourse, serious or fanciful, on all manner of subjects, was wholly a joy to him.

After a day or two at Kreutznach, he continued his course in a leisurely way by Heidelberg, Baden, and Strasburg, to Paris, where he spent some time, and applied himself in his own thorough-going fashion to seeing as much of the place and the people as he could.   The impressions he formed were not favourable.

"Paris," he writes to his recent fellow-traveller at Kreutznach, "with its good things and innumerable bad things, is a place where there is no medium course.   You wander through grand churches and feel awed and spiritualised, and you leave them only to stumble at the first step over some example of the essentially voluptuous, atheistic, and depraved character of the Parisians, a people whose intensely demoniacal passions must ever and anon find vent like the imprisoned fires of the earth in the volcano. In Paris you are ever tossed from heaven to hell, or *vice versâ;* you find the finest and most delicate taste associated with the vilest.   The whole character of the people is repugnant to me.   I would rather live in Central Africa yet than in Paris."

He returned from Paris in time to attend the funeral of Darwin, and in the middle of May we find him back in Edinburgh, a profoundly interested auditor of the memorable Robertson Smith heresy case in the Free

Assembly—his sympathies being of course warmly on the side of those who stood for liberty in the application of scholarship to biblical questions.

The months of summer he spent amid the ever interesting scenes of his native Nithsdale, at one time poring over such compacted stores of thought as Darwin's 'Origin of Species' and 'Descent of Man'; at another romancing and moralising in wood or pass or linn; or yet again exercising himself and keeping up his "form" in pedestrian excursions that seemed to others phenomenal. It was on one of the hottest days of that summer that he walked from Gatelawbridge to the top of Criffel and back, a distance of at least fifty-five miles (and in effect very much more on account of the laborious effort needed in the ascent of the hill), indulging cheerfully in a dance after his return, as though he had been having a quiet day with no particular exertion. In the exuberance of his health and animal spirits, he seemed in those days ready for any exhibition of staying power.

In that year the meeting of the British Association was fixed to take place at Southampton in the end of August. As one of the men who had made his mark upon the map of Africa, Joseph Thomson was urged by the president of the geographical section to come and take part, a request to which he very willingly acceded.

The subject of his paper was, "The Geological Evolution of Lake Tanganyika." Beginning with a consideration of the aboriginal conditions of the African continent south of the Equator, he asked what was the testimony of the rocks on the subject. He thought that that testimony pointed to the existence at one time of an immense central sea, cut off from the ocean by the elevation of the continent, and almost coterminous in extent with the present drainage area of the Congo. An elevated ridge was then upheaved along the eastern boundary of this sea. By and by the centre of this ridge collapsed, originating the trough of Lake Tanganyika, and subsequently the central sea draining away to the west left Tanganyika isolated. The speaker then proceeded to explain how the secondary characters of the lake arose, and how its scenery was moulded by the action of the sub-aërial denudation on rocks of different resisting powers. After accounting for the peculiar marine-like type of its shells, the origin of its outlet, the Lukuga, and the freshening of the water of the lake, he referred to the curious intermittency of the outflow. This he explained by the probable fact that in ordinary years rainfall and evaporation nearly balance each other; but sometimes there occurs a series of years in which the evaporation exceeds the rainfall, thereby lowering the level of the lake to a point beneath that of its outlet. A more or less long period must then elapse before it regains its former position, and the Lukuga resumes its function.

The reading of this paper was the prelude to a little stirring of the waters in another sense, which formed one of the incidents of the meeting. The discussion turned upon the last point in the paper, namely, the long-vexed question of the nature of the Lukuga outlet. Cameron held quite a different theory, and was there ready, after his own vigorous fashion, to do battle for it. The junior explorer, however, was not to be lightly disposed of. He had by his own observation disproved the other's theory, and he stood to his guns with equanimity and self-possession, showing that he had abundant reasons for the faith which was in him. There was a large assemblage of "armchair" geographers. In a matter like this, however, there was, even for the greybeards of the science, nothing for it but to leave the field to the two experts and watch the interesting encounter.

At the conclusion of the discussion the president referred to the fact that Joseph Thomson was returning to Africa to renew his explorations. He assured the traveller of the sympathy and good wishes of the geographers gathered there, in which sentiment none joined more heartily than Lieutenant Cameron himself.

Joseph Thomson's last public appearance, ere he set off on his new enterprise, was in Glasgow. There, on the 2nd of November, before a very large audience, he inaugurated the winter course of science lectures in St. Andrew's Hall, his subject being "Leaves from my African Sketch Book." And now all his thoughts were focussed upon a task for which all his previous work was but a preliminary and indispensable apprenticeship. This new enterprise, as he said in the closing words of his lecture in Glasgow, was to be his Tel-el-Kebir.

# CHAPTER VI.

## THROUGH MASAI-LAND.

MODERN exploration in East Africa had its starting-point at Mombasa. From the year 1844, when the missionary Krapf (whom the kindly Sultan Seyed Said described in his letter of recommendation as "the German good man who wishes to convert the world to God") settled in that ancient and interesting place, there had been kept up for well nigh forty years a persistent forthgoing of endeavour towards the wresting of the secrets of the Dark Continent. The efforts put forth, more especially in the latter half of that time, had been most encouraging, and sometimes even brilliant, in their results. Tract after tract had been brought to light by the pioneers of geographical inquiry; and wonder after wonder had been unveiled to stimulate men to fresh research.

In 1858 Speke and Burton had penetrated to Lake Tanganyika; and immediately afterwards Speke, travelling alone, set eyes upon the great Victoria Nyanza. In 1862 the same traveller discovered the sources of the Nile, having previously, in company with Grant, reached the important country of Uganda, which has ever since been a centre of more or less deep interest to Europeans. Further to the south also Livingstone was by this time beginning that wonderful series of exploratory journeys which, in the course of the next ten years, were to bring such vast regions of barbarism within the ken of the civilised world,

But while in this way light was being made to penetrate the inner recesses of Africa, there was one tract that remained sternly and stubbornly closed to every approach of inquiry; and, curiously, that tract lay quite contiguous to the original starting-point. With the exception of a couple of hundred miles in from the coast line, there was no district in the whole mysterious continent more thoroughly a *terra incognita* than that which lay between Mombasa and the shores of the Lake Victoria Nyanza.

This was in no sense due to that impractical spirit which sometimes makes men neglect things near at hand for things far away. Nowhere had more persistent attempts been made by explorers than just here. From the days of Krapf's settlement at Mombasa, one after another had tried to tear aside the veil of mystery which hung so tantalisingly almost at the door of the Mission.

From 1846 to 1851 Krapf, and his equally devoted colleague Rebmann, pioneered earnestly, often enduring extraordinary hardships. In 1847 Rebmann penetrated to Teita, and in 1848 he discovered Kilimanjaro. In 1849 Krapf explored Ukambani almost at the cost of his life, and in this journey he caught a far-off, shadowy glimpse of Mount Kenia—this being the first time in which European eyes had rested on that remarkable mountain. But with all their self-sacrificing efforts they had only been able to reach the outskirts of the exclusive district.

The task essayed by these patient workers was taken up ten years later by Baron von der Decken, who, in the three journeys he made (1861–1865), added considerably to men's knowledge of the country between the coast and Kilimanjaro, but found, like his predecessors, that that great mountain marked for him the limit of possible attainment. A similar tale had to be told of the missionaries Wakefield and New, and of the German travellers Brenner, Hildebrandt, Denhardt, and Fischer, who, from 1865 to 1882, strove in one direction or another to break through the charmed circle. No district of untrodden Africa had had a greater number of able and courageous pioneers knocking at its gate for entrance, and yet, after forty years of labour and sacrifice, there was none concerning which geographers knew less.

The difficulty in the way of the pioneers lay not in the physical features of the country but in the character of the inhabitants. It was occupied by a powerful tribe of arrogant, fierce, suspicious, and intractable savages, in presence of whom no white man's life was safe, unless he could surround himself with a protecting force such as explorers are rarely able to command. Those haughty and truculent warriors were a terror to all their neighbours, and again and again strong heavily-armed trading caravans had met with disaster, and even annihilation, in attempting to pass through their lands. It almost seemed as if the geographer, in view of the certain perils and enormous risks of exploration in that dreaded region, must content himself with such a knowledge of it as might be obtained by vague rumours or native description—although those rumours and descriptions were just of the sort to whet curiosity, telling as they did of snow-clad mountains and active volcanoes and new lakes and wonderful caves.

But other eyes than those of the mere geographer were turning to this region. When Gordon was Governor-General of the Sûdan, he perceived, with the instinct of a practical genius, that the true route to the head waters of the Nile lay in a line that passed from the Zanzibar coast right through the territory of the terrible Masai; and, if he had not been checked by the peremptory orders of the British Government, he would promptly have proceeded to clear the way by force of arms.

Meanwhile the Church Missionary Society were directing their attention inquiringly to the same quarter. For the thorough prosecution of their christianising enterprises in the interior, it was becoming a matter of increasing anxiety to find a healthy and direct route from the coast.

Masai-land seemed to offer at least the possibility of such
a route.

Thus, for once, the geographer, the politician, and the
missionary were united in their desire—if only the right
man could be found to realise it!

At this crisis the Royal Geographical Society seriously
took up the question, and their thoughts at once turned
to Joseph Thomson. His brilliant success in his first
expedition, with its record of courage and tact and
patience, pointed him out as the man to face a forlorn
hope.

Hence, shortly after his return from the Rovuma trip,
there came to him the request to report on the practica-
bility of taking a caravan through the Masai country.
The idea was not new to him. He had often, in his
dreams of possible exploration, dwelt upon it, and hoped
that circumstances would permit him some day to work it
out. When, therefore, his favourable report and plan of
operations were received by the Council, and he himself
was asked to undertake the venture, he responded with a
prompt and hearty acceptance. It was precisely the kind
of emprise to chime in with his likings; for, if it presented enormous difficulties, he had both experience and
the fulness of youthful strength with which to meet them,
and, to his daring and chivalrous spirit, the manifest perils
of it were rather an attraction than otherwise. Besides,
the thought of succeeding, where failure seemed a foregone conclusion, appealed to the romantic element in his
nature; moreover, if he could succeed without resorting
to force, where men like Stanley felt that a thousand
rifles were needed, would he not have scored a point in
favour of Christian and civilised methods?

It was not with the light-heartedness of mere blind
impulse that he set about making his preparations, but
with the calm courage of one who has a full view of all
the dark possibilities of his mission. His letters at the
time show that he had his moments of pensive foreboding,

although there was always the brave heart to rise above them. Writing from London to the companion of his Rhine trip, he says :—

"I have been sitting for the last hour steadily looking into the glowing fire and, with feet extended *à l'Americaine*, watching in a pleasant reverie the old days troop past, recalling tenderly the various special events which have characterised my life thus far. On the eve of a great and dangerous undertaking one's mind somehow tends to become retrospective, and recalls with a sweet melancholy the past, as if something delightful had gone, the like of which would never return again, as if all behind were an Eden and all in front a stern dreary world into which fate had driven us forth. . . . It is very wrong of you to wish me so ill as to incapacitate me from going again to Africa. Why, if I were to stop now I would simply be forgotten and drop out of sight. . . . And yet, after all, I hardly know myself what I am aiming at, or what will be the upshot of it all. You predict for me ' a bright future.' If you mean by that that I shall be to some extent famous, you may be right. If you mean that I shall have a happy and pleasant future, then I am afraid you are mistaken. To me the future, when I think about it, which I very seldom do, seems anything but pleasant. My lot will always be that of a wanderer. It is my fate, and towards it I involuntarily drift. But, there! such thoughts don't often come to me. Don't suppose me steeped in melancholy or in depression ; or, if you do, ascribe it to my liver. I look forward with eagerness and expectation to my journey. I enjoy my life at present, because I never allow myself to dwell upon the dangers."

In a letter to his "dearest father and mother," on the eve of his departure, he writes :—

"The last night of my stay in Britain has come, and

somewhat unexpectedly. I only learned on Monday that I must go on Wednesday if I wanted to spend any time at Cairo; so I had to bundle everything together and prepare for the last great step.

"I am a prey to very conflicting emotions. You will understand my pleasure at feeling that soon my shoulder will be at the wheel again. But you will also, on the other hand, appreciate my feelings on seriously contemplating the fact that I am at last fairly launched on an enterprise the end of which no man can see, however high may be one's hopes or sanguine one's beliefs. . . . The one great thing which renders me unhappy is the thought of the pain and anxiety I am causing you. If I could but imagine you looking forward as sanguinely and hopefully to my return as I do myself, I would go forth with a great burden off my mind. Unfortunately, I can but imagine nights rendered sleepless and days filled with your forebodings over my fancied sufferings. I know, however, that you have brave hearts, and I beseech you to throw off such spectres. Let your panacea for care be, Joe will turn up all right covered with renown! Look forward always to the time when I shall once more appear in 'the auld house,' the same old boy."

These somewhat grave notes, however honourable as a revelation of his filial tenderness, simply reflected his mood as he waited and wearied for action. Once he was fairly afloat (he sailed on December 13th, 1882), he could have said "Richard's himself again," ready for any diversion that might be going.

His one desire was to be on the field as soon as possible, and, as the voyage on this occasion was a particularly quiet one, he set himself to make it as short as possible by reading. He tells a correspondent that he devoured *en route* no less than eleven novels. The monotony of his outward journey was pleasantly broken, however, by a sojourn of ten days in Cairo—days of entire happiness and good fellowship.    In a letter to his friend Anderson, he says:—

"I wish I could work myself into the proper spirit to describe to you all my impressions of Cairo and my experiences.   The climate is simply delicious at this time of the year, making it a joy only to live.   The last time I was there I made it my duty to 'do' everything about the place; this time I resolved to make it a pleasure, and in this I have succeeded far beyond my expectations. . . . I was introduced to all the notables of Cairo, from Alison down to Baker Pasha, and from Dufferin down to the minor Egyptian minister.   I had also the honour of being invited to a grand banquet given to General Stone, on his leaving Cairo, by the Geographical Society of which he was president.   I was specially marked out by having my health and success proposed, to which I had of course to reply—the best of the joke being, however, that all the speaking was in French, only the general sense of which I was able to take in, and on that I had to frame my answer in English.   Fortunately I got through it all right."

He arrived at Zanzibar on the 26th of January, 1883, and, full of high hopes and pleasurable anticipations, at once set about making his arrangements for the journey. At any time when he had an important affair on hand it was not his way to "let the grass grow beneath his feet"; but in this case he found an additional stimulus to the hastening of his preparations in the fact that, shortly before his arrival, the German explorer, Dr. Fischer, had set out with the intention of covering the very route which he had marked out for himself, and thus he was "threatened with the misfortune of reaching a second-hand goal by roads already pioneered."   Fortunately, Government had done everything to smooth his course, and everybody, including even the Sultan (whom he had expected to find still sulky at the memory of his shattered hopes of coal), was anxious to help. Everything therefore went well until he came to the engaging of the porters.

At this critical point, however, he had an experience which might well have filled a less resolute man with misgivings. In the first place, he had fallen upon evil days in the matter of time—quite a number of important caravans having left just shortly before, taking with them the pick of the available men. Then, among such desirable porters as remained open for engagement, the very name of a caravan for Masai-land was enough to make every one fight shy of it. It was only when, in his despair of getting a caravan, he offered to engage men at higher wages and ask no questions, that he could make headway at all.

But then poured in upon him a flood of Zanzibar villany, and out of this ruck of Oriental rascaldom he had perforce to make his selection. After doing his best he could only look upon the result with a sense of shame. Fortunately, he had engaged as his headmen and caravan assistants half-a-dozen first-rate men, including Muinyi Sera, who had been with Stanley; Makatubu, who had twice already been in his own service as headman; and James Martin, a Maltese sailor, who could jabber in a dozen languages and make himself handy in a hundred ways. But as for the rank and file, never had such a morally ragged, disreputable crew left Zanzibar on any serious undertaking—not to speak of an undertaking beset with such surpassing difficulties as that upon which Joseph Thomson was now setting forth.

As illustrating the young leader's tact in dealing with men, and the shrewd insight into character which stood him in such good stead, a fact may be mentioned in this connection which he related to an interviewer:—

"I tried," said he, "a rather hazardous experiment this time, which was justified by its complete success. The question arose what I should do with one of my men who had in the earlier expeditions been the ringleader in every mischief. He was a magnificent worker when he liked—a great power in the caravan for good or evil; and, though it had been hitherto chiefly for evil, I was loth to part with him. I did, instead, a risky thing—I made him one of my head overseers. The result was that during the whole of the expedition he worked as hard for me and against the rebellious spirits as he had hitherto done in the opposite direction. Throughout I have been fortunate in my leading men, but perhaps none has served me more faithfully than this one."

The caravan was in all a hundred and forty strong, some eighty of the number carrying guns. A preliminary trip of inquiry had been previously made, and everything else was in readiness by the time the engagement of the men was completed. Within five weeks of his arrival at Zanzibar the explorer had his company on board a Government steam tug bound for Mombasa, and in three days more everything was in order for the final start.

On the 15th of March the journey, around which so many dark possibilities gathered, was begun in earnest, and, leaving behind the picturesque palm groves of Rabbai, the company filed away into the wilderness.

The leading of such a caravan as his through the two hundred miles of desert which lay between the coast and Kilimanjaro was in itself a task to try an explorer's quality. This great tract is almost entirely uninhabited, and seems the very ideal of a God-forsaken land. There is not a pleasant feature to relieve its forbidding aspect. Only here and there a scorched clump of bush and tangle, or "a weird and ghastly assemblage of thorns and gnarled trees" emphasises the monotony of sterile soil or glaring red sand. Nowhere, except at the mountain oasis of Teita, which lies half way, is there a drop of water to be found, except where, perchance, the last rain may have left traces of itself in small evil-smelling holes.

VICTORIA NYANZA
INDIAN OCEAN
Equator
Thomson's Route shown thus
English Miles

Through this forbidding land had to be forced a company of men, debilitated with previous idleness or debaucheries, ready for any treachery, fully intending to desert if they could, and only deterred from doing so by the guns being nightly stored and by the most bloodthirsty orders being ostentatiously given to the guards. Under the pitiless blazing sun the caravan pressed on day after day. At one point they had to endure all the horrors of unrelieved thirst for two days and a night, when it seemed as if every man must sink on the burning sands and die. But, by dint of tremendous exertions on the part of the leader and his headmen, that nightmare of travel gradually glided into the past, and the toil and terror were exchanged for the delights of Taveta, which was reached just a fortnight after leaving the coast.

After what they had thus passed through, Taveta, nestling in the shade of its tropical verdure, seemed to the explorer "a veritable dream of Arcady."

"Its majestic trees sheltered under their luxuriant foliage a wealth of graceful curving palm and tender plant; while from trunk and branch swung numberless creepers, binding the forest giants in fantastic bonds. Here was grateful shadow; there floods of sunshine. On all sides were murmuring streams. Glimpses there were of huts embowered in bush and creepers, of plots of ground cultivated for the use of man, of banana groves loaded with golden fruit. Cool, too, it was, for beside it rose the majestic mass of Kilimanjaro, its summit capped with eternal snows from which come icy streams and refreshing breezes to temper the heat of lower levels."

In this idyllic spot, amid a pleasant and hospitable people, whose only bad point was their "excessive lack of common morality," he rested his wearied men for a couple of weeks.

This time did not hang heavily on the leader's hands.

Loads of beads had to be strung, and cloths made up to suit Masai ideas—a process which afforded abundant illustration of the scoundrelly propensities of his men. Duties of this kind, however, were agreeably varied by trips for the study of the botanical and geological features of the district—a work so marvellously interesting that he could with delight have spent a much longer time in the prosecution of it, if there had been no sterner duty pressing. It was on one of these trips that he got his first view of Kilimanjaro and found it to be the perfect realisation of "majestic grandeur and god-like repose." This is how he describes it in one of his letters :—

"To the east is the dreary desert, and to the west—ah! well, to the west you probably see nothing but a great bank of clouds. But wait till the morning, just after the sun has risen, and you will then see a sight. There! You behold at one glance a mighty mountain mass rising to a height of 19,000 feet, capped with a silver crown of snow, glancing like burnished silver in the morning rays. Majestic, snow-white, *cumulus* clouds roll grandly across the face of the former great safety-valve of the region, which times without number has throbbed and groaned with the imprisoned heat of mother earth, till, with some grand effort, it has relieved itself with showers of stones, explosions of steam and rivers of molten rock. And now the snow lies undisturbed on the once fiery summit, and the clouds roll calmly over it. But, even as we look, the *cumulus* gives place to the *stratus*. Ere we are aware the mountain has vanished, and we see but the blank hazy distance. And that is the great pillar which marks the boundaries of the unknown and the untrodden—the great sentinel placed to guard the mysterious land beyond."

The fortnight of rest swiftly glided away, and now came the hour for entering upon the critical part of his great venture. The near view of the reality was not calculated to lighten his anxiety. If distance and the mere spirit of hopefulness had cast any glamour of enchantment around the enterprise, the inquiries diligently pursued at the very threshold of the inhospitable land, rudely and promptly dispelled it. He had had abundant evidence of the wretched character of his following; but now he learned from experienced traders that, even though his caravan had been of picked men instead of mere " wastrels," it was ridiculously small. Then he had for guides two men, Sadi and Muhinna, whom he knew to have the worst of characters, and whom he dared not trust (though that fact had to be carefully concealed); a state of mind only too fully justified by facts, for very soon they did prove to be double-dyed traitors. All things seemed combining to present his anticipations of success in the light of a mere Quixotic dream. But it was no faint heart that he bore, and, even when he had counted the cost to the full, he indulged no wavering thought. The circumstances only braced him to sterner resolution.

It was to the no small dismay of the men that the marching orders were given; for, the more they had heard of the Masai, the more their fears had grown. Fain would they have used their last chance of deserting; indeed, it was only by extraordinary precautions and watchfulness that this danger was forestalled.

The route chosen was by the southern and western slopes of Kilimanjaro, with the remarkable volcanic cone of Mount Meru on the left. Almost at the very outset, however, they encountered a provoking experience of detention. A large war party of Masai was reported to be immediately ahead, and, in turning aside to avoid this supposed danger, they fell into the hands of the notorious chief, Mandara of Chaga. It was impossible to decline his embarrassing and by no means disinterested hospitality; so the situation had to be accepted as philosophically as possible.

The days of enforced delay were turned to good purpose

in further geological examination of the neighbourhood,
and in a botanical trip up the great mountain, which he
climbed to a height of nine thousand feet, returning with
a wealth of interesting specimens and much scientific
information, the value of which subsequent explorers
have warmly acknowledged.   Of his geological work at

MANDARA'S WARRIORS.

Kilimanjaro, Dr. Hans Meyer, in his ' Across East African
Glaciers,' writes thus :—

"Starting from Moji, the kingdom of the notorious
thief Mandara, Thomson was unable to do more than
penetrate the forest region to a height of about 9000
feet; but in an excursion to the district of Shirwa, and

subsequently while pursuing his route towards Masai-land, he covered much new ground and gathered materials for a clear and comprehensive account of the particular origin and main geological and geographical features of the mighty volcanic mass. Thomson was the first to give us any information regarding the northern aspect of the mountain, which he describes as 'a solitude owing to its extremely precipitous nature' with 'no projecting platforms and no streams,' and his sketch of its physical history—of Mawenzi as the original seat of eruption, the subsequent upheaval of Kibo during a late phase of volcanic activity, and the formation of the numerous parasitic cones and of the terrace of Chaga, as the final manifestation of a gradually decaying volcanic energy—was a yet more important contribution to scientific knowledge."

Released from Mandara at last, after an involuntary parting with a quantity of his all too scanty goods, he once more proceeded on his way. For several days the caravan marched through a country rich with streams and grassy glades and forest patches, teeming also with big game. On the 3rd of May they crossed the threshold of Masai-land.

In the meantime the reported party of Masai was supposed to have passed, and thus there was behind the caravan a terror that operated more effectually to prevent desertion than any precaution the leader could devise. To him this seemed only a cause for self-congratulation, as now he would be able with a less distracted spirit to turn to other pressing concerns.

His satisfaction, however, was short-lived. To his intense chagrin, he found that, after all, he had just hit upon Dr. Fischer's route, and that that gentleman in his dealing with the Masai had left him a most unwelcome inheritance of troubles.

Presently he made his first acquaintance with the much

talked of warriors, in all their unctuous glory of red clay and grease, and with their great shovel-headed spears. Even in his opening experiences of them, he saw in their overbearing swagger and fierce rapacity sufficient to prove that they had not got their evil character for nothing; indeed, in the very first interview one man attempted to stab him. Matters rapidly became ominous. Fischer's party had been fighting, blood had been shed, the whole country was in a state of dangerous excitement, and he and his little party were evidently marked as the victims of their revenge.

Clearly, in face of all the facts, it would be mere foolhardiness to push on further in this direction. A policy of sensationalism might have its attractions, but here it could only spell disaster. Retreat must be the order of the day, and some other door of entrance must be tried. So, under the friendly veil of a dark and stormy night, the men silently struck their tents, shouldered their loads, and headed for Taveta, which they reached after five days of steady travelling.

It was a bitter disappointment to the young explorer to find his first attempt thus baffled. But he was not the man to take a first defeat as other than a preparation for ultimate victory, even though the odds seemed overwhelming against him. He *would* succeed; but in order to compel success he must remedy some obvious defects. More goods and men must be got, and that meant a journey to the coast.

Selecting ten of his best men, therefore, and camping the rest at Taveta with due precautions against desertion, he once more faced the trials of the wilderness. In this journey he surely, for speed, "broke the record" of all known African travel. The distance of about two hundred and thirty miles he covered in five and a half marches, in one of which he and his men walked over seventy miles, having been twenty-two hours on their feet without food or water.

Having gathered with infinite difficulty a small caravan of sixty-eight men, he retraced his steps in another series of swift marches, and after a variety of adventures, in one of which he narrowly escaped being carried off by a lion at midnight, he re-entered Taveta to find all safe. A vivid glimpse of his experiences in that second wilderness journey, and of the frame of mind in which he was contemplating the immediate future, is obtained in a letter written on the 24th of June, and headed " Halfway to Kilimanjaro."   He says :—

"We started at 12 A.M. under a fiery sun, and pushed on till sunset, when we stopped to rest without food or water.   In three hours we went on once more, the men fast getting tired with their enormous burdens.   Ever and anon would be heard the dull thud or sharper rattle of loads thrown off the head—the only sounds which broke the deep silence of the night.

"On throughout that glorious moonlight night we pushed—or rather, I pushed the men—the most unpleasant task the white man is called to perform, as circumstances make him feel for the time like a slave-driver.   First two men, then another man, deserted, and added to the difficulties of our already overloaded caravan. Morning at last came, to find us in despair, and water still a great distance off.   We entreated, reasoned, raged at the men to make a spurt; but it was no use.   At last, towards midday, seeing the task hopeless, I myself pushed on with one or two choice spirits, and in about three hours reached a mountain, at the top of which water was to be got.   Towards night I rushed back with the pure element, helping a considerable number, and then carried a load into camp.   One half the men, however, were not relieved till far into the night, and had to camp in the wilderness.   Each man carried from seventy to ninety pounds, and in one march covered quite fifty miles.

"There is a trial of endurance for you! And now it is that, after such a feat, I find myself writing this letter.

"You will, long ere you get this, have heard of my principal adventures; how I have been amongst the Masai, and had to flee back to Taveta, and from Taveta had to return to the coast. How bitter that pill was, and is, to me, you will understand from the fact that; but for a slight accident, I might at this present moment actually have been on the shores of Victoria Nyanza. It was sufficient to crush any one. However, I am made of indiarubber, and though sat upon for a few days, I soon recovered my wonted sanguine spirit. Within the next three weeks I shall once more pit myself against the Masai, and this time I shall make sure that it is success or complete disaster. It won't be a question of retreat for renewed effort, but victory or the collapse of the expedition."

The safety of his camp at Taveta was better news than he had dared to hope for on his return. But the joy it brought was heightened by other tidings of a welcome sort. A great trading caravan, bound for Masai-land, had arrived from Pangani. It seemed a special providence. If he could only, in their company, get into the heart of the country, he had no fear of being able to shift for himself. Before the day of his return from the coast was finished he had managed to arrange terms with Jumba Kimameta and the other traders; and by the 17th of July he was once more on the road for the goal of his hopes.

This time the course taken was by the east and north sides of Kilimanjaro. As they rounded the slopes of the vast mountain a beautiful country opened out before them. It was manifestly of surpassing fertility, but quite uninhabited through dread of the Masai. Day by day they gradually rose in altitude, until at last they reached a level of about 5000 feet. And so for a month they journeyed on without hindrance; but not without lively experiences. Hardly a day passed without some excitement or other. Now it was a rhinoceros scattering the caravan, now a fierce old buffalo bull making havoc in the camp, now lions attacking the donkeys in the night, now a jungle conflagration enveloping them in its

LAKE CHALA, KILIMANJARO.

fiery embrace. As there were no inhabitants except in the mountain fastnesses, there had to be much hunting for the supply of food; and as Joseph Thomson was no lover of sport for its own sake, he was brought into more perils from wild beasts than he cared for, though happily with no hurt to himself.

When at last they did again come into touch with the Masai, it was to learn from a few old greybeards the pleasant news that the warriors of the district were away on a distant expedition. Thus relieved, for the present at least, from fear of trouble and extortion, they entered upon the great Njiri Desert.

The sights of the next few days were weird in the extreme—for the party were passing through a land blasted and barren; yet through the quivering heat-haze everything was seen with a spectral glamour upon it. Ever and anon the mirage played strange pranks with the landscape, making game walk in mid-air, and filling up the prospect with illusory lakes and ponds, while north, south, and east, the mighty mountain masses, seen afar through the pulsating sheen, dominated the horizon.

The passage of the Njiri plain brought the explorer to the base of Donyo (Mount) Erok, and to the beginning of his real troubles; for from this point he had to play "a high chess game" with the savages in all their diabolic genius for provocation. No single night dared they camp without a formidable *boma*, or wall of thorns, being erected around them. Surrounded by such a palisade, with its bristling spikes, it would doubtless have been diffi-cult for even the Masai to attack them successfully. But there was a very real danger indeed in the possibility of their being surprised on the march. The caravan, ham-pered with heavy burdens, would certainly have been at a terrible disadvantage, and an attack in such cir-cumstances could hardly have failed to be serious in its consequences. It was under the constant shadow of such a peril that the daily progress had to be made.

Every day brought some new distraction to the leader's brain, or humiliation to his spirit. To the aggressive and ferocious-looking warriors the white man was an object of curiosity; but that was no protection, for theirs was a curiosity quite fearless and undisguisedly contemptuous. It wanted a coolness, a self-control, a ready resource far beyond common to ward off disaster. Each waking hour had to be spent in the presence of elements that might, through an ill-considered word or act, have developed into a sudden catastrophe.

Ten marches through the unlovely, but densely inhabited district of Matumbato, and along the verge of the great waterless plain of Dogilani, gave opportunities more abundant than welcome of becoming acquainted with the

MASAI WOMEN.

character and habits of the Masai. And a most interesting subject of study they proved to be, although the facts about them had to be acquired often by dolorous experience.

They are a people of quite a distinct race; brown in colour (when through the greasy coating of red clay the true hue is reached), and with sloping eyes. Tall also they are, and of magnificent physical proportions, which is not a little surprising in view of their universal and hideous immorality. Up to thirty the men are warriors and unmarried, dwelling in separate kraals with the young unmarried women, and leading a life of an unspeakable sort, all the time partaking of absolutely nothing but a diet of meat alternating with milk—the necessary salts being obtained by the drinking of the warm blood of animals. After thirty the men leave off war, marry, and settle down to domestic life after a free fashion, and to the keeping of the enormous herds of cattle which constitute their wealth. The exigencies of pasturage for these, and the necessity of varying the scene of the young warriors' cattle-lifting raids, foster a nomadic habit. But wherever they go they bear themselves as lords of creation, all other tribes being simply looked upon as fit subjects for their rapacity and cruelty. Such was the nation of swaggering, aristocratic thieves into the midst of which the expedition had come.

A sojourn of a fortnight on the plateau to the right of the Masai plain brought them into touch with the Wa-Kikuyu. These they found to be quite as intractable and treacherous as the Masai, and after a lively time in which the caravan was brought several times to the verge of ruin, a return was made to the plain.

This plain of the Masai, though associated with unpleasant experiences, presented to the young geologist features of very great interest. It is a curious meridional trough dividing the coast water systems from those of the great central lakes. On its right or east side frown the escarpments of the Kaptè and Lykipia plateaux, and on its left those of Maū and Elgeyo—these great natural walls rising to a height of from 6000 to 9000 feet above sea level. Throughout its length this remarkable depression gives most striking evidence of its volcanic origin. Thermal springs, and steaming rents, and lakes and cones and craters, all tell their tale of igneous disturbance. One

of the most remarkable of the many craters is that of
Donyo Longonot, which rises to a height of 3000 feet
above the surrounding country. The summit, where the
explorer reached it, was found to be a perfect circular cup,
two miles across and several thousands of feet deep, with
a rim so sharp that he actually "sat astride of it, with one
leg dangling into the abyss below and the other down the
steep face of the mountain."

Alternating with sensations like this the daily experience
of being harassed and plundered, he literally bored his
way past Lake Naivasha to El-Meteita. At Naivasha he
found himself once more upon Dr. Fischer's route. That
explorer had reached the lake before him, only, however,
to give up in despair the attempt of pushing through the
country.

Finding himself thus, therefore, in sole possession of
the field, Joseph Thomson braced himself up for a still
more determined prosecution of his purpose. Now it was
that he resolved upon an enterprise which seemed to the
traders nothing less than mad in its daring. This was to
form a picked company of thirty men (as he had done at
Tanganyika) and to visit Mount Kenia by a dash through
the Masai of Lykipia—the general body of the caravan
being allowed to go on with the traders to Lake Baringo.
It was clearly a case of taking his life in his hand; but
he could not be within eighty miles of that great mountain
around which hung so much both of interest and mystery
without at least a bold attempt to see it for himself.

He had scarcely well started on his audacious mission
before he discovered that it was more perilous than even
he had dreamed of. All through the region to be traversed
a portentous pestilence was decimating the herds. And as
the savages saw their cattle dying by thousands on every
hand, they were not only in a most truculent mood, but
ready to blame the strange visitor for the lamentable
visitation.

It was only by a stratagem that he could make headway

at all—he posing as a great *lybon* or medicine man, who
had come to make spells for the healing of their cattle.
This *rôle* of thaumaturgist had its humorous aspects, but
it was not without its dangers and drawbacks among a
people so unimpressible and fearless as the Masai—as for
instance when one of the savages nearly wrenched off the

MASAI WARRIORS.

explorer's nose, having got the impression, from a trick
which he played with a couple of false teeth, that he was
made to come to pieces if need be.

Space does not permit us to recount the incidents of
that excursion over the lofty equatorial plateau, amid
scenery more suggestive of Europe than of tropical Africa.
Suffice it to say that, after weeks of worry unspeakable,

and of a physical and mental strain that would have broken down all but an indomitable spirit, he stood at the base of the heaven-kissing mountain, "entranced with its awful beauty as the snow pinnacles caught the last rays of the sun and shone with crystalline beauty."

On the way to Kenia he had made the interesting discovery of a magnificent range of mountains running to 14,000 feet in height, which he named the Aberdare Range, after the president of the Royal Geographical Society. This discovery formed an additional and much prized reward for his labours.

The object of this *détour* having been accomplished, his one thought now was how to get back most quickly to his men. His position among the Masai of Lykipia had become absolutely intolerable, and he once more resolved upon the expedient of a night flight. After eight marches through an uninhabited forest in the direction which, it was supposed, would lead to the conjectural Lake Baringo, he had the joy of emerging at the edge of the plateau to survey in actual fact the lake's isle-besprinkled expanse gleaming some thousands of feet below him.

An adventurous couple of days followed, in course of which he got separated from his party and was thirty-six hours without food; but at last, to the great delight of the caravan, he rejoined them at Njemps near the southern shore of the lake. He had expected his trip to occupy ten days. It had in fact extended to a whole month, and the caravan had become seriously concerned about his non-appearance.

The quiet and plenty of the camp at Njemps were like a glimpse of Paradise, after the maddening trials and incalculable hardships from which he had just escaped, for not only had he had to endure wearing anxiety on account of the people, but for the whole time the sole food which he and his men could procure was the diseased flesh of cattle which were sold to them only when at the point of death. The Wa-Kwafi who were settled here were, like their kinsmen at Taveta, a kindly, peaceable, honest people. Amid the exquisite scenery and the glorious sense of freedom, therefore, he could give himself up to pure rest and enjoyment for a season, and so prepare himself for the second part of his great undertaking. During the six months of his journeying from the coast he had enjoyed almost uninterrupted good health ; consequently it required only a week or two of the delicious *dolce far niente* which Njemps afforded to give him perfect recruitment and re-invigoration.

The task of traversing the unknown region which lay between Baringo and Victoria Nyanza was one to which rumour attached even more risk and toil than that which had characterised their course hitherto. Certainly, disaster had dogged the footsteps of the last three caravans which had attempted it, and each had lost more men than he proposed to take with him altogether. The only one of his guides who had been through the district was so terrified at the idea of being taken, that he feigned extreme illness in order to be left behind. These things did not of course in the smallest degree shake the leader's purpose, for he was now more convinced than ever that there was no hindrance incapable of being overcome by patience and self-restraint.

Taking with him all the men who were physically fit— about a hundred in number—he marched away from Njemps on the 16th of November. Scaling first the sharp Kamasia range and then the precipices of the great Elgeyo escarpment, he pressed westward for many days at an altitude of from 7000 to 8000 feet, through an uninviting country swarming with game. On the 28th of the month he arrived at Kabaras in Kavirondo. This region he found to be rich in good things, and populous to an extent surpassing all his previous experience of African lands.

After all that he had heard, he made his first advances with some anxiety ; but his experience did not belie his

VILLAGE OF KABARAS, KAVIRONDO.

faith in gentle methods. A rash or wilful man would indeed instantly have made trouble for himself, for the Wa-Kavirondo were evidently mercurial in temper, and their experience of traders had made them suspicious of this curious phenomenon, the white stranger. It only, however, wanted a little tactful treatment at the outset to make the nude savages his friends, and as his good fame went ahead of him, he had his way comparatively smoothed onward to the great lake.

The 10th of December saw the triumphant completion of his outward journey; for on that day he passed through the gently sloping country that leads down to Nyanza's reed-covered, marshy shores, and, after bathing in its waters, watched the light from the westering sun stream in effulgent splendour over its vast expanse.

He was at this point only forty-five miles from the Nile, and would naturally have liked to look upon the beginnings of that wondrous historic river; but from this point the fates were unpropitious. He was, for almost the first time in this chequered journey, struck down with fever, and his goods were all used up. This of course would not have stayed his progress. But, just at the last moment, he learned that the King of Uganda, objecting to the idea of the white man entering his kingdom by a back door, had laid a trap for him. To make light of a risk like this would have been an act of perilous, if not fatal, foolhardiness on his part (as indeed poor Hannington found afterwards to his cost). Joseph Thomson, though fearless in what he deemed to be duty, was no madcap and no spectacular adventurer. So, thinking it better to do some further useful exploration than to languish in durance vile in the hands of a savage potentate, he at once resolved to begin his return journey.

Before doing so, however, he made some careful observations which proved that the map of the north-east portion of the lake required to be very considerably altered; for nearly the whole of Upper Kavirondo occupied a space which was hitherto supposed to be covered with water.

In place of simply retracing his steps he resolved to return by way of Mount Elgon, whose noble contour loomed so loftily in the north. He was fortunate in having so chosen, for there he discovered some profoundly interesting remains of a former civilisation—enormous caves which had been skilfully cut in an extremely hard conglomerate rock, and which extended far into the heart of the mountain, forming shelters in which the modern savage dwellers build their villages.

The next day after his departure from Elgon was the last of 1882, and it seemed like marking also the close of his career. As he was hunting to supply food for his men, preparatory to entering upon a long stretch of uninhabited country, he had shot—fatally as he thought —a buffalo bull. In proceeding to secure his spoil, he found the ferocious creature sufficiently alive to project him skyward with its mighty horns, and, when he came to his senses a few moments later, it was to behold the avenger standing over him ready to complete its deadly work. This without doubt it would have done had not the opportune shots of his followers distracted the brute's attention in the last moments of its fast-ebbing existence, and given him the precious opportunity of dragging himself away from his awful position. He was seriously wounded and had lost an enormous quantity of blood, but in the evening he so far rallied as to be able, in a spirit of grim pleasantry, to celebrate his deliverance in soup made from the flesh of his bovine adversary.

Beginning 1883 in this crippled condition, he had to be carried on a stretcher across the wilderness. Three weeks later he reached Njemps, and by that time he had so far recovered as to be able to walk a little.

There remained yet one more exploring excursion, which he longed to make before resuming the perilous coastward journey through the Masai country. As soon,

therefore, as he was fit for service, he was off to examine
the region to the north of Lake Baringo. In this trip he
gained much valuable knowledge, geographical and scientific, besides having hunting successes to his heart's
content, and when he returned to his men he came laden
with spoil.

This marked the practical close of the mission of exploration for which he had been sent out. In the course
of his wanderings he had rescued from the realm of
mystery manifold secrets which the world of inquirers
had long been waiting to welcome. But at what a cost to
himself was the prize of knowledge obtained! From its
very start his expedition had been one long adventure in
which every quality of his manhood had been strained
to the utmost. He had lived every moment in the
presence of death. So constant were the perils that he
had come to look upon them as commonplace facts and to
walk among them with a strange sense of mirthfulness.
Indeed, even in the most trying situations he was all
alive to the ludicrous element, and the joyousness of his
nature would have its outlet. Keenly as his wits were
aware of the stern realities around him, he could have his
laugh and enjoy the point of a practical joke, even when
destruction was visibly jogging at his elbow. The whole
enterprise, in fact, seemed to him a grim game, in which
intellect and civilisation in his own single person were
pitted against the overwhelming odds of savagery and
Nature's forces, and he had a lively though quaint satisfaction in getting the better of them in the contest.

But Nature had its revenges, too, and these of a terrible
sort. For long, illness was held at bay, and it seemed as
if there was to be a contrast to the experiences of his first
expedition. At last, however, hardships began to tell
upon his constitution, weakened as it was for the time by
the effects of his almost fatal misadventure. The dread
disease dysentery began to reveal its ominous symptoms.
From the time of his return from the north to Njemps, in

the middle of February, there ensued a three months' struggle for life, through which nothing but a magnificent constitution, and an unconquerable resolve not to die, could have borne him. The story of that illness was a record of unimaginable misery and of suffering heroically endured.

He started resolutely on the homeward march, but by the time he reached Naivasha further progress was impossible, and there for several days it seemed as if only a fatal issue was to be looked for. Gradually, however, he

MASAI HUTS.

rallied, and hope smiled upon him once more. But as the exigencies of the caravan required a removal to the plateau for food, a relapse immediately followed. There, therefore, in the solitary darkness of a native hut, on the sleet-swept heights of Mianzini, with nothing to subsist upon but clear soup made from the half-putrid meat of diseased cattle, and with swarms of the murderous Masai prowling malignantly around the camp who would only too gladly have massacred the whole company, he lay for two long months, hovering on the verge of the eternal world.

But at the end of that dolorous time he had still a sufficient spark of resolution left to insist that he should be carried coastwards. It was a last desperate expedient; life or death. But life had the mastery. As they journeyed on, the wave of vitality began to pulsate more strongly, and hope gradually brightened. His men, now thoroughly regenerated and devotedly attached to their leader, bore him heroically through the dangerous and famine-stricken countries. Enduring hunger and thirst and manifold perils, they pressed cheerfully on, week in week out, over long and trying marches, until at last they reached the outposts of civilisation. By this time it was the beginning of June, and the stricken man could stand on his feet.

After fifteen months of silence, the knight errant of science emerged out of the unknown land, but it was as the very ghost of his former self. Let those who saw him at the beginning and again at the close of his journey tell their impression.

"One day, in the spring of 1883," wrote Mrs. Wakefield, the wife of the devoted missionary at Rabbai, "it was our pleasure to receive as our guest for a few days the noted young traveller, Mr. Joseph Thomson. Full of life, energy, and hope, he was about to start on his memorable Masai journey, and with intense interest did we listen to his plans and watch the gathering of the porters from the Mombasa district. We well knew how dangerous was the mission on which he was entering, while we admired the courage and enterprise which were spurring him on. We were with him when he turned his back upon the coast; we heard the cheers of the sailors on the steam launch which had brought him from Zanzibar as they uttered their fervent, 'God bless you, sir,' and waved their kindly farewells. Our boat conveyed him up the creek, and soon after we said, 'Good-bye,' adding our best wishes on behalf of a prosperous and happy issue for his journey.

"We saw him again when compelled to return from Taveta for more men and goods, and then there ensued about fifteen months of silence, during which we often wondered what had been the fate of the expedition and of its gallant leader.

"At length one day a note came from our friend and neighbour the church missionary at Rabbai, with the glad intelligence 'Thomson has returned,' and asking us to send our boat to meet him, at the head of the creek. In a short time we were grasping his hand. He had endured and suffered much, but had mercifully been preserved and brought back even from the gates of death. His form was fearfully emaciated; strength and spirit were well nigh spent. But his work was done, and well done. All the toils and dangers were behind him, while before him lay home, rest, and well-earned laurels."

# CHAPTER VII.



IT was indeed a narrow escape that Joseph Thomson had made. His unconquerable will and magnificent constitution had enabled him to fight death *à outrance*, and to reach the coast alive; but it was manifest to any discerning eye that it would take months of care and tendance to restore the shattered physical powers. It was indeed a question whether he could ever be the same man, or able with the same buoyant cheerfulness to face hardship and toil. He had now, however, returned to scenes where rest and home comforts could be enjoyed, and where there was no lack of tender ministries. Even if there had been no sentiment of friendship to inspire the impulse of kindness, the admiration which was aroused by his chivalrous mission would have been sufficient to secure for him every possible attention.

He did not linger at Mombasa an hour longer than was necessary. One unpleasant duty, however, had to be done, and that was to hand over to justice the traitorous guides Muhinna and Sadi. These men had been necessary to him in the circumstances, but their treacherous spirit had been a continual source of danger to the expedition. More than once they had brought it to the verge of ruin, and the leader had to be ever on the watch to checkmate their game. With all their duplicity they themselves had never suspected that they were fully understood, and they were simply thunderstruck when they were brought face to face with the evidence of their guilt. It would have been wrong not to have exposed them in the interest of other possible leaders, though there was more than a suspicion that their evil conduct had been originally instigated by the Governor of Mombasa himself.

On re-entering Zanzibar he found that Dr. Kirk had again returned to his post, and it was a quickening cordial to receive from his former mentor and friend the cheering welcome which he knew so well how to give. A short time of residence under the hospitable roof of the consulate, and in the enjoyment of Dr. Kirk's skilful advice, rapidly enabled him to pull together the faint remaining traces of his youthful vigour, so far as to permit him to contemplate the voyage home which he was so eager to begin.

It was thought that in his prostrate condition the lengthening of the voyage might be beneficial. Curiously, a means of securing this very opportunely presented itself through the arrival of a courteous invitation from the Sultan to accept a free passage in one of His Highness's steamers to Bombay. The possibility of thus combining the pursuit of health with the prospect of viewing, however cursorily, the scenes of our Eastern empire, was a boon not to be refused. The invitation was therefore gladly accepted, and for the third and last time he turned his back upon Zanzibar, a city which in the course of the past five years had been linked with memories of such varied interest for him.

In leaving East Africa behind, little did he anticipate that the very arena of his exploits during those years was so soon to be the focal point of European interest, in the diplomatic contendings of the western colonising nations for a recognised footing on that section of the Dark Continent. Still less did he dream that the outcome of his last enterprise there was to mean nothing less than the adding of a vast country to the British Empire, and that before a decade had passed the wilderness and the virgin scenes of his daring wanderings would have the prospect of echoing to the rush of the railway train and the shriek of the steam whistle.  Yet so it was to be. In his own purpose and aim he was but the pioneer of scientific inquiry, but all unconsciously he was preparing by his toils and sufferings for ministering to a nation's earth-hunger, and for transforming the destiny of many savage tribes.

The rest and the quickening influence of the long sea voyage were undoubtedly beneficial to him, but the effects of so dire an illness were not to be lightly obliterated, and when, a month later, he arrived in London, it did not require the eye of an expert to see that he had been wrestling with death.  But it was already as an inspiration of life to him to think of breathing the air of his native hills and of basking in the sunny pleasures of home. Steadily, if slowly, his strength returned, and soon with characteristic buoyancy he was making light of his ailments.

"You will have seen from the papers," he jocularly writes on July 26th to his friend Miss Noake, "that I have returned a sad wreck—only a few planks, as it were, holding together.  I had indeed almost hoped that you would have replied to my advertisement, 'Wanted a nurse, to take care of a shattered constitution ; must be amiable, have a low sweet voice with a soothing tone, and be able to strike pleasing attitudes when administering nauseous medicines.  None who are not sympathetic need apply.'  You will be pleased to learn, however, that I have been heard to laugh since I returned, and it is generally believed that, if afforded an opportunity, I might be able to sing 'Three Blue Bottles,' and dance in old time fashion a Scotch reel.  The truth is, there is hardly anything wrong with me, as you will find for yourself when you give us a visit."

But notwithstanding this optimistic account of himself,

he was only too conscious that such an experience as he had passed through meant so many years off his life. When he permitted himself in quiet to think of this, it would have been surprising if he had not had pensive moments. It is from this point that we begin to detect an occasional note of despondency in his correspondence—a note which strikes one with touching suggestiveness by its very contrast with the habitual brightness of his letters. Writing to his schoolmate, Miss Bennett, about this time, he says :—

" The thought seems to occur to me that my life will be short. I picture myself in a narrow defile from which there is no escape or back-turning, neither is there any halt. Slowly and surely I move on to the mouth of that defile, across which lies a gloomy chasm, into which fate will precipitate me. When I think of such a thing, 1 am not unhappy, only pervaded by a touch of melancholy. And yet sometimes my cogitations on this subject seem to be so ridiculous that I laugh aloud, and turning to the mirror, see neither a face and form that speak of the sad hue of melancholy, nor the cadaverous countenance of a man doomed to the grave ; and even now I can picture you with a comical expression of amazement as you read my mournful forebodings."

His panacea for these misgivings lay in hearty work, for he had ever faith in a good breeze of activity to drive away the shadowing clouds of sadness. As soon, therefore, as he could settle to his desk, he applied himself with what energy he had to dash off the narrative of his journey. The task, in itself, was most burdensome to him ; but he had a powerful stimulus in the consciousness that he had a tale of unique interest to tell, and in the evidences which he had that the geographical world was waiting impatiently to hear the novel revelations which it was known he had to make; for sufficient information had leaked out to make it clear that

not a few theories of arm-chair geographers were about
to be upset.

The full record of the fruits of his wanderings had,
of course, to be reserved for the meeting of the Royal
Geographical Society; but to a gathering of the Glasgow
Dumfriesshire Society (who had come on an excursion to
Thornhill, and entertained him as their guest) he outlined
in his speech a sketch of what might be expected, which
was well fitted to deepen curiosity.

By the end of October his health was, to a great extent,
recovered, although, as he admitted to an interviewer
from the *Pall Mall Gazette* (who was sent down to Scotland to see him), he "still had an occasional twinge to
remind him of the time when he had to be carried, like so
much luggage, on an improvised litter."

The meeting of the Royal Geographical Society, for
receiving the account of his stewardship, was fixed for
the 3rd of November, and it proved quite a red-letter
occasion for him.  His reception was more than flattering.
The large and brilliant audience which filled the theatre
of Burlington House waited upon his thrilling story, not
only with rapt attention, but with evident enthusiasm;
and at the close, men like Hannington, Cameron, Galton,
and Ravenstein vied with each other in tributes of admiration for the explorer, and in expounding the points
of novelty and of scientific value in the results of his
"wonderful journey."   These compliments were fitly
crowned with the closing remarks of the President:—

"Mr. Thomson," he said, "had proved, in his expedition
to the west side of Tanganyika, that he was admirably
fitted for encountering the tremendous dangers which it
was known he would meet with in the Masai country.
To have travelled among such a people under such difficulties, and to have escaped without having recourse to
violence, argued that Mr. Thomson was a man of undaunted courage, of extraordinary resources, and that he

K

possessed all the qualities necessary for African travel. He wished to congratulate both Mr. Thomson and the Society on the result of an expedition which had been looked forward to with so much interest. No doubt there were still dangers to be encountered in completing the geography of Africa, but probably no expedition remained to be made of equal interest to that which Mr. Thomson had just described."

The spirit of these various speeches found a hearty echo in the leading articles of the Press on the next day. The extraordinary character of the narrative had, indeed, manifestly created no small stir, and it was universally admitted that Joseph Thomson had won for himself an unchallengeable place in the very front rank of African pioneers.

"If for nothing else," said *The Scotsman*, "Mr. Joseph Thomson deserves the warm thanks of his countrymen for bringing back to us for a time the African age of romance. The story which the young Scotsman told last night to the assembled *savants* of the Royal Geographical Society was one that, at every paragraph, must have made old geographers prick up their ears. . . . He may be congratulated heartily on the magnificent record which he was able to lay before the Royal Geographical Society ; and his countrymen may be excused for congratulating themselves that, like other noble workers in the same field, he belongs in an especial way to Scotland."

"The existence of Englishmen like Mr. Thomson," said another leading paper, "ought to reassure any who are dejected by disquisitions on the decadence of the race. For no reward but the thanks of a learned society, he defied a year's perils of every conceivable description. Amid them all he bore himself with the cheerfulness of an Alpine tourist, and he relates them with no apparent consciousness that any remarkable faculties were needed to surmount them. . . . No explorer has more thoroughly deserved the triumphal reception, such as yesterday's in the theatre of Burlington House, which is, for his restless profession, what Westminster Abbey seemed to Lord Nelson."

Experiences like this might well have spoiled him, if he had been a less strong and simple man. If he had cared to let himself be "boomed" in society, he might have made a prominent public figure, and had the usual incense burned for him. But, with his unfailing modesty, he was the last to presume upon his fame, and when the moment of release came, he was glad to get beyond earshot of the chorus of praise, and to be allowed in quietness to think his own thoughts and renew his fellowship with old friends.

He who has won distinction, however, has this penalty to pay, that he is not allowed to be the master of his own movements. Claims come upon him by virtue of his record of work, which he is not at liberty to resist. As a matter of fact, therefore, his hands were kept as full of duties as they could well be. In the intervals of his bookwriting he had, as he says, to be "tearing around, everything by turns and nothing long—now a platform orator, anon an after-dinner speaker, then a newspaper letter writer, and next a lecturer—in fact, starring it generally," with the consequence of having his "humble self" discussed in a variety of newspaper articles, and even having his "life" written after a fashion.

In December of that year (1884) the Scottish Geographical Society was inaugurated, and of course it behoved him, as a Scotsman and an explorer, to be present. Mr. Stanley, who was the inaugural lecturer, was at that time vigorously playing his *rôle* of advertiser of the commercial prospects of Africa, and especially of the Congo; and he naturally used the opportunity of his various appearances to make glowing appeals to the mercantile imagination.

The hard predominance of the commercial note jarred upon the younger explorer. He felt that to make the interests of mere trade the only, or even the leading, motive in African exploration was to degrade it, and to depart *toto cœlo* from the spirit which had animated the greatest and noblest pioneers. At the banquet following the inaugural address, he got the opportunity of relieving his mind, and, wisely or unwisely, he used it in uttering a half-serious, half-humorous protest :—

"I have to express," he said, "the melancholy feeling I have for the last few days entertained, as I listened to Mr. Stanley, on seeing how the iron heel of commerce has entirely knocked romance out of African travel. There were days when there was romance in African travel, but the soul-less march of commerce has been gradually trampling out that, and we must apparently consider that the days of African romance are pretty well gone. It is pitiful that such should be the case. . . . We have come to look upon the palm-tree, not in regard to its artistic effect, but upon the quantity of oil that it is to produce. If this sort of thing is to go on, I should prefer to go to the North Pole."

This speech would perhaps have been as well left unuttered, seeing it was not taken in the playful spirit in which it was spoken. But to this extent it is interesting, that in its own way it reveals one of the characteristic traits of Joseph Thomson as a pioneer and explorer. His work was inspired all through with the spirit of romance, because it was done purely for its own sake and wholly for the love of it. To him exploring was *a vocation and an inspiration*, not a profession. He could not have done and dared what he did upon the motive impulse of mere commercialism. And he could not have borne and shown patience with savage peoples as he did, if he had penetrated into the dark places as the

mere representative of Mammon. The seeker after mere
profit is ever under temptation, in his haste, to make light
of men's rights, and even of their lives. He is apt to become the apostle of force and self-will, and to carry these to
uttermost lengths rather than be turned, even for a time,
from his purpose. But the man who goes simply as the
inquirer after truth and the student of the problems
presented by man and Nature, can afford to be gentle
and just in presence of even ill-treatment and suffering.
He can afford to respect men's prejudices, and to live
down their suspicions. And in the end he loses nothing
for himself, and he leaves no heritage of ill-will for those
who may come after him.

But while the fundamental motive of his exploration
was the love of knowledge, and the desire to extend the
boundaries of it, Joseph Thomson was, at the same time,
something more than the knight-errant of science. It
was in no impractical spirit that he had bored his way
through so many savage tribes, and traversed lands
hitherto closed to the ken of civilisation. He was keenly
alive to the questions which the world at home would
be asking, as to the resources and possibilities of the
countries through which his wanderings had led him.
He never forgot that the great money-making multitude
concerned itself little with the settlement of geographical
and other scientific problems, as compared with the
finding of new means of adding to its gain. The question with them was, Will it pay to exploit this or that
land? and Joseph Thomson ever looked with a shrewd
eye upon the various elements that go to the answering of
that question.

Now there are obviously several things that naturally
predispose an explorer to give a good, rather than an
unfavourable, report of the lands he has visited. It is
pleasanter to the man himself, it is popular with the
public, and, in these days of rampant company-mongering,
it pays. A man needs both conscience and force of

character to be perfectly honest in his representation of facts.

Joseph Thomson felt the strain to the full. But the result of his observations in each of the three districts of East Africa, had been unfavourable from the commercial point of view, and he must needs speak out the truth as it impressed itself upon him. It had been his fate to get "the gilt taken off the gingerbread" of his own dreams about Africa. Affected no doubt by the prevalent popular notions of that land, he had gone out predisposed to find it an El Dorado. But hard facts had disillusionised him. He found, especially in the sphere of his first and second explorations, the immediate resources of the country poor in the extreme, the wants of the people excessively simple, and the difficulties in the way of trade enormous. And if Masai-land itself did not present quite so barren and unproductive an aspect, there was there this enormous drawback, that the entire region was in the hands of a powerful people whose whole instincts led them fiercely to oppose the trader and all his works. As he expressed it to an interviewer from the *Pall Mall Gazette:* " You cannot trade in that region unless the Masai allow you, and at present they would rather have your head than the present of a linendraper's warehouse."

On the whole, his honest conviction was that, whatever development of commerce might emerge as " the long result of time," it would certainly neither be good for Africa itself, nor wise or safe for the capitalist at home, that money and lives should be poured recklessly into it, with the expectation of an immediate return.

To these views he gave energetic expression in a lecture which he delivered in connection with the Students' Union, immediately after the Stanley banquet. Thus Edinburgh had the somewhat bewildering experience of two admitted African experts speaking from diametrically opposite points of view, the one conjuring up glowing visions, the other a herald of caution. There can be no doubt as to which testimony was the more popular and acceptable.   It is for history to say which has most strictly justified itself by experience.

After his appearances at Edinburgh he lectured at Greenock, Thornhill, Dumfries, and then after enjoying the much-prized family gathering on New Year's day at home, he returned to London to appear before the Society of Arts.

Meantime, a new enterprise drifted into view on the horizon of his life, and in the end of the year (1884) his letters to his intimates began to throw out vague hints of "an important diplomatic mission to a Central African potentate."   To one he writes (December 24th) in a spirit of assumed melancholy :—

"The moment I would soar into the region of pleasant phantasy, I am rudely pulled down by my African Frankenstein.   Can you imagine me consigned in less than six weeks to the steam bath of the Niger, there putting on my autumn tints, as liver with lavish bile paints the burnished gold which speaks eloquently of jaundice and organic derangements ?   Is it not infinitely pitiful that the few planks saved from my last trip should be launched once more before the caulking and repairing has been thoroughly accomplished ?   Such is my fate—a poor waif lost on the bosom of a turbulent ocean, and tossed about by wind and wave !   To-morrow, possibly, I shall be mocked by numerous wishes for a happy Christmas.   That is how the rude heel of stern reality crushes out the little happiness I occasionally get— will-o'-the-wisps only making fun of me and leaving me at last in mire and darkness. . . .   Imagine *me* a coiner of money and an African trader, dispensing cotton for palm oil, measuring native damsels for suits of Sunday clothes !"

In the same gay manner, to his fellow-Dumfriesian

and faithful correspondent, Mr. Thomas McKie, he writes :—

"You are probably aware by this time that my fate is sealed, and that the fair (?) Spirit of Africa is standing with heaving bosom and outstretched arms awaiting my approach, with the vain phantasy of romance knocked out of me and bearing instead a trophy of Manchester goods, etc., symbolical of the blessings of commerce! Is not this a change? Will not H. M. Stanley be proud of me? . . . Would that I could tell you all about everything, but, alas! my lips are sealed. I myself get but a hazy glimpse into futurity. Does it not sound tip-top to speak about 'sealed orders'?"

Certainly in one aspect of it the character of this new mission was such as to make him laugh at the topsy-turveydom of fate. The explorer transformed into the expansionist; the declaimer against mere commercialism turned into the agent of a trading company! Was there not room for his making a little fun at his own expense?

But really the new engagement thus foreshadowed was one that appealed to him as having in it vast possibilities of interest. It would take him to classic scenes of African exploration, to a region redolent of thrilling memories, associated with the names of men like Park, Clapperton, Landers, Gallieni and Barth. It would enable him to see for himself new and contrasted phases of African life, and it would give him an exceptional opportunity of witnessing the semi-barbaric splendours of powerful states too far removed from the beaten paths of travel to impress themselves much upon the consciousness of Europe.

The genesis of the expedition was as follows. The company trading on the Niger as the National African Company found its valuable interests to be imperilled. It had been hoping, after its successful checkmating of French rivalry and the expenditure of much means and effort, to settle down to the quiet development of its resources, when in 1884 a new danger arose. Germany, waking up for the first time to the idea of colonial expansion, was casting her eyes upon this great waterway of West Africa as a possible scene of operations. The fact that the Niger was being exploited by a British company made the scheme of operating there all the more attractive to Germany, which at that time entertained feelings far from friendly towards this country. It came to the knowledge of the company just in the nick of time that a political envoy—Herr Flegel—had been appointed by the Germans to visit the Kings of Sokoto and Gandu and the other chiefs who controlled the destinies of the vast *hinterland* of the Niger. Instant action with the view of foiling this move was necessary, if mischief was to be averted; and the question was, whom to send for the securing of the desired treaties? Joseph Thomson's established reputation for energy and tact pointed him out as the very man for such a task as was proposed. Would he act as the Company's emissary?

His acceptance of the appointment was prompt and hearty, although it was only too clear that it involved for himself very grave risks with regard to health. He was far from having thrown off the effects of the illness which had so nearly carried him to a grave in Masai-land; and to enter such a deadly region as that of the Niger in a condition of impaired vigour, certainly wanted strong reasons to justify it. But when, in a manner, his patriotism was appealed to, it was quite like the man that he should chivalrously put all considerations of self in the background. He had his own passing qualms of doubt as to the wisdom of his going, but these he characteristically mentioned in his letters only in terms of seeming gaiety:—

"My book," he writes, "is being finally touched up and will be offered to an appreciative and eager public about the first week of January. Is not that a very hopeful commencement to the year?  I shall have some comfort in knowing that this interesting offering of my brain will remain behind me to comfort a sorrowing world."

Meantime, as these words indicate, the preparation of the narrative of his recent journey had been proceeding apace.  As he had been relieved of all anxiety with respect to literary revision and press correction, he had the advantage of being able to dash ahead, *currente calamo*, and to impart to his story all the vividness and sense of onwardness which come from a rapid telling of it.

Just on the eve of his setting out for the Niger, 'Through Masai-land' was published.  It was dedicated to his father and mother, and bore on its title-page a motto or foreword which his editor suggested as peculiarly descriptive of its contents, and which has become indelibly associated in the public mind with his entire life-record as an explorer: "*Chi va piano va sano; chi va sano va lontano*" (He who goes gently goes safely; he who goes safely goes far).  The book was at once received with every mark of approval and interest.  Indeed its success was assured even before publication, owing to the great and widespread interest aroused by his paper at the meeting of the Royal Geographical Society.

The perusal of the complete account of his journey only served to deepen in the public mind a sense of the notable character of the journey and of the value of its geographical and other results.  At the same time the foremost representatives of the Press warmly praised the literary quality of the book.

"Mr. Thomson," said the *Times*, "has no need to apologise for his want of practice with the pen.  His former narrative proved that he can tell his story quite as well as he leads his expeditions.  The present volume is marked by all the best qualities of its predecessors; a clear, swinging, vigorous style, rising into eloquence and even poetry under the stimulus of Nature's wonders, and abounding throughout with a sense of humour or rather rollicking fun, which does not even spare the author's own peculiarities. . . . It would be impossible to add to the interest of the narrative itself."

Precisely similar, and equally hearty, was the verdict from all other quarters. And so, amid a chorus of approval, which could not but be pleasant to the young explorer and author, he could set forth with fresh confidence to win new triumphs as a leader.

It may be noted in passing that, almost simultaneously with the publication of 'Through Masai-land,' came the agreeable notification that the Royal Italian Geographical Society had elected him as an honorary member. Meantime his name had appeared as one of the first quartette of honorary members of the Royal Scottish Geographical Society, the other three being the King of the Belgians, Mr. Stanley, and Lord Aberdare.

Here also (although it is a slight anticipation of the subsequent course of events) we may chronicle, in association with the Masai-land journey, what he regarded as one of the highest honours of his life, namely the conferring upon him in July 1885 of the Founder's Gold Medal of the Royal Geographical Society. The medal was given " in recognition of the great services he has rendered to geography by carrying out with admirable zeal, promptitude and success the two expeditions into East Central Africa with which he was charged by the Society."

In the absence of the explorer in West Africa, the medal decreed to him was received by Sir Rutherford Alcock, K.C.B. The president, Lord Aberdare, in announcing this to the meeting, said that " no more fitting person could be found for such a purpose, Sir Rutherford having been president of the Society at the time when Mr. Thomson was engaged to serve in the first expedition, and having taken a very strong personal interest in all its operations." The president in continuation said: "The successful completion of his second great African expedition must have prepared the Society for the selection of Mr. Thomson for the honour of receiving the Founder's Medal. His career as a geographical traveller has been singularly rapid and remarkable." Lord Aberdare then sketched briefly the story of the journeys the explorer had made, in which, said he, "he proved himself a born leader of men." His concluding words were these:—

"His account of the interesting and dangerous journey through the Masai country to Kenia and the eastern shores of Lake Victoria Nyanza must have been read by the most of you, and I will venture to say that it not only justified his choice by the Society as its leader but has stamped him as one of the ablest travellers that ever devoted himself to African exploration. The cheerfulness with which he endured hardships, delays, obstacles of every sort, and even insults from his barbarous hosts; the patient skill with which he converted his half-hearted and mutinous followers into a band of devoted and trustworthy friends, his quiet tenacity of purpose, his dexterity in dealing with warlike and aggressive tribes, and the accomplishment of this perilous journey without shedding a drop of human blood—all these qualities and deeds point him out as one in the foremost rank even of those distinguished travellers of many countries who have been selected by the Society for their highest honour."

In accepting the medal for the absent explorer Sir Rutherford Alcock said that Mr. Thomson had in his first journey added valuable fruits to geographical knowledge, but that, in his most recent journey, he "had made one of the most valuable contributions to the geography of the interior of Africa that had been obtained in modern times. He had well earned the highest honour that the Geographical Society could confer upon him. He was the youngest of the list of medallists, but, taking into account all the conditions and circumstances in which he worked

ROYAL NIGER COMPANY'S EXPEDITION, 1885.
MAP 4 
AIR or ASBEN
TIHRI
DAMERGHU
KANEM
L. Chad
or
Tsad
GANDU
SOKOTO
BORNU
ADAMAWA
YORUBA
BENIN
DAHOMEY
NIGER COAST
PROTEC.
KAMERUN
Slave Coast
BIGHT OF BENIN
GULF
OF
GUINEA
BIGHT
OF
BIAFRA
Thomson's Route shown thus ______
English Miles

and triumphed, the Society must feel that they could not have added to their number one who was more deserving of the honour."

It was the beginning of February before he was able to start for the Niger.  He had hoped to be half way to his new scene of operations by that time, but, unfortunately, and much to the trial of his own patience, his preparations had been delayed by an attack of inflammation in the lungs with an interlude of fever.

On the 2nd of the month he set sail from Liverpool in the ss. *Opobo*, along with a gentleman named Hamilton, who desired to have the privilege of being one of his company.  The voyage was entered upon amid somewhat gloomy and depressing weather conditions, and in various other respects it kept up the character of dreariness to the end.  As he was being borne into scenes and circumstances very different from those with which he had now become familiar in East Africa, he found sufficient matter of interest for a time in the study of his fellow-passengers and in little trips of observation at the various landing-places.  With the passengers, who were evidently a fair representation of West African society, he soon found himself standing on more agreeable terms than he had thought possible.  On the other hand, as they crept from point to point on the West African coast, he found at each new place something fresh to disillusionise him.  Here is the summing-up of his impressions :—

"My voyage along the coast and visits to all the principal places have astonished me profoundly.  I looked forward with pleasure to a study of the influence which a century of contact with civilisation has effected in the barbarous tribes of the seaboard.  The result has been unspeakably disappointing.  Leaving out of consideration the towns of Sierra Leone and Lagos, where the conditions have been abnormal, the tendency has been everywhere in the line of deterioration.  There is absolutely not a single place where the natives are left to their own free will, in which there is the slightest evidence of a desire for better things. The worst vices and diseases of Europe have found a congenial soil, and the taste for spirits has risen out of all proportion to their desire for clothes—the criterion with many of growth in grace.

"The inaptitude of the natives for civilisation is nowhere shown more distinctly than among the Krū-boys, a tribe which every one admits is the most docile, the most manageable and most intelligent on the coast. To a man the Krū-boys have spent years in contact with such ameliorating influences as are to be found in those parts, yet their tastes have risen no higher than a desire for gin, tobacco, and gunpowder. These they get in return for a few months' or a year's labour, to go back home and for a few short days enjoy a fiendish holiday. I visited one of their villages, and such a scene of squalor and misery I have rarely seen. . . . In these villages men, women and children, with scarcely a rag upon their persons, follow you about beseeching you for a little gin, tobacco or gunpowder. Eternally gin, tobacco, and gunpowder! These are the sole wants aroused by a century of trade and of contact with Europeans!"

The ravages of the gin traffic thus forced upon his attention at every new trading centre on the coast, aroused in him a feeling of shame and moral indignation. In his heart he made a vow that, if he was spared to return home, he would make his countrymen's ears tingle with an exposure of the outrage thus perpetrated among the native races in the name of civilisation. And he kept his vow. So scathingly did he expose the hypocrisy which, under the guise of introducing trade and other beneficent influences, was really ruining the natives body and soul through the diabolical traffic in strong drink, that the public began to feel the national honour to be imperilled. Certainly the recent awakening of the public conscience on this subject dates from his outspoken utterances; and, if healthful restrictions have been introduced in various important quarters, it is in no small degree a fact to be placed to the credit of his advocacy.

The voyage turned out to be much more protracted than he had been led to anticipate, and he began to be restless as repeated delays consumed the time which was so precious to him. But his impatience deepened into anxiety when he found that through some misunderstanding he was being carried past the mouth of the Niger. The next landing-place was Old Calabar, and the loss of the week, which must elapse before he could return to Akassa, might mean the frustration of the object of his expedition. He might, of course, have informed the captain of the situation, but his mission was a profound secret; so there was nothing for it but to swallow his annoyance as best he might, and keep up his *rôle* of a traveller visiting the Niger for his own pleasure.

At last, on the 15th of March (three weeks behind the anticipated time), Joseph Thomson and his companion crossed the bar at Akassa. Happily the lengthened voyage had one good effect; it enabled him in some degree to obtain a much needed recruitment of his physical health, and so to fit him for facing more hopefully the hardships and trials which might be in store for him.

Akassa with its sweltering, moisture-laden, debilitating atmosphere and its monotonous stretches of mangrove swamp, the very home and hunting ground of fevers, dysenteries and liver troubles, was not a place to linger in, especially for one who had so recently come from the very threshold of death. Three days sufficed to complete all necessary preparations, and the fourth saw them steaming out of the pestilential delta.

As they glided into the broad undivided stream, flowing majestically between rapidly rising banks, and winding in beautiful reaches between tropical forests of graceful palms, towering silk-cotton trees and other indigenous arboreal growths, he began for the first time to realise what a noble river the Niger is. Gradually, as one proceeds upwards, the river widens out until it becomes almost lake-like in its expanse. Coincidently the scenes and movements of savage life become more noticeable The stream is lively with canoes going and coming, while the banks every here and there are dotted with people bathing or drawing water or standing in animated groups watching the explorer's noisy flotilla of steam launches as they forge past with fussy clamour. Everything carried with it the suggestion of peacefulness, and woke in the traveller reflections as to the change which has stolen over the spirit of the scene in the course of a few years.

"It was along this stretch that the early battles of the Niger trade were fought; for here, as in the case of other places on the coast, the natives strove hard to confine the traders to the deadly coast line, and to keep the control of the interior trade in their own hands. The consequence was that to go up the Niger was to run the gauntlet of a shower of bullets. Now any white man may pass single-handed in a canoe from Akassa to Bussa, and feel himself as safe as any boatman on the Thames."

So they steamed on day by day, amid gradually improving natural conditions. The almost constant breeze blowing down the river pleasantly tempered the torrid heat, and they could enjoy dreamily watching the kaleidoscopic effects of the scenery. Now some native village with its barbarous inhabitants would attract the eye, cosily ensconced in the shadow of the primeval forest; anon there would be the sense of sharp contrast, as in a cleared space the whitewashed walls and corrugated iron roofs of one of the Company's factories would claim attention, glaring against the dark background of tropical trees, and the casks of palm oil would appear, ranged on the bank waiting for shipment. The quieter parts had their

own points of interest.   Here there would be the excitement of taking pot shots at a diving hippopotamus; there
a crocodile, basking by the river's brink like a stranded
log, would be the object of their marksmanship; while
everywhere the waterfowl, in great numbers, would attract
the onlooker.

As they neared Lokoja, the scenery suddenly develope l
into an Alpine character.   The escarpment of the inner
plateau now begins to reveal itself in " a picturesque
series of peaked hills, table-topped mountains, and rugged
crags."   Here, through a narrow adamantine gateway, the
Niger rushes in a swift current, and among the hidden
rocks the navigation is anything but safe.   These obstruc-
tions past, they presently steamed into " the lake-like
expanse formed by the intermingling of the dark waters
of the Binuè with the grey flood of the chief river."
Apart from the richness of the landscape, the sights that
met the eye were lively and suggestive of brightness.
" Canoes cleave the water everywhere, carrying homeward
the weary toilers from the fields, while smoke curling up
in various directions tells of industrious inhabitants, who
are further indicated by picturesque villages on the slopes
and by the gleaming whitewashed houses of the pioneers
of Christianity and commerce."

At Lokoja the travellers had reached the outskirts of
the King of Gandu's sphere of influence, and now the
period of action had arrived.

An obvious difficulty met them at the very threshold.
Malikè, the King of Nupè, although acknowledging the
Sultan of Gandu as his suzerain, was only too well aware
of the importance of keeping the Company from entering
into direct relations with his liege lord, and of retaining
for himself the profits of their trade.   If he should scent
out the nature of the mission that was now afoot, he
would, without doubt, do his best to thwart it.   Means
must therefore be taken to outwit him, so that the
expedition might slip through his country before he

should be aware of their presence or object. In place of delaying, therefore, to engage porters for the land journey, which was to begin at Rabba, it was resolved simply to make up the rank and file of the caravan by labourers from the various factories of the Company that remained yet to be passed, and to have everything ready

NUPÈ HUT AND FAMILY GROUP.

for an immediate march as soon as Rabba should be reached.

If haste had not been of prime importance, the explorer would have found joy in lingering at the various places of call—Egga, Lafiaji, and Shunga—to study the aspects of their wonderful commercial activity, and to learn something by personal observation of the manufacturing genius of the Nupè people in cloth, brasswork, and other articles of use and beauty.  It was impossible not to be impressed with the fact that, from Lokoja onwards, an entirely new state of things prevailed.  In the social life, the activity, and the enterprise of the inhabitants, everything was a complete contrast to what prevailed in the Lower Niger.  Up to this point Paganism reigned, but now Mohammedanism was the ruling influence; and the remainder of the journey bore the travellers through lands where the zeal of Islam glowed at a white heat and with astonishing results.

On the 7th of April the expedition landed at Rabba. To the surprise of the people and the confusion of the local chief, the caravan stepped ashore complete, all ready for the land journey to Sokoto.  King Malikè had been thoroughly hoodwinked, and before the news of their arrival in his country could be conveyed to him, they hoped to be far beyond his reach.

The caravan consisted of a hundred and twenty men chiefly from Elmina, Akra, and Brass.  There were also two educated native interpreters (an Arab and a Haussa), and an agent of the Company, named Seago, who made a very efficient assistant to the leader.  Ten horses rounded off the equipment.  All preparations had been made on the voyage up the river; hence, without an hour's delay, the company were *en route* for their destination.  Joseph Thomson was once more in his element, buoyant with anticipations of stirring and novel experiences; and of these there were certainly abundance in store for him in the course of the next few weeks.

The route chosen was very much like that taken by Herr Flegel a few years previously, when, under British pay, he had been quietly and industriously prospecting with an eye to German interests.

Scarcely had the travellers got out of sight of the gates of Rabba when an ill-omened occurrence beclouded the high spirits of the party.  By a fall from his horse

Hamilton broke his leg, and there was no alternative but to send him back to Rabba in charge of Seago.

At the first camping-place, Mokwa, while they waited for Seago to rejoin them, they had some unpleasant suggestions of the difficulties that might await them through their having no king's messenger. It was only by a good deal of tact and anxious diplomacy that they could persuade the authority of the place to sell them food at all; and clearly, if Malikè could only get orders sent ahead of them, he would almost of a certainty thwart the expedition completely.

That night a terrific tornado threw the camp into confusion, and it was with a considerably modified enthusiasm that the caravan resumed the march. A day of very trying experiences followed, in which the behaviour of the porters roused serious misgivings in the leader's mind. They, unlike the Swahili porters of Zanzibar, were entirely unused to the work of a caravan, and in a few hours were in despair. It was only with the utmost difficulty that they and their loads were got into the next camp, where the miseries of the previous night were repeated in the occurrence of another furious storm. Matters came to a head in the course of the second day's march, for then it became evident that the men had mutinously resolved to compel a retreat. What followed will best be described in the leader's own words:—

"For three weeks Mr. Seago and I had to struggle with our men for the mastery. They adopted every imaginable course to annoy us. They assumed the most insolent attitudes. They would travel only as they pleased, which meant going a hundred yards and resting half an hour. They would have their cowries to buy food, not as we were able to give them, but as they pleased to desire them. They would not have this food or that. It was no use to argue or explain; they would not listen, and our expostulations were received with jeers.  They demanded our biscuits or they would desert. We refused, and off they marched to a man.  Seago, in attempting to turn them, had a loaded gun aimed at him. To get them back we had to give in, distributing half our supply; and we might as well have given all, for the other half they afterwards plundered.  They amused themselves threatening to murder us, and one did actually try to stab me, the others looking quietly on while I struggled with the scoundrel.  We dared not sleep without our revolvers under our heads; and thus for a time we were made their laughing-stocks, and almost mastered. But though we were two pitted against more than a hundred, we were not to be frightened, and we only looked the more dangerous with our loaded revolvers and the more ready with our fists when other arguments were of no avail.  We were biding our time, which soon came. Having once got them well into the country, we began to turn the tables upon them, and presently we were able to resume our self-respect, which had been sadly shaken. The last spark of the mutiny was suppressed by their being starved for three days into doing what they declared they would not do.  During that time we were hourly surrounded by the men, who scowled at us and threatened all sorts of bloody deeds.  But we were determined this time to regain the mastery, or throw up the game; so we smiled at their scowls and threats as we toyed with our loaded revolvers, and in the end the mutiny utterly collapsed."

Thus, fighting for their purpose like men at bay, and putting forth herculean exertions, they reached the town of Kontokora on the 20th of April.  There they felt, at last, that they could breathe freely, so far as fear of King Malikè was concerned.

Worries and excitements like those through which they had passed, coupled with the pressing need of haste, left little opportunity for a close study of the country and

the people. In Nupè they were on ground traversed by
Clapperton fifty years before. But it was only too
visible that a sad change had come over the scene in the
interval. The former teeming and busy population had
been decimated, and mere villages marked the site of
ruined cities, once centres of abounding commercial
activity. The armies of the masterful Fillani had some
years before swept over the land, and misery and desolation had taken the place of prosperity. The presence of
Joseph Thomson's expedition in that land was, it may be
hoped, the harbinger of a return to the golden past, for it
was in a sense the pledge of the extension to Nupè of the
advantage of British protection, under which the natural
energy of the people may soon work wonders of industrial
and commercial revival.

The arrival of the expedition at Kontokora was the
occasion of a demonstration of welcome which was to the
traveller both novel and startling, while it had the added
interest of forming their first introduction to the remarkable Fillani people. Here is his own description of the
event :—

" Rounding the hill near the town, our ears were
suddenly saluted by wild weird music—shrill pipes, more
sonorous trumpet blasts, and tom-toms, the whole conjuring up in my mind a confused medley of memories,
reminiscences of Zanzibar, Egypt, Arabia. I looked
ahead, and was astonished to see an imposing band of
Fillani cavaliers grouped near a tree. . . . As we neared
them, they all at once set up a loud shout, and, each one
lifting up his arm as if to launch a spear, they charged
wildly down upon us, apparently bent upon utterly
annihilating us. In a twinkling we were surrounded by
nearly fifty horsemen, all dashing about as if in the thick
of a terrible hand-to-hand fight. This was their mode of
saluting us. A more magnificently picturesque scene I
have never witnessed. The wild plunging of the horses,

decked off with Oriental extravagance of trappings in leather, cloth, and brass; their riders in indescribable amplitude of dress—trousers, tob, and turban in great folds which would in their arrangement have been both the delight and the despair of the artist.   Seeing some venerable old men sitting under the shade of a tree, we rightly concluded that they were the chief and his men, and so

HAUSSA HUT, NEAR BUSSA.

without stopping we continued towards them as fast as the equine turmoil would allow us.   The pipes shrieked still more shrilly, the great six-foot-long trumpets blared out louder and deeper notes, and the tom-toms were more vigorously beaten.   At last we dismounted and approached the two sitters.   They proved to be the brother of the King of Kontokora and his headman, and they gave us a most ceremonious and hospitable greeting, with no end of compliments. This interesting episode over, we again mounted our horses, and surrounded by our lively escort, who kept up a mimic fight, we proceeded to our quarters. The trumpets, pipes and drums preceded us, accompanying a song of welcome chanted by an attendant. Crowds lined the path, or crowned the walls of the town, and thus, with an overwhelming amount of state and ceremony, we were conducted to the place which had been prepared on hearing that we were coming. Shortly after, heaps of food for man and beast enhanced the hospitable nature of our welcome."

As the direct road to Sokoto was impracticable, the expedition, on leaving Kontokora, struck W.N.W. through the country of Yauri, reaching the Niger again about twenty miles above the rapids of Bussa, famous in a melancholy sense as the scene of Mungo Park's death. Passing Ikung, they traversed the broad low valley, with its inhabitants of Pagan Fillani—an extraordinary contrast to their conquering Mohammedan kinsmen—and following the Niger up to the mouth of the Gindi tributary, they wended their way up that affluent to the town of Jega.

On this part of the journey the explorer was once more carried to the very point of death. The hardships and anxieties which he had had to endure in his partially recovered condition of health had brought back in full force the dire enemy dysentery. It seemed as if the close of his career had come at last. By vigorous measures, however, the alarming and dangerous malady was once more fortunately stayed in its progress, and soon he was again leading on towards his goal, although in a seriously weakened condition.

It was at this time that the murderous assault which has already been referred to was made upon him. Enfeebled as he had been by his terrible illness, he was in no fit state to cope with the furious fellow, and as not one

FILLANI NOBLEMAN AND ATTENDANTS.

of the mutinous porters would lift a finger in defence of their leader, it is only too probable that the struggle would have issued tragically for him, had it not been for the timely assistance of Seago.

At Jega a stay of only one day was made, as they wished to avoid being mulcted by the Sultan of Gandu before they had paid their visit to the still more important sovereign, Umuru of Sokoto.

Their road lay along the great trade route which connects Timbuktu and the Western Sûdan with Bornu and the kingdoms of the Chad region. As they proceeded, it was with a sense of wonderment at the contrast which forced itself upon their notice. As compared with the countries through which they had been hitherto journeying, the Haussa States, with their sights and sounds and throbbing rush of commercial life, burst upon them with all the astonishing effect of a transformation scene. It seemed as if they were no longer in Negroland, but had been spirited away to some Moorish or Algerian scene. The volume and variety of the traffic, too, were such as the traveller had never imagined possible in such a remote quarter of the African continent. "Native produce here intermingled with articles of trade from Tripoli, Morocco, Senegal, Sierra Leone, Lagos and Akassa. Timbuktu and the Western Sûdan sent their quota, as did Bornu in the east, Adamwa and Nupè in the south, Yoruba, Dahomey, and Ashantee in the west—all were represented in this great artery of commerce." The travellers by the way were no less interesting. There were the warlike Mohammedan Fillani "portentously picturesque in their voluminous garments," the vivacious and more simply clothed Haussa, the fierce-looking, spear-armed Tuareg Bedouins from the Sahara, with other types mingling and passing in bewildering variety. The country was densely populated, and the frequent occurrence of large tree-shaded towns and villages standing out like oases in the midst of the landscape, gave sure evidence of the fact.

Inside these towns all was animation and energy. Everywhere there were the tokens of a busy industrial life, differentiating itself into endless forms.

And these aspects of Sûdanese commercial and industrial life were not divorced from other and higher influences. Perhaps the most astonishing of all the unexpected sights in this land of the far interior was the evidence that abounded on every hand of a profound religious zeal pulsating through the entire life of the people. At every turn there was something to remind the visitors from the Western world that, whatever decadence Islam might be exhibiting elsewhere, here at least it was a living force and a universally controlling influence.

On the 21st of May the expedition made entry into the city of Sokoto. This they had expected to be the goal of their journey. They found, however, that Umuru had removed his court to Wurnu, and thither they must follow. During the brief stay in Sokoto one rather exciting incident occurred. The explorer's zeal for photographing led him incautiously to set up his camera in the market-place. Instantly the alarm was raised that some witchcraft was being attempted, and, before he realised what was happening, he found himself in the midst of a wild, excited mob, in whose surging fury not only the camera but his own person seemed likely to come to grief, and from which he extricated himself only with extreme difficulty.

The next day brought them to the outskirts of Wurnu. Their coming having been announced beforehand, a grand demonstration of welcome had been intended for them, after the manner of that which they had had at Kontokora. They themselves, however, unwittingly disarranged the programme, by appearing unexpectedly early at the gates. So they entered quite without ceremony, although not without demonstrations of popular interest—for they were the first Europeans that had been seen there since Barth, thirty years before, visited the city on his way to

Timbuktu.  The reception in other respects however was
right royal, and augured well for the success of their
mission.

No time was lost in the preparation for coming to the
point of broaching the business of the expedition.  A
necessary and very important preliminary was to secure

FILLANI COURTIERS.

the goodwill of the Wazir, the crown lawyer and general
adviser of the Sultan, and the real fountain of influence in
the State of Sokoto.  A visit of etiquette to this shrewd
personage, and the making up and sending of a present of
judicious value, occupied the afternoon on the day of their
arrival.  It was soon apparent that the Wazir had been

favourably impressed, for the intimation came that the Sultan himself would receive them in audience next morning.

As something depended upon an appeal to the eye of the Court, they tried to make as brave a show as possible. In due time they set off for the palace—the leader showing the way dressed in a fancy silk-and-wool shirt, white drill trousers, military helmet with puggaree, and canvas gaiters. Seago, similarly attired, followed with the two interpreters and other attendants—all resplendently got up according to native ideas of magnificence. Dismounting in style at the gate of the palace, and threading their way through a labyrinth of courts, filled with a crowd of retainers truly Oriental in their heterogeneous variety, they at last stood in the presence of his dusky Majesty, who was seated cross-legged on a raised dais in a large softly-lighted hall. They saluted him by simply taking off their helmets and making a bow, the interpreters prostrating themselves in native fashion. After a long preliminary palaver of etiquette between the Sultan and the interpreters, Joseph Thomson made his speech. He explained that he had been sent all the way from England to convey the salutations and compliments of certain English people, to thank the Sultan for the goodwill shown to their traders, and to express their wish to conclude a treaty with him. Such a treaty would be for the mutual advantage of both parties: for while the extension of trade would benefit those whom he represented, it would no less tend to enlarge and consolidate his own influence as a sovereign. He concluded by showing how rapidly some of the river kings, like Malikè of Nupè, had risen into power and wealth by their connection with the English traders.

Umuru was obviously pleased, and expressed his approval by punctuating the speaker's words (as interpreted) with a curious clucking sound of the tongue. He replied in a complimentary fashion, and seemed specially gratified at the idea that the envoy had come all the way from England to do him so much honour.

It was considered more judicious to refer to the details of the proposed treaty at a subsequent stage, and with due ceremony the party retired to prepare the Sultan's present, feeling sure that the grandeur of that present would be a very useful preliminary to the discussion of terms.  It was intended to take the present next day, but meanwhile the Sultan had got his curiosity aroused by reports of what the Wazir had received, and he was too eager to endure the delay.  Accordingly, in response to a message, the evening saw them as visitors again at the palace.  This time they were received with less of formal etiquette, but with notable cordiality, in what appeared to be the royal treasury.  What took place is thus narrated by the envoy himself:—

"The place where we were being too small to exhibit the articles, a large mat was spread in the court in which to lay them.  As this was being done, Umuru tried to put on an appearance of indifference becoming a great sultan and one 'accustomed to that sort of thing;' but now and then, as he got a glimpse of some magnificent object or other, he became fidgety and showed signs of allowing the royal dignity to give way.  Finally he succumbed to the fascinations of the various objects, and proposed to go out.  There, exposed in the yard, lay a collection such as had never greeted the eyes of any Sûdan sultan before.  There were gorgeous silks, satins, and velvets, beautiful embroideries, rugs, silver vessels, revolvers—everything of the most handsome and expensive character.  If the Fillani were a people given to dancing, doubtless His Majesty would have executed a *pas seul*.  As it was, he had to express his delight less demonstratively.  We had special pleasure in showing off a magnificent silk umbrella, of large dimensions, and loaded with gold fringes.  It had been intended by a

French company for a king on the Niger, and, need I say, it was composed of red, white, and blue, with a charming bow of the same colours on the handle; all, no doubt, intended to express in the most insidious manner not only how pleasing to the eye but how refreshing to the body it is to rest under the shade of a tricoloured umbrella. But the irony of fate has willed that once more 'perfidious Albion' will reap where the French wished to sow. On some hot journey Umuru will be gratefully blessing the British nation, unwitting that he is indebted to the ingenuity and the prudential efforts of their great rivals. We had every reason to feel encouraged by the effect of our display. The Sultan was quite overwhelmed with surprise at the unexpected magnificence of the present. We, of course, improved the occasion, and hinted that these were but samples of the thousands of articles which the English made, and which could be got through intercourse with them."

The result of the subsequent negotiations was all that could be desired, and better by far than had been anticipated. In consideration of a yearly subsidy, Umuru agreed to hand over irrevocably to the National African Company all his rights to the banks of the river Binuè and its tributaries to a breadth of thirty miles on either hand; to give them an absolute monopoly of all trading and mineral rights throughout his entire dominions, and to make the Company the sole medium in his intercourse with foreigners.

After a ten days' rest at Wurnu, during which he was treated with the most lavish of royal hospitality, Joseph Thomson passed on to visit the Sultan of Gandu, whose rule extends over the main river from Lokoja to near Timbuktu. From this prince he had an equally favourable reception, and obtained the same rights and privileges with respect to his empire which had been secured in Sokoto. Thus the Company was put in absolute command of the whole middle area of the Niger and the whole of the basin of the Binuè.

It goes without saying that the whole transaction was on both sides an intelligent and business-like affair; for the educated Mohammedans who granted the concessions were as wide-awake in guarding their own interests as the envoy was above all capability of trickery. in dealing with them. The treaties were written out in Arabic and carefully studied by the sultans and their counsellors before being signed and stamped with the royal seals.

These treaties in practical effect meant nothing less than the annexation of a vast and valuable territory to the British Empire. The explorer could now set his face homewards with a justifiable pride in the fact that he had not only opened a free way to the very heart of the Western Sûdan, along which the European visitor would henceforth be received with a hearty welcome in place of suspicion, but had brought within the reach of British enterprise an area of the greatest commercial promise. Doubtless the Germans were profoundly chagrined at being so thoroughly out-generalled; but even they had to admit that the conduct of this embassy was as far beyond reproach as its fruits were beyond recall.

Joseph Thomson's mission having thus been satisfactorily crowned, there was every reason against delaying his return. He had, indeed, not a few significant reminders of the fact that, by the self-spending involved in such a mission in his then state of health, he was seriously mortgaging his vital resources.

By the 7th of July the expedition had returned to Rabba. The most noteworthy fact in his homeward journey thus far was that at the Gindi River he had the great misfortune to be robbed of his diaries and notebooks. The loss was an irreparable and most regrettable one, for with the disappearance of his papers many facts of interest and value had slipped into oblivion.

M

We may fitly close this chapter with a quotation from a letter written at Abutshi to Miss Noake:—

"Here I am, and well down towards the mouth of 'the white man's grave' (the Niger) on my way home to re-organise my shattered internal machinery, before returning again to bask in the smiles of the fair spirit which rules over the heart of Africa.  At the expense of a few pounds and a demoralised stomach, I bring back to the English nation a present of incalculable value—but let me not anticipate these wonderful matters, but leave enshrouded for a while my mission to the great native empires of the Western Sûdan.  Enough that I have not disgraced my previous record, and that, successful beyond the most sanguine expectations, I return to civilised life.

"As I shall be in England as soon as this letter, I need not enter into any history of my movements...'Twere needless to tell how I traversed five hundred miles on horseback, and exactly three months from my leaving England reached the famous city of Sokoto, and there bloomed forth in all the glories of a diplomatist.  'Tis true, I might interest you here were I to tell you how I 'starred it' in great state and won immense applause from the native mob.  If you had seen me on those occasions, you would have had to ask yourself if this was the same person you had seen brandishing the mallet and the chisel in a Scotch quarry, clothed in moleskin.

"Well, we had a jolly and romantic time of it there.  Time was of too much consequence to allow us to stop longer than ten days; but in that space we negotiated certain treaties which may yet be famous.  From Sokoto we hurried off to Gandu.  There we completed our work, and another month brought us back to the Niger, down which we have come to this place in canoes.  In a few days we shall be at Akassa, and then I'm off to England once more—though but for that demoralised stomach I would have stayed somewhat longer."

# CHAPTER VIII.



In the beginning of September, 1885, he was once more at anchor in the haven of home. He sorely needed a period of rest and mother-nursing to rehabilitate his exhausted powers, and under the roof of "the auld house" he was glad to seek recruitment from his weariness. Native air and home ministries, with the joyous revisiting of familiar scenes, could do much for him; but, young though he was in years, he found that the recovery of his physical and nervous tone was to be a slower process than he had anticipated. He had resolutely defied his weakness; he had spent himself unreservedly; and he was now being reminded that Nature must have its reprisals. It was under the only too painful consciousness of such reprisals that he wrote at this time to one of his correspondents :—

"Alas, I find my inner man each year becoming more sensitive to climatic influences. Ah, well! I must console myself with the quotation of a saying which peeped forth in melancholy manner from the last letter I got from you before leaving England—'Whom the gods love die young.'"

For the first six weeks after his return he was really very ill; although, with his habitual tender thought for his mother, he tried resolutely to dissemble his condition and to make light of his painful symptoms.

M 2

Towards the end of October, however, he began to feel that he had " turned the corner," as he said, and that he was making for convalescence.  A short sojourn among friends in England—at Manchester, London, Brighton—greatly accelerated the revival of his strength, and by the time that November had run its course he was back again in Scotland, " quite a new man," as he somewhat sanguinely expressed it, and with his mind full of plans for work.

His first public appearance after the Niger trip was at Edinburgh, in connection with the opening of the second session of the Scottish Geographical Society.  Lieutenant A. W. Greely was the lecturer on the occasion, and the subject, his explorations in Greenland.  The honourable duty of moving the vote of thanks was entrusted to Joseph Thomson as a brother explorer.  Needless to say it was performed with cordiality.  It was, indeed, as he said, a very great delight to him, coming fresh from the tropics, to see and hear one who had made his name famous in the pages of Arctic research, and whose story of discovery had thrilled the heart of Europe and America with an emotion such as had been rarely evoked in the history of scientific progress.  Those who knew the mover of the vote of thanks would recognise a distinctly personal and characteristic note in his expression of admiration at the lecturer's exploits :—

" No one listening to such a story of suffering and daring as that told by Lieutenant Greely would think of asking, what is the use of it all ?  But if such there be, I would simply reply to him in the words of the American poet :—

> ' Whene'er a noble deed is done,
> Our hearts with glad surprise
> To higher levels rise.'

" We may be a nation of shopkeepers, but we have a warm heart to everything which keeps burning brightly the sacred lamp of that chivalry, in which there is as much daring, more self-denial, and a more tender regard for the weak and the oppressed, than was ever practised by the flower of ancient knighthood."

Meantime he had been requested, as an honorary member of the Society, to prepare a paper to be read before its various branches, at Glasgow, Edinburgh, and Dundee. He chose for his subject, " East Central Africa and its Commercial Outlook." He had a threefold reason for reverting to this subject. First, he felt that at least two of the cities concerned were peculiarly interested in commercial questions. Then he saw that there was at the time a mania of speculation in all things African, which was likely in more than one respect to be hurtful to the best interests of Africa, as well as fruitful of disappointment to many at home. Further, his experiences in his recent expedition up the Niger had only tended to crystallise and confirm the views about East Africa which he had already formed and expressed. In the circumstances he felt specially called upon to throw upon the situation so far as in him lay the sobering light of truth.

In his paper he pointed out, as the conclusions from his own wide and varied experience, that, whatever prospects of commerce there might be on the West of the Continent, in the Niger and Sûdan district, with its grand river waterway and comparatively civilised populations of keen traders, or in the Congo region, of which the possibilities had been so eloquently advertised, certainly East Central Africa, as an arena for trading enterprise, presented very few hopeful features indeed. To give *couleur de rose* descriptions of it as capable of yielding a return for European capital or effort would be to wrong the public. The land could only in a very few places be described as fertile, and in these the climate was for the most part pestilential. Then the questions of transport and of labour presented other very grave impediments to the exploitation of even the meagre possibilities of the country. On the whole, East Central Africa had practically very little to offer to those who were seeking for new sources of supply.

But what about this region as a market for European goods, and a sphere for the exercise of civilising influences? Well (his reply was), even here there was little hopeful to be said. The population were barbarous in the extreme and sparse everywhere. They wanted little of all that Europe could offer them, and they needed still less of the company and example and influence of the average European trader, as these in only too many instances tended more to demoralisation than to civilisation. Even to the missionary the field was one of the hardest and most unpromising to cultivate. Among races so degraded and of such low development, even the most devoted pioneer of Christianity must for long find the work depressing and the returns most meagre.

Such was the gist of his views on East Africa as a sphere for the merchant and philanthropist. It was not delightful for him to enunciate these any more than it was cheering to many of his hearers to receive them. But it seemed to him that, in the excited state of the public mind in relation to Africa, it was at once the most kind and the most honourable thing to speak out the facts as he knew them; and if his utterances were in some points just a little more *staccato* than they needed to be, that may be explained by the fact that he knew beforehand he would be attacked by interested parties, and he was therefore consciously speaking somewhat in the spirit of controversy. He would have no man misled through false impressions derived from him.

His paper was read at Glasgow on the 8th of January (1886), at Edinburgh on the 11th, and at Dundee on the 12th. Naturally, his relentless crusade against a popular delusion attracted a good deal of attention. The criticism of the press was friendly, and even where disappointment was expressed at the tale he had to unfold, there was frank appreciation of his courage in setting forth unpopular truths. He was glad, however, to turn his face southwards on a more pleasing mission.

At Annan on the 15th, and at Manchester on the 27th, before the Geographical Society, he lectured on his trip to Sokoto. In recounting the stirring details of his dash into the heart of the Western Sûdan, he felt once more that he had a congenial task in hand; and as in his own modest yet bright and vivid way he told his romantic story, there could be no doubt as to the enthusiasm of the listeners.

The reading of a paper before the Anthropological Institute on the African tribes of the British Empire completed the round of his public engagements at this time, and with the finishing of his four articles for *Good Words* on the Niger journey, he was glad to find himself released for the enjoyment of a spring holiday.

The effects of his recent illnesses and hardships were ever and anon making themselves unpleasantly felt. With all his buoyancy of heart and vigour of will he could not ignore the inward reminders of his need of further rest and treatment. Even his lungs were for a time under suspicion. That suspicion proved to be unfounded; but it was manifestly desirable that he should seek a more genial climate for a month or two. In the middle of February, therefore, he left for the Riviera.

Amid the sunshine and the social brightness of that lovely region. he, of course, found much to interest him and to help him in escaping, for a time at least, from the too insistent consciousness of his physical troubles. To him, with his intense love of nature and poetic sensibility, the varying aspects of the wonderful scenery were an unfailing delight. He loved to watch the mighty mountains with their rugged summits towering up into the blue, and to trace their descent, now by beetling cliff, anon by terraced, vine-covered slopes, till they glided out through orange groves and gardens to meet the opalescent sea. The combination of sternness and softness, of the elemental and the artistic, awoke a responsive symphony of the strong and gentle in his own nature. He was both stirred and soothed.

As was to be expected in his ailing condition, he at times felt somewhat keenly the want of companionship. But this only made him the more anxious to use his opportunities and to see what was happening around him. It was not in his nature to be of a sad countenance when others were frolicking. Despite all the terrible experiences he had passed through, his boyishness of heart was ever ready to assert itself. The season in which he had arrived at the Riviera was just the one to give scope to his love of fun. Writing from Nice in the end of March, he says:—

"I arrived here just in time for the Carnival. Need I say that, as I am not given to dissipating in the usual ways, I determined that for once I should cast off my melancholy visage and have a good all-round time of it. I accordingly threw myself with *abandon* into all the wild revelling going on, and, amid masquerades, battles of flowers, and the wild *mélée* of the *confetti* days, I was not found in the rear. It would be impossible within the limits of a letter to describe that week of unrestrained nonsense, or to tell you how I quite forgot that I had for some time assumed the *rôle* of 'the most miserable man alive,' who had come to conclude at twenty-eight that life was a fraud and a delusion."

But his high spirits were not to be indulged with impunity. Unsuspected, a chastening hand was there to summon him back to soberness. His constitution, rendered sensitive by his experience of African damps and hardships, could not bear the exposure at that treacherous season. On the last day of the amusements he caught a bad chill. For the next fortnight he was confined to his hotel with inflammation in the lung. An attack of rheumatism followed; but, fortunately, it so far yielded to treatment as to allow him in a few days more to resume his tour, though with more need of "setting up" than ever, and with aches enough to keep daily before his mind the lesson of caution.

It may well be supposed that with his ardent nature and his habit of making light of troubles, he did not take kindly to the restraints which he had to impose upon himself. They depressed him by making him feel that he had no longer the physical vitality which used to be such a joy to him. The consciousness of them also took no doubt something from the pleasure which he had anticipated for himself in exploring the treasures of each new place on his route. Perhaps it is this that explains the touch of cynicism, so uncommon in him, with which he hits off, in one of his letters, the impressions of his trip :—

"How can I, in the limits of a letter, tell you how, disgusted with Nice, I kicked the dust off my feet and fled eastward? Pleasanter would it be to linger under the sheltering buttresses of the Alps, lapped by clearest blue-coloured Mediterranean waves, in an atmosphere laden with perfume of violet and orange—everything tempting me to turn lotus-eater and no more return to my island home, with its shrouding fogs and bitter blasts. How pleasant also would it be to 'Cook' you through the marble palaces of Genoa with their artistic treasures—for which you find the appropriate expressions of rapture in the pages of your Baedeker and Murray. It is impossible to describe the sights and scenes of the birth-place of so much of the art of Italy, Florence, with its memories of Savonarola, of Dantè, Michael Angelo, and a host of others. Here you get your Madonnas by the acre, and Holy Families till you find yourself exclaiming,

Hang them! Still you soon come to talk learnedly of the merits of Andrea del Sarto, of Fra Bartolomeo, and others—and isn't it something to be able to cram a few names like these down the throats of less travelled acquaintances? Milan next came under my critical eye, and the Cathedral was so unfortunate as not to meet with my approval. Como, no doubt in compliment to me as a Scotsman, obscured its blue skies, and draped itself in Scotch mists, and kept up a drizzle of rain, so that I had the satisfaction of feeling myself on a Highland loch in Italy. The St. Gothard route was grand, however; and how shall I describe Lucerne? Words fail me. The weather was perfect, the scenery glorious, and the sunsets unequalled in my experience. I left with reluctance, passed Paris in contempt, and here I am in London."

This was in the end of April. In London he was detained some time in connection with the Colonial and Indian Exhibition, which was to be opened in the early summer, and to which he had promised a collection of his photographs and interesting curios, illustrative of the strange lands and peoples he had visited. The arrangement of his exhibit was a matter on which he spent much pains, as he was very particular about securing artistic effect. The time of his stay in London was made lively for him with *fêtes* and functions of various sorts—too lively, in fact. Dinners, garden-parties—including one given by the Princess Louise—and other like entertainments made somewhat severe demands upon his limited strength. As soon, therefore, as the duty in connection with the exhibition was off his hands he was glad to return to Scotland.

There, amid the healthful repose of the country and the cheering brightness of opening summer, he gradually regained much of his former elasticity, and with the revival of his physical tone came back to him a fresh sense of joy in the beauties of his native vale. In the renewal of old associations he could forget the years of toil and suffering and feverish stress, and be a boy again.

"How am I to see you," he writes, at this time, to a former companion, "and have at least some drives and walks about the old place, reviving our souls with the sentiment of other times, now so rare in these *blasé* days of ours, in which it is 'the proper thing' to be people of the world, which means that we are to have no beliefs, no emotions, no ideas, except those which are the fashion of the hour? Nobody, of course, can mix with the world without getting tainted to some extent with its artificial ways; but I always like to keep a warm corner in my heart, in which are treasured up my boyish enthusiasms —some corner where no echo of the world's cynicism and scepticism is allowed to enter. How delightful it would be to ramble with you up the Sandrum wood or in the more gloomy Crichope Linn, and give all these chivalrous notions a good airing before locking the door of that particular corner for another period!"

In the middle of this summer, Nithsdale, like the rest of the country, was in the throes of a general election, and in the wordy conflicts of the rival parties in the locality he could not but take a keen interest. He professed to be no politician, but he had really very decided Liberal sympathies. He could not help taking a side in a quiet way, especially as he felt that the circumstances of the neighbourhood in relation to the land question constituted a pressing case for reform. The Liberal candidate, Mr. Thomas McKie, was one of his own intimate and most highly-valued friends. No one who knew Joseph Thomson, therefore, was surprised when one day he appeared upon the public platform at Thornhill, and vigorously supported Mr. McKie's candidature.

As his vigour increased, it seemed as a matter of course to seek outlet in pedestrian exercise. Soon he was able to extend his walks for pastime to distances which few even of the most enthusiastic would think of attempting. One feat in particular may be mentioned, by which he celebrated his return to the ranks of the convalescent. In the middle of July he walked, one day, all the way to Edinburgh—a distance of seventy miles. On the journey of sixteen hours he made only one stop, namely, at Biggar, for breakfast. He arrived in Edinburgh early in the evening, and after tea sallied forth to the Exhibition, in which he rambled about for another couple of hours. Curiously, the extraordinary effort did him not the slightest harm.

But, indeed, this power of tramping over long distances without fatigue was with him quite a gift, and it had been developed to the full by the kind of life-work which had fallen to him. He had, of course, a love for this sort of exercise, and he had instinctively developed the method which enabled him to accomplish the most with the smallest physical expenditure. His feats in this way turned not so much upon strength as upon art.

In health-giving holiday exercises of this nature, varied with reading and a measure of literary work, the summer months of 1886 passed away. For the most part he remained bright of spirit himself, and an inspirer of brightness in others. Yet now and then a great feeling of restlessness would come upon him. Writing to his intimates in such moments of depression, he would accuse himself of seeing everything in a morbid light.

"It is so different," he would say, "from the old days of enthusiasm, when everything was so fresh and novel, so wonderful, so beautiful. Now there seems nothing worth working for, and still less worth living for."

"Why," he exclaims in one of these moods, "cannot we always remain with the same thoughts and feelings, the same romantic enthusiasms, and bright ideals, and noble aims, which characterised us about twenty? Then we first begin to live. The world seems so fresh, so new, so

very desirable.  How glorious everything looks.  A primrose pathway, fair with delights, appears to lead through
the world.   Alas!  we do not go very far before a hundred
delightful illusions vanish, and a hundred things we
fancied solid realities prove to be the veriest mirages.
Our road is strewn with burst-up hopes and Dead Sea
fruit.  And when we turn our longing eyes back to the
point we started from, it is only to find disappointment;
for we have eaten of the fruit of the tree of knowledge,
and what we enjoyed at the beginning of our journey
would now appear to be 'flat, stale, and unprofitable.'"

These, however, were but passing moods, the after-echo
of much dolorous experience.  Few even of those who
lived nearest to him had any reason to suspect him of
entertaining thoughts of sadness.

In the early autumn the British Association met at
Birmingham, and thither he went, according to promise,
to read a paper.  He took as the title of his address—
"Niger and Central Sûdan Sketches," and obtained a
very appreciative reception.  The *Times*, in a general
article on the work of the Association, specially noticed
his contribution, and described him as having "kept a
crowded and attentive audience enchained for more than
an hour."  In this paper, after recounting the sights,
incidents and impressions of his journey, he set himself
to discuss the commercial prospects of the country in
question, and to give reasons for the faith that was in
him.  His conclusion amounted to this : that " in all the
wide range of tropical Africa there is no more promising
field for commerce than this semi-civilised region which
forms the central area of the Niger basin," and that indeed it is " the only region in Central Africa which
presents any prospects whatever of development in the
immediate future worth speaking about."

A brief sojourn in London, after the meetings of the
Association, was devoid of incident, and in the middle of

September he returned to Gatelawbridge. It was only, however, that he might make preparations for a possible new move in life, thoughts of which he was beginning to entertain. In a letter written on September 20th he says :—

"There seems to be very little chance of any more exploring on the big scale. I would *like* so much to do some more, but Africa is played out in the meantime. In a week, therefore, I am going off to Paris, where I intend to stay till the end of the year, furbishing up my French in preparation for the final plunge into the Consular service."

Not that he had any positive prospect of employment in such service. Not, either, that he had any craving after it. Hardly any post, indeed, could have been less to his personal liking, in many respects, than that of a consulate. For a man of his active, ardent, energetic nature, accustomed, moreover, to form independent judgments and frankly to speak out his mind, the idea of being buried alive in some stagnating African seaport, and subjecting his individuality to the fetters of red-tape, was one quite without attraction. But, on the other hand, his varied experience had given him a unique knowledge of native races, their needs and ways, and his studies and the training of circumstances had so fitted him for usefulness in Africa, that, in default of a more congenial call, he thought he might look forward to this as a practical way of furthering the cause of civilisation.

In his schooldays, French was the only language which he had any liking for. He had only learnt it then, of course, in an elementary fashion, but in the subsequent years he had always casually been enlarging his acquaintance with it. Circumstances, however, had shown him the importance for a man in public life of being able to speak the language in a free and fluent way. To this object, therefore, he would now devote himself, while at

the same time gaining a little more knowledge of some
phases of life which had been hitherto hidden from him.
It was an additional element in his resolve to spend the
winter in Paris that one of his intimates, Mr. T. L.
Gilmour, then private secretary to Lord Rosebery, now
a barrister in the Temple, had laid his plans for a like
sojourn.

During his stay in the gay city he boarded in the house
of Madame de Préville, who occupied a flat in the Faubourg St. Honoré.

He was fortunate, in a sense, in having come into this
particular household, for it gave him an opportunity of
studying a very interesting *stratum* of Parisian society.
Madame de Préville was herself a descendant of the great
Mirabeau, and something of the glamour connected with
that romantic and notable figure lingered about her
family.  As one who, though poor now, had come of
ancient and noble lineage, she moved in a social circle
of precisely the like sort.  In fact the old lady reckoned
as many counts, marquises, etc., among her relations as
she did dollars in her purse—a fact of which she was
duly proud—and thus the young explorer was able to
make the acquaintance of people bearing names famous in
French history, and with whom it would not have been
easy otherwise to mingle.

Then Madame de Préville's house had also its literary
associations.  She was a near relative of the celebrated
authoress who, under the *nom de guerre* of " Gyp," amused
and interested her public with dainty satires on the
various phases of modern fashionable life, and whose
delicate art in the use of words was in itself an attractive study.  The family thus stood at least within the
fringe of literary Paris, and breathed something of the
atmosphere pertaining to the writers and writings of
the day.

The only other member of the household was
Madame's daughter Jeanne, a *Parisienne* of the religious

class, who went devoutly to church every morning, and was ready to dance and sing every evening—a very charming *demoiselle* after her kind, good-natured, bright, and an excellent musician. On the floor above dwelt another lady who professionally taught the language. With her he promptly arranged to become a pupil.

The situation had a dash of novelty in it which appealed to the romantic as well as the humorous side of his nature. At first there was great fun in the attempts of the ladies and their new boarder to make themselves mutually understood. For a time there was much delightful murdering of both French and English. The result was of the best, however, for his purpose; for the de Prévilles began to feel quite a personal interest in his progress, and presently he found himself, much to his amusement, and sometimes a little to his embarrassment, an object of educational attention to no less than three gracious ladies, each of whom was equally bent upon making *le jeune écossais* a proficient in the use of their beautiful tongue.

For the first six weeks or so there was no opportunity for his restlessness asserting itself. He worked systematically at the task he had set for himself, and not in vain; for by the end of one month he could converse intelligibly on ordinary subjects.

It may well be supposed that he lost no opportunity of seeing what was to be seen beneath the surface of Parisian life. Some aspects of that life interested him greatly, particularly the social amenities and amusements of the different classes. But in the main he found little to satisfy him, and much to depress him. The impression which he had already formed was only deepened by fuller knowledge. Paris seemed to him a sad place, with all its gaiety and sparkle—a place to visit, not to dwell in, a place to wonder at and pass on.

Gradually he and his work as an explorer began to be known to a widening circle—for in the same week in which he came to Paris a French edition of 'Through Masai-land' was published, and attracted considerable attention.  Flattering references were being made to his name as an explorer, and one evening he had the somewhat unique enjoyment of sitting unknown, as one of the audience, when a M. Paul Vibert eloquently and appreciatively discoursed the story of his Masai journey.  He could not quite remain hid, but he avoided publicity as much as possible.  Beyond giving an interview to M. Elisée Reclus, who was busily gathering material for his great geographical work, 'Nouvelle Géographie Universelle,' he, for the most part, avoided the recognition of geographers altogether.  He would, meantime, be true to his mission as a student, and content himself with his books, walks, and such social opportunities as he might have without being lionised.  "I am beginning," he writes in November, "to know a lot of very nice people, especially members of the old French aristocracy.  Often asked out.  To-night, for instance, I dine at one place, and afterwards attend a reception at another.  Was at the theatre on Thursday with a marquis and his family."

Regarding this Paris sojourn his companion Gilmour writes interesting reminiscences, which we may here quote :—

"Thomson soon became a great favourite with the small circle in which we moved.  His 'Through Masailand' had been translated into French, and his African adventures were a never-failing subject of interest and wonder to the visitors at Madame de Préville's.  I remember one amusing incident connected with the French edition of the book.  The French publisher, not content with the prosaic illustrations of the English edition— mostly reproductions of photographs—had commissioned an artist of imagination to illustrate the scene where Thomson was tossed by a buffalo.  The result was an exciting picture, with the explorer high in the air.  Some

N

unknown admirer had, at Christmas, sent him a number of photographs of this picture, and soon afterwards a French lady, whose mental attitude towards our country-men was, that nothing was too eccentric for us to attempt, nothing too impossible for us to accomplish, was heard to ask Thomson, in all seriousness, how he had succeeded in posing '*comme ça*'!

"We lived very quietly during those months, doing the various sights, and taking long walks in the sur-rounding country, much to the astonishment of our French friends, who to the last could never understand why we should walk from Versailles, when the railway was available. Thomson's easy gaiety of heart and exuberant spirits were really almost a revelation to the majority of our hostess's visitors. It was, on the other hand, a constant source of astonishment to him to find what extraordinary ideas the average middle-class French man or woman had of the inhabitants of these islands. They pictured us apparently as a morose and sullen race, living in an atmosphere, physical and mental, of de-pressing fog, and Thomson appealed to them as something almost incredible, since his buoyant good spirits ran so absolutely counter to all their preconceived ideas. Madame de Préville was wont to offer the explanation that the Scotch were a very superior race to the English — and we did not say her nay."

The only diversion from his French studies which he allowed to himself, in those early days of his stay in Paris, was in the writing of his article for the *Contem-porary Review*, on "Mohammedanism in Central Africa," which appeared in the December number.

As has already been noticed, he had been immensely impressed, while in the Western Sûdan, by the hold which Islam had taken of the people, and by the vital energy with which it moulded and controlled their entire social life. The way in which it had adapted itself to the negro character in those vast regions, and lifted men up from barbarism, not only to a measure of civilisation but to genuine religious fervour, had struck him with all the force of a revelation. The facts of the case, as they gradually unfolded under his eye, awaked in him new thoughts. As one having the interests of Christianity deeply at heart, he could not help asking how it came that the pure and sublime religion of the Gospel had, among native races, proved itself so powerless and unprogressive in comparison. With the noblest truths to proclaim, and the most devoted and most self-sacrificing lives spent in the dissemination of them, why were Christian missions quite unable to show anything like this in any of the regions he had visited? How was it, for instance, that Islam could quite eliminate the drink traffic and the horrors of slavery from the life of the teeming populations, while elsewhere, in presence of European and professedly Christian influences, these accursed things were rampant and apparently irrepressible? When a Divine religion advanced so meagrely in its visible influence, was it not time that its adherents were looking more critically at their methods of disseminating it, and asking whether they might not learn some practical lessons from their successful rivals? The religion of Jesus Christ *ought* to carry everything before it, and when it was not only not doing so, but barely holding its own, was there not a call for some new departure?

These were questions which pressed upon his own mind, and in his article in the *Contemporary* he simply sought to give voice to them, and to show that they were questions worth asking. The *rôle* of candid friend, however, is not a popular one, at least with the persons advised. It is not surprising, therefore, that the reception of the article was somewhat mixed. He did not expect it to be otherwise. But he was not a little grieved to find himself represented in some quarters as hostile to missions and missionaries. No suggestion could, in fact, have been further from the truth. It was repudiated with sufficient point and effectiveness by himself, in a letter which he subsequently wrote to *The Times* in connection with the controversy on " Islam in Africa," initiated in that newspaper by Canon Taylor.

" No one," he wrote, " is a more sincere admirer of the missionary than I ; no one knows better the noble lives of many and the singleness of purpose with which they pursue the course which they think to be the true one. They seem to me the best and truest heroes which this nineteenth century has produced. Nobody has more reason to speak well of them than I, and to rejoice that they have spread over the waste places of the earth. In the heart of the Dark Continent I have been received as a brother ; I have been relieved when I was destitute ; I have been nursed when I was half dead ; and time after time I have been sent on my weary way rejoicing that there is such a profession of men as Christian missionaries."

He had not a word to say against the men ; but he thought that none who had the christianisation of Africa at heart should be above examining their methods in the light of experience, or taking a useful hint from any quarter. He believed that if they would only condescend to adapt themselves to the mental level of the people, teach nothing but the veriest simplicities of Christian faith and practice, and bring the influence of religion more to bear upon the outward environment of the natives in the way of industrial training, and a relentless crusade against social evils like the traffic in strong drink, etc., " they might not only rival the success of Mohammedanism in the Western Sùdan, but far exceed it."

This, however, is by the way, and we must not digress.

As it drew towards the close of the year 1886, it became

evident that some new influence was coming in to pre-occupy his mind. It was just about this time that anxiety regarding Emin Pasha began to make itself felt, and the very mention of his need of relief was sufficient to stir the explorer's heart to eager interest and to turn all his thoughts once more to Africa.

It is unnecessary to recall the details of one of the most extraordinary chapters in the modern knight-errantry of travel—a chapter which combined, as few others have done, the story of high aims and simple folly, of daring and blundering, of tragedy and fiasco. We shall only mention so much as is necessary to explain Joseph Thomson's relation to the affair.

Emin Pasha, it will be remembered, was the person appointed by General Gordon to be Governor of the Egyptian equatorial provinces. He was a man of quite remarkable accomplishments and capacities—a qualified doctor, a gifted linguist, an acute diplomatist, a cultured scientist; and in the administration of the country put under his charge he had obtained a very striking measure of success. The unhappy events, however, which cul-minated in the death of Gordon at Khartûm, had the effect of quite isolating Emin, and, for at least three years previous to the time of which we are speaking, nothing was heard of him or his mission.

At last news of him reached this country. That news was of a disquieting sort. It was thus summarised at the time: For the past three years this distinguished man had been completely cut off from the civilised world. He had been attacked again and again by the rebels from the north; his soldiers had been reduced to absolute nakedness and to such scanty supplies of food that they had even gnawed their own sandals to still the pangs of hunger.

Suddenly the British public awoke to the fact that a brave man, and a trusted friend of the hero Gordon, was being culpably forgotten, and immediately the question of how to relieve him became the question of the day. The British public tends to extremes, and it was now as eagerly urgent as it had hitherto been apathetic. Day by day the newspapers were full of discussions on the absorbing topic.

It was beyond question that an expedition would require to be organised forthwith; and to lead such an expedition would have been a task perfectly after Joseph Thomson's own liking. His heart leapt up at the very thought of it. Nothing could have more delighted him than to undertake it without personal fee or reward. He felt, too, that he had good grounds to advance why his claims to lead such an expedition should be considered. Rapidity was obviously of supreme importance in any honest attempt to reach the beleaguered man; and for directness and shortness what route could compare with that through Masai-land which he had already traversed and made his own ? The same route had also the very great advantage of healthiness and of a climate that permitted of camels and donkeys being taken with perfect safety, while there were practically no topographical difficulties. By this route a caravan of four hundred porters, accompanied with fifty to seventy camels and donkeys, could be easily started within three months from the coast; in less than other three it could be at the north end of Kavirondo, and probably in one month more Emin could be reached. Such was his mental figuring out of the enterprise as he advocated it in a letter to *The Times* (24th November).

Other routes were proposed, and in the discussion that followed his interest deepened daily in intensity until it became almost a fever of excitement, especially when he saw or suspected that other motives than the simple desire to render speedy succour to Emin were coming into play in influential quarters.

The route which he advocated was so manifestly suited to the object in view, and he himself had given such abundant evidence of his courage and resourcefulness as a leader, that there were many powerful voices raised in favour of his being appointed. His friends, however, did not command the purse-strings, consequently they could only advise.

But their opinion could not be lightly set aside, and the effect was seen in the fact that, even after Mr. Stanley was chosen, the most strenuous efforts were made by the committee to induce him to go as his lieutenant. He was eager to help. But his judgment told him that this proposal would never do. Stanley's methods and his were simply the antipodes of each other, and no good could come of their being joined together in the same enterprise. So he held the committee off until within two days of the starting of the expedition.

How he was feeling at this time and what he did will best be described by quoting one of his letters written at the crisis. He says:—

"Can you imagine me in the sulks, or off my head, or somebody finding it necessary to tell me to 'Keep my hair on'? I am sure you cannot. Am I not the most philosophical of mankind, inclined to take ill-luck and good luck equally airily? However, all that has been burst up during the last few weeks. I have been wild at being out of this Emin Pasha business, and doing the most ridiculous things—sending off the most aggressive letters to *The Times* in the evening, only to telegraph next morning to have them stopped. The extent of my distraction may be gathered from the fact that, finding there was absolutely no chance of another expedition being got up or of my views being adopted, I actually came to the point of volunteering to go with Stanley, in spite of my opinion of him and my disbelief in his plans and route. Happily, however, I was too late. All their arrangements had been made."

He was fortunate, indeed, not to have been taken at his

impulsive offer, and as the lamentable story of horror and loss in connection with the expedition came gradually before the public, he saw only too abundant reason to thank God that he *had* been too late.  He continued, of course, to watch the progress of the expedition from the first with the closest attention.  But so convinced was he that the interests of Emin Pasha were being sacrificed to other considerations, that he had only the most melancholy satisfaction in finding his original contentions justified by the whole course of events.

Although the expedition had been finally, and, as he thought, fatuously, started on the Congo route, he did not give up hope of something being yet done by the route which he himself had advocated.  This hope was strengthened by the receipt, a month or two afterwards, of letters from Emin himself, in which he made it clear that he had no intention of abandoning his province, and that it was by the Masai route he was expecting assistance to come to him.  The appearance of these letters moved Joseph Thomson once more to appeal to the public through *The Times*.  He said :—

"My object in writing, is not to attempt to reopen the question of the routes.  That would be more than absurd with Mr. Stanley already on the way, though it may be interesting to note that Emin Pasha himself has effectually confirmed my contention that the Masai route was the one which should have been selected for his relief.

"The one thing to remark in reading Emin's letters is that he does not want to come away, and that he is only wanting means to enable him to hold on.  He writes, ' I repeat what I then said ; I shall remain there and hold together as long as possible the remnants of the work of the last ten years.'  He describes what he could do, and would attempt to do ' if we could only get a few caravans sent, *viâ* Mombasa, Masai, Masala, Uakolio, and from thence either here or to Kabarega.'    Again and again in his letters he appeals to the 'philanthropic spirit' of England, reminds her of her 'ancient traditions,' and asks if she will allow his province to sink back into the state of barbarism from which he in a manner has raised it. . . . .

"Under these circumstances, why not fulfil Emin's expectations and open up the route through Masai-land? Such a scheme should appeal to all Englishmen who have the interests and honour of their country at heart. Masai-land lies in 'the sphere of British influence'— that is to say, it is practically ours.    Are we to follow a dog-in-the-manger policy, and neither do anything to open that region up nor allow any one else to do so?    From the wreck of nearly twenty years' labour, carried out with admirable foresight, in the interests of Great Britain, Sir John Kirk has been able to secure for us Masai-land.    Are we to be content with the mere fact of possession? . . . .

"In utilising the Masai route the philanthropist will do a noble work in preventing the lapse of Emin's province into barbarism or the hands of Tippoo Tib, the geographer will add richly to the store of facts, the sportsman will find virgin fields for the exercise of his love of adventure, the trader, or it may be the colonist, new countries of some promise, and British influence—now so sadly on the wane in East Africa—revive once more, and become the reality it was before the Germans, with their new-born enterprise, stepped in and occupied the place which, for reasons incomprehensible to the outsider, our Government has caused to be vacated."

This letter elicited no immediate practical response, though probably it had its influence in stimulating the aspiration for the opening up of the Dark Continent which was finding expression after a fashion in the efforts of the Imperial British East Africa Company.

But we are anticipating the order of events—this communication having been penned in London on May 13, 1887, nearly three months after he had left Paris.

In December, 1886, he had been across in London in connection with the Emin relief business, and at New Year time he writes thus to his friend Miss Noake :—

"I need hardly announce to you the fact that the Channel separates us, and that once more I have shaken or brushed the mud of London from my feet, fled from its Hades-like fogs, and put myself under the flag of *la belle France*, to succumb to the witcheries of the fair ones who live and breathe under its protecting folds.

" A hundred times I have had reason to curse the fate which took me across to London. Ah well, there is nothing for it but to drown my disappointment in Parisian dissipation—of the respectable sort, of course— a ramble in the boulevards, a peep in at a theatre or a ball or a concert, a cup of coffee at a café, and other like innocent amusements, including of course pleasant evenings at 178 Faubourg St. Honoré, with Chopin, Liszt, etc., interpreted by Mademoiselle Jeanne with deft fingers.

" It was quite soothing to my wounded pride to find such an effusive welcome on my return—to find, in fact, the fatted calf killed for me. . . . I have hardly yet fallen into my old ways here, but am gradually picking up the broken threads."

To quell his own restlessness, he threw himself with a new zeal into the study of French literature, and as by this time he was pretty much at home with the language, he began to develop a real interest in many of the leading modern writers of fiction and poetry—an interest which only deepened in after years. The writings of Dumas, Zola, De Musset, Daudet, and Guy de Maupassant, were all more or less dipped into, and each had some point of attraction for him. The moral tone of some of these disgusted him, and he could not but feel that the sentiment of others was of the shallowest. But, as illustrations of the art of literature and of the varied use of perfect idiomatic French, the books of all were to him a constant subject of admiration, and the reading of them proved a new and powerful influence in relation to his own literary taste and style.

Thus the weeks pleasantly passed on to February. By that time he felt that he had obtained all that he sought from Paris, and that it would be well for him to be setting about some new employment. One of the closing experiences of his stay was a social function, which he thus describes :—

"Since I last wrote, I have been to another ball—this time a very proper one, and as staid as French people can make an affair of that kind. It was given by Grévy, the President of the Republic, at the Elysée. I never saw such a crowd of utterly insignificant men, and plain or ugly women, in my life. Among some five thousand people I did not see five women that I would care to look at twice, and not one really beautiful or even pretty, while the men looked like a collection of miserable tailors or shoemakers, with a sprinkling of convicts and other poor and weak specimens of humanity. Of course, it could hardly be called a representative gathering of French people, as the aristocratic element was entirely absent, as well as that part of the middle class which aspires to be fashionable. Neither of these will patronise the head of republican France. Everybody of course tried to dance with heroic persistence, and with a certain appearance of enjoying the results of their efforts. To the onlooker, however, it all seemed a failure. The crowd was so great that all they could do was to bob up and down from one foot to another, receiving with sickly smiles the weights of their neighbours on their favourite corns, or else driving from one elbow to another, but in the midst of it all trying as best they might to keep in harmony with the music. I myself, as the philosophic and disinterested outsider, inwardly digested the scene, and made many observations of great wisdom on the French, the queer ways people take to amuse themselves, and how frequently men and women are content with the appearance of pleasure."

In the same letter he says :—

"I am gradually working up my feelings to the point of being able to cast Europe and civilisation to the dogs, and burying myself for ever in the heart of my beloved Africa. I intend to leave Paris in the end of this month for home. After a few weeks I shall return to London to set about my next move in life; but what that will be I know not."

In the beginning of March accordingly he said his *adieux* to his pleasant French friends, and returned to Scotland.

# CHAPTER IX.



## OVER THE ATLAS MOUNTAINS.

THE "next move in life" did not suggest itself so readily as he could have desired. He was now fully restored to something like his normal health, and, with energy to spend, it was simply impossible for one of his ardent temperament to rest content in even temporary idleness. It is not surprising, therefore, to find him writing, shortly after his return, that at home he was "mooning about dissatisfied with himself and with everything around him," and jocularly adding that he thought he would "turn into the quarry to see if a little honest work would not be good for the spleen."

It was at this time that the idea occurred to him of making an incursion into a new realm of literary effort, namely, the writing of fiction. In May he writes from Gatelawbridge :—

"I don't know how long I shall remain here. It may be two weeks or two months. That will largely depend on whether I get started to an African romance which has been fermenting in my brain for the last two months. What do you think of me as a possible novelist, working out something thrilling on the slopes of the mighty Kilimanjaro and the plains and plateaux of Masai-land? In my heart of hearts I don't think anything will come of it. However, it amuses me at present."

Something did come of it. The idea gradually took

more definite shape and transferred itself to paper. Ultimately it claimed public attention in the form of 'Ulu,' by Joseph Thomson and E. Harris Smith.

The evolution of this romance will best be described in the words of his co-worker Miss Smith, now the wife of Dr. Hugh Calder, of Leith—a lady with whom, from her bright student days, he was, all through his own career, on terms of brotherly intimacy, and of whose literary abilities he entertained a high admiration :—

"The idea that we should write an African novel together," says Mrs. Calder, "originated accidentally one day whilst we were discussing some recent work of fiction—'She,' I think it was—which had stirred Joe's indignation by depicting Africa as it is *not*—the theatre of a thousand incidents and adventures appropriate only to a Baron Münchausen or the heroes of the Arabian Nights.

"'I've a great mind to write a novel myself,' he exclaimed, 'that shall be a protest against all this impossible stuff. Yes, I will, if you will help me!' 'But what do I know of Africa?' I objected. 'As much as I do of writing novels,' he replied—a retort that for the moment seemed convincing, however inadequate it might appear on after consideration.

"Carried away by his enthusiasm, before I knew where I was I found myself taking the projected novel as *un fait accompli*, and had lightly promised to 'look after the characters and the dialogue,' whilst he should 'take care of the local colour.'

"The 'local colour' was to be the feature of the book. The Kilimanjaro region having been fixed upon as the theatre of action, it was determined that the scenery, the inhabitants, the customs of the district should be described with the most faithful accuracy, as opportunity occurred. No incidents or adventures were to be introduced save such as might have happened to any one who chanced to be in that neighbourhood ten or twelve years ago. The characters, though not drawn from any actual prototypes, were to consist of just such a group as circumstances might very well have thrown together at a time when East Central Africa had as yet scarcely begun to be penetrated by the first faint rays of European civilisation. In a word, Africa and the Africans were to be depicted as they appear to the explorer, the naturalist, and the ethnologist, attractive or repulsive as it might happen, but in any case unadorned by a halo either of glory or of honour.

"The introduction of Europeans at all may be said to be purely incidental; and whatever may be the opinion of readers, to the authors it was in the development of the personality of Ulu herself that the interest of the story mainly centred.

"The character of the lovable, but untutored, little maid was intended to illustrate some of the best traits of an utterly uncivilised nature, and at the same time to show its limitations. Whatever good qualities Ulu possessed are inherent, and are by no means the result of the christianising and civilising influences to which she was subjected. Externally, the latter exercised a certain modifying effect, but only under circumstances in which they had undivided play. As her conduct on more than one occasion showed, she was ready at any moment to relapse into savagery, and at her best never attained to any higher religion than that of obedient and untiring devotion to those she loved. It is a religion which has claimed its martyrs in Africa, as elsewhere, and of these Ulu was one."

The writing and touching up of this story gave him pleasant though fitful employment, in the absence of the more distinctive work for which he longed and in which he felt he could use his powers to more purpose. In the course of the summer and autumn he varied his literary activities with changes of a holiday character. In July he was in London with his Paris companion Gilmour, in connection with the celebration of the Queen's Jubilee. Afterwards he visited Manchester, and addressed a public meeting on "The demoralisation of native races through intercourse with Europeans."

In this address he did not by any means uphold the stereotyped view of the advantage which the spread of commercial enterprise was supposed to bring to barbarous tribes. He thought it salutary and necessary to remind his hearers that there was a reverse side to the shield—a side which had often forced itself upon his attention as a traveller. There could, he felt, be no question as to the nobleness of the Christian aspirations for the good of the heathen, which found expression in manifold missionary efforts. But what hope was there of these aspirations ever being realised, in face of the high-handed action of various European nations, and very especially in face of our own national traffic with the natives in articles which, if a means of gain to us, are morally ruinous to them? The traffic in strong drink, above all, called for plain speaking. It seemed to him that the diabolical work commenced by the slave trade was being even more effectually carried on and widened by that in ardent spirits. We ourselves were doing our best, or worst, to make the missionary crusade a hopeless one.

"What," he asked, in effect, "is a missionary here and there compared with the thousand agents of commerce, who with untiring and unscrupulous industry dispense wholesale the deadly product so greatly in demand? What is a Bible or a bale of useful goods, for instance, on the West Coast of Africa, in opposition to the myriad cases of gin which compete with them? What chance has a Christian virtue, where the soil is so suitable for European vice—where, for every individual influenced for good by merchant or missionary, there are a thousand caught up in the Styx-like flood of spirit-poison and swept off helplessly to perdition?

"Ought we then to retire altogether and leave Africa and the African alone? No; we must not, and ought not if we could. We have reparation and atonement to make for the evil of the past, by destroying the gin and weapon trade. We brought the monster into being and we ought not to rest until we have checked its desolating career, and slain it outright. Here is a task which we as a Christian people cannot shirk. Conscience calls aloud that we should put ourselves as a nation in sackcloth and ashes, and set about sweeping our commerce free from the iniquities by which it has been hitherto characterised. Then will the way be clear for inaugurating the real work of civilisation, and making the nations feel that Christianity only means good and the uplifting of their life for them."

Such was the drift of his address. The subject was one on which he held very strong and earnest convictions, and he felt that it behoved him to speak with no bated breath, when opportunity offered in such a stronghold of commercial activity. The thoughts, which he here enunciated in a passing way, he afterwards embodied in an article, which was published in *The Contemporary Review* (March, 1890).

As the progress of the novel was suspended in August, owing to the death of Miss Smith's mother, he satisfied his pedestrian instincts, and at the same time revived his memories of schoolboy days in a walking tour through Galloway with his old classmate Robert Armstrong. Armstrong was like himself, though to a more measured extent, "a man of his feet," and the two had a happy outing—an outing none the less happy from the fact that, in the years since their schooldays, much of life's history had been made for each of them and their early ideals had undergone the test of varied experiences. The route followed was from Thornhill to Carsphairn, thence by the Deuch Water to Dalry, and through the beautiful valley of the Ken to Castle Douglas. From this place they worked down to Mainsriddel on the Solway, and thence by Dumfries to Thornhill again.

*A propos* of this tour an interesting glimpse of Joseph Thomson at this stage of his life is presented in reminiscences of a casual meeting with him, which were contributed by a writer to the *Dumfries Herald*:—

"It was in the summer of 1887, and I had gone to Carsphairn. On returning from my daily occupation of fishing in the Deuch Water I was told that two gentlemen had arrived from Thornhill on foot and were now at the hotel. As pedestrianism never was my forte, I looked upon this accomplishment of walking from Thornhill to Carsphairn as a great feat, and was anxious to see the two gentlemen who had performed it. When I entered the dining-room they were resting, and to my surprise one of them was a very intimate friend of my own. The other was Mr. Thomson, and to him I was at once presented. What struck me about him was his quick eye, shrewd but kind, which met my own inquiringly. His slender build made him appear tall. He was lithe of figure and active in his movements. He had not been in Carsphairn before, he said, and was anxious to know about it. Was it far to Loch Doon? Could he go there before dinner? I told him as nearly as I could the distance of Loch Doon, but considered it too far after his already long walk. He thought it would give him an appetite. 'The distance was a trifle,' he said. The trifle was nearly five miles long, single journey, and he had already walked more than twenty miles as the crow flies since his breakfast. Nothing would satisfy but that he would go to Loch Doon. So off the three of us set, Thomson chatting cheerily all the way. . . . I took notice

of his style of walking. His was not the exact measured
tread of the soldier, though it had all its rhythmic beat.
Certainly it was steady and regular, but there was a
departure from the military step in the tremendous fling
forward of one foot as compared with the other. The
body, too, inclined slightly to the one side, caused possibly
by the constant wearing of a side satchel over one shoulder
in his long tropic marches.

"When passing the *débris* thrown from the mines, and
heaped up on the hillsides, Thomson, with the instinct of
the geologist, was immediately attracted to them in the
hope of spoil, but he was much disappointed here, for he
found nothing of particular interest.

"We reached the summit of the hill at last, for Thomson preferred going straight over the top as the shortest
route (a way of his) rather than trending the height and
escaping the climb. Our companion elected to sit here
and wait for our return, for we had still half the journey
to perform. There was nothing of interest in our visit to
the loch. Suffice it here that Thomson had his desire in
reaching it. As we began the ascent on our way back
Mr. Thomson scanned the hill to find him who had
remained behind, for we had determined to go round
rather than over it again, as there was no great difference
in the distance. He soon spied the weary one resting
apparently just where we left him, but he failed to bring
him within my focus; and we walked a few hundred
yards, too, before I could distinguish him. Had he not
risen, I think I never would have seen him. Thomson
saw him even sitting. Even in his upright posture his
outline was no greater than a good-sized mantel vase, we
were so distant from him. How Thomson could have
seen him sitting is a marvel to me. If I remember rightly
he explained his powers of perception and penetration to
me at the time. If he did so, I have forgotten now, and
must put them down to his experience and 'gleg' eyes.
After dining together we visited the churchyard, which

contains some tombs of interest, and thereafter spent the evening together, listening to many an adventure told unostentatiously but interestingly by Thomson."

In September he came to Edinburgh, for convenience in the work of completing his part of 'Ulu,' and to this task he steadfastly devoted his days for the next two months. During this time he occupied rooms with Anderson in York Place. His evenings spent in company with him and like kindred spirits were replete with just the enjoyment he revelled in. To have his hands full of work, and a friend near to open his heart to or to discuss a point with, was all the happiness he wanted. Then was he a joyous spirit indeed, and the " flowers of the soul " (as he was wont to call his more exuberant or fanciful utterances) would spring to the birth. Not that he was by nature one who cared to use much speech, or who watched for opportunities of saying bright or striking things. It needed favouring circumstances to call out his powers. "I have often," writes his poet friend, " heard him confess regret that he had not the knack of expressing himself in small talk or the art of capping stories. But he had far better. Once get him on to his favourite subject or subjects, and his conversation was interesting in the extreme." In such moments his face would indeed light up and he would pour forth fact, fun, or fancy without effort, as his purpose might require it.

By the beginning of November he had finished the novel so far as he was concerned, and he began to look forward with interest to the appearance of the new venture. But as was to be anticipated, his release from literary labour was in one sense by no means a source of pleasure. It only brought him anew face to face with the fact that occupation in the line of his liking and training was in no haste to present itself. The immediate consequence was a fresh contest with himself, and a fit of depression in spirits. He felt it so hard to possess his soul in patience, eager as he was to be up and doing. The reaction after the mental strain of the past two months no doubt tended to aggravate the depression.

On the 28th of November he writes, in his half-laughing, half-serious style :—

"I have had an awful fit of 'the blues,' which curiously had the effect of making everything look *black*. For the time being I loved not the light but sought the darkness. In the midnight hours I might often be seen flitting like Hamlet's ghost round about Arthur's Seat, or at eerie times, when contented people were snoring in bed, I would go off for an eighteen miles' walk, to listen in melancholy desolateness to the weird night sounds, the rustling of dry leaves, the sighing of the trees, etc.

"What crimes have I committed which require thus to be expiated? Is my name of Joe to be confounded with that of Jew, and am I to be henceforth spoken of as a re-appearance in the flesh of the unfortunate wanderer?

"'Ulu' was finished and sent off to the publishers last week. I shall be very much surprised if Miss Smith does not yet make her mark as a novelist. As for myself, I have no intention of doing any more in that line for some considerable time to come. It won't be my blame if I am not off to Africa before the New Year has advanced far."

In a similar vein he writes, two days later, to another correspondent :—

"Here I am about to write a letter to you in a most unfit frame of mind for the pleasing task. One's fancies should be free and light as air, one's soul expansive, and imagination somewhat excited, to write in a manner worthy of the fair reader. But none of these conditions prevail with me. For the last week or two I have been enjoying a most delightful fit of the blues; and, still worse, I have been writing to a religious paper, which has

been deliberately telling some lies about me. . . . Now
my trouble is this : I have not been able to say in set
terms to the editor that he was telling lies.  I have only
'corrected' him.  Conceive then the amount of suppressed
passion there is contained in this 'buzzum' of mine—
making me feel like a volcano, when rather I should
imagine myself some babbling streamlet meandering by
primrose-clad banks or sweet hay-scented fields.  When
I ought to soar into the ideal I feel impelled to wallow in
the real, and wish to call a spade a spade without any
circumlocution.

"I wonder if you expect to get any news from me !  If
so you are mistaken.  I never write anything but nonsense, or croon something in the manner of the melancholy
Jacques.  For instance, it gives me a certain amount of
melancholy comfort to compare myself at present not to a
volcano or a stream, but to a ship which has broken loose
from its moorings, and with but one man on board to
steer—not a soul to set or trim the sails—with the
consequence that sometimes it goes safely in the right
direction, but when contrary or violent winds rise then
the steerer is helpless, and the ship, now in the trough of
the sea, now submerged under a wave, drives helplessly
hither and thither.  Now I frequently ask myself, shall I
ever come to anchor again, ever ship an able-bodied crew
of human virtues and good intentions to assist the steerer,
conscience ?  Every day I am saying to myself, I must
mark out a course and steer towards my goal with
unflinching determination."

A brisk walking tour in the direction of Melrose and
the Scott country supplied the necessary tonic for any
atrabiliar tendency.  Presently he was his old self again,
as vivacious and sparkling as ever.  The perfect corrective
of dolesomeness came to him, however, in another form,
in the opening up of a prospect of further exploration.

On the 28th of January, 1888, he lectured in London

at the Royal Institution, taking for his subject "The Exploration of Masai-land." There was a large and brilliant audience by whom he was exceedingly well received. *A propos* of this he writes :—

"You will see from *The Times* report that I still retain a little touch of fancy and have not quite succumbed to the prosaic influences of the age. I have come to the conclusion that life would not be worth living if I got completely rid of all my little poetical fancies, my illusions and the strain of romance which still hangs about me."

To Mrs. Gray-Hill he writes about the same time :—

"Did you see that I had been lecturing at the Royal Institution here a week ago? It was a great success. Imagine, however, my feelings a couple of days after on seeing a leader in a new evening paper in which it was frankly stated that they had never heard of me or Masailand before, implied that the world was equally ignorant, but ended by soothing my feelings with the flattering advice that I should write a book. Such is fame—and London journalism !

"My most interesting news is that I am going to explore—if possible—the Atlas Mountains. I am going this time entirely on my own account, as I am thoroughly tired and disgusted with life in England. I am rusting rapidly into the heart, and if I do not get thoroughly rubbed up by action I shall commit suicide or do some other startling thing."

Ever since his visit to the Sûdanese kingdoms of Sokoto and Gandu, he had vaguely cherished in his heart a wish to explore Morocco. The marvellous development of Mohammedan activity in those central regions, and the striking illustrations of the civilising influence of Islam which he had there witnessed, had made him anxious to observe at its fountain-head the force whose results were felt so far away.  A people who could make the impress of their religion, arts and industry so visible and real across the dread Sahara—never to speak of the part they had played in European history itself—must, he thought, be a people worth visiting in their native fastnesses.  His desire to see the Moors at home was only intensified by the fact that it could not easily be realised.  Sir Joseph Hooker, one of the very few who have penetrated any distance into the land, had described it as " the most diffi-cult of all countries to explore."  This fact, which had availed to keep it practically a sealed recess, though lying at the very gate of prying European nations, only whetted his craving to be at the heart of the mystery.

It was not the people alone that he was anxious to study.  There was the grand range of the Atlas Moun-tains still offering virgin soil to the explorer who should have the courage or the good fortune to penetrate its glens and passes.  The part of its secret which had been wrested in the plucky journey of Hooker and Ball, and later in those of Lenz and De Foucault, had only em-phasised the fact that the range as a whole was practi-cally unknown, and that whoever should first traverse it thoroughly would make geographical science his debtor.  Might not he have that honour and privilege ?

But for long there appeared not the least likelihood of his aspiration being realised in this quarter.  Any pro-posal which tended that way was in general emphatically discouraged by those whose interest he was fain to arouse.

At last he seems to have come to the conclusion that if the usual sources of help remained closed, he would make a bold shift, and essay the enterprise at his own charge.  This resolution at once cut the knot of difficulty.  There were now quite a number willing to lend a hand in making the proposed expedition a success, and in lighten-ing the monetary responsibility he was assuming.  The Royal Geographical and Royal Societies, and subsequently the British Association, promised subsidies.  The Foreign

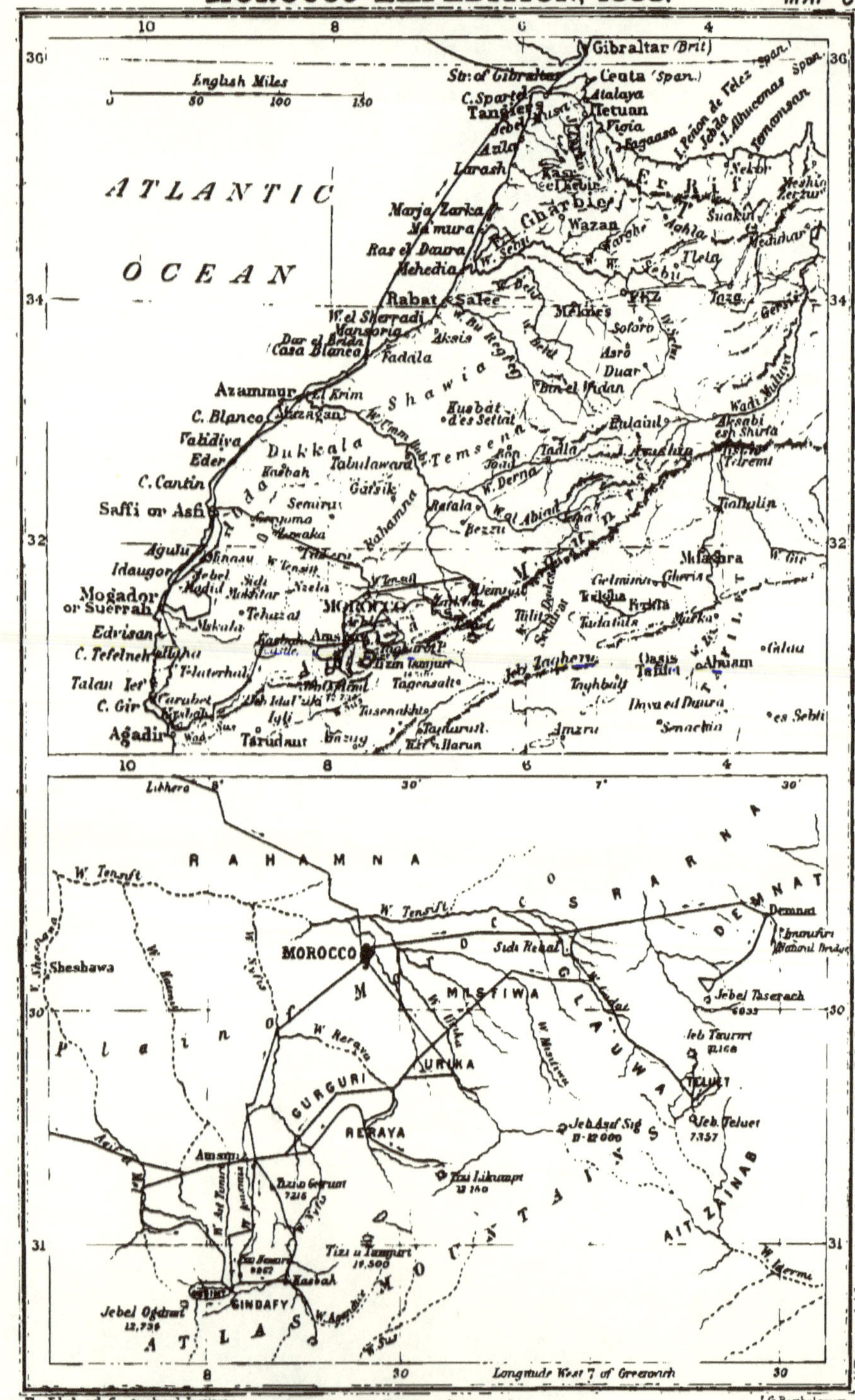
English Miles
0    50    100    150
ATLANTIC
OCEAN
Gibraltar (Brit)
Str. of Gibraltar
Ceuta (Span.)
C. Spartel
Atalaya
Tangiers
Tetuan
Jebel
Figia
Azila
Sagaasa
I. Peñon de Velez (Span)
Jebda
I. Alhucemas
Tomsan (Span)
Larash
Kas el Kebir
Nekor
Heshid
Zertan
Marja Zarka
Gharb
Wazan
Mamura
W. Sebu
Targhe
Johla
Suakin
Ras el Daura
W.
Mechthar
Mehedia
W. Sebu
Tlela
Rabat
Salee
Taza
Gersif
W. el Sherradi
Mansoriga
Meknes
Dar el Beida
Casa Blanca
Akais
Soforo
Asro
Fadala
Bin el Widan
Duar
Azammur
El Krim
Kusbat
d'es Settat
Eulaiui
Aksabi
esh Shirta
C. Blanco
Mazagan
Shawia
W. Umm
Temsenn
Tadla
Tahidiya
Dukkala
Tabulawara
Taurirt
Eder
Kasbah
Gatsik
W. Derna
C. Cantin
Semiru
Rahamna
Rafala
W. el Abiad
Saffi or Asfi
Bezru
Agulu
Shnasu
W. Tensift
Tidzerti
Mlachra
Idaugor
Jebel
Nzela
W. Tensift
Jemut
Gelminn
Giheria
Mogador
or Suerrah
Sidi Mukhtar
MOROCCA
Tililtz
Krita
Murka
Edrisan
Mskala
Tehuzat
Kasbah Amsmiz
Ajrurt
Jeb. Inghero
Oasis
Tafilit
Ahsam
C. Tefelneh
Talybu
Tizin Tamjurt
Taghbult
Talau Ier
Taterhult
Tagensalte
Umm el Daura
C. Gir
Gurubet
Taylurut
Amzru
Senachia
es Sebti
Agadir
Wad
Tarudaut
Enzag
Kis el Harun
Sus
Libhere
RAHAMNA
DSRARNA
DEMNAT
W. Tensift
W. Tensift
Demnat
Sheshawa
MOROCCO
Sidi Rehal
Imnukri
Natural Bridge
Jebel Taserach
Plain
of
MSFIWA
GLAUWA
W. Reraya
Jeb. Taurirt
GURGURI
URIKA
TELUET
RERAYA
Jeb Asif Sig
Jeb. Teluet
Amsmiz
Tizin Tamjurt
Tizi u Tamjurt
ATLAS
MOUNTAINS
AIT ZAINAB
Jebel Ojdant
GINDAFY
W. Agadir
ATLAS
W. Sus
Longitude West 7 of Greenwich
The Edinburgh Geographical Institute
Thomson's Route shown thus ———
J. G. Bartholomew

Office also willingly undertook to bring its great influence to bear in the most important quarter, in the way of obtaining facilities for travel. The result was that, before much of the year 1888 had run, Joseph Thomson found himself on the verge of another great venture, and busy with the manifold worry and excitement of preparation.

"Once more," he writes in the beginning of March, "it is my fate to move on, driven by a resistless demon within me—a species of Frankenstein which I have called into existence and cannot now get rid of. I was only two days at home, and in that time had to gather all my traps together, see a lot of people, write as many long letters (business), and last, not least, write my last will and testament. Now that I am back in London, as much lies before me. Inquiries have to be made, people interviewed, camp equipment, etc., got together, a lengthy correspondence on Moroccan matters kept up, and finally, the proofs of 'Ulu' corrected. It will be out in the beginning of Easter, so, you see, I won't be here to witness the joy of an impatient reading public on having this wonderful work put into their hands. I have been nearly run off my feet, and the number of farewell dinners that have been given me has been sufficient to complete my demoralisation, though it has been pleasant to find I was so much thought of."

On the 9th of March he left England for Tangiers. For the first time in an expedition of exploration, he took with him a European companion, in the person of Lieutenant Harold Crichton-Browne, who was anxious for once to get off the beaten tracks of travel under the auspices of an experienced pioneer, and who gladly undertook to share the expense.

On the evening of the 17th he arrived at Tangiers from Gibraltar. He felt that he had suddenly been transported

from a scene suggestive of everything European to one
as thoroughly contrasted as though separated by a few
thousand miles. In Gibraltar there was everything to
remind him of British rule and British ways. A few
hours of troublous tossing on the uneasy waves of the
blue strait, and, lo, he is in the midst of the Orient!
This is how he describes, in a letter to Gilmour, his
approach to the scene of his new quest, :—

"The sun was nearing the horizon as we steamed into a
small bay. It was as if a pillar of fire hung over Tangiers
to hide it from our infidel sight; for so dazzling was it
that nothing could be seen, strain as we might. Finally
we glided into the shadow of the low hill, and then, as
in a beautiful transformation scene, the town was revealed
to our longing eyes. While I looked and admired, before
I was aware the anchor was down, we were surrounded
by numerous boats propelled by Moor and 'nigger.' A
few more minutes, and we were on the beach beset by a
gesticulating crowd anxious to relieve us of our belongings.
Then I felt at home. With that expressive and awe-
inspiring wealth of language which never fails a Britisher,
I drove the picturesquely ragged crew to the four winds
of heaven. Our luggage was peered at by grave and
reverend Moors who sat cross-legged on the ground.
Then we 'processed' through some narrow streets, our
feet falling softly on the wealth of offal which carpets the
ground. We stealthily peered into glorious gazelle-like
eyes, which peeped from behind veils held coquettishly in
front of the face. As in a dream we passed on, feeling
everything delightfully Oriental. A few more steps, and
in a twinkling we were once more back in Europe—back
at least in a European hotel."

The sense of novelty naturally suggested sight-seeing.
As soon as dinner was finished, therefore, he and his
companion were off, *à la* Haroun Alraschid, with a native
guide bearing a lantern, to explore the quaint, sewage-

scented streets, and to get at least a glimpse of the night life of the place. After so long a period of enforced inaction the prospect of movement and adventure had an electric effect upon his spirits. He felt for the moment like a schoolboy let loose, and he had all the schoolboy's unaffected heartiness in the enjoyment of his liberation.

At Tangiers he had a longer time to become acquainted with Moorish city life than he either bargained for or desired. For, despite the friendly exertions of the energetic British Minister, Sir Kirby Green, it was full three weeks before the necessary written permit from the Sultan could be obtained. The time of enforced delay was, of course, not idly spent. In addition to further exploration in and around Tangiers, he made a trip on horseback to Tetuan, fifty miles off. There he stayed two days in a Jew's house, eating unleavened bread—it being Passover time. In his return he had to make his way in a terrific storm of rain, now fording swollen streams, now floundering over quagmires and ditches, anon climbing rocky hills, to reach Tangiers only after twelve hours in the saddle. The result was a severe

AN ITINERANT MUSICIAN.

cold.    But then he was feeling once more in his element, and he was happy accordingly.

At last the Sultan's letter came.    It was a disappointment.    There was the anticipated diplomatic expression of friendliness towards the enterprising *protégés* of the British Government.    But the document, duly read between the lines, simply meant that the Sultan's faithful *kaids* were to take good care to prevent the travellers from visiting the very places they wanted to visit; and the soldier, who was sent under the name of an escort and protector, was merely a messenger of his Shereefian Highness to secure that the royal letter should not be misread.    There was nothing for it but to accept the permit for use as far as it would prove helpful, and to quietly register a secret resolve that by the help of Providence and his own wits he would considerably widen the programme.

On the 5th of April he sailed for Casablanca *en route* for Mogador, which was to be his real starting-point.    In the overland journey to the latter place the travellers were accompanied only by the soldier guide and one Moorish attendant.    Their way carried them, at first, through a long stretch of undulating country, treeless, monotonous, and almost devoid of inhabitants.    The one striking feature in the otherwise uninteresting expanse was the floral display; but that in its brilliance and variety was nothing less than marvellous.

A fifty miles' ride brought the party to Azamor, where they camped in the open for the night, and enjoyed such fragmentary snatches of sleep as were possible between the howling onsets of a mob of ravenous and aggressive dogs.    The next hundred miles lay through a like featureless tract—the soil rich in possibilities, but practically unexploited, owing to the blighting misgovernment under which all Morocco languishes.

After resting a day at Saffi, where they obtained not only warm hospitality, but valuable advice from Mr.

Huriot, the British vice-consul, they pushed on over the remaining distance to Mogador. Crossing the River Tensift, which was in flood, they entered a country more broken and picturesque, but for the most part utterly barren, owing to the adamantine calcareous crust under which the soil is sealed up. The only relieving tone of green was in the forest tracts of the oil-bearing Argan-tree, which seems to be able to flourish under the most disadvantageous conditions.

On the afternoon of the 17th, they came within sight of Mogador. At the same time there leapt into view the object towards which the thoughts of the leader had been hopefully turning. For there, on the far horizon, gleamed crystal-like, and sharply projected against the sky, one of the snowy peaks of the Atlas. It was a gage of promise, to appeal to his imagination and to lure him on.

At Mogador he began to realise at close quarters some of the difficulties which were to beset his enterprise. Here it was that he must engage the necessary servants and purchase horses, mules, etc.; but it was only after a most exasperating experience of delay and shuffling that he found himself ready for the road. Such qualities as haste or business promptitude were quite unknown in the depressing, enervating atmosphere of the place—an atmosphere in which the appropriate thing was to do nothing. Despite the valuable assistance of the British consul, it was almost impossible to get any matter brought finally to the point of settlement. At last, however, he did get to the end of the negotiations, with the result that he had a caravan secured of five men, five mules, a camel, a donkey, and a horse.

On the 5th of May he gladly left Mogador behind. He did not, however, take, as might have been anticipated, the direct road to the interior. His experienced eye had already seen enough to arouse in him a suspicion of trouble ahead with his men. He thought it well, therefore, to make a little preliminary test of the stuff he had got in hand, and to measure himself as leader against the possible elements of obstruction.  For this purpose he chose a circuitous route back to Saffi.

The revelations of that short journey were far from encouraging.  What could he hope to accomplish of a task, hard and hazardous at the best, with such a party of lazy, insolent, gluttonous liars about him?  The matter could not be mended at this stage, but clearly, unless some changes were made, there would be more than scope for all his tact, and resource, and patience.  How he viewed the situation, and what was the ultimate issue of it, are thus described by himself in a letter to Gilmour written two months later from Morocco:—

"I had not been two days on the march before I discovered that the greatest danger to our eventual success would be, not the mountaineers, nor even the opposition of the government officials, but the half dozen men who formed the *personnel* of our small party.  On first learning what they were, and what they were capable of, a horrible feeling of despair almost overwhelmed me.  How, I asked myself, could I ever become master of half-a-dozen men all bound together by common ties and interests, when my sole means of communicating with them was one of themselves?  And yet master of them, ay, and complete master of them, it was absolutely necessary to become before I could hope to penetrate a mile into the mountains.

"The struggle that ensued, and which lasted for a month, I shall not trouble you with.  It has been one of the most disgusting and painful experiences in my rather varied life.  Suffice it to say that they started from Mogador in the belief that they had got a new European greenhorn to plunder and make do as they pleased, and they found a Tartar.  I did succeed in breaking their power, and in the end they were all crushed and brought completely under my thumb, though up to date they never ceased trying to thwart, by every means in their power, all my attempts to go to the mountains—happily with but small result. And now I have the happiness of sitting here in Morocco to look back upon success as great as I dreamed of in England, and to reflect that so far I have carried out the exact programme which I sketched for myself before leaving."

But to revert to the course of events. On the journey from Mogador there was an interesting interlude in the ascent of the Iron Mountains (Jebel Hadid), and the examination of the ancient iron workings there. These were in the form of an enormous pit on the summit of the ridge, from which ran an underground passage into the very heart of the mountain. Two days were spent in the exploration of the pit and passage, and in the course of that exploration the leader's geological zeal led him into some experiences which were more venturous than comfortable. A spice of excitement was further added to this same journey by the crossing of the flooded River Tensift, which was only accomplished after three hours of perilous work.

Saffi was at last safely reached. There some slight relief in the situation, as between leaders and followers, was obtained. Two of the most objectionable of the Mogador men were dismissed, and two new men obtained by Mr. Hunot were substituted. There was thus secured at least a division, and so far a weakening, of the obstructive forces. But the outlook was not promising. The explorer could only cheer himself with the thought that he had never yet failed to get command of his men, and that if his record was to be broken down now, it would only be after a few startling things had happened.

Thus, then, in a spirit of mingled misgiving and resolution did he set his face towards the goal of his desires. That goal was for the present a secret of his own inner consciousness; for well he knew that if it were once understood that the Atlas was his objective, he might reckon on failure as a foregone conclusion.

It was on the 19th of May that he left Saffi for the interior. In the next few days' marching there was little of interest or beauty to note in the landscape. For the most part the country was treeless, and though the soil was marvellously rich in character, it was hardly cultivated at all. The frequent ruinous droughts partly account for this; but without doubt the main cause is the unspeakable system of misgovernment under which the wretched inhabitants live. Ground down and plundered mercilessly by the greedy *kaids*, the poor people have no heart for enterprise or industry. They are sullenly content to live in the uttermost squalor, leaving the land with all its vast possibilities to run to waste.

In his resolve to evade the Sultan's restrictions, and get beyond the limits marked out for him, Joseph Thomson thought it best to pass by the city of Morocco in the meantime, and push straight on to Demnat. He might propose, but his men, suspecting his intention, resolved to dispose. Pretending to take the route he wished, they simply led him by a difficult and circuitous path right into the place he wished to avoid. It was an unpleasant taste of their quality. But, though it irritated him exceedingly, it did not daunt him in his purpose to be upsides with the rascals.

Accepting his preliminary defeat in silence he entered the city, presented the Sultan's letter, and was received with lavish professions of good will and hospitality. A night's rest revived his hopefulness, and enabled him to form fresh plans and resolutions. He was more determined than ever that he would see the Atlas at close quarters before he should set his face homeward.

It certainly wanted all the sanguineness of his temperament, however, to keep his hope from failing. The difficulties were sufficient to disconcert any ordinary man,

and they seemed to grow at every step.  How to keep his
men absolutely in the dark with regard to his intentions,
and yet obtain sufficient information as to the country
and the roads into the mountains, so as to render him
independent of their guidance, was a problem not to be
easily solved.

But happily, just when the solution seemed well nigh

JEWS OF THE ATLAS.

a thing to despair of, light began to dawn.  His own
interpreter was utterly to be distrusted, but fortunately
he fell in with a Gibraltarian named Bonich, who in the
most kindly way offered his services as interpreter during
his stay in the city.  By this friend's timeous aid,
knowledge of the most valuable and practical sort was
acquired; and in the prospect of getting the direction of
things into his own hand, the explorer's spirits rapidly rose.

P

Still more relief and good fortune came to him in the arrival of a mountain Jew from Saffi, accredited from Mr. Hunot there, and warranted not only brave, faithful, and intelligent, but quite an expert in his acquaintance with the mountains and their inhabitants. This was truly a godsend. To know that he had at least one reliable man in his company was to feel that his mission was not altogether a forlorn hope.

Four days were spent at this time in Morocco. Pre-occupied as he was with matters pertaining to his further journey, he could only make a hasty survey of the city and its life. But that was sufficient to dispel some illusions. He describes his first impressions thus :—

"As we passed beneath the battlemented gateway which gives entrance to the city we were full of bright hopes and eager expectations. For were we not entering a city with a history—a city which had been the theatre of wars and sieges and the residence of sultans? Its very name threw a glamour over its yet unknown features, and connected it with all the past glories of the empire.

"How different and disappointing was the realisation! As we wandered through street after street, and lane after lane, enclosed by red clay-built walls, we saw much indeed of the 'havoc' but little of the 'splendour' of the East. Morocco was a city grown slattern, very much out at the elbows, and utterly careless of its personal appearance.

"It seemed incredible that the people who, at the very dawn of their national life, reared such works as the Alhambra, the aqueducts, bridges, and mosques, which to this day remain the chief wonder of southern Spain, are the same as those who are content in the present day to live in shapeless, almost unornamented, clay-built barracks, with no higher thoughts than the unlimited indulgence of their sensual appetites.

"Throughout Morocco there is nothing more disappointing

FOUNTAIN IN MOROCCO.

to the traveller than the signs of the decadence of the distinctive arts which in past times made the Moors famous. One naturally expects to find all sorts of beautiful and quaint objects, to see picturesque and enduring buildings, and get glimpses of the most delightfully fanciful interiors. That some such things existed in early days is, every now and then, made apparent as we wander through the town. But to know that an object is beautiful, that it shows careful and loving workmanship, and reflects the graceful fancy we associate with things Moorish, is also to know that it is old. In everything else we see there is evidenced a frightful degeneracy in genuine workmanship and artistic taste."

This was but another obvious result (added to the many he had already observed in his progress through the land) of the frightful misgovernment. How could beauty continue to live in a city, or prosperity in a country where security of property and common justice were quite unknown?

Meantime, however, he had no mind to linger for the study of the city. He hoped his opportunity would come afterwards; and it did. His thoughts were on that mountain range thirty miles away, which, as it towered up in heaven-kissing magnificence, daily appealed to his wondering gaze. "Before us," he says, "loomed the majestic front of the Atlas. Our eyes roamed from its dark bush and forest-clad base over its lower ranges to the snowy masses which broke through a zone of grey cloud and, above it, gleamed in dazzling whiteness against the deep blue sky. Seen from our distant coign of vantage, the Atlas had an air of dominating and impressive grandeur." To look upon that wondrous sight, and to think of all the mystery that brooded over its peaks and glens and gorges, was to have his curiosity whetted to intense eagerness,

But prompt action was necessary if he was to avoid defeat, for every hour spent in the city increased the risk of obstacles being thrown in his way. His fear in entering the city was that there, under the pretence of seconding the Sultan's professed anxiety for his safety, more soldiers might be attached to his party to watch and checkmate his movements. To prevent this he suddenly, to the surprise and chagrin of his men, took French leave of the place on the 27th. Pushing on rapidly past Sidi Rehal, at the base of the mountains, he rested not until he reached Demnat, which place he proposed to make his headquarters in his preliminary essays at mountaineering, working gradually westward along the range. He had now obtained information as to the various routes, and could act without consulting his men, as one having authority, who knew where he was going and what he meant to do.

At Demnat he was, for the first time in his trip, on unexplored ground. The town itself he found to be delightfully situated in the centre of a valley lovely beyond description. Enthroned on a projecting spur of the Atlas, and cooled by pleasant breezes from the mountains, the town overlooks a landscape possessed of almost every conceivable charm. Here, then, he plunged into the real work which he had come to do. For that work the way was unexpectedly smoothed at the outset by a cheering piece of good fortune. This was the discovery of a Jew of Demnat, David Assor by name, who had once lived in London, and who spoke exceedingly good English. As he was willing to accept the post of interpreter, he was at once gladly engaged, and his services proved simply invaluable. For the first time the explorer had the joy of feeling independent of his treacherous followers.

The story of the labours and perils which Joseph Thomson encountered in the course of the subsequent weeks can only be briefly outlined here. The natural difficulties to be faced were enormous, and tried to the full his hardihood and physical strength,  But these had to be overcome in defiance of dogged official obstruction, and despite the never-failing knavery of his men, the fanaticism of the inhabitants, and the risk of death itself which hovered about him everywhere. It was a hard-earned pleasure that his triumph brought; but he *had* his triumphs, and they were to him a sufficient recompense. Before he closed his exploration the central crest of the great range had been reached at seven independent points, the heights attained exceeding those of any previous travellers by as much as two thousand feet; several new glens had been examined, six passes crossed, and the general configuration of the Western Atlas finally fixed.

From Demnat he made two interesting excursions across the secondary heights of the great range. In the first of these he discovered at Iminifiri a very extraordinary phenomenon—an arch of rock springing at a height of over one hundred feet from one side of a mountain gorge to the other, and serving the purpose not only of a bridge but an aqueduct. In the second, despite the resistance of his soldier guide, he scaled a peak six thousand feet high, from which he commanded a view which he felt to be nothing less than enthralling in its impressiveness.

His first grand *coup* was the crossing of the main axis to Telnet. Coming westward for this purpose to Sidi Rehal, he managed by a clever ruse to throw his men off their guard and to enlist the services of the local sheik by telling him that he was the bearer of a letter from the Sultan to his chief the Kaid of Glauwa.

Striking the glen of the Wad Gadat and toiling up a path of the most rugged and dangerous description—now winding along the verge of a dizzy precipice, now passing through some deep ravine or awesome gorge—he reached, at the close of the first day, the very heart of the Atlas

Range, and there he camped in a scene of unspeakable desolation. Resuming next day the trying task, he crossed the pass at a height of over eight thousand feet, with the mountains towering up two thousand feet higher on either side.

At Teluet the party were most hospitably entertained for ten days by the Kaid of Glauwa. But they were soon made to feel that they were under the strictest supervision. It was only with the greatest difficulty that excursions could be made. One morning, when Thomson slipped out with only one attendant, he was nearly shot by armed mountaineers. The ascent of Jebel Taurirt, 11,168 feet high, was the principal achievement of his stay here.

Finding to his great chagrin that the exploration of the southern aspect of the chain from this point was rendered impossible by the revolt of the tribes and by the stern resistance of the Kaid, he resolved to return by the same pass to the north side. In one or two forced marches he reached Amsmiz, from which he proposed to make a new attempt on the mountain fastnesses. Here again fortune favoured him. The Governor was away, and the same tactics were used with his lieutenant which had been so successful at Sidi Rehal, the happy result being that a guide was supplied without question to lead him to the Kaid of Gindafy on the other side.

It was at the outset of this trip that he had one of the most extraordinary sights of snake-charming ever recorded. Meeting a follower of Sidi Aissa (one of the most revered saints of Morocco) he invited him to give his performance. Moslem scorn was great, but Christian silver had its power too. The fanatic cursed the tempter, but could not resist the lure. Taking a snake from his basket which he carried he began his incantations. With glaring eye he slowly fascinated the reptile, his own excitement gradually rising. Suddenly the spectators were horrified to see him bite off the snake's head and chew it as a sweet morsel. Presently their disgust was succeeded by alarm, as he rolled on the ground in agonised convulsions which seemed to bring him to the point of death. But the alarm was changed to astonishment when, an hour after, the charmer sat up and began lifting pieces of burning charcoal between his fingers from the fire, blowing them to a white heat and popping them into his mouth to chew and swallow them at his leisure. He repeated this several times as if he quite enjoyed it, and as if it were the most

ABOVE THE CLOUDS, ATLAS MOUNTAINS.

natural thing in the world to eat his dinner raw and then send after it the fire that was to cook it.

Following the Wad Amsmiz to its source, they once more began the arduous ascent of the main axis. It was no holiday work this scaling of the terrible mountain path, for it was the most dangerous yet attempted. But despite many anxieties and a few thrillingly narrow escapes, the pass of Nemiri was at last safely surmounted at a height of about ten thousand feet. A descent of five thousand feet brought the toil-worn party to the Kasbah or Castle of Gindafy.

At Gindafy he was by no means so hospitably treated as at Glauwa. In the days which he spent there he was only able to make one trip, namely, to the cañon of the Wad Agandice. This gorge he found to be of a remarkably imposing character—the crystalline limestones and sandstones rising with savage ruggedness on either side in a series of beetling cliffs, and leading up to jagged peaks and table-topped rocks four thousand feet overhead.

At Gindafy his companion was unfortunate enough to be badly bitten by a scorpion, and had to leave the place in an invalided condition. A return to Amsmiz was made by the pass, Tizi-n-Gerint, 7215 feet high.

From Amsmiz, where Crichton-Browne had to be left to recruit, another dash was made upon the central range through the glen Asif-el-Mel. The objective in this case was Jebel Ogdimt. The climax both of peril and physical exertion was reached in this attempt. It was made in defiance of the Kaid, and in spite of the protests of the soldier guide and the alarmed machinations of his attendants. Finally, the ascent developed into a race for life, in which it was no small marvel that he escaped unhurt amid the bullets of the pursuing natives. Gradually dropping his assailants, however, scaling difficulty after difficulty, and passing through the zone of clouds itself, so that he could look athwart their upper surface as upon a vast white sea in which the mountain peaks shot up as islands, he at last stood upon the sky-piercing summit exhausted but triumphant. When he recovered sufficiently to take his observations, he found that he had attained a height of no less than 12,734 feet, and had outdone all previous records by at least 1500 feet.

This peak, however, was not the highest to be climbed, and he was eager to outdo his own feat. But meantime, his mountaineering was broken in upon by his finding it necessary to visit the city of Morocco.

This interlude, which he intended to be brief, extended from one cause and another to six weeks. The time did not hang heavily on his hands. He used his opportunities to the full for a study of Moorish social and political life, and for obtaining a closer acquaintance with the city and its ways. It need not be said that he refused to content himself with the sights open to the ordinary visitor. The spice of danger involved in visiting various out-of-the-way places was an attraction rather than a deterrent, and not a few spots were boldly ventured into which were supposed to be absolutely sacred to the tread of the faithful. Of

A MOORISH AUDIENCE.

course, such adventures had necessarily to be made in Moorish dress. Without such a disguise, his sight seeing, so far as the inner life of the people was concerned, would have been limited in the extreme.

In this way he made acquaintance with the interiors of some of the mosques. Thus also he visited the *hammum*, or bath, from whose holy precincts such as he were strictly debarred. There, in a loathsome cellar heated up to 150°, and through which ran an open sewer emitting the vilest of vile smells, he was baked and kneaded in the most vigorous Turkish fashion, and thereafter solaced with the sight of a set of dancing girls going through their Terpsichorean entertainment—a set of vertical rhythmical movements very much like stamping on a hot plate, and decidedly more vigorous than graceful. He even managed, by dint of diplomacy, to find a way of visiting a harem, and of seeing for himself the interior arrangements of one of the households of the faithful—the proprietor himself being, despite all social rules, the obliging introducer of the "Christian dog" to take note of his domestic amenities.

He did not, however, leave the city without a characteristic illustration of the measure it prefers to mete out to the hated Nazarene. Both he and his companions, in fact, came perilously near being done to death.

It was on the occasion of the Aïd-el-Kebir or Great Feast, which marks the close of the ceremonies connected with the pilgrimage to Mecca—a time when the faithful hold high holiday and when their zeal is at fever heat. After witnessing the remarkable ceremonies in connection with the religious celebration of the day, they were setting forth to the Powder Play which crowns the day's proceedings, when it became unpleasantly manifest that they were the subject of hostile attention, and that it wanted but a spark to kindle a blaze of fury about them. That spark was supplied by the impulsive act of their hot-blooded young interpreter, in rashly resenting with a blow insulting words levelled at him. Instantly the passion and fanaticism of the mob overleapt all restraint. Murder was in every eye, and the little party had to fight for dear life. It seemed as if they must be hopelessly over-whelmed. But, letting out the huge lash of his hunting crop and throwing all his force into one blow, he swung it round furiously in the faces of the assailants. For a moment they fell back with howls of pain and rage. Now, however, he was the centre of attention, and the cry was, "Stone the Christian dog!" From every quarter the missiles came hurtling. In a minute he was black and blue with the stunning blows, though happily his skull remained untouched. It seemed as if any moment might end matters with him; and so doubtless it would, had not the other two bravely set themselves to create a diversion in his favour, and given him a chance of slipping into a café. Before the crowd could break in the door the sharp clatter of hoofs told that a company of cavalry had been sent to the rescue. They had come not a moment too soon. If they had delayed only a little longer, Joseph Thomson's Morocco visit would have ended in a tragedy.

Resuming his mountaineering programme after this interval of varied interest and excitement, and going back to a more easterly point than Jebel Ogdimt in the selection of his new object of attack, he began with an attempt to penetrate the glen Urika, his aim being to scale the prominent peak of Jebel Asif Ig. In this he was completely foiled by a large party of mountaineers. As it would have been madness to attempt, even with the help of the Kaid's escort, to force their way through, in face of the determined resistance of fully armed men entrenched behind rocks and thickets, he had to swallow his disappointment as best he might and return to the plain.

He had his consolation, however, in the complete success of his next venture. Proceeding by way of the glen Reraya, the most striking in its frowning desolation of all the valleys they had as yet penetrated, he was able to achieve no less a feat than the ascent of the mighty Tizi Likumpt. The toil was of course tremendous, but the result was a full compensation for it all. Standing finally at an altitude of 13,150 feet among wreaths of snow, he gazed upon a scene of indescribable sublimity, "a bewildering, awe-inspiring assemblage of snow-streaked elevations, sharp jagged ridges, and deep glens and gorges," while to the westward there shot up to a height 2000 feet above his lofty standpoint the rugged peak of Tizi-n-Tamjurt, the king among these mountain Titans.

For a second time he had thus broken the record of mountaineering in the Atlas.

One more crossing of the range remained for him to accomplish, namely from Imintanut into the dreaded country of Sus. In this also he succeeded, although amid circumstances of the most trying sort, for his men were in terror at the very idea of the trip, and owing to a quarrel that had broken out among the tribes, bloodshed and robbery were rampant everywhere.

And so concluded his mountaineering exploits in this noble range. He had by means of them added largely to both geographical and geological science, and, so far, he could look back upon them with a measure of satisfaction as not unworthy of his past. But the accompaniment of ceaseless worries with his men had been a soul-sickening experience, and he was glad now to hasten to the coast that he might free himself from the intolerable incubus. He hoped with a new set of followers to start again at Fez and explore a more easterly section of the range. That plan, however, was unexpectedly cut short by a call to another undertaking which gave promise of being very much more to his mind.

So far as the country and the people of Morocco were concerned, the observations of the past months had been in all respects a saddening revelation to him. Every hopeful anticipation which he had permitted himself to entertain had one by one vanished. Socially, politically, and religiously the country was found to be everywhere in the most pitiful case.

Reference has already been incidentally made to the hateful misgovernment under which a few human leeches suck the life-blood of the nation and make enterprise impossible. Oppression in every conceivable form is rampant. Between the official class who grind him down and the money-lending Jews who, like flies upon sores, batten on his distress, the Moor in his own country has not the life of a dog.

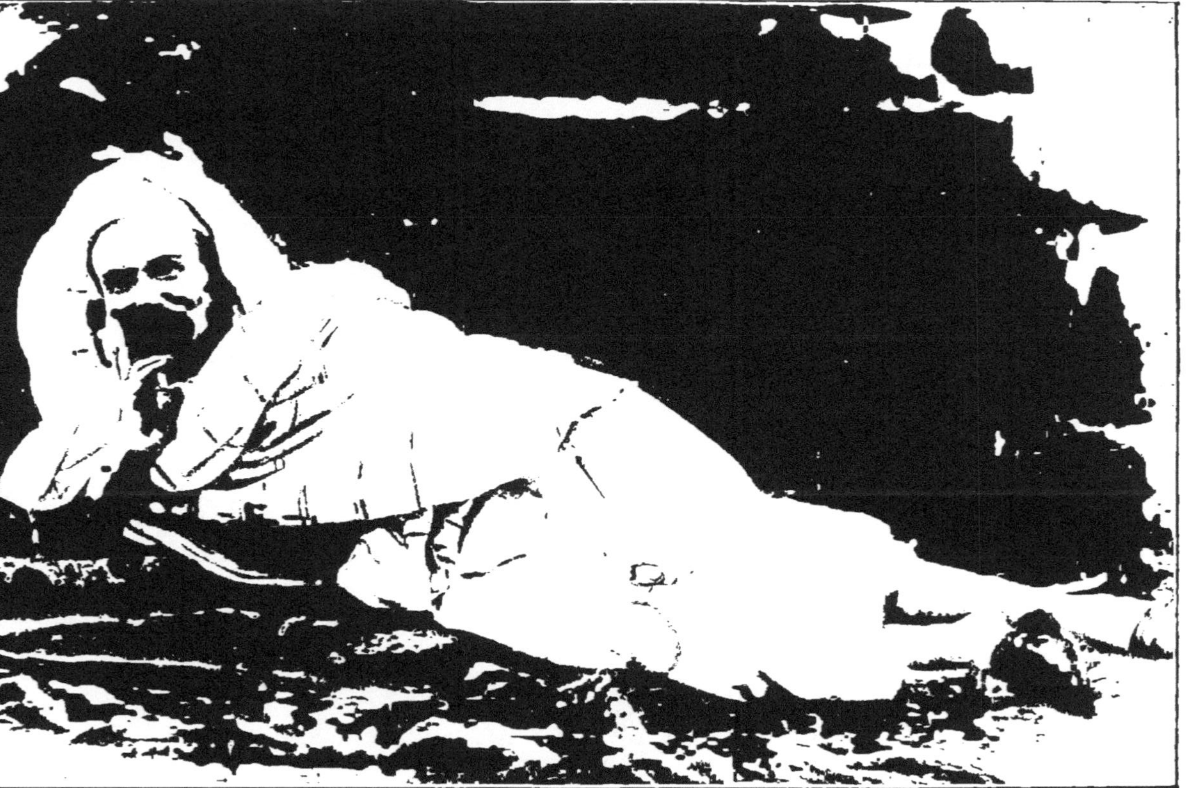

*From a photograph by]*  JOSEPH THOMSON IN MOORISH COSTUME.  *[J. Fergus, Largs, N.B.*

It is but the natural complement of this, that the physical life of the people should be lived amid the unhealthiest and filthiest conditions. If the Moor ever was "heart clean" with respect to his domestic surroundings, adversity and the experience of hopeless injustice have driven common sensitiveness out of him. The pestiferous abominations that are tolerated alike in town and country, never to speak of such unimaginable dunghills as the *Mellahs* or Jews' quarters in Morocco and Mogador, are significant marks of a nation having lost self-respect. Even where the Moor does betray some vague hankering after sanitation, his ideas take shape after such a perverted fashion as to emphasise his demoralised condition. For instance, at Mogador he has gone in for a sewage system; but in how strange a style! The primitive system, under which garbage and filth were deodorised in the open air and borne out of sight by the ubiquitous canine scavenger, would be infinitely preferable; for here he has simply got the length of cutting open drains in the middle of the street, into which every festering and evil-smelling thing is thrown, until at certain seasons the place becomes a deadly focus of pestilential influence.

But the ignorant and savage fanaticism which universally reigns, makes it hard to extend to the Moor a simple pity. The explorer found him everywhere somewhat of a dangerous animal, only restrained from furious demonstrations against such "Christian dogs" as himself and his companion through fear of consequences. Indeed, not even that availed to shield them from harm, as their experience in the city of Morocco proved, and if the like violence was not offered to them elsewhere, they had unpleasant enough evidence that it was not for lack of the will to hurt. Everywhere they had to run the gauntlet of scowls and curses.

As an object-lesson on the effect of Islam, the religious condition of the people was a salutary if unwelcome piece of education, and Joseph Thomson, with his habitual candour and honesty, was not slow to note the lesson and to proclaim it.

" If in the Sûdan," he says, " we found Mohammedanism instilling a new life and vigour into barbarous races and setting them on the road to spiritual, moral, and material advancement, in Morocco we found it doing quite the reverse.  Here it was preventing all advancement, suppressing all higher and nobler impulses which happen to be alien to its spirit, cutting off 'the believer' from all outside genial influences, and acting as a blight upon his whole nature.  Superficially it presented a fair and seemly spectacle — unquenchable faith, scrupulous attention to ceremonial duties, and most absolute submission to the will of Allah — but underneath all was maggots and rottenness . . . It was difficult to grasp the fact which had been gradually boring its way into our minds with growing knowledge of Moorish life, that absolutely the most religious nation on the face of the earth was also the most grossly immoral.  Among no people are prayers so commonly heard, or religious duties more rigidly attended to.  Yet, side by side with it all, rapine and murder, mendacity of the most advanced type, and brutish and unnatural vices exist to an extraordinary degree. . . .

" The very force which made the empire great in the world has now, in its corrupt and degraded form, become the agent which will prove the empire's destruction. . . . Chiefly through its influence Morocco has become a noxious backwater cut off from the healthy current of advancing civilisation, and there it develops its poisonous germs and collects its rotting pestiferous weeds."

In view of this moribund state of religion, and the utter paralysis of moral force among the people, he felt driven resistlessly to the conclusion that there is no hope for

Morocco save in the application of the strong hand and drastic measures from without. "To talk of reforms is to talk to the idle winds. . . . Morocco must either become absolutely a European province, or be placed like Tunis under the protection of a Christian government sufficiently powerful to compel reforms, not merely to urge them."

# CHAPTER X.

### MORE BOOK-WORK.

In the end of October, 1888, Joseph Thomson was once more in London, having, as already indicated, abruptly cut short his programme of operations in the Atlas. The occasion of his sudden change of plan was the receipt of communications from the East Africa Company indicating that there was an opening for him in the scene of his former labours, and that they wished to engage him for a term of two years.

The precise object in view was not stated; but naturally his mind at once leapt to Emin Pasha, and to the fact that, so far as was known, he was yet unrelieved. A year and a half agone Stanley had vanished into the unknown, and absolute silence rested upon his movements. Not a word of news lightened the mystery of whether he was alive or dead. The only echoes from the ill-starred expedition were those terrible stories of The Rearguard Camp, which came to haunt as a nightmare the philanthropic public, and to shake the simple-minded confidence with which they had relied upon the scheme of so-called relief.

Could this new "opening" mean the adoption of his plan for reaching Emin through Masai-land? Could it be the tardy response to his letter in *The Times* (May 13, 1887) in which he had urged the development of the East Coast route to the Equatorial Provinces? There seemed but one answer possible to these questions. With a rush all the old interest in the Emin Expedition again took possession of him. Promptly he answered the call in person, glad in a sense to leave Morocco behind.

His surmise as to the purpose of the Committee was quite correct. For his acceptance of the leadership of such an expedition terms were very easily arranged. The fact of his original contention being thus endorsed, even at the eleventh hour, was in itself almost a sufficient compensation, especially as he had received a very significant confirmation of his former doubt with regard to the *bona fides* of the Congo Expedition. Shortly after his meeting with those who had called him home, he writes to Gilmour:—

" You are probably aware that I am back from Morocco to take an expedition through Masai-land to Emin, which shows that all things come to those who can wait. . . . What a pity those letters I wrote in Paris did not appear. Everything I said then proves to be true. De Winton kindly told me that Stanley had taken the Congo route by command of the King of the Belgians and in the interests of the Congo State !

" By-the-bye here is an interesting piece of news. Captain E. C. Hore, of the London Missionary Society, has just returned from Tanganyika after seven years' residence there. On his way to Zanzibar, accompanied by his wife and child, he was never molested or insulted by the Arabs or natives, who all expressed the greatest friendliness to the English, but an undying hatred of, and a determination to fight the Germans. This state of things our Government seems bent on upsetting in the interests of a German trading company.

His delightful anticipation of going upon his new mission of rescue was unhappily, however, destined not to be realised. Notwithstanding that he had made a great personal sacrifice in cutting short his work in Morocco and accepted the Company's proposal, in full reliance upon their honour, the arrangement very soon began to hang fire. A change was apparently coming over the spirit of their dream. After a brief period of hesitation, there was a complete *volte face*, and the enterprise was practically dropped.

The reason vouchsafed was that, owing to the German attempt at colonising in East Africa, the whole of that part of the continent had been thrown into a state of excitement and opposition to white men, and that the directors objected to risking his life there.

It is needless to say that the explorer's disappointment was very great. The excuse as to the risk he thought quite hollow; and in view of the sacrifice he had made and the trust he had reposed, he felt that he was not being honourably dealt with. He had been wantonly, as he thought, led on a fool's errand, and he was indignant accordingly. In a letter to Mr. McKie (December 2) he says: "The Company in any case have treated me scandalously, and with an infamous want of consideration." This resentment was not diminished by the measure of compensation offered to him. Ultimately, however, "the hatchet was buried" by the acceptance of terms, and so ended the one disagreeable experience he had with any public body.

In the meantime he was being occupied about other matters also, which helped to withdraw his mind from these worries. The writing of an article for *Good Words*, and the preparation of his Morocco paper and map for the Royal Geographical Society, gave him at once an occupation and a welcome anodyne. This paper was read to the Society in December with the usual pleasant accompaniments to which he had become happily accustomed in that quarter.

For once he was again able to take part in the much prized family gathering under the paternal roof, with which the new year was invariably opened, and from

which he had perforce to be so often absent. He counted
this a great privilege; for, wander where he might, his
heart was ever warm to the memories and ways of the
home circle.

In the January number of the *Contemporary Review*
appeared his article on "East Africa as it was and is."
It was an impassioned indictment of the Government of
the day for the base and blundering policy (as he considered it) which had been followed, and which had not
only sacrificed the rights and the influence of Great
Britain in East Africa, but betrayed the cause of civilisation in that region. He had been watching the course
of events and the evolution of international competition
there with a deeply interested mind; for the country
so closely identified with his own past career was,
in a manner, an object of affectionate concern to him.
Gradually, as the time went on and the unhappy trend
of affairs became more evident, his misgiving had deepened
into disgust, and he felt that he must speak out in protest
against the dishonourable entanglements into which the
country was allowing itself to be dragged.

He had formerly spoken out—too vigorously as some
thought—in deprecation of the carefully nursed delusion
that East Africa was an unexploited mine of wealth, being
sure that such an idea was likely to be hurtful to the
interests of East Africa itself. But events had afforded
a justification of his fears more emphatic than even he had
anticipated. In the years preceding 1883, Britain had
been able in a quiet way to do great things for that land.
Under the wise educating and guiding policy of Sir John
Kirk at Zanzibar, the slave trade had largely disappeared.
Our Indian subjects with their industrious ways and keen
trading instincts had been encouraged to settle in large
numbers, to the benefit of all concerned. Commerce in
a natural and healthy way had been fostered. And above
all, our missionaries, at the cost of immense sacrifice, had
begun to breathe a new life through the whole region.

They had made the name of Englishman revered and admired throughout the length and breadth of East Central Africa. They had roused unbounded confidence in his word and his good intentions. All this time Germany had been doing absolutely nothing for the country, and the extent of her influence and interest was represented by a single trading house which acted as an intermediary between Europe and the British Indian merchants at Zanzibar.

"But in 1884 all this began to change. In that year the preposterous views expressed by various travellers about the commercial possibilities of Africa began to find general credence. Tickled by such nonsense as that in Africa the world had 'a new El Dorado,' and 'a second India,' and that its proposed railways were to be the finest paying commercial speculations in this century to a world athirst for wealth, the nations of Europe pricked up their ears, and then commenced *the scramble for Africa*. Innocent chiefs were defrauded out of their lands by bogus treaties. An innocent and ignorant people at home were found ready at the beck of glib company promoters to put their money into all sorts of schemes.

"In this general gilding up, East Africa came in for a share, and soon there was nothing heard of but treaty making and planting of flags. To back these enterprises up, companies were promoted in Germany. The sovereign rights of the Sultan of Zanzibar were violated in the most shameless fashion. He was treated as a barbarous chief, and as an obstacle to civilising influences."

In those days history was rapidly made. The Sultan's resentment, the appearance of Germany's threatening ironclads, the unblushing violation of international law and equity, the appointment of a commission to delimit the Sultan's territories, his trust in Britain as his representative, and our betrayal of him, and, finally, his untimely death as a man despoiled of his rights, followed each other in rapid succession. Then came still more unfortunate entanglements for this country; and now, what was the situation we had to contemplate in East Africa? This:—

" Some thousands of British subjects have been ruined and driven from their homes, without hope of redress. All our interests have been handed over to Germany. After spending much money and many noble lives, the work of our missionary societies has been ruined. We have agreed to make our anti-slavery policy subservient to the colonising schemes of Germany, to the detriment of the good cause and of our country's best interests. The country has been thrown back into a worse condition than that of twenty years before. European travellers, however well armed and protected, cannot now go where formerly a solitary individual, armed only with an umbrella, could pass with safety."

His fear was, that things would get into a still more deplorable position, in which the exigencies of an unfortunate policy would further imperil the honour and interests of this country. Hence this outspoken article.

He hardly expected that his protest would be treated by the Government as other than a Cassandra cry; but he had at least relieved his own conscience in calling attention to the facts of the situation.

The preparation of his book on the Morocco journey now absorbed his entire attention. He made fairly rapid progress with the work; but, whether it was owing to a more fastidious criticism of his own composition, or to some other reason, he had more than the usual sense of toil in it, and less of that conscious fluency and freedom which were characteristic of him—although no one would suspect this from the actual style of the book itself. In

February he writes from Edinburgh, where he had settled down for the purposes of his literary work :—

"I have had a fairly lively time of it in the evenings, though during the day I have been writing like a slave. I have not got half so easily on with this book as with my previous ones. There seems to be no inspiration in it, or in myself, to hurry me on. The book is promised for the end of March, and it is only half written. I think, however, it will take when it does come out. . . . I must confess I am getting restlessly eager to be off to Africa, though I must now anchor here till my book is out."

Perhaps this closing confession may, to some extent, throw light upon his sense of drudgery. He had the fever of Africa in his veins. He was ever dreaming of active service, and longing for new outlets for his exploring enthusiasm.

The monotony of book-writing was pleasantly broken by other engagements of a public sort. In the end of February he lectured on his explorations in the Atlas before the Scottish Geographical Society in Edinburgh and Glasgow; and, on the 7th of March, a still more agreeable task awaited him.

The unveiling of a bust of Livingstone in the Wallace Monument at Stirling was fixed for that date. The donor of the bust was Provost Donald, Dunfermline. Mrs. A. L. Bruce, Dr. Livingstone's daughter, performed the formal ceremony, and Joseph Thomson, as a Scottish explorer and an avowed follower of the great missionary philanthropist, had the duty assigned to him of pronouncing the oration which the circumstances called for. No duty could have been reckoned by him more honourable. He had a sincere enthusiasm for his subject, and therefore spoke out of a full heart, as befitted the occasion. As there was an element of self-revelation in the speech, it will not seem out of place that we should quote the closing part of it :—

"After all, it is not so much what one does of himself which specially distinguishes the great man. It is rather that stimulating and living force which goes out of him and becomes imparted to others—firing them to follow in his path, and stimulating them to better deeds and nobler lives. There can be no real greatness for the man who does not possess this quality ; without it, however largely he may bulk in the public view, he is but a meteor blazing across our horizon—one moment dazzling all, the next nowhere. Applying this criterion of real greatness to Livingstone, we find at once how prominent he stands before us. As missionary, traveller, and philanthropist, he has done great, nay, herculean deeds ; but as a transmitter of the spirit which burned within him he has done, through others, infinitely more. He was one great living accumulator of force, which he could not possibly expend himself. He was full of the electric currents which tend towards self-immolation for the good of others, to deeds of high Christian emprise, to everything that is great and noble. No one could come in contact with him without feeling a stimulating shock. Hence the enormous influence for good he has had upon our times—an influence which, however paradoxical it may seem, grows with time and in proportion as it is spent.

"Livingstone was great as a missionary, but the work he performed is small compared with that accomplished by those he imbued with his spirit. To what part of Africa can you turn without seeing his influence in missionary enterprise ? To him you trace directly the foundation of the Universities Mission in East Africa, and the Scotch one on Nyassa. Indirectly, he led to the establishment of the various missions on Victoria Nyanza, Tanganyika, and the Congo. It is the charm, too, of his life and work which still largely stimulates and fires new men to go forth to carry on the holy war and fill up, with undaunted courage and self-immolation, the ranks of the fallen.

"As an explorer his influence is as marked. No single traveller ever did so much for the opening up of Africa as Livingstone, yet the accumulated work of those he brought into existence bulks more largely in view. If there had been no Livingstone, should we ever have heard of Stanley or Cameron, and a host of minor travellers who have done something in the exploration of Africa? In this respect I can speak feelingly, for I am one of the band. It was the boyish desire to emulate his deeds that undoubtedly led me to the Dark Continent and made me what I am.

"Single-handed, Livingstone could do nothing to suppress the slave traffic, but none the less he it was who sounded its death knell. He laid bare its horrible character, and infused men's minds with his horror of it till its destruction was decreed. Years have passed since Livingstone preached the anti-slavery crusade, and it might be supposed that but little had been done to accomplish this great end. In reality, there has been much. Christian Europe is gradually arranging its forces and taking up positions to grapple with the hydra-headed beast; and before the century closes we may hope that the appalling horrors of the slave route will be things of the past. Would that we could say there will not be a slave or slave-owner left; but that is more than can be expected.

"It is not, however, in Africa only that Livingstone has left the benign impress of his moral greatness. That such a man has lived at all is a distinct and precious gain to the civilised community and humanity at large. The mental and moral forces which he so strikingly displayed have contributed largely to the upraising of our own level. Circumstances have only permitted the few to emulate his deeds, but thousands upon thousands have thought the higher of their kind, and have profited in unthought-of ways. Every warm glow of feeling which a knowledge of his work has evoked has been so much to the good of the person touched. Every wish, though unfulfilled, to follow in his footsteps is a stepping-stone to a higher and more unselfish life. . . .

"Among the sordid cares which envelop us, and the soul-deadening pursuits, which threaten to engross our every thought, we have each year more and more need of a Livingstone to break in upon us and remind us of a higher and nobler life. Livingstone is no longer with us in body, but his spirit lives in an undying force, ever vivifying our hearts and minds with ennobling influences. This bust will have failed of its true function if it imparts not to all who look upon it some of that spirit. We stand in a monument to Wallace, the true type of a country's patriot and choicest hero; but before you is the bust of an even higher type of hero, one who drew no distinction of country or race, who fought not for self, or home, or fatherland, but for Christ and the all-embracing brotherhood of men."

Resuming work upon his book he plodded away steadily. By the end of March he could report that his writing was nearly finished, although he had also to add that he was "heartily sick of it." Fortunately, the habit which he maintained in his exploring career of recording all impressions and incidents day by day, while the memory of them was fresh and vivid, formed an excellent guarantee against dulness, even though in the putting together of the materials he had the irksome sense of being "like a writing machine." As a matter of fact there is none of his narratives of travel more racy; none which bears upon it more of the impress of reality, giving the reader the sense of seeing and sharing all the humours and excitements of the expedition.

The volume, dedicated to his "very dear friends Dr. and Mrs. Calder," was published in May, and was at once accorded a hearty welcome—the critics vieing with each other in saying kind things of it. "Thomson," wrote one, "is the ideal of the geographer and explorer. Little tit-bits of information are served up with quaint humour. The scientific diversions in his chapters take the shape of joking lectures to his travelling companion Mr. Crichton-Browne, and never bore. The realistic truth and satiric comment are delightfully varied, buoying up the immense mass of material contained in this concise and handy volume."

While seeing this work through the press he visited Manchester, and on the 9th of April lectured to the Geographical Society there, his subject being "Some Impressions of Morocco and the Moors."

The completion of the book and release from the strain was followed, as in a previous case, by a sharp reaction. Writing on the 14th of May he says : "I have been in the depths and swimming hopelessly in the floods of Styx, eager not to be just yet cast on the shores of Hades."

"After that," he adds, "you will wonder to hear that I have been tickling the ears of bishops at Lambeth Palace, telling them their duty in certain matters—to receive the encomiums of the archbishop, who presided, on my Christian sentiments. You see you have much to learn about me ! And what wonder, when I am only beginning to get some clue to the solution of my own character ? I am devoured for the time with a thirst to know myself, though, so far as my investigations have proceeded, I am not flattered with the result."

The summer of this year he spent at home, doing his best, by a course of reading and an occasional spurt of pedestrianism, to stave off his insatiable thirst for action. At one time during this summer he seems to have had some prospect of being sent out on a mission to Damaraland. Nothing came of it, however, and he must needs endeavour to possess his soul in patience a little longer.

His study of African affairs was keen and constant; but in those days there was little pleasure and much vexation to be got from it. "I can do nothing but rage over the turn events are taking in Africa," he confesses to one of his correspondents. And little wonder that he should have been so moved; for then it was that news began to reach this country of Dr. Peters' filibustering expedition through Masai-land and Kavirondo, with its record of deliberate robbery, violence, and bloodshed. From his point of view indeed almost everything seemed to be going wrong in East Africa. The "scramble" for territory there was proceeding apace, with consequences most disappointing for the interests both of Africa and of this country.

Joseph Thomson sincerely believed—and not on patriotic grounds alone—that Great Britain had a mission to fulfil towards the Dark Continent in securing the well-being of its peoples and developing its resources, a mission which no other nation could discharge. Naturally, therefore, he was anxious to see this country alive to the necessity of widening its influence there, and ready to recognise its responsibilities wherever it had a sure footing. For this, however, he looked in vain. While such countries as Germany and France were eagerly pushing to the forefront in African affairs, and with purely selfish objects, Britain was contenting herself with philanthropic professions to the neglect of obvious calls for energetic action, and with sleepy quiescence letting the shameful game of "grab" go on.

Facts like those chafed and vexed him; and, as the march of history made matters more urgent, his anxiety deepened into impatience. In his heart he had a grievance to vent against "Downing Street," and against the whole system of inert, mechanical red-tapism in relation to Africa which it represented. This grievance he had already so far voiced in his article in *The Contemporary* a few months before; and now again he felt impelled to utter it anew, and with a still sharper emphasis, in an article in *The Fortnightly*.

The article appeared in the August number and was entitled, "Downing Street *versus* Chartered Companies in Africa." It was based upon his own personal experience in East and West Africa. His observations, he said, had shown him that on both sides of the continent "Downing Street" had been stupidly and guiltily apathetic. In East Africa it had simply thrown away its heritage and had barely saved for itself a sphere of influence between the seaboard and the great lakes. In West Africa it had not only allowed itself to be forestalled in many desirable quarters by jealous rivals, but, even where it retained power and place, it had done its utmost by mechanical and unintelligent restrictions upon trade with native races, to crush out the spirit of enterprise and to prevent the vigorous development of commerce—except, perhaps, as regards the one sad instance of the traffic in gin and gunpowder.

What was the remedy for these mistakes? His answer was this. Let the government, under proper safeguards, hand over to its own interested people powers which it was officially neither fitted nor minded to exercise aright. Let it give to men of means and intelligence some inducement to put their strength and their wealth into the work of developing Africa's resources. "There are," he said, "but two ways to administer and develop the resources of such regions as Central Africa, viz., either the French method, in which the Government does everything—acts as pioneer, makes roads and railways, establishes markets, experiments on the products of the country, etc.—or else Chartered Companies."

For the latter he declared unhesitatingly. A chartered company, he held, has every interest to put money freely into the country; it can carry on the administration at the very cheapest rate by men of practical experience; it can keep up a continuous policy which the natives soon come to understand; and it can maintain an effective control over the traffic, finding it for its advantage to check everything that is deleterious.

This, he held, was no speculative theory. Experiment had justified his argument, and he could point to the sphere of the Royal Niger Company, in its contrast to the remainder of the West Coast under British rule, as a sufficiently encouraging proof of what good fruits a charter could secure. That company, even before its chartered days, had done wonders in a private capacity within its restricted sphere of operations. But now that its sphere had been so enormously widened, as the result of his own mission to Sokoto and Gandu, and its position rendered secure by charter, it had, in a most spirited and successful manner, tackled the problems of the situation. There was vigorous life and movement over the entire sphere, and already results of a most beneficent and promising sort had been attained.

The facts of this case, he thought, were in themselves proof sufficient that it would be not only safe but wise to apply the principle of devolution everywhere in Africa. Let "Downing Street" denude itself of functions which it was unable or unwilling adequately to discharge. Let public enterprise have reasonably free scope, and who could doubt that there would be a salutary forward movement in other undeveloped parts of the continent?

Having thus unburdened himself of his manifesto, he resolved to treat himself to a holiday. Accordingly, in the end of July, he set off with his friend J. M. Barrie for a ramble on the Continent. This trip occupied six weeks, and, as may well be supposed, the two had "a good time." Their route led them up the Rhine to Constance, thence through the Austrian Tyrol, and across the Stelvio Pass into Italy. After resting awhile at Lake Como, they returned by the Splugen Pass to Lucerne, where they

R

spent three days. Thence they wended their way to Paris, in which they sojourned for five days, "doing" the Great Exhibition, and seeing the sights of that gay time.

Shortly after his return, he once more took up quarters in Edinburgh for a fresh bout of literary work. Thence he writes to a friend in the end of October :—

" For the last three weeks I have been pegging away at the 'Travels of Mungo Park, and the Story of the Niger,' till the sight of pen and ink makes me sick. Writing is not my vocation. Rather fifty miles on foot in an African desert than ten miles described on paper ! "

The new volume, the commencement of which he thus impatiently chronicles, was one which he had undertaken to write for *The World's Great Explorers* series. The aim of the editors was to secure that each biography in the series should be written by the highest authority available. Naturally, therefore, Joseph Thomson, as the most recent traveller amid the scenes of Park's triumphs and sufferings, was marked as the narrator of his life-work, and of the various efforts of exploration and commercial enterprise which followed upon it under the auspices of men like Denham, Clapperton, Landers, and Barth.

He had another and quite as vital a qualification for writing the life of the great pioneer as that of having visited the Niger for himself. That was a profound personal admiration of the man, and a keen sympathy with his spirit as an explorer. Park, next to Livingstone, stood out before his mind's eye as the ideal of what a pioneer among savage races should be. One cannot read Joseph Thomson's estimate of Park, knowing the writer's own character and aspirations, without feeling that the qualities described were, so far as they went, very much those which he was ever striving to reproduce in his own career. This is what he says of his hero, and it will show the point of view from which he approached the task of writing about him :—

"For actual hardships undergone, for dangers faced and difficulties overcome, together with an exhibition of the virtues which make a man great in the rude battle of life, Mungo Park stands without a rival. In one respect only—that of motive—does another surpass him. Here Livingstone stands head and shoulders above his predecessor. . . . Not that Park was altogether wanting in all that tends towards the spirit of self-sacrifice. On the contrary, throughout his whole narrative we fail to find the faintest trace of vulgar ambition or ignoble self-seeking. He deliberately suppressed incidents which would have added greatly to his fame. . . . His whole nature shrank from notoriety. . . . As little was he actuated by the desire of gain. . . . The spark that quickened his manhood to heroism, and fired him to 'scorn delights and live laborious days,' was the worthy ambition of a noble mind to work for the good of his country and the advancement of knowledge, rewarded solely by the approbation of his own conscience and the esteem of good men. . . . From what we know of his intense religious convictions and kindly nature, Park, had he lived at the present day, would probably have been a missionary, aflame for the cause of Christ, and ready to lay down his life for it, or a traveller preaching a crusade, not only against the slave trade, but against the gin trade likewise."

With a subject like this, upon which he could dilate with full knowledge and fellow-feeling, it is not surprising that he made rapid progress, however irksome to him the mere penwork might be. By the end of November the book was half written, and he was indulging in somewhat confident hopes that he would be able to make a good story, although he felt a vast difference between writing his own travels and writing other people's.

The inevitable "blue mood," as he called it, would once in a while visit him.   In one of these he says :—

"I have been sitting for the last hour or so trying to imbibe some Emersonian lore, with but poor success. My mind was too much in a wild frenzy—electricity-charged clouds hanging portentously over life's firmament, and throwing a gloom over all things here below.  I am feeling like a caged lion."

It was the old story—the feverish hunger to be once more out in the open, and to be pouring forth his un-slumbering energies in some new mission.

"I am," he confesses, "beginning to fret very much to be up and doing—off and away to my adopted Continent ; but of course I am sadly tied down by my book.  Till it is finished, I have to do my best to sit upon the wild longings that will effervesce whether I will or no."

Happily for the restoration of his good spirits, he was not to languish long under the prospect of hateful in-activity.  Before the year 1889 was finished, a new call for his services was apparently beginning to make itself articulate, and already he was anticipating the joy of finding himself once more in the field of action.

On Christmas Eve he writes to Mrs. Gilmour in a manner sufficiently indicative of restored buoyancy :—

"There would be clear evidence that the guiding hand of the overruling Providence, which watches over the errant—if not erring—footsteps of danger-pressed African travellers, was hopelessly astray if it did not cause me to enlist the services of my pen to convey my Christmas greetings and good wishes to you and such as bask in the sunshine of your presence. . . . I regret that I am not in town with you to tell you in my own particular way how much I desire for you all good things appropriate to the season, and ply a knife and fork once more at your table in a fashion not unbecoming one who has dined on rhino and sucked the marrowbones of elephants.

"Of news I have got none—for am I not vegetating in a backwater of the current of life, graced with lilies and irises, it may be, and overshadowed and decked with sweetest ferns, yet still with mud gathering and mephitic gases generating therein, and sleep, death and the grave beyond?

"But happily the time is approaching to be once more up and doing. Mungo Park has nearly received his complete suit of new clothes, and, released from the tailoring task, I mean to take on a coat of luminous paint and burst one of these fine days upon you all, meteor-like, portentous with the fate of—myself."

We have no definite information as to what were the particular prospects or purposes which he had to confide to his friends; but, in all probability, the "fate" to which he refers had some relation to a mission upon which we find him setting out three months later, and which he thus announces in a letter to Mr. McKie:—

"I'm off to the Zambesi to do for that region what I accomplished on the Niger—that is to say, secure it from other people."

It may have related to another matter, for there was more than one candidate for his services at this time. In conveying to another correspondent the above news, he adds:—

"Curiously enough, the East Africa Company have been almost going down on their knees to me to go out for them, to checkmate, if possible, this new move of Emin. I have been rather pleased than otherwise to say, 'No,' to them, considering the way they treated me after bringing me back from Morocco."

Be this as it may, he now decided to go out in the

employ of the British South Africa Company, who, in their proposals, were not only offering to him an opportunity of action wholly congenial, but, in the matter of remuneration, treating him in a liberal and honourable spirit. Not that he set great store by the mere question of payment—for no one was ever more easy-minded about money matters; but, of course, it was encouraging to feel that he had men to deal with who were ready to put a respectful estimate upon his services.

In view of his new enterprise a few of his more immediate intimates in London assembled on the 12th of April at the Holborn Restaurant to dine in his honour and to give him a friendly "send off." The names of his hosts on that pleasant occasion were as follows: P. B. du Chaillu, Dr. Hans Meyer, Edward Clodd, John Bolton, J. M Barrie, E. G. Ravenstein, J. Thomson, T. L. Gilmour, George Philip, J. S. Keltie, and J. Jackson Clarke.

On the 18th of the month he sailed for Cape Town, and so entered upon what proved, alas, to be his closing effort in African exploration.

# CHAPTER XI.



To Joseph Thomson as an advocate of the principle of Chartered Companies in the opening up of Africa, the British South Africa Company had from its formation been an object of special interest. It had only been a year or so in existence at this time, but already by its masterly enterprise it had laid broadly the foundations of what might turn out to be a great empire. By treaties and other means it had secured sovereign rights over an enormous tract of territory, reaching north as far as the River Zambesi. But it was not content with this. It was believed that in the great unexplored region extending up to Lake Moero there were lands of much value and promise, which under proper administration might prove a means of enrichment to the Company.

If this possible acquisition was to be obtained, however, very prompt and vigorous action was necessary. Not only were the Portuguese thoroughly wakened up to the fact that their influence in East Central Africa was in peril, but other eyes were being turned desiringly to the territory in question. It was in urgent circumstances like these that the directors of the Company proposed to enlist Joseph Thomson's energies in their favour. His past achievements as an explorer, the notable success of his humane methods in dealing with savage races, and his tact and capacity in negotiating treaties with native potentates, which had been illustrated so signally in the Niger and Western Sûdan region, marked him out as the man for their purpose in their character of commercial pioneers.

On his part there was everything to prompt a ready response. There was not only the delight of being put upon his mettle in a function demanding both courage and address, but there was the prospect, dear to the heart of every explorer, of filling up a blank space in the map. Moreover—a fact not without its interest or importance to his romantic nature—there was the opportunity offered in connection with the proposed expedition of visiting spots rendered classical in the history of African travel by their association with the last days of Livingstone.

It was with high anticipations, therefore, that he once more left his native shores behind. Hitherto he had penetrated to the hidden heart of Africa thrice from the east, once from the west and once from the north. Now he was to complete his round of pioneering by attacking it from the south.

After a quiet and uneventful voyage he arrived at Cape Town. There he was received with much cordiality by Mr. Noble, clerk to the House of Representatives. He had first met Mr. Noble in 1878, when he was just on the eve of setting out on his first expedition with Keith Johnston. Subsequently they had renewed their acquaintance in 1889 in the house of their mutual friend, Sir James Anderson, when Mr. Noble cordially invited him to call upon him if ever his travels should bring him to the Cape. Now that he was in a position, a few months after, to take advantage of the invitation, he was not only welcomed but urged to make the house in Montrose Gardens his home for the time; and there he received at the hands of host and hostess, both then and subsequently, the greatest consideration. He had further, during his stay in Cape Town, many valuable services

LUAPULA
LAKE
BANGWEULU
Mare Myoro
MANICA
LAND
BASENGA
BANYA
WEST NYASA
CENTRAL
ANGONI
SOUTH NYASA
UPPER SHIRE
WEST SHIRE
LOWER SHIRE
Thomson's Route shown this
English Miles

rendered to him by a brother Scotsman, Sir James Sivewright, who, besides "putting him up to the ropes generally," entertained him more than once at his charming residence, Somerset West. Sir Henry Loch also showed him much kindness.

The first step in his programme consisted of a run to Kimberley to confer with Mr. Cecil Rhodes, then "the uncrowned king of those parts," from whom, as the managing director of the Company, he was to receive his final orders. This conference was entirely satisfactory to himself—his own manly, straightforward nature enabling him to appreciate the blunt, unloquacious manner of his master for the time being, who showed equal business capacity in the plan of campaign which he indicated, and shrewdness in the measure with which he left him a free hand to carry it out.

On this visit to the diamond capital he had the fortune to meet several men whose names have become more or less prominent in connection with the subsequent development of Zambesia. Among these were Mr. A. R. Colquhoun of Asiatic fame, Mr. Rochfort Maguire, Mr. J. W. Moir, manager of the African Lakes Company, and Mr. (now Sir) H. H. Johnston. He also there became acquainted with Colonel Pennefather of the Enniskillens, and his secretary and aide-de-camp, Sir John Willoughby, who were on their way to Mashonaland in command of the Company's Police Force; besides such financial magnates as Messrs. Robinson, Wulff, and Beit, of the De Beers Company.

It was on this visit that he also met Mr. J. A. Grant, son of the late Colonel Grant, a young man in whom there was recognisable much of his father's vigour of character, and who was only too glad to throw himself into any adventure which would enable him to follow in the parental footsteps as an African traveller. Joseph Thomson's proposal that he should accept the position of his lieutenant in the new expedition was at once heartily agreed to, and the arrangement was never regretted on either side.

Before returning, he seized the opportunity offered to him of being taken down the diamond mines, the working of which interested him greatly. " It is a most wonderful sight," he remarks in his journal, "to see the thronging hundreds of naked natives rushing along with the trucks, or working like gnomes or evil demons in dimly lighted corners, while white men with fierce oaths and fiercer gestures urge them on or correct them."

Returning to the Cape towards the end of May, he proceeded forthwith to make his final preparations in the purchase of stores and of ammunition for the use of his men, when he should have reached the interior. These being completed, he with Grant set sail for Quilimane on the 1st of June, arriving at his destination on the 15th.

At Quilimane he had to encounter the first serious difficulty of the expedition. In view of the manner in which the Portuguese had been checkmated and out-manœuvred by the Chartered Company, official suspicion was in a state of high sensitiveness, and, not unnaturally, any one who seemed at all likely to be an agent of the Company was the subject of special scrutiny. How to pass not only themselves, then, but their stores, and above all their guns and ammunition, through the customs without ultimately finding themselves inmates of a Portuguese prison, was a problem involving no small anxiety. Suffice it to say, however, that the thing was accomplished. Thanks to presence of mind, hard work, and a spice of audacity, they found themselves, with their embarrassing (but fortunately unsuspected) bales of goods, safely stowed in boats on the Kwa-Kwa and ready to get under weigh for Vicenti on the Zambesi.

At Quilimane, thanks to the good offices of Mr. Churchill, the British consul at Mozambique, there were fifty-five stalwart Makua porters sent to him. With this nucleus of a caravan he set out from the coast on

June 26th. Some days of toiling through sweltering mangrove swamps, which gradually gave place to firmer and more healthful land, and they glided into the great river. There the steamer *James Stevenson* awaited them, and to it they transferred their goods.

They were not yet by any means safe from risk of detention; but happily, beyond requiring frequent exhibitions of their passports in their assumed character of independent hunters and travellers, the Portuguese officials gave them no serious trouble; and in two days more they were steaming energetically up the Zambesi.

On the 6th of July they reached the limits of the Portuguese authority at the point where the river Ruo joins the Shiré. There they expected to have again to run the gauntlet of examination. The *James Stevenson*, however, passed through the lines without even being challenged, and was already discharging her cargo before the Portuguese became aware of the fact that they had been caught napping.

The circumstance was no doubt fortunate for the travellers; but it led to a demonstration of anger on the part of these officials which might have had serious consequences. Not only was the *James Stevenson* captured in descending the river and her officers promptly sent to prison, to the imminent risk of trouble between this country and Portugal, but Thomson himself was made the subject of a dangerous outrage. In passing in a boat with three of his men down the British side of the Ruo, he was exposed to a murderous fusillade on the part of a couple of thousand of native soldiers under the command of Lieutenant Coutinho. His escape with his life and a whole skin, amid such a whizzing shower of bullets, was somewhat of a miracle. Yet, as he presently glided into the shelter of the Shiré banks, his anxiety gave way to laughter at the comical futility of the outrage, and as at the last moment the big guns began to boom out, he could not resist the temptation to lift his cap and bow in ironical politeness to the military rabble who had vainly spent so much good ammunition upon him.

In passing from Chiloma, at the confluence of the rivers Ruo and Shirè, to Blantyre in the Shirè highlands, he thought it best to strike out a new route for his party. Scaling with much labour the mountain barrier which frowned above Chiloma, they reached the summit at the height of four thousand feet. Here they entered upon rich grassy uplands having features of beauty which were quite a surprise to the leader. Nature on every hand was opulent in its aspect, and gave promise of a large return to the planter who should seek to exploit its resources. Up to that time, however, the teeming soil had been left untouched by the white man, and even native tillage was then a thing unknown. About the time of Livingstone's first journey, the devastating Ajawa had unpeopled the whole district, and thenceforth the spirit of the wilderness had been supreme. Over this fertile tract they pushed on amid a silence too eloquent.

In four days Blantyre was reached, and here surprises of another kind were in store for him. The scene that unfolded itself as he approached Blantyre offered everywhere heartening signs of life and industry. Populous native villages with well-tilled fields first proclaimed the change from the forsaken, if beautiful, wilderness. Then the gardens of the planters added an object of fresh interest. Presently house and store, church and school, crept into view. Finally a genuine, well-made, homelike road was struck, which led the party "into the cosy comfort of a Scottish home, where the Glasgow accent reigned in delightful supremacy."

Blantyre mission station he found to be truly a place of light and leading, a centre of hope and promise in the great moral desert of East Africa. The more he recognised the influence that was radiating from it, the more was he cheered and thankful. Here at least was one place where

the advent of the whites was an unmitigated blessing to
the natives; and here was being carried on a work for
Africa entirely after his own heart's desire. The African
Lakes Company, while practically a failure as a business
concern, had been operating hand in hand with missionaries as wise as they were earnest and as practical as they
were devout. The result was a revolution in the social
and industrial as well as in the religious life of the
district—a revolution which seemed likely to have a
salutary effect far and wide.

The moving spirit of the place was the Rev. D.
Clement Scott. In him he recognised a missionary
entirely according to his long cherished ideal, a man
magnetic in personality, cultured of mind, broad of view,
perfectly understanding the native character and knowing how to adapt himself to it, a man tireless in his
energy, and equally at home in a score of occupations.

Writing of the first Sabbath spent at the mission, the
explorer says:—

"It was interesting and touching to hear church bells
ringing over the country from Blantyre, quite a homelike
feeling of quiet and peace reigning around. Inside the
church I was surprised to note a Church of England air,
the candlesticks in the shape of a cross, embroidered
tablecover and lectern. All else, however, was Presbyterian. The Lord's prayer was repeated aloud. There
were over twenty Scotch worshippers, and thirty or forty
Blantyre servants. The natives turned out in their
holiday costumes. Some of the women and children
looked very nice in their Swahili dress, white with blue
sash round the waist, or blue with white sash. A special
and largely attended service for natives was held in the
afternoon, and then in the evening another service in the
church. Mr. Scott's sermon was highly interesting,
revealing the intellectual scholar in the impassioned and
enthusiastic preacher."

Though there was much interesting and worthy of study at this place, the circumstances forbade delay, and he must needs push on. At Mandala, the headquarters of the African Lakes Company, he was hospitably received by the acting manager, Mr. John Moir. From the meagre stores of the company he was able to purchase a few additional necessaries for his caravan, and from among their employees he secured the services of Mr. Charles Wilson, a young man who as a helper proved invaluable to the expedition.

On the 21st of August the caravan left for Matopè on the Upper Shirè, whence they were to be conveyed on the lake steamer *Domira* to the real starting-point of the main journey, Kota-kota.

As Joseph Thomson, now in health and comfort, steamed into Lake Nyassa, he could not but recall how, on his first great journey ten years before, he had stood footsore and toilworn on the heights at its northern end, and surveyed with mingled emotions its glittering expanse. How much had been crowded into that decade, which now in the retrospect seemed so short! Through what varied scenes and sufferings had those years borne him! And what would the next similar space of time have in store for him? Ah, well it was that the veil of secrecy now rested upon even the next few months of his adventurous career, and how much more was it well that mystery enfolded the years of trial that were to follow!

The week's delay at Kota-kota, which they had planned in order to secure additional porters and get things into order for the new plunge into the unknown, was lengthened out to a month, through a mishap to the *Domira* which was bringing the new men from Bandawè. But at last the time of weary waiting ended. On the 23rd of August, they left the blue waters of the lake behind them and wended their way westward.

The caravan consisted of a hundred and forty-eight, namely, the three white men, the fifty-five Makua porters from Mozambique, and ninety Atonga from Bandawè. In all there were but twenty of the company carrying guns, so that the power of the caravan either for offence or defence was decidedly limited.

Rising gradually from the lake by a stony and difficult track, they reached the summit of the lower plateau after four days' marching. They were then at an altitude of nearly 4500 feet. Before them stretched a landscape entirely uninteresting and unpromising. Over this commonplace country they marched for a fortnight until they reached the plain of the River Loangwa. During this time, they, for prudential reasons, directed their route through a kind of debatable land between the territories of two powerful chiefs, Mwasi on the north, and Mpesini, a dreaded Zulu despot, on the south. The route had one disadvantage. The natives, ever the subject of attack on either hand, were exceedingly suspicious. Every now and then they gathered excitedly in threatening attitude. Joseph Thomson, however, was a past master in tactful dealing with demonstrations of this sort, and again and again the warlike gestures were transformed into manifestations of welcome, through the exercise on the part of the strangers of a little self-control and gentleness. Here, as elsewhere in Africa, he found that the courage of patience smoothed the way, even where the situation bristled with provocations to bloodshed.

The descent into the densely-populated plains of the Loangwa on September 8th brought a very different country into view. Here, amid rich alluvial lands, the Babisa chief Kabwirè rules over a kindly and contented people. By this chief the caravan was very hospitably entertained, and with him the first treaty on the journey was made.

At Kabwirè's occurred one of those exciting emergencies which beset the African traveller. The Atonga porters, fearful of being taken into the unknown country beyond, had resolved to desert in a body. Happily the plot was discovered in time to be thwarted; but it wanted all the leader's experience and resource to deal with the crisis, and he had for a time no small anxiety until he had his men fairly across the river and once more on the march.

The Loangwa was forded ten miles below the point where Livingstone had crossed in his last great journey, and, after a few marches through a country of pleasant aspect, tropical alike in its luxuriance and its heat, they once more ascended the escarpment of the plateau forming the so-called Muchinga Mountains, and rising to the normal height of over 4000 feet. The explorer, with his eye ever open for beauty, was fascinated with the scenery that unfolded itself, as they toiled up the romantic glen of the Mpamanzi on their way to the summit. Here is his picture of the view :—

"We look up 2000 feet and see grey crag and rugged precipice break in many a wild and threatening shape from the green forests, which struggle for a foothold on the nether slopes. Below flows the river (Mpamanzi), here sweeping past a dense brake of waving bamboo, there lingering to lave the roots of palm and tree-fern bending streamwards, enamoured of their own mirrored loveliness. Anon it seems to sleep in some rock-bound basin, and over it the lilies spread their green leaves and budding flowers, till, waking suddenly again, it sweeps onward under an archway of leafy trees or dashes itself to foam among the obstructing rocks. At any moment the dreaded buffalo may rush from that dense brake; there the monkey swings from tree to tree; above, the baboons clamour noisily, safe on their distant perch; while the green parrot flits screaming past, striking a discordant note in the softer music of the wind and stream."

On arriving at the summit of the plateau, his first thought was to look with expectant curiosity for the

Lokinga Mountains.   They were apparently non-existent; but in their place this was what he saw :—

" Before us spread, as far as the eye could reach through a clear atmosphere, a billowy country like the swelling sea, its every feature clad with an unbroken forest, its winding hollows traversed by numerous streams.   On this pleasing landscape lay the rich colours of a dawning spring, gorgeous yet delicate, surpassing anything to be seen in the autumn glories of our own woodlands, or in the flowery splendours of a Moorish summer.   Ruby and crimson—the distinctive tints of the young mimosa leaves —prevailed, and, massed together, glowed under the tropic sun like a field of living flame.   Interwoven with these, and tempering their brilliancy to a delicious harmony, were the yellows and browns and greens of every subtle tint and tone that marked the foliage of the passing year —growth and decay, life and death

> 'Alike in glorious livery dight,
> And fair to see.' "

From dreams of beauty, however, he was rudely recalled to the anxieties of a leader.   The Makua porters had had their Mohammedan prejudices outraged by some trifle in connection with the killing of a goat, and to a man they mutinied, marching indignantly out of camp.   Fortunately the disaffection was wholly confined to this portion of the caravan, as the pagan Atonga men had no sympathy with the ideas of the Makua.   A little vigorous action together with a judicious assumption of calm indifference, soon brought the deserters to their senses, and presently they found themselves compelled, crestfallen, to resume their duties.

Through scenes of varied interest they plodded on for several days over the cool and fertile though, strange to say, uninhabited uplands, gradually ascending until, at the base of the Vimbè Hills they reached an altitude of 5300 feet. Here they were on the watershed. Behind were the streams flowing towards the Loangwa; in front were those seeking their destination in Lake Bangweolo. Two marches beyond this point—in one of which they had to cross a swamp, wading for an hour waist-deep— brought them to Kwa-Nansara, the village of a female Babisa chief.

The 21st of September, the day of their arrival here, proved to be a sadly memorable date in the history of the expedition; for then it was they discovered to their alarm that they had to reckon with the deadly scourge of those regions, small-pox. The calamitous outbreak occurred without the slightest warning. Within twenty-four hours eleven of the porters were *hors de combat*. The one course open to them was to leave the smitten men behind— making all possible provision for their maintenance and comfort—and to press on in hope that they might escape from the pestilence. It was not for long, however, that they dared to cherish that hope; for in the marches that followed man after man succumbed to the loathsome disease. At first the loads of the ailing porters were distributed among the healthy; but very soon that process reached its limit, and loads had to be hidden by the way and sent for from the next camp.

So they toiled on, forlorn and anxious, through the unpeopled, trackless, forest-clad wilderness that had to be crossed in order to reach Lake Bangweolo. Meanwhile their food supply failed, and as the dolorous way lengthened itself out, through the discovery that the maps were all wrong, and that day by day the expected lake was "receding before them like the mirage," the burden on the leader's spirit was fast becoming one of despair.

To the intense relief of all, on the 29th of September, they descried signs of human habitations. Presently they entered the village of Chitambo. Never was haven more joyfully welcomed by trouble-stressed men, and there amid plentiful provisions they were only too glad to rest and recruit.

The name of Chitambo was familiar as that of the scene of Livingstone's death. It was soon found, however, that there were two villages so designated, and that the classical bearer of the name was no less than twenty miles away to the east. Fain would Joseph Thomson have gone in person to visit the great explorer's grave. But in the sad condition of the caravan it was simply impossible that either he or his assistants could leave it even for a day. The only alternative was to send an intelligent and trusted headman to see the place and report. "He returned," says the explorer, "with the account that the tree under which Livingstone's heart was buried still spreads its protecting branches over the spot, displaying the inscription unharmed cut deep into its bark"—a part of which bark the visitor so far exceeded his instructions as to bring with him.

It is right to note, in passing, that doubt has been cast upon this man's report by the late American explorer Glave, who claims to have seen and photographed, *at Ilala* further westward, the veritable tree, with the bark pared off for a space of about two and a half feet square, and the inscription deeply cut into the hard solid wood. What the real facts are it is impossible, without further evidence, to say. Only Joseph Thomson quite positively makes this statement, as the result of personal inquiries: "Livingstone did not die in the district of Ilala, but in that of Kalindè" (in which Old Chitambo is situated).

The same circumstances which prevented the explorer from personally visiting Livingstone's grave availed also to hinder him from making a scientific survey of the south end of Bangweolo; but such observations and inquiries as he was able to make furnished material for important corrections. Two facts at least were brought out: the level of the lake was much lower than had been supposed, and neither in the dry nor in the wet season did the lake reach anything like so far to the south as the maps showed.

The few days of rest at Chitambo were days of deepening gloom, so far as the small-pox scourge was concerned. In those days six men were buried, and when once more the caravan marched forth on the 5th of October, it was with a melancholy rear-guard of fifteen men in all stages of the loathsome disease. The situation is thus depicted by the leader himself:—

"It would be impossible to describe the worries and troubles which now dogged our footsteps. It was bad enough to be hampered for lack of healthy porters and harassed by necessary attendance on the sick, but when we began to be boycotted by the natives, it seemed as if we would be utterly crushed. Only by a determined show of arms were we enabled to proceed, while each camp claimed its victim, and on each march some poor wretch slunk into the jungle to die in peace. The men who were healthy grew dispirited and worn out from overwork. They rebelled continually, demanding to be taken back, and only by daily threats and promises could they be forced forward."

It was thus that they dragged their weary steps westward. Had they been in a position to enjoy them, the sights that daily met their eyes were pleasing in the extreme, for they were passing through a delectable land for natural advantages, a land overflowing with plenty and swarming with all kinds of game, which mingled gracefully to the view amid tropical foliage, or gambolled in the grassy glades. Now they traversed the verdant plain of the Lohombo; now they threaded their path for days on the banks of the majestic Luapula, sweeping on to become itself the Congo; now they passed over the flower-bedecked rolling uplands of Iramba.

After three weeks of marching, in which dolour was strangely mingled with delight, they found themselves at

Kwa-Kavoi, a small village situated near the watershed of the country. This proved to be a turning point in the journey in more senses than one. Further progress westward was stopped by a vast, trackless, uninhabited forest wilderness, for which no guide could be got, and through which in their desolate condition it was hopeless to attempt to pass. A similar condition prevailed also towards the south. There was no choice left therefore but to strike out in a direction east by south, in the hope that they might outflank the forest and reach their objective—the River Kafuè—in a roundabout way. But these disappointments were trivial in comparison with the calamity which here befell; for now it was that the leader himself realised, after some days of suspicious symptoms, that he was in the fell grasp of some grievous disorder.

To himself the trouble was mysterious, and it was only long afterwards, when medical experts were able to take the case in hand, that the history of it could be traced. The beginning of the mischief had been laid in Morocco. In the course of his journeying there a riding accident had occurred in which he was nastily wounded upon the pommel of his saddle. The wound had healed freely, but in such a manner as to leave a certain liability to future trouble. The labours and hardships of this new journey supplied precisely the conditions likely to turn the risk into a reality, and now he was subjected to the wearing and overmastering agonies of acute *cystitis*.

In these perturbing circumstances he set his face to the new route. It, too, led them into a forest tract, but they trusted to a guide to lead them through it. Presently, however, they found that he had deserted them. For four days they marched on with deepening solicitude. Already they were beginning to feel the pangs of hunger and dismay, when to their joy they suddenly emerged on the edge of an open cultivated country. There at least they could procure a supply of food.

But it was a case of "out of the frying-pan into the

fire." The district had been again and again harried by the Portuguese slave-raiders, and now was repeated the experience which he had had ten years before on the west of Tanganyika. Wherever the caravan appeared throughout this country the natives in a frenzy of suspicion mustered in hostile array. So critical was the situation at times as to make it no small marvel that bloodshed was avoided.

On the 4th of November the village of Mshiri was reached. Here the crisis in the affairs of the expedition became acute. It was the leader's purpose to strike westward from this point, in hope to reach Sitandas in Manica-land — Selous' furthest point north. But the small-pox plague had now returned with renewed viru-. lence—as many as six being attacked in one night—and already it had destroyed quite a third of the caravan. Then whenever the Atonga found that the order of march was to be again westwards, they in a paroxysm of home-sickness broke all bonds of discipline. They became quite reckless in their determination to return and run all risks, although they well knew that these were enormous. Quietly at night they made their preparations, and the next morning dawned upon an almost deserted camp.

The situation was one of the most galling and vexatious conceivable. A leader could scarcely have been in a harder case. With the mere remnant of his caravan, nearly all of whom were sick and dying men ; with the rainy season about to begin, increasing tenfold the difficulties and hardships of travel; and with his own strength on the verge of complete prostration through the sufferings. he was undergoing—what was left for him to do except to submit to the inevitable, and take what measures he could to stave off utter disaster?

The Atonga, overtaken by hastily despatched messengers, agreed to pause for a palaver. Neither appeals nor bribes, however, availed to turn the desperate men from their purpose. He thought himself fortunate in the end when, in his eagerness to save this part of his plan from hopeless defeat, he succeeded in striking a compromise. The main body of the men would camp there under Grant and Wilson (who would be as hostages for his return), while a small party should accompany himself to Sitandas.

Everything in his circumstances counselled haste in this business. As soon, therefore, as he could get his selected following ready for the road, he was off under pressure. Footing it at the rate of over twenty miles a day, he traversed the country of Urengè, reaching the borders of Manica-land at the village of Kwa-Chepo. There he had hoped to make the desired treaty with the chief Chepepo. That chief, however, had been driven to settle in a new place twenty miles further to the north, owing to the raids of a Portuguese ivory and slave-trader from Zumbo—who, by the way, was met at Kwa-Chepo, his compound significantly crowded with the fruits of his last raid, boys, girls, and cattle.

At Chepepo's, whither the explorer now hastened, he learned that the chief Sitanda was dead; and, as it was thus useless to proceed further, he once more set his face towards the camp. Travelling resolutely on, with no guide but his compass, and amidst the anguish of a rapidly increasing illness, he re-entered Mshiri's on the tenth day, having covered during his absence a distance little short of two hundred miles.

If his return to the camp was beclouded by anxious forebodings about his own condition, it was not brightened by the news that met him. Not only had the epidemic continued its ravages among the men, but it had spread to the natives, and, to the horror of the people, even one of the chief's sons had fallen a victim. A new peril had thus been incurred, which could not be ignored. There must be no delay for rest. They could not leave the place an hour too soon.

Thus, under the most dolesome conditions, the return

journey was commenced on the 18th of November. Happily for the men the epidemic had apparently spent its force; and with reviving spirits, as they knew themselves facing homewards, they soon began to improve. It was all the other way, however, with the stricken leader. With a resolute heart he strode on for a short time determined to set an example of endurance, although "every step was marked by a throb of pain." But there were limits beyond which even his brave will could not sustain him, and soon it became plain that the only condition of progress was that he should submit to be carried. A hammock was hastily constructed, as comfortable as their scanty resources would permit, and in this he was borne over the remaining six hundred miles to Blantyre.

The story of what he endured in those dreary weeks that followed, and of how, amid the distractions of his sore trouble, he had to do his endeavour to direct the affairs of the caravan, and fulfil by the way the objects of the expedition, need not be dwelt upon in detail. A sufficiently suggestive glimpse of the predicament is given in the following quotation from a letter, subsequently written, to Miss Noake :—

"It would have given you a proper 'scunner' to have seen my caravan at some stages, with its long tail of disease-struck beings, although I have no doubt you would have been moved to greater pity if you had seen my men carrying my skeleton in a hammock on the last stage of the journey, when I had tramped on until I had thus indecently disrobed my bones of their proper covering, and exhausted all the vital force belonging to me. I really believe you would have objected to put your hands on such fevered remnant of a brow as was then left me. ... You can imagine what a jolly Christmas and New Year I had, with my men playing pitch and toss with my remains!"

Thus, in a grim race with Death, he steadfastly agonised towards his goal, pressing on over ridge, and dale, and swollen flood in the mountainous land which separated them from Lake Nyassa. They crossed the Lunsefra River and its tributaries, traversed the hundred and fifty miles of toilsome up-and-down country between the Chifukunga Mountains and the Muchinga Mountains, reaching the River Loangwa on December 5th.

It was hoped that from this point they would be able to strike straight east to Blantyre. But, as in the Kafuè Basin, the Portuguese slave-traders had transformed the country into a pathless and silent wilderness, into which no man would venture as their guide. The only course remaining for them was the unwelcome one of proceeding by way of Mpesini's.

The aspect of the country they had now to cross was interesting in the extreme—interesting in its charmingly picturesque variety, interesting, above all, in the evidence which every mile afforded of its great natural resources and abundant possibilities. A teeming population, and the appearance on every hand of vast flocks and herds, sufficed to show that here at least want was unknown. But if Nature was attractive, man was very much the reverse. Numbers and abundance had fostered arrogance, and in the overbearing attitude of the natives there were unpleasant omens of trouble in store for the caravan. As for Mpesini himself, it was not without cause that he had got his evil name. He proved, in fact, to be an arbitrary and bloodthirsty savage; and his attitude towards his British visitors was not ameliorated by the fact that he had at his ear, as adviser, a man in the pay of the Portuguese. Be that as it may, there was no getting to terms with him, and every hour of delay seemed to make his hostility more pronounced and his conduct more unpleasant. When at last they were compelled, after three days, to move on from the immediate neighbourhood of his kraal, they were attacked for plunder on the way by a party of warriors, and it was only by the most vigorous resistance, under the direction of Grant, that they were able to drive their assailants off.

Their relations with Mpesini were not to end with this *fracas*.  It had happened, unfortunately, that in the defence one of the assailants had been speared.  The incident roused the Zulu bully to fury.  Presently the alarming news came to their ears that an onslaught in force had been planned, and, if they were to save themselves from disaster, prompt measures must be taken.  With the leader *hors de combat*, and the caravan weakened and demoralised by its troubles, besides being very insufficiently armed, it was vain to think of making a successful stand in fight.  The only alternative was flight.  Under the cover of darkness, therefore, they silently disappeared, though not without repeated narrow escapes from detection, and, marching all night and far on into the next day, rested not until they had left Mpesini's country a long way behind.

It wanted but two days of further effort to bring them into the kindlier atmosphere of Mwasi's village.  There they rested for two days—the last of 1890 and the first of 1891.  On the 4th of January they stood once more on the escarpment of the plateau, looking upon Lake Nyassa with its verdant bordering plain.

At Kota-kota, which the remnants of the caravan entered on the same day, the journey was practically at an end; and not a moment too soon for Joseph Thomson.  He had been brought to the uttermost stage of exhaustion.  It was only his manful tenacity of spirit that had enabled him thus far to keep body and soul together.  Indeed, but for the invaluable relief from many of his cares, afforded by the devotion of his assistants, Grant and Wilson, he would almost certainly on this journey have found his grave in the continent which he had done so much to open up.

He was sorely in want of medical treatment.  But for

that he must needs wait, with what resolution he could summon to his aid, for a whole month, pending the arrival of the lake steamer, *Domira*. Thanks, however, to the rest and the good milk supplied by the chief Jumbè, he was enabled to regain sufficient strength for the final effort. On the 14th of February he signalised his thirty-third birthday by resuming his course to Blantyre, and after five days of further painful travelling he was borne into that hospitable haven, to find a sympathetic welcome from the missionaries.

From leaving Kota-kota till his return to it five months later he had travelled at least 1250 miles, about 950 of which represented entirely unexplored territory; and through the treaties which he had been able to conclude with chiefs by the way, he had secured for his employers the entire political, trading and mining rights over an area of no less than 40,000 square miles. From an agricultural point of view, this vast territory was by far the most promising he had seen in Africa. A large proportion of it is simply holding its riches for the incoming of the planter; and as the climate is for the most part excellent and the mineral indications favourable, no one can foresee the extent to which, in the near future, colonising work might be carried on over the area thus acquired.

As soon as possible after the arrival at Blantyre, Grant was despatched to the Cape with the fruits of the expedition in the shape of treaties. Meantime, Joseph Thomson was fain to submit himself to the skilful attentions of the medical missionary, Dr. W. Scott. That gentleman, by such measures as were available, was able to alleviate considerably the prostration of the sufferer and to mitigate the most distressing symptoms. But it was soon evident that the case was of too serious a nature and too badly complicated to be adequately dealt with except by surgical treatment at the hands of a specialist. The immediate aim, therefore, was to get up his strength sufficiently to permit of his attempting with safety the journey home.

In this, some small headway was made; but in the exceedingly adverse physical circumstances in which he was placed, his advance towards convalescence could not but be of the slowest.

On the 26th of April he wrote to his friend, Mr. Noble, at Cape Town:—

"Our trip would have been a pleasant one if it had not been for that loathsome monster, small-pox, which persistently dogged our footsteps. Then the illness which laid hold of me made life a weary and painful burden to me during three-fourths of our journey, and has left me even yet with but the shadow of my former strength.

"I am glad to say, however, that I have vastly improved since I came to Blantyre, and might, indeed, have been a little better but that for the most part I have been without a doctor—he having gone to Quilimane as escort to Mrs. Scott, who has been sadly shaken by the recent series of disasters, which have so crippled the staff of the Blantyre Mission. Happily, Dr. Scott is expected back every day now, and once he is here I hope to push ahead a little faster.

"I must conclude that, for an African traveller, my lines have fallen in pleasant places. Blantyre is really a charming place, picturesque in aspect, delightful in climate, not lacking in good society or in the more material good things of this life. I have been very much struck by the excellent way in which the mission is conducted here. The church that has been built is to me the most wonderful thing I have seen in Africa, when it is considered who planned it and the people who built it.

"Since Grant left us a rather melancholy incident has happened here. A fine young fellow, called Wilson, was with us in our expedition and had the best of health all through—was, indeed, a stone heavier on his return. I sent him off to do a bit of treaty-making work to the west, which he accomplished successfully. He had almost

re-reached Blantyre when he got such a dose of fever that
he was brought in nearly dead. He did, in fact, die,
despite our best efforts, in a few days. He was a capital
fellow, and I had looked forward to taking him again with
me. Such, however, are the ups and downs of African
travel.

" I often wonder how you are all getting on at the Cape
—I mean my friends of course. I have had serious
thoughts of coming south for a change, and may yet do
so if I do not get better a little faster."

The loss of Wilson above referred to was, indeed, an
occasion of real distress to him, for he had become sincerely
attached to the young man as well as to his other assistant,
Grant. " It would be impossible for me," he testified
elsewhere, " to over-estimate the character of Mr. Wilson.
He possessed all the qualities to make him successful in
the life he had chosen, and I am sure a more willing and
cheerful worker never travelled in Africa. . . . It was the
oft-told African story of a bright and promising career
brought prematurely to a close."

In the beginning of May a telegram from Mr. Rhodes,
telling him to await further instructions, made him aware
that some new project was afoot. Not till July, however,
was his curiosity satisfied; and then curiosity gave place
to anxious perplexity. The instructions came in the form
of a characteristically laconic letter from Rhodes :—

" Thanks for your letter. You seem to have had the
plagues of Egypt.

" I want you to get M'siri's. I mean Katanga. The
King of the Belgians has already floated a company for it,
presumably, because he does not possess it. Next time
you arrive there no doubt Arnot will be there, so matters
will be all right. . . . You must go and get Katanga. If
you are too seedy send Sharpe with Grant.—Yours
C. J. RHODES."

Joseph Thomson was, indeed, at that moment "too seedy" for anything. He could, in fact, do very little more than move about the place in invalid fashion, and the root of all his suffering was still undealt with. It seemed like marching to death to set out on such a mission. But in his chivalrous view of things duty was more than life. Sharpe was not available, and a task so difficult and delicate wanted an experienced hand to deal with it. He would go himself! though he should have to be carried all the way, as, indeed, seemed most probable.

Having once settled this matter with himself, he at once set about his preparations with all the vigour of will, if not of body, which was characteristic of him—making sport the while at the only too evident tokens of his weakness. It is in this vein of apparently rollicking high spirits that he writes at the time to a literary correspondent in London. Here, parenthetically, we may note that meantime Mr. H. H. Johnston had been appointed to represent the majesty of England in Nyassaland; and those who are acquainted with the new commissioner's published views as to the luxuries and amenities necessary in a pioneer life will understand the playful references of the letter.

"A couple of days ago I was preparing for a run south to the Cape—a run which probably would not have ended till I had precipitated myself, if not upon your manly breast, at least into the bosom of your family. To-day all that is changed, and I am preparing for another run north and west—opening the way, as it were, for the approach of the 'neat, elegant, and debonair figure' of a gentleman not unknown to the columns of *The Times*. My change of route is due to a letter from Rhodes which rang in my ears like the bugle call to an old cavalry horse. So here I am on the prance.

"Of course my object, as you have already informed

a discerning public, is to consolidate the treaties with which I have already littered M'siri's kingdom, and so raise an impassable barrier to all comers who may have the impudence to venture into those parts, which an all-wise Providence has clearly designed for those who sail under the colours of the B. S. A. It is to be hoped that Providence has also designed me as the humble instrument; for, alas! Joseph is not as he has been. The 'cancers,' the 'internal tumours,' and such like diseases to which he is a prey, will be sadly against him doing the seventy miles a day in which he rejoiced of old. These colossal strides must now give place to modest marches of fifteen or twenty miles *carried*, ye gods! in a *machilla*.

"However, I hope to come up smiling by taking care to supply myself with marmalades, jams, and other luxuries of that nature to which I have been accustomed. I would like to have adopted a higher level, but alas! Grant has stupidly brought up with him only two tins of *paté de foie gras* and one tin of *caviare*. However, we shall keep these, in case of our having H. H. J. to dinner, so that he may be deceived into supposing that such is our daily fare, and that we don't belong to the marmalade class. Sheets for our bed are beyond us, and I don't know about table napkins. . . .

"To tell you the truth, I am very far from being in a fit condition to travel, and hence the late intention of going south. Certainly my recovery has been going on at a dreadfully slow pace. During all these months I have been here, I have only twice walked as much as a mile, and my days and nights have been anything but delightful. . . .

"I expect to leave here about the 20th, and if all goes well, I shall be back in January, if not December. I shall then proceed to the Cape, and home to be renovated and generally overhauled, while I bask in the smiles of my fair friends and enjoy in a reflected way the sweets of other people's domestic bliss."

In a fortnight the arrangements for the new journey were complete.  Another day, and the caravan would have been *en route*.  But, just at the last moment, there was an unexpected interference, apparently at the instance of the British Government.  As in a dissolving view the situation was transformed.  The expedition to Katanga, happily as it turned out, was at an end.  So, unhappily, was also Joseph Thomson's work in Africa, although as yet he knew it not.

A month later he said good-bye to Blantyre, leaving in that interesting community, as everywhere, the kindliest memories of his stay; and on the 18th of October he once more landed on English soil.

# CHAPTER XII.



THE explorer's arrival had been anxiously anticipated. In his letters home he had, with instinctive considerateness, made light of his bodily troubles. But the long unexplained delay of eight months at Blantyre was ominous, and meantime evil rumours of various sorts with respect to his condition had leaked out. It was variously reported in this country that he was suffering from cancer, tumour in the bladder, and other things. These circumstances had prepared his friends to expect a change in his appearance, and, when he did arrive, it wanted no skilled eye to note the traces of much sore suffering. He had left for the Zambesi the picture of health and strength, but now, despite the fact that his rest at Blantyre had done much to improve his physical condition, he was but the shadow of his former self.

It was with a sense of unspeakable relief that he reached once more his father's fireside; for with his wonted hopefulness he assured himself that his native air and the treatment of experts would speedily put matters to rights with him. Merciful was the cloud that veiled from his knowledge the immediate future— the weary months and years of stress for body and mind which lay before him. Strong man as he was, even his

T

brave heart could not have borne the anticipation of his coming experiences.

In his active career the courage of a manly soul had been tried in a thousand forms by privations and hardships and difficulties, by wild beasts and savage men. But not less terribly was his courage to be tried in another way. For now he had entered upon his "Valley of Shadows," when, amid the consciousness of weakness, the depressing sense of enforced inaction, and the never-ceasing burden of pain, yet with intellect clear and aspiration unquenched, he could but stand and see his hopes crumbling, and his bright dreams of further usefulness vanish into thin air. For him at many a coming eventide too real was to be the feeling thus voiced by another great sufferer :—

> "The day is over, the feverish careful day;
> Can I recover strength that has ebbed away?
> Can even sleep such freshness give,
> That I again should wish to live?
> Let me lie down!....Give me a quiet grave;
> Release and not reward, I ask;
> Too hard for me life's daily task."

A month at Gatelawbridge enabled him to overcome the more immediate effects of his long and trying voyage, *via* Cape Town, to this country. In November he removed to Edinburgh for the special treatment to which he had been looking forward. There he remained for the next seven months, six of which were spent at 3, Cassells Place, Leith, the house of his loving friends Dr. and Mrs. Calder, who devoted themselves with every art of tender ministry to the alleviation of his miseries.

It was hoped at first that ordinary medical remedies might secure the object aimed at, and enable Nature once more to bring about healthful conditions. A few weeks, however, were sufficient to prove the necessity of more heroic measures. An operation presented itself before him as a thing inevitable.

When he had once made up his mind to this "short cut" to health (as he punningly called it), he must needs do his best as in other hard cases to exercise his wit upon it.   In December, he writes thus to Gilmour :—

"You will no doubt be asking prosaically : ' But how are you getting on ?'   As if I, in my impaired health, could endure any such abrupt demand to stand and deliver my news!   Why not let my soul, under the influence of the friendly muse, get away from its inflamed surroundings and seek peace, if only momentary, in a more serene and genial environment ?   Must I always remain in a vale of tears—always a subject of exploration and medical treatment ?   No : ten thousand times no !   Though you cut my wings and pile leaden ballast upon me, yet will I aspire to rise on such angel pinions as I can borrow ! . . .   Still borrowed wings are hard to work, and despite them I sink back to earth and the weary woes that mar its beauty.

"And now must I be realistic, and lift up my voice and weep over the evil days that have come upon me ? In my sore affliction, sitting as it were in ashes, clothed in sackcloth, shall I give my language something of the inflammatory quality which characterises part of my inner man, giving vent, as it were, to the music of the lower spheres ?   But no, I will be calm. . . .

"Possibly you have heard through Keltie some coherent statement of my case.   In general health I have nothing to complain of ; but in regard to my special trouble I can only write in groans.   There must have been some improvement ; nevertheless, in one of my most harassing symptoms the reverse seems to be the case.   I have rarely half an hour's peace of mind night or day, and that keeps me much reduced bodily and mentally.   I get out for a short drive now and then, but get mighty little pleasure from it.   Cold affects me very keenly. Without some more drastic treatment, this sort of thing may go on for months.  But my patience has got to the end of its tether.  I have quite made up my mind to undergo an operation."

To Miss Noake he also writes about the same time:—

"I have now been two months in the hands of the doctors, who have done precious little to relieve my tortures. I have finally resolved to submit to the surgeon with the beginning of the year.  The prospect is not a pleasant one, but the shortest cut will be the best.  You will now understand what a jolly time is before me for Christmas and New Year—drowning my sorrows in soda and milk, feasting on slops, having 'a high old time' in the delightful seclusion of my bedroom, charmed with the occasional visits of my doctor and nurse.  Well, it is a poor heart that never rejoices, and I am going to rejoice in the thought that matters might be worse with me. . . .  It is certainly rather difficult for me at present to take a cheerful view of life, but unless one goes in for suicide there's no use moping."

In the same spirit he writes a week later :—

"My Christmas has been made additionally merry by a sore thumb.  Nothing could be more jolly than to be confined to the house with a complication of troubles, and not to be allowed through pain to bite one's own thumb, and otherwise enjoy one's self as may be thought proper.  However, I shall take comfort in the thought that that is nothing compared to the fun that is in store for me on Monday week and the days that follow, when I shall have the opportunity of drawing what I like on my bedroom ceiling, when I am tired of reading novels and counting my fingers.  Truly I have much to be thankful for, when I think of the people who can go out in the cold and the rain and make pretence of enjoying themselves, while I, nicely tucked up in bed, have no fear of

cauld blasts' or other accompaniments of winter in
puir auld Scotland.

"How shall I thank you for the flowers you sent to
gladden my heart and my olfactory organs?  There was
a time when I would have soared high in answering their
nice message.  But, alas, a heavy weight clings to my
feet; my poetical wings are cut and singed, and I can
only flop about like an ostrich trying to fly!"

In the beginning of January, 1892, he removed to a
private nursing home in Forres Street, Edinburgh, where
Professor Chiene was to operate upon him.  It was
thought that a fortnight would suffice to fit him for
a return to his friends in Leith.  But here a new disappointment was in store for him.  The operation was
quite successfully performed, but owing to the low condition to which the vital forces of his constitution had
been reduced, the healing process advanced only with
the most tantalising tediousness.  It was full six weeks
before he had the happiness of saying good-bye to the
room which he had come to look upon as a veritable
prison-house.

The net result of the drastic treatment was, as he had
to confess to himself, not cheering.  The original illness
remained in as irritating a form as ever.  Every day,
moreover, a weakening malarial fever, running to 102°
to 103°, returned persistently upon him.  Still he
struggled away bravely against his depression.  "I have
not much to boast of," he said, "yet I must be hopeful
that with time I shall once more be able to take a walk
*somewhere*, if not across Africa."

This was written on the 16th of February; but not
many days after it seemed as if even this modest hope
was doomed to summary extinction.  One after another
the demons of trouble, begotten of his African hardships
and toils, were finding him out in his disabled condition
and, vulture like, settling upon him as their prey.  In

this case it was some malignant complication in connection with liver  and kidneys that suddenly developed. The illness was as alarming as it was sudden.  It brought him to the very door of death, and it was long before he crept away from that undesirable neighbourhood.

"I have had a bad time of it," he writes to Mrs. Gilmour in the end of March.  "However, matters are better again, though every now and then another attack of fever throws me back.  You would hardly recognise me if you saw me now.  I am almost a skeleton, and as weak as a baby.  To some extent this is due to my lack of sleep.  I see nothing before me but long, painful, or rather worrying, months of convalescence.  It is all sufficient to make me despair.

"We had a visit from Barrie last Friday on his way north.  He says he is going to start a new novel at once —scene chiefly in London.  His visit was of course quite the best of stimulants for me, bringing as he did such a budget of news about all my London friends.  Heigho! When shall I get down to see them all ?

" You must excuse me if I don't write any more, as I am still in a brain muddle and hardly know how to write."

Independent of his own weakness and suffering, there were other circumstances to cast him down, especially the death about this time of several intimate acquaintances, such as Colonel Grant, and II. W. Bates, whose friendship and wise help had so cheered him in the beginning of his career as an explorer.  To Edward Clodd, who subsequently acted as the biographer of the latter, he thus speaks (10th April) of his sad experiences :—

"My new illness happened on the day of dear old Bates' funeral, so that I nearly started off to search for him and otherwise explore the Elysian Fields.  However, thanks to the ' best advice ' that Edinburgh could offer,

I was dissuaded from proceeding there for the time being. From that illness I have never quite recovered. Daily attacks of fever, along with the eternal worry of my original trouble, keep me crushed to the ground. I am little better than a bag of bones. The specialists are quite at a loss what to make of my case. They are at present having a series of investigations made to see if the real seat of the trouble is not in the kidneys. If it proves to be so, then that will mean another operation, and where it is all going to end the Lord only knows. Meanwhile I have not lost sight of my project to explore the Elysian Fields."

The conviction that his case had quite bewildered the doctors grew upon him. He felt that he was merely the subject of experiments. And, as the weary days dragged on with their monotony of suffering, and the end of the spring found him still at mental and physical zero, through continuous pain and nervous distraction and sleeplessness, he resolved to take the law into his own hands. He would see what the quiet, the sunshine and the country air of home would do for him. The journey of four hours was a heroic measure in his exhausted condition, and his proposal to undertake it alarmed his friends; but there was no turning him from his purpose. The beginning of May therefore saw him rolling homeward in charge of his brother, with his temperature at 104°. His resolute spirit triumphed once more, and he reached his destination without complete collapse.

The change and the invigorating influence of home did have a reviving effect upon him. Anew the stirrings of hope began to be felt. In acknowledging a gift of roses sent to him from the sunny south he writes to the sender:—

" I can now find breath to thank you for your delightful present—though in some respects the sight of them makes me sigh at my inability to fly to where the roses grow and the east wind does not blow, . . . The doctors have practically given me up, but the roses tell me to be of good cheer, for the spring, such as it is, has come and the summer is at hand, and all things bloom and become green.   And why, then, should I not regain the freshness of other days and flourish like the green bay tree ? "

The sight of the country bursting into summer life and beauty was itself a quickening influence, and fain was he to respond to the spirit of life asserting itself all around him.

" We have had rain," he says, " for the last three days, and the benefit produced has been enormous.   It has been like springing from winter into summer, so far as the vegetation is concerned.   I am longing to be able to walk up as far as the White Quarry, and over to Crichope Linn.   The one must be beautiful with primroses—the other with newly bursting ferns.   But this fever and all the other worries are too much for even my will or my wishes, and like an old worn-out man I must sit over the fire, or try to find better rest in bed."

Slowly the general tone of his health improved, although the fundamental mischief obstinately refused to give way. Presently he was able to take a gentle drive now and then, whenever, in the course of an unpropitious summer, the sun would deign to shine and be genial.   On such occasions how his heart swelled with the joy of Nature !
In July he writes :—

" The country is looking superlatively lovely.   The wild flowers never displayed themselves in such profusion and beauty, nor the ferns in such luxuriant grace.   Woods and fields alike are in the richest greens, so that it is a continual delight to drive about in spite of cold and clouds."

The revival of strength very soon, as was to be expected, revealed itself in the rejuvenescence of his spirits, and presently he was blossoming out according to his wont with new " flowers of the soul." To his friend Keltic he thus unbosoms himself :—

" For some months back I have meditated over the idea of sending you a few notes of the Great Northern Wail, instalments of which I have from time to time sent south during the past winter. . . .

" The Wail has now less of the tone of despair—a wail with a something of promise in it, calculated to play upon the ear-drum of some fair damsel as with the eloquent melancholy of sighing woods, rippling streams, and other sounds of Nature. Consider me then as a sweetly sad Voice in the wilderness, on quest for ' beds of amaranth and moly '—a Voice ever ringing with a clearer and more inspiring note as it nears the Land of Promise—no longer echoing the bleat of mountain sheep or circling whaup, but gradually adapting itself to fill the air with the triumphant soaring song of the joyous lark.

" To return from the clouds and metaphors which may be mixed—the genuine Thomsonian blend—let me tell you in plainer language that, though I am still in the Vale of Tears, it no longer wears the aspect of a Valley of Death. The clouds are breaking overhead, and in the distance a way out appears. Each day finds my lungs better inflated, while I am putting on flesh and gradually re-acquiring the Adonis-like proportions so satisfying, let me hope, to the eye of my lady friends."

It was also inevitable with the quickening of the pulse of life that he should begin to crave after some employ-ment, if it were only to release him from a depressing self-consciousness. At this time a very pleasant distrac-tion suggested itself in the fitting up of a little museum, wherein he might bestow the many *souvenirs* of his travels. This offered scope not only for his ingenuity but for his artistic taste ; and for a time the directing of the workmen and the arranging and grouping of the various trophies gave full outlet for all the little energy he had to spend. When the work was at last complete, he felt quite proud of his show-room. And, indeed, in the quaint and beautiful treasures which it contained, it presented an exhibition quite unique in its way—an exhibition which gradually got to be known as one of the sights of the neighbourhood, and which he was delighted to explain to visitors. There, too, at times he rejoiced to sit amid the memorials of his varied exploits, and dream himself anew into fellowship with the stirring days of the past.

By the beginning of August he had so far pulled himself together that he thought he might venture upon a brief visit to the British Association meeting at Edinburgh. He was craving to see old friends and have speech of them, if it were only for an hour or two. The pilgrimage was still trying, but he returned without mishap. To find himself brought once more into touch with the stream of scientific life operated as a tonic for his mind. We do not wonder, therefore, to find him, immediately after his return, beginning to make plans for renewed literary activity. An elaborate report for the British South Africa Company, two articles on Morocco for a magazine, a paper on his last journey for the Royal Geographical Society, and, finally, an article for the *Contemporary Review* on "The Uganda Problem," abundantly, and withal healthily, occupied all the available hours of his autumn sojourn at home.

As the latter subject was keenly stirring the public mind at the time, he felt that, having been the first to open the way to Uganda (by his Masai-land journey), he was called to say something upon it.

The Uganda problem amounted simply to this: Shall we retain it, and if so, how shall we best administer it?

To the first part of the problem he had but one possible answer to give: certainly we should retain it. Disastrous blunders had been committed and golden opportunities thrown away through the neglect of his repeated warnings and appeals at the time of the Emin Pasha Relief Expedition. But there we are (he said), and there we must remain to retrieve, if possible, past mistakes. The country demands it, and our honour is involved in it. Commercially, indeed, Uganda is at present of no great value. Yet some day something will be made of it, and we must look ahead and secure scope for the enterprise of coming generations. There could be no doubt, however, that *morally* our holding of that great central province would be an enormous gain —a giant's step forward in our anti-slave-trade policy.

In answering the second part of the problem, he stood forth once more as the advocate of Chartered Companies. Direct government from the Foreign and Colonial Office he had seen reason profoundly to distrust, as simply a laying of the dead hand on the development of Africa. The East Africa Company had indeed erred and suffered in many things, but it had gained experience, and in the light of what the Niger Company and British South Africa Company had accomplished elsewhere, he had not lost faith in the principle of chartered companies, even as represented in East Africa. Let the East Africa Company, therefore, be empowered and encouraged to deal with the situation, and doubtless the best interests of civilisation would be served.

What then about a railway to Uganda? Well, the answer would depend upon how far this country would feel repaid by *moral* results. On the commercial side of the undertaking, he would say there was no prospect of profitable returns for a very long time. But, as regards moral effects, there could be no doubt that its influence would be of simply incalculable value. Next to holding Uganda itself, the construction of the railway would be the most killing blow to the slave trade which the end of the century would be able to show—in doing away with the need of porters, and rendering the administration at once cheap and effective in its action. If three millions would provide such a railway, this country would be abundantly rewarded for the expenditure, in the good which would thus be done in the opening up of the continent. Such were his views.

By the time these articles were off his hands, the raw fogs of late October were beginning to assert their chilling influence, and he was "wearying to be off with the swallows after the blessed sunshine." Physically, he had still been steadily, if not rapidly, reaching forward to convalescence, although never allowed to forget for a day or night that the root trouble still remained to be dealt with. The cheering consciousness of greater strength nerved him to a new resolution to face further surgical treatment. Haply it might even yet be given to him to have days unmarred by pain and nights no longer rendered miserable by involuntary vigils!

With this prayerful hope in his heart, he hied him to London in the beginning of November, and there in another nursing home he invoked the skilful attentions of Dr. Buxton Browne. Thanks to his improved physical state, good results were immediately apparent, and every day brought with it some further cheering symptom. It was with no small measure of grateful joy that he could say in a letter (November 20th) to Mr. McKie:—

"I have once more escaped from quarantine. I am greatly improved, and I once more find life worth living, with Africa looming up invitingly ahead." In that same letter he says: "I have been lunching with Rhodes, and last night I dined with Nansen, the Arctic explorer, so you see matters are beginning to look up with me."

The outlook was indeed brightening. Already the prospect of fitness for active employment was an influence which tingled with thrilling force through all his being, stranded as he had so long been in helpless unquiet idleness. In his eagerness to be up and at some work, he was almost impatiently counting the moments till the call would anew come to him. Indeed, he even sought to anticipate the call, by offering himself to head the new mission to Uganda which the Government had resolved upon. He did not really expect the appointment in his partially convalescent state; moreover, he had so plainly spoken out his mind about Government bungling, that he was quite well aware he was not a *persona grata* in official quarters; but the application helped to keep up the pleasant feeling that "things were moving" again in his life, and so far it answered its purpose.

On the 22nd of November he once more appeared before the Royal Geographical Society, his paper this time being entitled, "To Lake Bangweolo and the Unexplored Region of British Central Africa." He had his wonted gratifying reception, a crowded meeting and generous applause, followed by an embarrassing multitude of invitations; he had indeed frequently to "flourish the hospital flag" to save himself from his friends.

His application with reference to Uganda came to nothing, as he had anticipated. But he had already another string to his bow.

"Rhodes," he informs his friend McKie, "has been sounding me about going out as the manager of a great territory north of the Zambesi, but to the west of my recent travels. This will suit me very well, and Rhodes as a 'boss' is of all bosses the most satisfactory to work for, the very antipodes of McKinnon, who is a man with imperial views and a parish grasp of them, and who expects to have slaves to deal with, not *men.*"

No doubt it was with reference to this new proposal that he announced to another correspondent: "I expect to be off again to South Africa about March for new adventures, and no doubt new diseases, to keep my mind and body occupied."

The words were in a sense prophetic; but the fulfilment was sadly different from his anticipation. He did go to South Africa in March; but it was as a disheartened invalid on a new health-quest. He had just begun to drink the cup of happiness, in his anticipation of being able to do some further good and useful work for the world, when it was suddenly dashed from his lips.

*A propos* of a smart and flattering word portrait of him in a society paper, which tickled his sense of humour greatly, he wrote thus to one of his intimates :—

"You have no idea what a great man I have become, or you would treat me with more awe than you seem disposed to do. What do you think of me having blossomed out into 'the best dressed African traveller in London?' There's fame for you! I blush, however, while I quote further that I am 'a deuced handsome fellow,' with 'frock coats built by the best tailor money can procure, and standing over six feet in his patent leathers.' No wonder it is a mystery to the writer 'that Joseph Thomson of Africa has up to this escaped matrimony,' for he is 'blessed with a plenitude of good looks, and has a tidy sum of siller!' After that there is nothing for you to do but fall down and worship. Fame, however, has come so suddenly that I have not been able to realise it properly, and I am going off to the wilderness of Eastbourne for meditation until Monday. . . . I have been very much bothered with a cold these last few days, which has prevented my appearance in Piccadilly to give tone to that haunt of fashion."

The cold, which he thus light-heartedly referred to, proved to be more serious than he imagined. When he reached his friends at Eastbourne, he had to confine himself to the house all the time. The attack was further aggravated by the return journey, and he was only fit for his bed. In the evening after his return he entertained Dr. and Mrs. Hugh Robert Mill at dinner in his rooms. He had promised to attend afterwards the hundredth representation of his friend Barrie's play, "Walker

London," and, when his guests were leaving, he would insist on keeping his word, notwithstanding the earnest remonstrances of both. The result was an attack of severe pneumonia.

The New Year of 1893 dawned upon him lying in uttermost prostration, hovering between life and death. The illness was one quite exceptional in its character, no definite crisis ever being passed, and curious complications arising, due, as the doctors thought, to the presence of African fever. One thing, however, was only too soon evident to those who were in attendance, and that was that the lung was seriously affected. In the whole circumstances, the case was felt to be peculiarly grave. The only hope for him lay in his being able to gather sufficient strength to allow of his facing a voyage to South Africa. From Africa he had come fifteen months before to be cured, and now, in the new situation of things, he must simply reverse the process.

It seemed to the medical experts very much a forlorn hope; but, weakened though his magnificent constitution was, from the almost incalculable strain of his troubles during the past two years, there was still in him a reserve of vitality which surprised his advisers. By the end of January he had rallied sufficiently to be taken to Bournemouth in charge of a nurse. Thither the writer of this narrative hastened also, in the hope that a breath of the home fellowship might cheer the sufferer's hours of prostration, and keep him from being quite crushed in spirit by his misfortunes. Other devoted friends, such as Dr. Calder, Mr. Thomas McKie, and Sir James Crichton-Browne, likewise rallied around him, personally or otherwise, and planned to show that loving sympathy which he so sorely needed.

As may well be supposed, he had little heart, as well as little strength, for correspondence with even his most intimate acquaintances. Only one of his notes, scribbled with a trembling hand, we give here, for the sake of the little self-description it contains.    It is to Mr. McKie (February 18) :—

" Your last letter, extolling the curative merits of Nature to the mind and soul diseased, found a most sympathetic reader in me.   From my boyhood upwards, I have been a kind of pantheist, revelling in the primrose banks, the singing of the birds, and the wimpling of the burns over stony beds.   Would that the primroses were there, and I fit to lie among them!   But there will, I am afraid, be many weary months before my eyes are gladdened by the golden glory of the simple flower.   To-day, here, one might well think they ought to be out and flourishing, so bright is the sunshine, and so balmy the air ; but, unfortunately, it is only the first good day we have had for over a week.

" Matters are with me much as when I wrote last.   It is a little discouraging to think that I have been here for over three weeks and can hardly say that I am any stronger than when I left London.   Whenever will I get to South Africa at that rate ?   However, I must hope for the best.   I trust you will soon let me have another of your inspiring letters."

His progress continued, indeed, to be tantalisingly slow. In London he had shrunk from the idea of going to South Africa.   Now he was longing to be off, seeing that even the genial climate of the south coast could do so little for him.   But, apparently, if he was to get away at all, he must resort to heroic measures, and set off weak or strong. With this resolution in his mind, he returned to London in the middle of March, to consult with his medical advisers.   They had much misgiving as to his proposal, for, as a matter of fact, they scarcely believed he could reach South Africa alive.   But, as he was determined in his purpose, they gave their reluctant consent.   Immediately, he arranged, therefore, to set sail in the *Hawarden Castle*

on the 25th. In his good-bye letter to Mr. McKie
(March 19) he says :—

"My next Sunday will be at sea, entering the dreaded
Bay of Biscay; but I shall be glad to have got away from
Modern Babylon, even as Lot no doubt rejoiced to find
himself safe out of the cities of the plain.

"My plans, after reaching the Cape, are still a trifle
hazy. Only I have to go up somewhere to the plateau,
and there spend two or three months on my back in the
open air. Isn't that a most agreeable prospect, in a place
where there are no primrose-banks, no shady trees with
singing birds, no wimpling burns, no grass even—only the
purest and driest of air, the bluest of skies, and sometimes
the hottest of suns?

"My news, as usual, are of the scantiest. For the time
being, the world circles round *me*, and I see and do
nothing. How I envy you your varied activities and
useful works! As for me, with a considerable part of my
lung gone, my African career is practically ended, and
what to turn to next is more than I can imagine. My
best plan will just be to stay out in South Africa, and do
my best to commence life anew. This is not exactly what
I had pictured for the latter half of my life."

Happily, the fears of his friends with respect to the
voyage were falsified. He stood it astonishingly well; in
fact, he improved day by day.

"Providence," he wrote, "was kind, and partly tempered the winds to the shorn lamb, and partly adapted the
shorn lamb to the stormy winds, so that I escaped, for the
first time in my experience, without an hour's sea-sick-
ness. Then everybody was very obliging, and Sir Donald
Currie and Sir Charles Mitchell (who were also taking the
voyage) vied with each other in doing everything they
could for my comfort."

At Cape Town Mr. and Mrs. Noble were waiting to

bestow upon him, as before, their hospitable attentions. In that place, however, it was not fitting that he should linger. On the advice of Dr. Douglas, he decided to hasten on to the station of Matjesfontein. The journey was, as far as possible, shorn of its discomforts, through the very kind invitation of Sir Charles Mitchell that he should go on with him in his special train. He describes his impressions on the journey thus :—

"The route from Cape Town to Matjesfontein lies along a narrow valley or glen enclosed by rugged barren rocky mountains of the most impressive and picturesque character. These grow wilder as we penetrate the country. Other changes occur simultaneously. The sky takes a deeper blue, the air grows cooler and drier, till it becomes perfectly exhilarating. At last, at an elevation of over three thousand feet, the track reaches the edge of the Karoo, and a few miles further on Matjesfontein, a little artificial oasis in a barren narrow valley, lies before us. Matjesfontein consists of a station, and a conglomeration of houses, which collectively form Logan's Hotel. Round these have been planted a number of eucalyptus trees, kept alive by irrigation. All else is monotonous, grass-less. The sole attractions are the matchlessly pure air, the floods of bright sunshine, the marvellously deep blue sky, and, at sunset, colours which transform the stern mountains into things of beauty and an endless joy. Yet here we have our electric light, our swimming-bath, and our lawn tennis ground."

In this lonely and secluded spot he spent a couple of months, getting what amusement he might from reading, watching the passing trains, and studying the varied characters who visited the hotel. Some of these were not a little interesting. For instance, he writes thus to his father :—

"There is a Mr. —— here, who, before he was twenty, had been in the diamond trade, a lieutenant in the French

army during the great war, a war-correspondent, a farmer
in Normandy. At twenty he had got out to Kimberley,
and since then he has been diamond-digger, gold-miner,
ostrich-breeder, engine-driver, farmer, clerk, newspaper-
reporter, editor, and finally, secretary to a millionaire,
who had commenced life selling oranges on the street,
and laid the foundations of his fortune in buying stray
diamonds out here. Then he has written a novel, divorced
a wife, shot a man, lost a hand, got every bone of his body
broken, or nearly so, and is now pretty nearly a physical
and moral wreck, thanks to his too great love for whisky.
That shows you what queer people one meets in such
places as South Africa."

A notability of a very different sort here made her
home—Olive Schreiner. He was very anxious to become
more closely acquainted with a personality so interesting;
but, concomitantly with a bettered condition in his general
health, he for some weeks lost his voice, and his conse-
quent inability to keep up a conversation, together with
the lady's natural reticence, almost entirely thwarted his
wish.

By the middle of June he had obtained all the advantage which Matjesfontein seemed likely to give him, and
the monotony of the place was beginning to have a
depressing effect. Mr. Rhodes, hearing of this, did an
exceedingly kind thing. He wrote, advising him to go
on to Kimberley, where there was equally healthful dry
air, and more life and enjoyment for an invalid. He
offered to place the De Beers house at his disposal as
long as he wished to remain, and even in a delicate way
proposed to make him free of his purse also, if there
should be any occasion for using it.

A proposal so generous and unexpected acted as a
tonic to his spirits.

"Talk of striking gold!" he writes laughingly to his
mother; "that is something like striking it rich! Only

a matter of putting out your hand—no mining, no trouble. Just like natural gas or petroleum, it comes right away. How nice and soft, too, to find such a portly bag between me and 'the rocks'!  I must really hurry up and get through my own humble purse, so that with a better grace I may attack his.  Meanwhile, I am going to be content with his house, which will have many advantages over an hotel, and I will take my meals at the club, which is just about opposite.  It is really very good of Rhodes to make me so free of his house and purse, considering that, after all, what little I have had to do with him has been purely on a business footing."

On June 19th he writes to his father :—

" Here I am once more in Kimberley, safe and—I was going to say sound—but for that I shall have to wait some time longer.  I hadn't well left Matjesfontein before I began to feel the benefit of the change, and I quite enjoyed the journey.  I have got a charming cottage all to myself, with a man and his wife at my command. This of course makes me very independent.  I am only sorry I did not come a month sooner.  Here there is greater warmth and steadier weather, and it is delightful to sit out in the veranda all day, though in the mornings the temperature falls to freezing point. . . . One thing is certain, I am sleeping and eating as I have not done since I landed in South Africa—and what better signs could a person have ? "

A medical examination led to a report which cheered him greatly.  Already the dry and equable climate of South Africa was telling beneficially upon him.  This was, no doubt, all the more distinctly the case owing to the fact that he had no hereditary weakness or predisposition to lung trouble to reckon with, and the natural soundness of his constitution was even now telling enormously in his favour.  These encouraging circumstances, with the quickening influence of the life and movement around him, brought back, for a time at least, something of his old spirit of jocularity. He must, in imagination, have a laugh with a kindred spirit, even though his own ills were the subject of his fanciful sallies. It is thus that he discourses to Gilmour (26th June):—

"For the last two months my soul has been in sore travail. I have been dying to write to you, and yet written I have not. My one hope is that you have divined why. . . . During all these years I have devoted myself to writing about nothing but geography, and now when geography fails me I am stumped. Thus doth Nature revenge herself for neglect!

"But why look back? With career closed and heart speechless, with my inside being gradually etherealised, and my outer man fading away, there is but one course open for me, and that is to prepare for an appropriate end in the warm, all-embracing Heart of Africa. With my knowledge of the country, I can foresee exactly every step of the road, every incident even unto the end; and to prevent mistakes I mean to sketch it all out and leave it behind. I am not going to run the risk of having some future biographer make out that I died of cramp in the stomach, when in reality I died (if I may say so while still alive) with the Spirit of Africa at my lips. You weep, *mon ami;* but dry your tearfu' ee. Let your soul only be possessed with a sweet melancholy till the right time comes.

"How will this title do? THE LAST TRAMP, or *How Thomson found the true Spirit of Africa, and pegged out his last claims on the Dark Continent.*

"How clearly it all rises before me! The uplifting of the 'banner with a strange device,' the pocket spittoon, and the bottle of cod-liver oil safely stowed away—the Ideal in one eye, Enthusiasm in the other. There! the supreme moment has come. On my bosom blazes a

placard, on which he who runs may read ' Excelsior ! "
with the announcement that I have got a cold, to explain
the absence of 'clarion notes.'  But it is on the closing
scene that I pride myself, and I flatter myself it will
' fetch ' the lady fellows of the Geographical, if there are
any.  I shall not spoil it, however, by even hinting what
it is like.

"But you doubtless want to know something of me.
What a fall is there to turn from the thought of Quests,
Destinies, and Spirits to *me!*  Why ask me to look back
on my movements, when the forward and future ones are
so much more romantic ? . . .

"I now write to you under the electric light, with
a good log fire blazing beside me.  I write, indeed, at
fever heat—a personal temperature of 103° in the best
shade my inner man can supply—so you might think I
did not need fires.  You will be interested to learn that
a kindly Providence has provided me with a counter-
irritant.  My kidneys have so far forgot their proper
duties that they have taken to manufacturing stones,
which with the sweat of my brow and sad groans, I
contrive to quarry and get to the surface.  Can this have
anything to do with early associations ?

"However, amid all the ups and downs, one thing is
quite clear; there is always gradual progress.  My last
week's experience of Kimberley has been most promising,
so in another month I may continue my journey north—
perhaps as far as Mafeking or Johannesberg."

A continuance of the healing process gave him some
heart to mingle with the society of Kimberley and to
interest himself in the life of the place.  At the club
where he took his meals there was always a competition
for seats at his table, and although he could seldom be
induced to give any reminiscences of his pioneering
exploits—a thing he always disliked doing—he was ever
ready to enter into discussion, or to take part in the

banter that was going; and, with his courteous ways and keen good-humoured badinage, he rapidly made friends all round.

The members of the club with whom he was more especially intimate jokingly spoke of him as "Topson." The reference was to a little incident that occurred at the club before it had become generally known who he was, and which a friend thus narrates: "On one occasion when the talk had drifted on to the native question, a leading legal luminary of Kimberley said in Thomson's presence that he had just been reading in an Eastern Province paper a remarkable article in which was mentioned 'Joseph Topson of Masai-land fame,' and remarked, 'I suppose that is the famous Thomson, the great African explorer.' He was rather nonplussed when he was confirmed by the 'great African explorer' himself. Thenceforth the name Topson stuck to him and was a kind of password on the lips of his familiars."

The time of his sojourn in Kimberley was coincident with the Mashonaland crisis and the expedition against the Matabele, which issued so victoriously and—as it seemed at the time—finally, for the Chartered Company's forces. In the questions involved in that crisis his sympathies were wholly with the Company. He felt indignant at the vacillation and irresolution of the home Government, and saw in the brilliant success of Rhodes and his little force a notable object lesson as to the usefulness of Chartered Companies. Rhodes, he thought, had proved himself in that affair "a born ruler of men," and he was heartily at one with all Kimberley in singing his praises. "In my opinion," he said, "there never was a more justifiable war, nor one more humanely carried through." He grew quite warm in inveighing against what he considered the "scandalous misrepresentations" which appeared here in such papers as *Truth*.

"It has," he remarked, "been a constant wonder to me,

who have always been a great admirer of the really splendid work that Labouchere has done at home, how in this case he has been seized with such a strange fit of madness, using recklessly any foul weapon that came to hand, so that he might blacken the character of the Company and their servants. More than once I have been on the point of writing to *The Times*, to do my little best to enlighten the public at home, who on things of this sort are so easily misled."

And again :—

"There is no better answer to all the attacks on Rhodes than the absolute faith reposed in him out here. If he is only working for himself, it is the people of these parts who should know it best, and who would suffer first. But they give their confidence, their money and their sons without stint into his keeping, satisfied that he is working in the best interests of the country, although not over-looking his own interests."

Joseph Thomson had, of course, had good reason personally to be favourably impressed with Mr. Rhodes. But he was too wide-awake and independent, and withal too conscientious a man to be an indiscriminate eulogist. A phenomenon like this "South African Dictator" was a subject that challenged a critical study ; and it was not difficult (especially when he came to see more nearly the man's influence and action in relation to the politics of the country) to recognise many things strange and even repellent in him.

"You mustn't imagine," he writes to Mr. McKie, "that I am an an out-and-out admirer of Rhodes. He is a man with terribly grave faults and many weak points. He is unscrupulous to a degree in carrying out his schemes, although no one who knows him properly can fail to be struck with intense admiration at the greatness of his plans and ideas. His education is that of the mining camp grafted on a University training, and he consequently often expresses himself and acts in a manner calculated to shock people at home, accustomed to the refined statesman full of suave language. How can you at home appreciate the character of a premier who delights to hang about a club bar, drinking whiskies and sodas, while with a word here and there between he settles the affairs of a country half the size of Europe. He would be an impossible person in England; but for South Africa he is simply the ideal man, and throughout the length and breadth of the country he is recognised as such."

The rapid healing of the lung secured for the invalid an increasing margin of strength, which he could pleasantly spend in outdoor exercise. In studying the various aspects of camp life about Kimberley, in driving and walking on the veldt, or down to Beaconsfield and the Pan, he found at first sufficient scope. Gradually he widened his rambling sphere. Drives out to the Vaal River Diggings, twenty miles off, to Mr. Paton's farm on the Hartz River, fifty miles off, and to the Jagersfontein Diamond Mines, eighty miles off, show the rising scale of his roving ambitions.

His advance in health was, however, not without its chastening interruptions. The glare and dust of Kimberley developed a very painful ulcer on his eyeball, and for two months, under bandages, he had to do without the sight of his friends or the solace of books. Then the old wearing bladder trouble returned upon him with its agonising worries, giving him further unwelcome opportunity of searching for "the soul of good in things evil." Few men have ever been more tried by a terrible concatenation of life's ills. Surely, if he had not been possessed with a heroic patience, and an almost phenomenal bravery of heart, he could hardly have survived his manifold baffling disappointments.

It is not surprising that in such circumstances he should have craved with a great hunger for the sympathy of those he loved, and that he should often have counted the hours till letters should come to keep up the sense of fellowship with friends in the home country. Here is one of his appeals to an intimate whose letters he prized, but whose absorbing occupation made his communications less frequent than was desired—and beneath the bantering pleasantry of it the undertone of yearning is sufficiently evident :—

"A thousand thanks for all your good intentions to write to me. Hardly a mail has passed without my hearing from some one or other that you were going to send me a letter. You have in this manner laid up much treasure for yourself in my heart. I mention this now because you may have thought that I did not sufficiently appreciate your aspirations. Some people, of course, would prefer a little performance to much aspiration—but you and I know better! Let us leave to the prosaic worm the satisfaction of looking back upon its little spiral of earth. For us, the clouds for chariots, hitched on to stars and comets! What though we become lost in space? We have for the time been nearer to the gods and the gates of heaven.

"With our friend Browning we know that to value a man we must take into account his aspirations as well as his acts. Thanks then, my dear ——, for all the letters you have intended to write. Thanks for the budget of news, the good stories which you have noted in your mind to communicate to me. How pleasant it has been for me to picture you from time to time—a glass of whisky at your side and a cigar between your teeth, your face lighted up with the virtuous intention of writing to me 'to-morrow, or the next day, or at least some day soon.' Such pictures as these keep a fellow from becoming pessimistic.

" 'Tis sad to think, however, that life is too short for performance.

> ' Le jour est brève ;
> Un peu d'espoir,
> Un peu de rêve,
> Et puis bon soir.' "

It was inevitable that the consciousness of reviving vigour should turn his mind to thoughts of action. His craving to be of use somewhere and somehow was irrepressible, and however often it might be thwarted, was ever anew asserting itself. Mr. Rhodes had given him to understand that as soon as he should be fit for work he had a mission for him in Mashonaland. The nature of that mission he did not know, but he kept it before his mind's eye with an ever-increasing eagerness to be launching his whole self into it. The life of an incipient colony, with its manifold unlovely features, was indeed a thing which he had no joy in contemplating, and with which he had no craving to identify himself. But, as he somewhat bitterly put it, "broken-down African travellers, like beggars, could not be choosers."

"You will not be surprised," he writes to Edward Clodd (December 4th), "that my thoughts are more and more turning towards Mashonaland, not as a thing to be looked forward to with pleasure, but as something inevitable, as my fate. After having given fifteen years of the best of my life to Africa and sacrificed my health in seeking ' the bubble reputation ' in its noxious wilds, I find I am only fit for Africa, having learned nothing that the world at home can make use of. I must therefore ' dree my weird ' with the best grace and heart possible, and bury up my hopes and dreams as quickly as I can. We are expecting Rhodes here soon on his way south from his victorious campaign, and I shall then have a talk with him and find out what sort of job I may look forward to. He has been extremely kind . . . I certainly have been extraordinarily lucky in finding so many good and generous friends wherever I have gone. That fact has, I think, kept me from becoming altogether soured by all the calamities I have experienced lately."

The opening of 1894 came to find him anxiously waiting for his marching orders. It was not till the beginning of February, however, that he got speech of Rhodes at Kimberley on his way south from Mashonaland. But it was just the height of the election fever, and "the great man" was surrounded by a crowd of people pushing their several interests, and had his mind occupied with a thousand other concerns. It was only a word, therefore, that he could get from him, and that pointed to further delay pending the settlement of matters with the home Government.

To have his hopes of getting once more into harness thus thrown back affected him, as may well be understood, with a profound feeling of disappointment. But when the first keen pain of this was past, the new delay had the effect of throwing him in upon himself in the way of self-questioning. Was he really sufficiently recovered to face afresh the hardships of pioneering life? And, now that his lung was practically cured, might it not be beneficial to consolidate his recovery by a summer spent in the atmosphere of his native place? The more he meditated on the matter, the more the longing grew upon him to visit once more the home scenes, and to look upon "the old familiar faces."

A month or two longer he lingered on enjoying the unrivalled weather of the South African early winter. But at last he took his resolution, and thus writes on April 10th to his friend Clodd:—

"I had made up my mind to go north this year, but unfortunately, as the time has come near to take the necessary steps, I have been compelled reluctantly to come to the conclusion that such a movement is quite premature. I find that, though in a measure practically cured, I have as yet accumulated no reserve of strength and health such as is essential to any one who means to face the hardships that still await the traveller even in Matabeleland. I foresee that I would run great risks of once more breaking down—and to break down again would be the death of me.

"In these circumstances I have made up my mind to run home and once more see my friends under happier conditions than I saw them last, and under their inspiring influence lay in a supply of courage to face whatever life may have in store for me, as also the necessary fighting material in the way of blood and muscle, and refitted organs.

"If nothing unexpected comes in the way, then, I shall be with you all in the beginning of June. Pray that there be sunshine and dry bracing breezes to greet me on my arrival, and make me feel that England is still the country for me."

From Cape Town, on May 16th, he said his farewell to Kimberley, and also to Africa, in the following telegram: "Just leaving, with grateful recollections of Kimberley Club, climate, hospitality, and good fellowship. Good-bye, till we meet again."

# CHAPTER XIII.

## THE CLOSE OF THE PILGRIMAGE.

It was with no small regret and misgiving that his friends in South Africa saw him preparing for so soon leaving its shores. They feared, not without reason, the effect of the humid and uncertain climate of the home country upon him, and did what they might to change his purpose. But when he had thought over a plan and come to a resolution, he was not easily to be moved from it. It was one of the defects of his qualities. He had been forced by the very circumstances of his career to rely so entirely upon his own judgment and to decide so constantly for himself, that he had almost lost the habit of submitting to advice. He was grateful for the solicitude shown, but he thought it best to adhere to his purpose. In the sanguine hopefulness of his spirit, he pictured himself returning in the near future with body and mind invigorated, to render some further service to his beloved continent.

The passage home was an ideal one for health and pleasure. Not a ripple from Cape Town to Plymouth. Day by day bright sunshine, and balmy breezes, and everything to make the time pass agreeably. It was an experience to inspire him with cheering anticipations. Alas, that the prologue to his home-coming should have been so delusive! The warm and bracing weather which he had bespoken in his heart was never realised. The summer of 1894 proved ungenial and precarious beyond common. Gloomy skies, cold damp winds, and general miserableness were the things that awaited him; and upon the sensitive constitution of one in his semi-invalid condition they told with a depressing and hurtful effect.

His renewal of acquaintance with the home climate was inaugurated fitly though unfortunately by a bad wetting as he was leaving the ship at Plymouth. In the joy of his arrival he paid no attention to it at the time. But he was soon reminded by the return of his fever that the untoward circumstance was not to pass without effect. So high did his temperature rise that another attack of pneumonia seemed imminent. Happily the illness fell short of that; but already he was realising that the dry and sunny south was the only safe quarter for him. Pity that he did not content himself with a flitting visit home and a mere hurried glimpse of loved ones, and then immediately retrace his course to Africa. For, as it was, every step of the way now was marked by failing strength, and slowly but surely the possibility of return was passing beyond his reach.

His health-quest of the past thirteen months had issued in great improvement; but what he had gained was from the very first mortgaged in the attempt to act as if he were no longer an invalid. He had so many warm friends in London, all anxious to show by hospitable invitations and otherwise their joy at his convalescence, and he himself was so fain to respond, that he quite overtaxed his strength. By the time he was able to set his face towards his destination in the north country, he had lost more than he could afford of the little treasure of health which he had so slowly gathered. He himself did not fail to note the fact. On the eve of his leaving London (June 14), he writes to Mr. Noble in Cape Town :—

"I have been going on very rashly since I came home. It is a marvel I have not come a genuine cropper. However, that is at an end now. To-morrow I am off to Scotland, where I shall be in peace and quietness under my mother's wing for a time. . . . The doctors recommend me to leave the country for the winter. I shall, therefore, probably go to North Africa for a change, and then, if all goes well, I shall be out next year *en route* for the Barotse Country and a grand final burst up."

The journey to Scotland proved too much for him. He arrived quite exhausted, and forthwith he found himself once more in the deep waters of affliction, the victim of a continuous fever which confined him to bed. It was grievously disheartening. He was naturally unwilling to let himself believe "that there was not a land of promise ahead," but there was only too obvious cause for disquiet. His old troubles were returning upon him, like insatiate birds of prey which had only been temporarily frightened away from their quarry, and it was not long before he had to confess himself completely overwhelmed. No wonder that he should have, for the moment, lost heart amid so many calamitous reverses. On the 31st of July he writes to Edward Clodd :—

" I am in a very bad way. Since I came to Scotland I have been nearly completely prostrate, mentally and physically, thanks to fever, starvation, and a harassing throat cough. In three weeks I have lost twelve of my precious pounds of flesh and I have never regained them. The cough happily has been subdued, but the fever sticks to me. I would just like to have some sort of ordinary painful illness and be laid up in bed; but this feeling of simple collapse sickens me. I cannot even read. For some days I have had Kidd's ' Social Evolution ' beside me, and for the life of me I cannot muster up courage to open it. . . . How I wish I were going to Norway with you. I believe the sea voyage in those bracing parts would be the saving of me; but I cannot move at present."

But, though he might be in the depths, what he felt in the way of depression he scrupulously concealed from those about him. He was magnanimous in his consideration for those he loved. As he moved about the old home wearily passing the long days of that inclement summer, he knew how hearts around him were suffering in sympathy, and he ever strove to dissemble his miseries for their sakes. His silence did not deceive those who were eager to cheer him with affectionate ministries, and his attempts at airy lightness in replying to the daily inquiries only touched them with a sense of pathos. But never would he suffer a complaint or a word of fretfulness to pass his lips. One day his mother, hungering, mother-like, to lavish tender attentions upon him, gently remonstrated with him for making so little call upon her sympathy. His reply was characteristic: " Mother, why should I sadden you with the story of my ills ? They are a thousand and one."

In the close of the summer he so far pulled himself together as to pay a brief visit to Greenock and Edinburgh. This effort over, he lingered for a few weeks more at Gatelawbridge, where at last the sun was condescending to become cordial in his shining. But when the sharper air of late September began to make itself felt, it came as a pointed reminder that he must seek a more southerly clime. A last lingering look at the scenes of boyhood's happy memories, a quiet good-bye in which one hardly dared to utter words—and the oft-broken chapter of his life in lovely Nithsdale was finally closed.

It was as " a subdued and disheartened man " that he resumed his pilgrimage, and he went forth, as he had never felt himself to do before, with a profound sense of loneliness. For a few days he lingered in London. On the 4th of October he set sail for Naples. He chose to go by sea in the hope that the few days of sailing would have a reviving effect. The hope was not fulfilled. He arrived in a very prostrate condition, and he landed only to find Naples under the unhappy influence of a sirocco. For days the deep blue sky which he had longed to see was hidden in a dull haze, and sea and mountain were alike invisible.

A little time, however, brought alleviations without and within, and he was enabled, though in a forlorn way, to wander or sit in the public gardens and enjoy the shade of pine, palm, and evergreen oak. Sight-seeing at first was of course beyond him. The one impression of Naples in those first days which he was pre-eminently conscious of was the prevalence of evil smells; but in writing of this he added, with a gleam of his old humour: "Even the stinks have a certain melancholy interest for me, as they indicate that there are microbes with which as yet I have made no acquaintance, and which may enable me to die in the odour of—well, let us say sanctity."

Even one thought of drollery was so far a favourable sign, and as a matter of fact he was conscious of slowly rallying—an augury for the future which he was only too eager to note. "I mean," he writes, "to pick up the shattered fragments of hope and piece them, as well as I can, together again." Doubtless the resolution helped to a certain extent to secure its own fulfilment. Be that as it may, he did gain ground. Cooler and more healthful weather also helped to put him on his feet again, and presently he could write of himself as "hastening with his *Murray* and a thankful heart" to see the lions of the place. The churches and the museum were special objects of interest to him. In them he spent much of his time. It was his good fortune here, as everywhere in his wanderings, to fall in with agreeable friends. Sir Wemyss Reid, whom he had met on the voyage out, was extremely kind in his attentions. A number of companionable and warm-hearted Americans also helped wonderfully to do away with the sense of tedium so oppressive to an invalid. One of these knew his chum and fellow-explorer Du

Chaillu, and that itself was a bond of friendship to draw them together.

As his various internal enemies became more quiescent, he was glad to seize opportunities of venturing out into the open and feasting eye and heart on the natural charms of the neighbourhood. His keen relish for the beautiful in scenery never failed him; indeed there was nothing that took him so perfectly away from himself or so helped to quicken the languid pulse of life. In December he writes to his sister-in-law at Greenock :—

"Naples is a place to see and leave, not a town to live in. Its streets are narrow, noisy, foul-smelling, and sunless, without a single building having the slightest claims to architectural beauty. They swarm with shrill-voiced hawkers, clamorous cabmen, and loathsome beggars. But outside, how different! There Naples spreads itself out, a thing of beauty. Its mean square villas and so-called palaces become picturesque, seen scrambling up the sides of the hill singly or in groups. The dirty whites and measly yellows become transformed under the magic influence of the brilliant mid-day sun, and glow with a marvellous beauty in the more witching light of the setting sun. And beside it stands Vesuvius clothed in purple, like the protective giant it is, while the blue sea cools its feet in lapping wavelets, and the blue sky spreads over all. But all this is seen from a little distance. Go inside and you will find that you have been admiring a painted sepulchre."

In the middle of December he left for a short sojourn of ten days in Capri. This charming island captivated him at first sight, though he had not the good fortune to see it under the best of weather conditions. It seemed to him the very "pearl of the Mediterranean—a place made only for sunshine and balmy breezes."

" This," he writes to his mother, "is the most delightfully
X 2

picturesque island you can imagine. Enormous cliffs, overhanging the bluest of blue seas, orange and olive groves with vineyards nestling in all sorts of snug corners, old castles and ancient Roman palaces crowning every height, while quaint whitewashed villages spread themselves out on the sunny slopes. Most wonderful of all, there are no beggars, no hawkers to weary the life out of one, none of the vile smells nor the viler sights of Naples —every one clean and bright and tidy, and every one cheerful and polite, so that Capri seems a veritable little ocean paradise in these southern seas."

After leaving Capri he spent two days in surveying the beauties of Sorrento, and then returned *via* Pompeii to Naples. At Naples the weather was lovely, but he had had enough of the place and was not tempted to linger in it. He had made up his mind to spend his Christmas at Palermo, and thither he sped as soon as possible.

The warmer air of Palermo suited him well, and if he could only have had the warmth which his heart more and more craved for—the warmth of loving fellowship— he would have been quite satisfied. As it was, the return of the festive Christmas season, with its reminders of family and friendly gatherings in the home country, painfully emphasised his sense of separation.

"I suppose," he says in a letter to Mrs. Gilmour, "I should be more or less discontented wherever I went, playing the *rôle* of the invalid. It is not a stimulating one, and becomes indeed frightfully wearisome when enacted companionless in foreign parts. The incessant change of faces, acquaintanceships nipped in the bud by the signal to move on, which is the characteristic of hotel life, the feeling of being more or less alone in all this seething current—these are conditions which prevent me enjoying myself. It is all so different, of course, when one is in really good health, for then one is a world in one's self, independent of everybody, and only evilly affected by the weather.

"You can understand then how at this time my thoughts wander back to my friends in England, till I become green with envy at the thought of their fireside gatherings with delightful interchange of gossip and thought and fun. How happy you all seem with your fogs or rains or snow outside, and your cosy rooms, bright fires, and all the rest inside! If you think of me in brilliant sunshine wandering through olive or orange groves, seeing this picturesque scene or that wonderful building, do not envy me for a moment. Do not wish that you also were there; but with all your heart thank goodness that you are where you are, and wish that I was with you."

With the advent of 1895, the weather in Palermo completely broke down, and there ensued a comfortless time of gloom, and cold, and wet—sleet-showers driving people from the streets, and clothing the hills around with a wintry white; while even inside the house it seemed almost impossible to get warm. In these circumstances he was only too glad to strike his tent once more, and steal away after the sunshine.

Taormina was his next resting-place. This he reached by way of Catania.

"There never was a more fortunate change of residence," he writes on January 26th, to Mr. McKie. "For three weeks I have been here, and all the time it has been the most delightful weather imaginable—nothing but cloudless blue skies, bright warm sunshine and soft caressing breezes.

"And what a landscape to look at, by merely turning my eye from this paper! A many-coloured sea, with a lovely curving shore, stretching away south to Syracuse; Etna, rising from the rippling waters, with its mantle of snow and its heart of fire. Nearer on the left are the picturesque crags and bold limestone peaks of Taormina, crowned by Norman castles—the town itself forming a straggling zone of mediæval churches, monasteries falling into ruins, dilapidated Gothic palaces, from which beggars look out at the windows, battlemented walls, Greek theatres and temples, Roman aqueducts and tombs taking back one's imagination to the dawn of history—and a score of other points of grandeur, beauty, or historic interest.  I am sure that there is not such another spot in all Italy.  To add to it all, the Hotel Timeo is most delightfully situated, most cosy, clean, and thoroughly well managed—has in fact but one fault: nothing to read."

To all these charms of Nature and art he gave himself up with growing pleasure, looking down with dreamy restfulness upon the blue, ever-sounding sea, giving his cheek to the caresses of the soft air, and bathing in the warm sunshine, " to the intense disgust of his microbes," as he facetiously put it.

His plan of tour forbade him to tarry in this bright spot, and at the end of his three weeks he must needs press on to Rome.  But here, again, he was only too unpleasantly conscious of a return to less suitable weather conditions.  When, therefore, his allotted time there was up, he was nothing loth to set his face westward once more, bound for the Riviera.  His idea was to stay in the Riviera until he should find himself able to slip back to London without too much danger, and then at once sail for Cape Town, which, he was now only too well aware, he had been rash in leaving so soon.

The first news of him that followed his departure from Rome was a shakily-written letter received by his mother in the beginning of March, from Mentone, announcing that he was " down with a very bad fever, and compelled to keep his room."  This was followed a few days later by an intimation from another source that he was lying in peril of his life with a new attack of illness.  Without an hour's delay, the writer hastened out to him, and found him in the hands of doctor and nurses. He had been seized with influenza, and pneumonia had supervened. In any case this would have been serious, but, coming as a new link in the long terrible chain of afflictions, it was enough to extinguish hope. The immediate crisis was past, and there were signs of rallying, but even love could not refuse to admit to itself that the approach of the end was ominously near.

During the three weeks of the writer's stay at Mentone with him there was a slow revival of vitality; but it was not until the middle of May that he was able to be removed, under the charge of one of his nurses, to London. He arrived there, at 3 York Gate, the house of his friend Mr. S. W. Silver, more dead than alive.

His marvellous spirit of resolution once more came to his aid, but alas, it was only to prolong the conflict for a very little longer. In July, according to his desire, he was removed to Cromer, in the faint hope that even yet the bracing breezes of the Norfolk coast might reinvigorate him so far as to enable him to take the voyage to South Africa. There was a temporary improvement, but it was only a passing impulse of quickening to the flickering life-forces. As the end of the month drew nigh it became only too manifest that a crisis was approaching. On the 28th he got himself propped up in bed to write two little notes to his dear and faithful correspondents, Mrs. Calder, Leith, and Miss Noake, Lymington. With the finishing of the note to the latter he laid aside the pen for ever. Here is what he wrote :—

"Just a line to tell you that your flowers arrived blooming and beautiful, like all things from your hands. They find me as helpless and hopeless as ever. My fever is always with me, making my days and nights alike miserable, and leaving me in much perplexity as to what to do next. I have much need of some one to take possession of me and think and act for me.  Excuse this note, but I am writing in bed in an uncomfortable position.—Yours affectionately,                    "JOE."

His need of "some one to take possession of him and think and act for him" was soon answered.  A telegram from his nurse brought the writer to his side with all possible speed.

He was indeed sadly changed.  It required no seer to discern the seal of death upon his wasted features.  But the mind was unclouded and the will firm as ever.  He had taken a great longing to be removed to London, where he would feel that he was not wholly surrounded by unsympathetic strangers, but was breathing the atmosphere of friendship and kindly human feeling.  The risk was great, with his life flickering on the verge of extinction.  But he was resolute, and who could deny a last wish like this?  Hastily preparations were made, and all possible means taken to smooth away the trials of the journey.

And so the arms that had so often carried the little brother in childhood's days once more bore him—alas, too light a burden and feebler than an infant—into carriage and train, and through the strident bustle of a London station, till at last, after an anxious journey, they laid him to rest in the hospitable home at York Gate.  It was with a sigh of grateful relief that he found himself under the roof of one who had always treated him with affectionate kindness, and he could contentedly lie down and wait for his release.

Of the three days that followed, and the little tender talks that now and then interrupted the stillness of watching, this is not the place to speak.  No reader can think of them as the writer does.  Suffice it to say that they revealed the man unchanged—gentle, unmurmuring, and now as ever thoughtful of others.  He loved life and would fain have rendered more service to his generation, had that been permitted. This was touchingly shown when on the day before his death he said with a brightening light in his eyes: "If I could put on my clothes and walk a hundred yards, 1 would go to South Africa yet!" But when it became clear that for him the end of the way had come, there was neither faltering nor complaint.

About mid-day on Friday, the 2nd of August, the signs of a near change were unmistakable, and the writer spoke to him of this in such words as he could find for the trying duty. The sufferer flushed slightly, looked for a moment with that straightforward, inquiring glance of his, and then calmly said, as the laboured breathing would allow him: "I have been face to face with death for years, and I need not be alarmed at it now. . . . We must all cast ourselves upon the mercy of God. . . . I am quite prepared, and quite satisfied."

These were his last words. Quietly he turned on his side and fell into a slumber, out of which he glided, with an almost imperceptible passage, into the sleep that closed the long agony. Thus, at the early age of thirty-seven, ceased a life, brave, pure, strong, and true among the truest—a life unsparing in its self-sacrifice, loyal to its ideal, unmarred by the memory of a single meanness.

The dying of the best makes but little stir in the public mind. But there were not wanting signs that thoughtful men felt the ranks of the world's true helpers to be the poorer for the loss of Joseph Thomson. The obituary notices which appeared in the newspapers everywhere voiced, with a singularly impressive unanimity, admiration of a life-work worthily and beautifully done. Manifestly, if he had not posed ambitiously before the public, he had at least secured a place for himself in the appreciation of those who had an eye for earnestness and moral enthusiasm and manliness.

The day of his death was coincident with that of the closing of the International Congress of Geographers, which had been holding its meetings in London.

"When," said one of the public journals, "it became known that Mr. Thomson had succumbed to the illness against which he had fought so long and so gallantly, the greatest sympathy and regret were expressed amongst the geographers assembled at the Imperial Institute. Many of those attending the Congress were personally acquainted with him, some had followed in his footsteps in Masailand or other parts of Africa where he had done previous work, and all were unanimous in expressing their sense of the great loss that his untimely death had inflicted on the continent in which he had done his life's work. . . . A brilliant young explorer has been cut off in what should have been the prime of his days, though not before he had accomplished an amount of work which has won for him an imperishable place in the roll of African explorers."

On the day following his death the body was removed to the paternal home in Scotland. There until the funeral the coffin was fitly enshrined in the little museum, amid the many unique trophies which silently told the story of his wanderings, and upon whose arrangement he himself had spent so much loving care.

On the 6th of August—one of those warm bright days of early autumn which make the valley of Nithsdale look its loveliest—he was buried in Morton Cemetery. The whole district had been moved by his death, and a great concourse of mourners assembled to do reverence to his memory. Many also came from a distance to pay their last tribute of respect. Among those who stood around the grave and joined with the sorrowing father and brothers in laying their friend to rest were J. M. Barrie, Alexander Anderson, and his old fellow student Wallace Williamson—each of whom, no doubt, had his own thoughts of sadness in recalling memories of "the voice that is still."

Thus, after the toils and sufferings of his strenuous

career, Joseph Thomson has found his quiet haven where of all places he would most have desired to find it, in the centre of the valley he loved, and amid the sights and sounds that were dearest to his heart. The sun rising over the shoulder of Queensberry, and sending his bright messages athwart Crichope and Gatelawbridge, seeks out the spot among the first. At the sleeper's head is the sheltering woodland, through which come now the cooing of the cushat and the warblings of the song-birds in their season, and anon, borne by the western breeze, the sighing sound of the Nith, as it flows on over its pebbly bed. And there, over against the place, stands sentinel the Burn Hill, up whose rough sides his boyish feet have so often clambered, and on whose heathery heights he dreamed his youthful day dreams, while he surveyed the glorious panorama spreading beneath him, and through it saw with the mind's eye the wonders of the great unsearched world beyond.

# CHAPTER XIV.

## AN APPRECIATION.

THE reader who has perused with attention the foregoing pages will probably feel that little more needs to be said in order to convey an adequate conception of the man whose career they portray. Yet it will be well that some things, which are, as it were, in solution in the narrative, should be crystallised into positive statement.

To merely casual acquaintances Joseph Thomson as a man was not known. Such might be attracted by his thoughtful look and grave, courteous demeanour—for he had in no slight degree the gift of captivating men's confidence at first sight—and they might note in the sparkle of his frank eyes some suggestion of the sunshiny nature that lay behind. But the veil of modest reserve concealed much of his individuality from all but his friends. Yet there are few men whose qualities would better bear a near scrutiny, or whose character was more decidedly worth observing at close quarters.

Those who were most perfectly intimate with him will probably think of the single-minded simplicity of the man as one of his most prominent characteristics. Whatever else he might be, he was at least transparently honest and sincere. Those who knew him felt safe to trust him to the uttermost. There was in him none of that suspicious *finesse* or diplomatic vagueness which suggests the possibility of unpleasant surprises, and compels a sense of uncertainty. Disguise was alien to his nature. His words were "trusty heralds to his mind." What he said, that he thought; and what he consciously permitted himself to seem, that he was.

It was one aspect of his honesty that he stood at every moment with heart and mind full open to the light. No one ever more earnestly desired to be free from the influence of mere prejudice. Prejudice in any sphere of life seemed to him the paralysis of usefulness there. Therefore he held himself ever ready to receive new truth. That is not to say that he set lightly by the opinions he had been led to form. On the contrary, he always held and stated his views with decision. Some men thought him even dogmatic, and in a certain sense, perhaps, so he was. But his emphasis of statement was never that of the man who thinks he has attained to ultimate certainty. It was the emphasis of one who feels that he is responsible for the use of the light he has, and that he is bound to impart that light to others.

Mr. Bartholomew, in his thoughtful obituary notice of his comrade in the *Scottish Geographical Magazine*, has said that " to those who knew him best a spirit of true chivalry seemed the keynote of his life." If chivalry be taken to mean the generous subordination of self and its interests to the fulfilment of a duty or the advocacy of a cause, the remark is singularly apposite. If in any circumstances it appeared to him that there was a service which he ought to render, all thoughts of self were summarily swept aside. Where the worldly-wise would have cautiously considered the consequences to their safety or prospects, he only thought of stepping into the breach. The prudential person, more astute than he, said it was Quixotic; but it was the Quixotism of conscience and high-mindedness. And if there was now and then a touch of the romantic in his self-forgetfulness, is it not well that the prosaic monotony of the commonplace should at times thus be broken in upon?

It hardly needs to be said that the dominating influence in Joseph Thomson's life was his interest in Africa and the Africans. This was the focal point of all his thoughts and energies. "My beloved Africa" is a phrase that every here and there crops up in his correspondence; and the phrase was with him no empty one. The pity for the dark tribes of that vast continent, which the reading of Livingstone's works had roused in his heart as a boy, deepened steadily as he got a near view of them until it became a passion which wholly possessed him. The uplifting of Africa was his constant dream, his accepted vocation; and in his yearning for that consummation he was possessed by as pure and reverent an enthusiasm as any fabled knight of chivalry in his quest for the Holy Grail. For this he counted no sacrifice too great. For this he dared all. For this he spent himself unto death.

It was the very intensity and simplicity of his passion for the elevation of the African that made men sometimes misunderstand him. If he denounced methods of wilfulness and bloodshed in exploration; if he spoke scathingly of the hurtful influence which unworthy representatives of civilisation were exercising; if he uttered words of fierce indignation against a selfish and demoralising commerce like that which fostered the drink traffic; if he protested against "the scramble for Africa" in which governments and individuals robbed the simple tribes and overrode their rights; if he strove by the blunt presentation of unwelcome truths to thwart the unscrupulous speculator who would make Africa the mere *corpus vile* for his experiments;—it was always for the one reason that in these things men were acting as enemies of the great cause he had at heart. On the other hand, if he upbraided our own government for its apathy about things African, it was because he believed that Providence had given Britain a mission for the good of Africa which she was sinfully neglecting. And if he even ventured to criticise the methods of some missionary societies in their work upon

the Dark Continent, it was because, in his eagerness for
the success of their beneficent object, he longed to see all
wise efforts made to quicken the pace. To speak pleasant
things all round would have been more popular, and sometimes more profitable to himself. But he was too much
in earnest for the advancement of his object to let his
influence fritter itself away in mere empty compliments
and futile generalities. He had decided views as to things
that were standing in the way of his ideal, and he must
needs say out what was in his heart—even though he
should be as a voice crying in the wilderness.

It is, of course, specially as an explorer that he has
accomplished the great work of his life; and as one of the
last and most successful of the African pioneers, his name
can scarcely fail of perpetuation. But if he has a claim to
be remembered by the magnitude of his record in opening
up new lands, he has still a more notable claim in respect
of the spirit which inspired his entire career.

He had all the qualities which go to make an ideal
explorer. He had the vigorous well-knit physique and the
splendid constitution which fitted him for effort and endurance; the fearless spirit which enabled him to look at
any danger calmly; the energetic will which gave him
perfect control of himself, and made him dauntless in face
of all difficulties; the keen sense of humour which kept
him cheerful alike in peril and suffering; the inquiring
spirit which rendered the discovery of the new a thing
worthy of any self-denial; and the enthusiasm, scientific
and moral, which abode with him as an unfailing fountain
of impulse. These are fundamental qualifications, necessary more or less to the success of any pioneer. But
to these Joseph Thomson added other attributes which
have secured for him quite a special standing among
explorers.

There was, for instance, his unique geographical instinct
—a natural gift sedulously trained. So highly developed
was this faculty, and so keen, rapid and true were his

powers of observation and of topographic discernment, that, in the opinion of another explorer, they "amounted almost to genius." It was no uncommon thing for him to check and set right even his own native guides. His companion in the Morocco journey thus testifies: "He was never at fault in deciding which of several routes across unknown country it was best to pursue in order to reach a desired point. Many times in the Atlas Mountains, when our guides were purposely misleading us, his quick insight came to our rescue. He used to guess the heights of the mountains we climbed before we commenced the ascent, and observations on the summit almost invariably proved his estimates to be correct within a few hundred feet."

Not less distinctive was his tact and practical insight in dealing both with those under him, and with savage and suspicious natives. He was a born leader and master. Not infrequently in his caravans he had the most intractable elements to reckon with; but he hardly ever failed to mould his men to his purpose, and, while winning their loyalty, to get out of them precisely what he wanted. Even more notable, if possible, was his success with the tribes through which he passed.

The quality, however, which has been recognised as perhaps overtopping every other in his character as an explorer, was his extraordinary gentleness and self-restraint. The natives, times without number, subjected his temper to the most severe strain, but he never failed to keep the mastery of it. To him they were but wayward and untutored children to be treated with compassion, with kindness if possible, but certainly with justice and charity. The result was, that almost everywhere he disarmed suspicion, and, despite all trials, was able to present the story of his daring journeys without a single stain to mar it in the eyes of humane men.

And he has his reward. Men who have the enthusiasm of humanity and who know the difficulties which beset the path of the explorer, speak of his example as one to be imitated. No higher encomium could his warmest admirer wish for him than that which has been penned by the President of the Royal Geographical Society (Sir Clements R. Markham), in a letter referring to the explorer's death :—

"I am anxious to convey to the parents of our Gold Medallist, and, I must add, of our highly valued friend, the assurance that we share in their sorrow. For Joseph Thomson was bound to the Royal Geographical Society by specially close ties. He commanded two of our most successful expeditions, and, speaking with an experience of thirty-five years, there is no other African explorer, alive or dead, to whom I would have entrusted the command of an expedition with equal confidence, either as regards scientific attainments or fitness for the command of others. Joseph Thomson had the high and glorious distinction of never having caused the death of a single native. This is a proof of very rare qualities in the leader of an expedition, and places him in the very first rank of explorers."

In view of such a tribute from one who could speak with the highest authority, it is not surprising that the public press, in referring to him at the time of his death, should have done so in terms like these :—

"England," said the *Pall Mall Gazette*, "has never yet realized what a stalwart and sterling son she had in Thomson. . . . With him dies the only traveller of our time who, as regards his pluck, his persistence and his methods, is worthy to rank with Livingstone. . . . It is such as he that have built up and maintained our great Empire." "Taken as a whole, he was," declared *The Speaker*, "distinctly the greatest African explorer of our time—immeasurably the greatest, if one takes into account the smallness of the resources at his command when he accomplished his greatest feats." Precisely parallel has been the universal testimony of those who could claim to speak with knowledge.

Y

The practical usefulness of Joseph Thomson's efforts as an explorer, has no doubt been enhanced not a little by his felicity in the use of the pen. His excellences as a writer have been widely acknowledged. He had a rare facility in self-expression, and a quick ear for the music and rhythm of a sentence; moreover, he put into his writing much of his own individuality—his sincerity, his frankness, his poetic fancy, his humour. The result is a style of a most racy and home-coming sort. His descriptive passages, especially, are always graphic and picturesque. He had the power of seeing in a landscape precisely the salient features that go to make up a picture; and as he could describe those features not only with the special knowledge of the scientist, but with much of the artist's keen insight into beauty, his accounts of the strange lands he visited convey to the reader not a little of the vivid enjoyment of a personal experience. One of the great charms of his writing is the utter absence alike of self-consciousness and of effort. He never thought of style at all, in the sense of making a careful and calculated adjustment of his words. He simply dashed down on the page his ideas as they rushed upon him, writing " by ear," if we may so speak, and leaving grammar and syntax to take care of themselves. Yet his pen-work is always fresh and forcible. By a wide and discriminative reading of good books, he had made his mind a full storehouse of apt words and allusions. Thus in what he wrote there was always at least the material out of which, with a little judicious editing, genuine literature could be made.

In his more private and personal relations Joseph Thomson was of a very winning and kindly character. No son was ever more tender in his devotion to his parents. The home fireside was the pole to which the magnetic current of his affection went constantly forth. Father and mother were ever his foremost confidants in all his aims and plans and doings; and however great might be the burden of his anxieties or the demands upon his time and strength, the regular letter to " the old folks " was never forgotten.

As a friend, too, he drew people to him with a more than common attachment. All his friends were devoted friends, for the better they knew him the more they found in him to attract them and give them pleasure. His unselfishness, his modesty, his healthy humanness of feeling, his brightness of spirit, his unaffected enjoyment of good fellowship, as well as his shrewdness of intellect, all charmed his intimates, and kept ever wide open for him the door of welcome. In many a circle he is missed and mourned as only the well-beloved are.

We cannot more fitly close our introductory notes than by quoting from ' Personal Recollections ' penned by one of his familiars.

" Those of us," says this writer, " who enjoyed the privilege of his friendship, honoured him no less as a hero that we loved him as a genial, true, and honourable man. Upright he was and honest to a degree that won for him not a few enemies—diplomatic directors and chairmen of companies mainly, who detested him for proclaiming truths they did not wish to hear. But these were interested parties, and count for nothing as compared with the host of friends he made wherever he went, and none of whom he ever forgot, however humble, however separated by time and distance. In his native shire, in Edinburgh, in London, in Cape Town, and regions yet more remote, there were many hospitable doors always open to him and a warm welcome always ready. When in London, in the happy days before sickness and hardship had undermined his marvellous constitution, it was his daily custom to lunch at the Criterion with a small band of congenial spirits, geographical and otherwise, which at various times included such well-known names as those of Du Chaillu, Nansen, and J. Scott Keltie. To them came from time to time such wandering celebrities or favoured friends as might be passing through the metropolis; and many were the tales and merry the jests that accompanied the post-prandial cigar. Thomson himself was not a smoker, however, and to the genuine lover of a good Havana it was painful to witness his futile attempts to keep his cigar alight, and the number of times he would wantonly knock off the ash. Though not a pledged abstainer, a more abstemious man it would be hard to find. Every one knows the story of how he carried a bottle of brandy with him to the very heart of Central Africa and brought it back intact, a feat which in some people's estimation almost rivalled that of the journey itself. . . . . .

"Thomson was not without his kindly, human weaknesses. Some of us were wont to rally him not a little now and then upon his nice taste in neckties, and a predilection for silk linings and luxurious smoking-jackets. These were the Bohemians among us, however, and, in graver and more philosophic moods, we agreed it was only fitting that one who always did his best, and gave his best, and lived his best, should likewise wear only the best. . . . .

"His was a strong personality and his words carried conviction and elicited a ready obedience. But above all he was a man of high ideals and lofty practice, generous to lavishness, honest to a fault, chivalrous towards all women, honourable and magnanimous towards all men. For those who counted themselves as of the inner circle of his friends, by whom can the vacant place ever be filled ?"

And now, with these simple forewords, it is time that the writer of this narrative should stand aside and let others, who knew the subject of it, and who have followed with varying interest his public career, speak their thoughts concerning him.

### The Man.

Of Joseph Thomson as a companion Mr. J. M. Barrie writes as follows:—

"I think I was proposing the toast of the Army, Navy, and Reserve Forces, coupled with the name of Mr. Brown, or the Agricultural and Landed Interests, coupled with the name of Mr. Black, when Joseph Thomson, then lately arrived, very red, from Africa, walked into the room; and I finished my speech abruptly because the company had turned from me to look at him. The year must have been 1880, and we were members of an Edinburgh university debating society, then holding our annual high revel, with two speeches apiece, and mine, as you will perceive, on subjects that sparkled of themselves. That was my first meeting with Mr. Thomson, who had probably been a member of the society some years earlier, when he was a student at Edinburgh; and I remember how we gathered round him as if we were an African tribe, and how openly pleased he was at our pride in him, and how modest and bashful when called upon to speak about himself. At that time he had the high spirits of a boy—it was his great good fortune to retain much of the generous exuberance of boyhood to the end—and my most vivid recollection of that night is, that he laughed throughout it—when we lavished praises on him, when he spoke of the privations he and his caravan had suffered, even when he was singing a painfully tragic ditty. But from the knowledge I had of him afterwards I am sure we bored him considerably before the night was far spent, for we were all men, or would be men by-and-by; and I remember his confiding to me once, what I had already discovered for myself, that he never knew a man whose society did not pall upon him in time, nor a woman whose society did. This he told me upon the deck of a Rhine steamer, which was crowded with newly-married people; we two, who were travelling in company, seemed to be the only bachelors on the boat, and every time he looked at the companions of the other men his eye wandered contemptuously to me, and he groaned.

"Do you remember how the light went out of his face when the ladies retired from the dinner-table, and how he yawned until we rejoined them! The ordinary after-dinner talk made him irritable; if it was about sport of any kind he lapsed into silence (with a wistful eye on the door). When in Africa he delighted in the sport that kept his caravans in health and good humour and provisions, but sport at home did not interest him at all; he scarcely knew how the popular English games are played. I recollect his only cricket match, and how he played in pyjamas, and had to be told why you changed your position in the field when some one called 'over,' and that when batting it had to be explained to him that he must try to keep the ball off the wickets. Then he did not smoke, which no doubt was another reason why he thought the departure of the ladies a mistake. Men, I think, who did not know him well, sometimes misunderstood him, but women never; at least, women of parts did not, for he was a remarkably good talker of that rare class who must exchange views instead of merely giving them. The woman who speaks what is really in her mind is probably much more refreshing than any average man similarly communicative, but it is no inconsiderable feat to induce her to do so, and I think Mr. Thomson performed it more successfully than any other man I have known. I suppose women felt that it was a compliment to be admired by this man—and I am sure it was, he was so brave and modest, there was so much chivalry in his attitude toward them, he was so ready to be their champion. Who was more scornful than he for men that spoke lightly of women, or more ready to give them a piece of his mind? And all this, it seems to me, could be read in his frank, wholesome face, which was stamped with honesty. Add to this that there was a dash of the sentimentalist about him, and that on occasion he had a roguish eye.

"I believe he would have gone to the stake rather than tell a lie. He could not even 'beat about the bush.' Such and such were his views, and if he was asked for them he must reply 'straight from the shoulder.' There were times when these views were not palatable to those in authority, when it would have been better for his own interests that he should tone them down, or make believe to change them, or at least keep them dark; and one hears it said that he was no diplomatist. I suppose he was not, in the poor conventional meaning of the word; but again and again events proved that, had his advice been taken, it would have been better for our interests in Africa. Surely that is not to his discredit as a diplomatist. I think, however, it can be fairly urged that he tended to be hasty and impatient in his dealings with men in this country, which makes his success in Africa the more remarkable. His patience there stands only second to his humanity, he seems to have been tolerant and conciliatory beyond almost all who have headed caravans, and to have left a sweet name behind him among all the tribes with whom he had sojourned. It is reasonable to presume that his straightforwardness and his boyish high spirits were responsible for much of his popularity with the natives. Whatever their faults, they too, were straightforward and gleeful, and so he had something in common with them; he and they found it easy to understand each other. I am sure he delighted in exchanging views with their ladies, and enjoyed dancing with the native belles, and was as courteous to them as though they were the beauties of Mayfair.

"I suppose one expects an explorer to be a reader of men rather than of books; but he was a great book-reader. On his return from Africa one of his first questions, after he had shaved his beard (he liked to bring his beard home with him), was, 'Are there any good new books?' He kept up with the literature of the day as well as though he lived within walking distance of the British Museum. He read a great deal of poetry, and among modern novelists Mr. Meredith and Mr. Hardy were his favourites. I went to Southampton with him to see him start on one of his last voyages, and I remember how, after the gangway was raised, he came to the side of the vessel and shouted, 'Remember to send me "One of Our Conquerors" as soon as it comes out.'

"I have known few men whom I have esteemed as much as Mr. Thomson."

## The Geographer.

The geographical work of Joseph Thomson is thus estimated by the veteran cartographer, Mr. E. G. Ravenstein :—

"In judging my late friend Thomson's achievements as geographical explorer two things must be borne in mind: firstly, the fact that he travelled as a pioneer, and that the knowledge which proved so useful to his successors had first to be acquired by him; and secondly, that he was generally alone, and had to attend in the first instance to the business requirements of his expeditions, thus curtailing the time left for scientific observation.

"Each of the six African expeditions upon which Thomson was engaged yielded geographical results of interest. During his first journey in 1879–80, when he so pluckily carried out the objects of the expedition fitted out by the Royal Geographical Society, after his leader, Keith

Johnston, had succumbed to the climate, he, as the first European, reached the northern end of Lake Nyassa from the Zanzibar coast; he traversed the plateau lying between that lake and Tanganyika and pushed far into the mysterious region lying beyond that lake. The results achieved at once won for Thomson, at the time a mere youth, a prominent place among African explorers, and fully justified the Council of the Royal Geographical Society in choosing him as the leader of an expedition which was to traverse Masai-land in the direction of the Victoria Nyanza (1883–4). He fully justified their choice. This journey proved by far the most important from a geographical point of view ever undertaken by him. He first beheld the eastern flank of Mount Kenia, established the independent existence of Lake Baringo, hitherto supposed to be an arm of the Victoria; visited the cave-dwellers on Mount Elgon, and as a crowning achievement reached the north-eastern corner of the greatest among the African lakes.

"A journey to Sokoto, which he undertook on behalf of the Royal Niger Company, led through districts already fairly well explored, but nevertheless yielded a few latitudes which proved of service in the construction of the map.*

"Far greater results were achieved by a short visit to Morocco in 1888, when Thomson was accompanied by young Mr. Crichton Browne. Not content with visiting the city of Morocco and other places readily accessible,

---

* These latitudes, which, as far as I am aware, have never before been published, are as follows :—

| | | |
|---|---|---|
| Kontokora . . | 10° 23' 20" N. | Gigo . . . . | 11° 44' 40" N. |
| Ikam or Gungu . | 10° 48' 56" N. | Shingebo. . | 11° 59' 49" N. |
| Fufu Ndigi . . | 10° 58' 51" N. | Mungadi. . . | 12° 5' 39" N. |
| Zaria . . . . | 11° 12' 56" N. | Alieru (8 m. E. by | |
| Zaga . . . . | 11° 22' 51" N. | N. of Jega) . | 12° 15' 46" N. |
| Kunde (S. of | | Tamboel . . . | 12° 23' 0" N. |
| Zaga) . . . | 11° 30' 0" N. | Bodinga . . . | 12° 48' 41" N. |

Thomson delivered several successful assaults upon the High Atlas, crossed that mountain range thrice, and ascended several of its virgin peaks.  It was in Morocco that Thomson contracted the illness which brought to a premature close the expedition which he conducted on behalf of the British South Africa Company to Lake Bangweolo (1891–2).  Still, even under these adverse conditions, and whilst suffering the pains of martyrdom, Thomson attended to his geographical work, and the resulting map proved of high value.

" As an explorer Thomson exhibited an admirable facility for appreciating, at a glance, the broad features of the countries he traversed.  His sense of locality was strongly developed, and his maps, although not as full of detail as are those of some other African travellers, present us with fair delineations of the regions they claim to portray.  Thomson's routes can be laid down without difficulty upon the most recent maps, embodying all the information derived from the more leisurely explorations of his successors—a test of general accuracy to which the work of many of our more famous African pioneers cannot be successfully submitted.  It is to be regretted, nevertheless, that Thomson never thought it worth while to acquire topographical methods more perfect than those almost instinctively employed by him, and that his knowledge of astronomical work never passed beyond an elementary stage.  His attempted determination of two longitudes during his famous Masai journey proved an utter failure.  How important such an observation would have been may be judged from the fact that Mount Kenia, although placed by him approximately in its true latitude, is nearly a degree out in longitude.  Fortunately the latitudes determined by him during this and the succeeding expedition, although received with some distrust at the time, have stood the test, and proved of great service in the construction of his maps.

" The very important services rendered by Thomson

to geology will be referred to by Dr. Gregory. That he was competent to deal with geographical subjects not immediately connected with his own explorations is shown by his work on 'Mungo Park and the Niger,' which a German critique pronounced the first satisfactory biography of the great African pioneer ever written.

"Before concluding this short notice of the work accomplished by one of our most successful and sympathetic African explorers, I feel bound to draw attention to the fact that Thomson succeeded in almost every instance in establishing friendly relations not only with the men in his own service, but also with the natives whose territories he was the first to explore. Not a page of his eventful history as an explorer is stained with native blood, and he never appealed to the *ultimo ratio* of kings and certain African travellers. He owed this success not merely to his high courage, decision of character, and promptness of action, but more especially to a naturally kindly and genial disposition, which showed great forbearance under provocation, and patience under difficulties. It was these qualities which enabled him to overcome obstacles from which others recoiled, or which they overcame only by a display of brute force."

### The Commercial Pioneer.

With regard to the influence of Joseph Thomson's expeditions in the commercial opening up of Africa, Mr. J. Scott Keltie, Secretary of the Royal Geographical Society, says :—

"I have been asked to write a few words as to the commercial value of my friend Joseph Thomson's various African expeditions. His two great expeditions, undertaken at the expense of the Royal Geographical Society, and on the results of which his enduring fame will rest, had for their sole object geographical discovery; yet indirectly they have been of great practical importance. His first journey, when by the sad death of Keith Johnston, he, a boy, was left alone in the heart of Africa, and with characteristic pluck determined to go forward, led through territory which has since become partly German, partly British, and partly Belgian. Young as he was, his observations on the country through which he passed were made with intelligence and accuracy, and have proved of utility to those who have, during the past ten years, been endeavouring to turn this great region of Central Africa to practical account.

" Still more has this been the case with his memorable expedition through Masai-land. It should be remembered that he was the pioneer explorer in a country which has since become a portion of the British Empire, and that while he was making his way northward to Mount Kenia, Stanley was on the Congo organising the Free State, and Germany was preparing for that *coup* which led to the scramble for Africa. Thomson's discoveries as to the character of much of the region beyond the waterless and desert coast belt, were a revelation to those inclined to regard tropical Africa as hopeless, so far as European commercial enterprise was concerned. It became evident from Thomson's careful observations as to the character of the country between Mount Kenia and Lake Victoria that it was capable of being turned to excellent account under white superintendence. He was the first to tell us of the 'Great Rift Valley,' which forms so formidable an obstacle to railway construction, as he told us of the facility of transit across the country between the coast and the valley, through which, he declared, one could drive a Cape cart. Thomson's observations have been the basis of all subsequent work in this region, geographical, scientific and commercial.

" With the exception of the Morocco journey, which was

purely geographical, all Thomson's other work in Africa had more or less directly practical objects in view, was connected with the exploration of Africa for commercial, industrial, and colonising purposes. But it must not be inferred that Thomson believed in the possibility of colonising Africa in the proper sense of the term. He was too honest, too experienced, and too intelligent to advocate any such idea. That Africa could be developed only under white direction he was convinced; but he never countenanced the belief that tropical Africa could be made the permanent home of Europeans.

"The Rovuma expedition was undertaken on behalf of Seyed Burgash, Sultan of Zanzibar, after his expedition to the Great Lakes. The object of the expedition was to discover if the coal, which was reported to exist on the Rovuma river, was of any commercial value. Had Thomson been a shade less honest and a little more tactful, the result might have been very different. As a geologist he was convinced that the stuff which he found on the Rovuma was not coal at all, or at least was of so inferior a quality as to be practically valueless. So he reported, much to the disgust and anger of the Sultan, who seemed to think that it was Thomson's duty to make coal, if he found none, or at least to say that the genuine article was there. But Thomson was no diplomat. He reported frankly what he believed to be the truth, much to his own detriment so far as his pocket was concerned. Thomson's report has been essentially confirmed by subsequent investigations.

"The great Niger expedition was a triumph so far as the commercial interests of England were concerned. By his determination and promptitude he secured one of the richest regions of Africa for the British Empire. He knew that Germany was at his heels, but he carried out his mission with entire success, and Thomson's treaties with the native potentates and chiefs have, on many occasions since, stood the Royal Niger Company in good stead.

"Thomson's last journey, that fatal journey on which he contracted the illness that ultimately led to his death, was undertaken at the request of Cecil Rhodes, for whose qualities as an empire-maker Thomson had the greatest admiration, and who, we know, had a high opinion of Thomson as a pioneer explorer. Thomson was sent mainly to report on the value of the territory to the north of the Zambesi, lying within the British sphere, and over which the British South Africa Company had claims. To Thomson himself, as well as to others, the results of this expedition were a surprise. He found over the greater portion of the area visited by him a high plateau-country, healthy as the Blantyre Highlands, and capable of enormous development, both for plantations and stock-rearing, if only rapid and cheap communication could be established with the coast. Thomson, as we have seen, was not a man to 'cook' a report to suit company-mongers and syndicate-makers, nor, as has been pointed out, had he any belief in the possibility of permanently colonising Africa by Europeans. His report, therefore, on the economical value of this enormous stretch of British territory, is all the more valuable, and undoubtedly added greatly to the value of the assets of the company with which Cecil Rhodes is so intimately connected.

"Alas! that he has not lived to bear a further hand in the opening up of Africa to British commercial enterprise. Had he lived, there is no doubt that Mr. Rhodes would have been only too glad to have made further use of his services in helping to develop that enormous territory, the progress of which has only been temporarily checked by recent events.

"While Thomson's fame will rest mainly on the work which he did as an explorer in Africa, it will not be forgotten that he rendered important services to the commercial development of a continent which he loved, and which claimed him, as it has done so many others, as a martyr."

### The Leader.

Joseph Thomson, as a leader, is thus portrayed by Mr. J. A. Grant, who served under him in his last expedition :—

" It is not without misgiving that I undertake to make some remarks on the character of the late Joseph Thomson as a leader, for I fear that my pen is incompetent to adequately describe its many fine qualities. But at the same time it is indeed a pleasure to me to endeavour to put on record even a part of the admiration I felt for one to whom I was so much indebted.

" My intimate acquaintance with Thomson was confined to an expedition he undertook in Central Africa for Mr. Cecil Rhodes. The work he was given to do on this occasion was political as well as geographical, in a hitherto unexplored region to the west of Lake Nyassa ; and its entire and complete success bore testimony to Mr. Rhodes' insight in the selection of a leader—a position which could only be successfully held by a man of tact, great endurance, experience, and courage. Starting from the delta of the Zambesi, Thomson took his expedition up that river and the Shiré to Lake Nyassa, where he disembarked at Kota-kota on the western shore. Here we began marching westward to Kwa-Chitambo, where Livingstone died. After following the River Congo for some distance we struck southward, touching the Kafué, one of the upper tributaries of the Zambesi. Thence our course was generally eastward, until we at length came back to our starting point on Lake Nyassa. Unfortunately this was the last expedition poor Thomson was destined to take part in, for, some months after we started, he contracted an illness from which he never entirely recovered, and thus indirectly added his name to the long list of his co-patriots who have died in making their country stand forth as the pioneer of light and civilisation.

"No doubt he had undertaken more eventful journeys where his skill was more constantly needed, and journeys where he found circumstances more novel and interesting to the outside world; but I doubt if any traveller ever underwent a more trying time than he did upon that occasion. Nothing but indomitable perseverance like his would have carried him through. Struck down by an acutely painful internal disease, far from any medical assistance, Thomson never for one moment resigned the work he had undertaken; he struggled on gamely day after day, refusing to be carried until he was worn to a shadow, and had at length to submit to a rough-and-ready hammock. But still he retained command of his caravan, never relaxing his attention and care of everything, until he brought his expedition to a satisfactory conclusion and resigned himself to the generous and kindly care of the Church of Scotland missionaries at Blantyre.

"Thomson was not one of those African explorers who considered the force of arms a necessary accompaniment of successful travel. He from the first grasped the fact that the African savage, although ever ready for the fight, with few exceptions, prefers peace, and that tact is quite as powerful as the rifle in African exploration. Consequently he was a prince among pioneers, for those who followed him were looked upon as friends, not enemies.

"In no circumstances that I can imagine are greater opportunities offered to one for forming a just estimate of a man's character than those offered by the long companionship of a Central African journey. No veneer could hide the genuine characteristics of a man when you can see him daily being subjected to the many trials to which the leader of an African caravan is liable. The mere catalogue of Thomson's achievements is sufficient to testify to his ability as an explorer and leader of the first rank; and, from my personal experience, I believe he attained to

this position by the charm and strength of his character.
The greatest difficulty, the most extreme danger, was met
with a smile on his face which was the outward sign of a
singularly even temper. Naturally a quite fearless man,
he was never reckless, and was always ready to appreciate
the timidity of a subordinate. If any danger was to be
run, Thomson invariably performed it himself; but at the
same time he expected his men to do their duty, and any
dereliction of it was instantly dealt with. His indomitable energy never allowed him to spare himself the
smallest trouble or pains, and a natural inquisitiveness
combined with such a nature was the cause of the stores
of information which may be found in his works."

## THE SCIENTIST.

On the contributions made by Joseph Thomson to the
'Geology of Africa,' Dr. J. W. Gregory, who after him
travelled for scientific study in Masai-land, makes the
following remarks :—

"The contributions to our knowledge of African geology
made by the late Joseph Thomson may be divided into
five groups: first, the geological appendix in 'To the
Central African Lakes and Back'; second, his examination
of the Rovuma Basin; third, the various geological notes
in his book 'Through Masai-land' and the map published
in the earlier editions of that work; fourth, his observations on the former glaciation of the Atlas Mountains in
Western Morocco; and finally, his study of the region to
the west of the Nyassa during his journey to Katanga, of
which the results were summarized in a paper on 'The
Evolution of the Tanganyika Basin.'

"In 1879, when Thomson so pluckily and successfully

carried through the expedition begun by Keith Johnston, very little was known of the geology of the *hinterland* of Eastern Africa.  The Zambesi Valley had been examined by the geologist Thornton, whose paper in 1862 marks the beginning of real work in this region ; the coastlands had been explored by Baron C. C. von der Decken, whose collections revealed the main facts in their geological structure.  In regard to the Nyanza and Tanganyika basins, however, and to the plateau that separates them from the sea, there were only the few geological notes of Burton and Speke, and the observations made by the keen eyes of Mr. Stanley during his two journeys to Tanganyika (1871 and 1876).

"Thomson showed himself equal to any of his predecessors in accuracy of observation, while he had the benefit of training in geology at Edinburgh.  He was therefore able to construct a definite geological section across the country from Tanganyika to the coast.  This section formed the basis of all subsequent geological work along that line, and was not materially corrected until the publication of the results of Oscar Baumann's ' *Zur Nil Quelle* ' in 1894.

"Thomson showed that the area between Tanganyika and the sea is a vast plateau of gneiss, schist and granite, which is separated from the coast by a broad belt of sedimentary rocks.  These beds he identified as Carboniferous, assuming them to be the northern continuation of the coal-bearing deposit of that age, found by Thornton in the Zambesi Valley.  He pointed out, moreover, that volcanic rocks are often deposited on the gneisses in the interior, and supported the view that both Lakes Nyassa and Tanganyika lay in depressions formed by faults.  These conclusions were published in an appendix to the volume containing the narrative of the expedition which was Thomson's first piece of geological work, and was probably his best and most important.  The main lines he laid down have been abundantly supported, and

subsequent workers along this traverse have only had to
fill in the details, except in regard to two points. The
first of these was the age of the sedimentary deposits along
the Rovuma Valley. Thomson's identification of these as
Carboniferous helped to encourage the hope that coal
would be found there, as it is in the Carboniferous
deposits of the Zambesi. The Sultan of Zanzibar accordingly sent Thomson to examine the district in greater
detail. No coal was found, for the beds are probably not
of the age supposed. The Sultan of Zanzibar appeared
so greatly annoyed at the failure to find coal, that it was
at one time thought likely to prejudice Thomson's chance
of organizing the caravan for his expedition to Masai-
land.

"This was Thomson's most famous piece of geographical
work, but the geological results were less completely
worked out than those of his first journey. Travelling in
the lands of the Masai and the Kikuyu is a more arduous
undertaking than among the Bantu tribes further south.
Hence so much of Thomson's time was occupied by the
work of feeding the caravan and pacifying natives, that
there was less opportunity for steady geological work.
Moreover, Dr. G. Fischer had a few months previously
marched along almost the same line as that followed by
Thomson, nearly as far as the northern boundary of the
Masai, north of Naivasha. Thomson promised a geological
report on the country, but this does not appear ever to
have been written, and we have only some notes scattered
through his volume and a sketch map. He pointed out
that gneisses and schists are extensively developed in the
interior of British East Africa, and that upon these are
piled great sheets and cones of volcanic materials.
Blandford had shown that the lavas of Abyssinia are
referable to two different dates, and Thomson tried to
group the East African volcanic rocks into the two corres-
ponding series. Considering the difficulties under which
Thomson laboured, it is not surprising that his attempt to

z 2

classify the complex lavas of the interior of British East Africa was not successful.  Moreover, Thomson relied only on observation in the field and did not collect specimens ; he seemed to think it unnecessary.  The igneous rocks of Masai-land cannot however be named properly in the field and require microscopic examination ; hence, unfortunately, not all of Thomson's lavas from the plateaux were correctly designated, and in some cases the errors were very misleading.  Hence Gustav Fischer—although a zoologist and not a geologist—was able by careful collecting to bring home material, which, worked out by Mügge, gave a more reliable idea of the geology of this region.

"Thomson's later journey up the Niger gave no scope for geological work, but in Western Morocco he was able to make valuable observations on the former glaciation of the Atlas.  The evidence adduced is perhaps not entirely convincing, as geologists are so tired of having gravel ridges called moraines that they are likely to suspend judgment until detailed maps and sketches of the ridges are available for examination.  But as Thomson's eye was so good and he had been educated in a glaciated country, his judgment on this question is very weighty.

" His last contribution to African geology was a geological sketch map of the Tanganyika basin, given in the report on his expedition to Katanga in the Proceedings of the Geographical Society.  He pointed out that the upper Congo basin was filled by sedimentary deposits which accumulated in a depression to the west of the East African gneiss plateau.  Here again his main facts were undoubtedly correct, although Cornet's recent detailed descriptions of the deposits (1894) are not quite in harmony with all his conclusions.

"It is impossible to read Joseph Thomson's writings without feelings of mingled admiration and regret—admiration at his brilliant insight, and his power of at once reading the structure of a country, and regret for the fact that his geological work had so often to be done under pressure of haste, a fact which of necessity at times lessened the value of it. One cannot follow in his footsteps without feeling that Thomson had a remarkable instinctive capacity for geographical work; he could learn more of a range or peak by a view from a distance of twenty miles, than many men would do by an actual ascent. This keenness of sight and his knowledge of the general accuracy of his conclusions, probably led him to trust to methods which no ordinary man would have dared to use. He was unfortunate in having been trained in geology in a district of which the geological conditions were totally different from those in the remarkable area in Africa where most of his best work was done. He had been trained moreover at a time before the work of Americans in the Western States, and of the Vienna school under Suess had greatly influenced European geologists : when we remember these facts, it is not surprising that some of Thomson's geological work has failed to stand the test of subsequent revision, and that it is on his contributions to geographical science that his fame will ultimately rest. In this department, however, his genius was at its best and his achievements were magnificent. The six African journeys have placed him in the front rank of African travellers, and his name will be remembered so long as the graceful *Gazella Thomsoni* gambols over the steppes of the Masai plateaux which he explored so well."

Writing of Joseph Thomson as a *Botanist*, Mr. G. F. Scott-Elliot, himself also a traveller for scientific purposes in East Africa, gives this testimony :—

" Joseph Thomson was one of the few individuals who still uphold the traditions of English scientific travellers in botanical matters. His main interest seems to have been geology (he was a very distinguished geological student in Edinburgh), but during his many dangerous and critical expeditions he managed under very difficult circumstances to make most valuable collections.

"No one who has not had personal experience of the same kind can have any conception of the dangers of African travel to botanical specimens. An overloaded canoe, a day's neglect, or even a careless porter, may completely destroy the accumulations of months of patient and self-denying labour.

"Unfortunately his collections have for the most part not yet been described in a thorough and complete manner, and hence many are still unnamed in the national *herbaria*. Yet there are sufficient to hand to show that, in the entirely new countries which he visited, he was the first to discover many interesting forms.

"Amongst these is a new species of *Pentas* which I have named *P. Thomsonii*, and if I am right in my estimate of his work, there are not more than two or three Englishmen of our own times who have made as many valuable discoveries in Tropical Africa.

"He managed, when exposed to the extraordinary perils of Masai-land, to carry a large collection safely home, and this must have been at very great personal discomfort to himself, for many of his own private comforts were abandoned instead of these valuable scientific collections.

"It would be a great benefit to science if there were more men of his stamp able to follow the example which he set."

These notes by Mr. Scott-Elliot, with reference to Joseph Thomson's botanical work, may fitly be supplemented by the words of another high authority. Writing in *Nature* (Sept. 12, 1895), Mr. W. Botting Hemsley, of Kew Gardens, expresses himself as follows :—

"During his too short career Thomson presented three considerable collections of dried plants to Kew. The first which appears to have been made on his own initiative, chiefly between Lake Nyassa and Lake Tanganyika, was secured for Kew in 1880, through the instrumentality of the late Colonel J. A. Grant, F.R.S. This was not the subject of a special paper; yet it contained a number of interesting novelties, some of which have from time to time been published in Hooker's *Icones Plantarum*, and elsewhere.

"Before going out again Thomson carefully studied the means by which his collecting opportunities might be turned to the greatest advantage. Armed with this knowledge, he collected even more successfully in the Kilimanjaro and other mountains of Eastern Equatorial Africa. This second collection reached Kew in September, 1884, and proved of the greatest scientific importance, being the first adequate illustration of the mountain *flora* of that region. It contained scarcely one hundred and fifty species; but the specimens were selected with admirable judgment, and were sufficient for all purposes. It was worked out by Sir Joseph D. Hooker and Professor D. Oliver, and the very important results recorded in the twenty-first volume of the *Journal of the Linnæan Society*. This paper and Thomson's collection will always rank among the classical documents for the study of the phytogeography of Central Africa.

"Subsequently Mr. Thomson sent to Kew the botanical fruits of his journey to the Atlas Mountains, and, although they contained very few previously unknown plants, they were none the less instructive as a sample of the *flora* of that comparatively little known part of the world.

"Had he preserved his health Thomson might have taken his place in the first rank of botanical explorers. He had acquired the rare gift of selection in collecting; of knowing what to secure and what to neglect."

Joseph Thomson's contributions to other branches of science were not unworthy of recognition. For instance, regarding his collection of shells from Lakes Tanganyika and Nyassa, Mr. Edgar A. Smith, of the British Museum, testified that it was "one of the most remarkable additions to the *Conchological fauna* of Central Africa that has ever been made." "I feel bound," he added, "to bear testimony to the admirable manner in which the specimens have been preserved by Mr. Thomson, to whom the greatest praise is due in contributing such a fine addition to our knowledge." *

Similarly his work in the department of *Natural History* is thus referred to by another writer:—

"A fact connected with the late Mr. Joseph Thomson has been brought to my notice which is worth relating, as it serves to recall some of the work which the young explorer accomplished in the field of natural history during his too short life. While on his expedition to explore the River Rovuma in 1881, Mr. Thomson made a very good collection of natural history specimens, especially of birds. These he sent home to be described by the well-known ornithologist, Captain G. E. Shelley, who was able to add interesting new species to the African *avifauna*. One of these he named after Thomson; and as the nearest ally of the new species had been previously called after Living-stone, the names of the two travellers will, not inappro-priately, be often remembered together in connection with the study of the *ornithology* of the continent which both did so much to develop. The specimens collected by Mr. Thomson are now in the national collections at South Kensington, where they will be preserved for all time." †

These various testimonies of experts, whether taken singly or collectively, surely need nothing to add to their weight; and men who have the vast and varied interests of science at heart will not fail to note their significance.

---

* 'To the Central African Lakes and Back,' vol. ii. p. 295.
† In *The Scotsman*, August, 1895.

He was cut off, alas! too soon. So, at least, would love and friendship say, which knew his aspirations, and which saw at once his gifts and the world's need of them. But far beyond the limited circle of friendship the sentiment of regret for his untimely removal finds echo. The world is never so rich in men who join high endowments with pure ideals that it can afford to look with indifference upon the loss of even one such worker. There is always pathos, too, in the thought of a life extinguished in the very noonday of promise, when its best fruition seemed yet awaiting it, and when there was the eager crave to be up and doing in the service of mankind. In presence of the mystery and the pathos we can but fall back upon the faith so grandly voiced by Mrs. Browning—grateful that an assurance containing such depths of light and comfort lies open to us:—

"I smiled to think God's greatness flowed around our incompleteness,—
Round our restlessness, His rest."

.

# APPENDIX

## I.

### A LIST OF THE PUBLISHED WRITINGS OF JOSEPH THOMSON.

1877.   The Origin of the Permian Basin of Thornhill. *Transactions of the Dumfriesshire and Galloway Natural History Society*, 1879, p. 43.

Notes on a Glacial Deposit near Thornhill. *Transactions of the Dumfriesshire and Galloway Natural History Society*, 1879, p. 70.

1879.   Notes on the Geology of Usambara. *Proceedings of Royal Geographical Society*, September, 1879, N.S. 1, p. 558.

Notes on the route taken by the Royal Geographical Society's East African Expedition from Dar-es-Salaam to Uhehè. *Proceedings of the Royal Geographical Society*, February, 1880, N.S. 2, p. 102.

1880.   A Trip to the Mountains of Usambara. *Good Words*, 1880.

Toiling by Tanganyika. Two articles: *Good Words*, 1881.

Journey of the Society's East African Expedition. *Proceedings of the Royal Geographical Society*, December, 1880, N.S. 2, p. 721.

Notes on the Geology of East Central Africa. *Nature*, 1881, 23, p. 102.

1881.   To the Central African Lakes and Back. London: Sampson Low, Marston & Co., 1881.

The same in German. Jena: Hermann Costenoble, 1882.

1882.   Notes on the Basin of the River Rovuma, East Africa. *Proceedings of the Royal Geographical Society*, February, 1882, N.S. 4, p. 65.

1882.  Adventures on the Rovuma.  *Good Words*, 1882, pp. 240, 398.

On the Geographical Evolution of the Tanganyika Basin. *British Association Report*, 1882, p. 622.

1883.  Report on the Progress of the Society's Expedition to Victoria Nyanza.  *Proceedings of the Royal Geographical Society*, 1883, N.S. 5, p. 544.

1884.  Through the Masai Country to Victoria Nyanza.  *Proceedings of the Royal Geographical Society*, December, 1884, N.S. 6, p. 690.

1885.  THROUGH MASAI-LAND.  London : Sampson Low, Marston & Co., 1885.

The same in German.  Leipzig : F. A. Brockhaus, 1885.

The same in French.  Paris : Librairie Hachette et Cie., 1886.

1886.  Sketch of a Trip to Sokoto by the River Niger.  *Journal of the Manchester Geographical Society*, 1886, 2, p. 1.

Niger and Central Sûdan Sketches.  *Scottish Geographical Magazine*, October, 1886, 2, p. 577.

Up the Niger to the Central Sûdan.  *Good Words*, January, February, April and May, 1886, pp. 24, 109, 249, 323.

East Central Africa and its Commercial Outlook.  *Scottish Geographical Magazine*, February, 1886, 2, p. 65.

Note on the African Tribes of the British Empire.  *Journal of the Anthropological Institute*, vol. 16, p. 182.

Mohammedanism in Central Africa.  *Contemporary Review*, 1886, p. 876.

1888.  ULU—a novel written in collaboration with Miss E. Harris-Smith.  London : Sampson Low, Marston & Co., 1888.

A Masai Adventure.  *Good Words*, 1888, p. 94.

1889.  East Africa as It Was and Is.  *Contemporary Review*, 1889 p. 41.

A Journey to Southern Morocco and the Atlas Mountains. *Proceedings of the Royal Geographical Society*, January, 1889, N.S. 11, p. 1.

How I Reached My Highest Point in the Atlas.  *Good Words*, 1889, p. 17.

Explorations in the Atlas Mountains. *Scottish Geographical Magazine*, April, 1889, 5, p. 169.

1889.  How I Crossed Masai-land.  *Scribner's Magazine*, 1889, p. 387.

Travels in the Atlas and Southern Morocco.  London: George Philip & Son, 1889.

Some Impressions of Morocco and the Moors.  *Manchester Geographical Magazine*, 1889, 5, p. 101.

1890.  Downing Street *versus* Chartered Companies.  *Fortnightly Review*, 1890, p. 173.

The Results of European Intercourse with Africa.  *Contemporary Review*, 1890, p. 337.

Mungo Park and the Niger.  London: George Philip & Son, 1890.

1892.  A Central Sûdan Town.  *Harper's Magazine*, 1892, p. 220.

The Uganda Problem.  *Contemporary Review*, 1892, p. 786.

To Lake Bangweolo and the Unexplored Region of British Central Africa.  *Geographical Journal*, February, 1893, 1, p. 97.


## II.

## A LIST OF THE HONORARY TITLES CONFERRED UPON JOSEPH THOMSON.

Fellow of the Royal Geographical Society.
Honorary Member of the Royal Scottish Geographical Society.
Honorary Member of the Manchester Geographical Society.
Gold Medallist of the Royal Geographical Society.
Honorary Member of the Royal Italian Geographical Society.
Honorary Member of the Netherlands Geographical Society.
Silver Medallist of the Royal Scottish Geographical Society.

# EXTRACTS FROM REVIEWS.

"Joseph Thomson was the Bayard of African travel."—*The Times*.

"Joseph Thomson has a front place in the ranks of African explorers, beside his countrymen, Mungo Park and David Livingstone. . . . A worthy and substantial memorial of a noble character."—*Scotsman*.

"A most interesting narrative."—*Daily News*.

"The charming and sympathetic biography which the Rev. Mr. Thomson has written of his famous brother, whose death Britain and Africa mourned so sincerely a year ago, is the best thing that has been produced by fraternal piety since Thomas Hughes composed his delightful 'Memoir of a Brother.' It tells the story of a fine and memorable life in simple and well-chosen language, and will be a precious possession to all who are interested in exploration, but especially to Scotsmen who are proud that so excellent a man as Joseph Thomson was their countryman. Like that of most of the pioneers of the Dark Continent, Mr. Thomson's useful career was cut short by the privations and dangers that he dared so lightly in the path of duty, which was for him also the path to glory, as it has been for so many in 'our rough highland story.' Yet he began so young that a life of only thirty-seven years in all included thirteen years of active work in Africa. In those years he not only set a nobler example than any traveller since the heroic Livingstone, but he achieved results which the best judges describe as 'magnificent.' He sprang almost at a bound to a place in the front rank of African explorers. His books and papers remain a record of the geographical work he did ; it is well that his brother has given us this account of that much greater thing—his simple, strenuous, and heroic life. The main facts of that life—how the lad of twenty-one seized the opportunity thrust upon him by the death of the leader of his first expedition, how he explored the Central African lakes, and led the way amongst the savage Masai, and saw Mount Kenia, and climbed the mountains of the Atlas, and finally assisted in the exploration of the districts about the Zambesi before coming home to a lingering death-in-life—these facts are sufficiently fresh in men's minds for us not to need to dwell upon their story, here told in succinct but fascinating words. The influences that moulded Mr. Thomson's character and the secret of his success are of more interest to us just now. On these his biographer throws a pure and brilliant light."—*The Glasgow Herald*.

"The Reverend Mr. Thomson's book, which is well equipped with maps, is, in its simplicity of style, brevity and directness, a model of what such a biography should be. . . . A very interesting and valuable book."—*The National Observer*.

"The record of Thomson's career, as given by his brother in the work before us, is singularly healthful and stimulating. . . . The biographer has done his work admirably, and the narrative is of engrossing interest from beginning to end."—*Westminster Gazette*.

"When the late Joseph Thomson died, last year, we pointed out that this country had lost 'the only traveller of our time who, as regards his pluck, his persistence, and his methods, is worthy to rank with Livingstone.' A perusal of this modest and sympathetic 'Life' merely confirms our opinion expressed at the time."—*Pall Mall Gazette*.

"The late Mr. Joseph Thomson, whose premature death last year, at the age of thirty-seven, robbed geographical science of one of her most distinguished and intrepid explorers, has found in his brother a very competent biographer."—*Literary World*.

"Mr. Thomson has told the story of his brother's career with brevity and skill, and the book cannot fail to attract many readers."—*The Spectator*.

"Books of travel are unusually numerous at this season.  One of the best is the 'Memoir of the late Joseph Thomson.'"—*Echo*.

"The story of the life of such a man as Joseph Thomson cannot fail to be of interest, and no one could be more fit to undertake the work of writing his biography than the brother who had assisted him in his first literary efforts. . . . An excellent feature in this book is the manner in which the biographer ignores himself. . . . He devotes himself entirely to bringing out the distinguishing features in his brother's character, and thus admirably succeeds in the task he has undertaken."—*The Field*.

"Very infrequently, I should imagine, does it fall to the lot of a reviewer to deal with a contribution to South African literature so altogether stimulating and interesting as is the Rev. J. B. Thomson's life of his brother Joseph. . . . The author has done his work well, and with an impartiality and conciseness seldom attained by the relatives of biographical subjects."—*The African Critic*.

"The biography of such an explorer was well worth writing, and in these pages this work has been accomplished in a manner altogether satisfactory. . . . Joseph Thomson must have many admirers, both in this country and elsewhere, and to all these, as well as to all interested in heroic exploration, we heartily commend this work."—*Manchester Guardian*.

"The biography will soon, we confidently anticipate, be one of the most popular books of the year, as Thomson will ever be a hero to all who know his life-story."—*The Independent*.

"The handsome volume recording the life and travels of Joseph Thomson, the famous African explorer, comes opportunely while his memory is still green, and while attention is being more than ever directed to the great continent which he did so much to open up.  The biographer has done his work well, and in the volume of 350 pages—which is none too long—he presents Joseph Thomson to us as a most interesting personality. . . . The work is finely printed and bound."—*Edinburgh Evening Dispatch*.

"This is, beyond question, one of the finest bits of biography that the British public have had given to them for a long time.  The subject is, of course, an excellent one ; but the execution leaves nothing to be desired. . . . The Rev. Mr. Thomson has made, in every respect, a notable contribution to our standard biographical literature.  As was said of one of Joseph Thomson's own books, we may say of this book : 'It would be impossible to add to the interest of the narrative itself.' . . . Our readers must procure the book. They will be richly repaid."—*Greenock Herald*.

"Not every biography is so interesting as that of 'Joseph Thomson, African Explorer.' . . . It is less the history of a life (and it is that in a full and accurate degree) than a romance of adventure."—*Glasgow Evening News*.

"In this handsome and handy book the Rev. J. B. Thomson has told in clear language, without undue embellishment, and with an admirable sense of proportion, the main incidents in the life of the gallant young explorer, who in his short span of thirty-seven years had packed many and great achievements."—*Greenock Telegraph*.

"This is one of the books of the year, and it is likely to remain a permanent addition to the biographical literature of the century. . . . The book is admirably planned, and the writing is maintained at a high level throughout. . . . The peculiar charm of the biography consists of the story of his boyhood, and the glimpses we get from correspondence and narrative of the bypaths of his life."—*Dumfries and Galloway Standard*.